# THREE PERFECT LIARS

Heidi Perks worked as a marketing director before becoming a full-time mother and writer. Her first novel, *Now You See Her*, was a *Sunday Times* bestseller and a Richard and Judy Book Club pick. Her second novel *Come Back for Me*, was also a *Sunday Times* bestseller.

Heidi is a voracious reader of crime fiction and thrillers and endlessly interested in what makes people tick. She lives in Bournemouth with her husband and two children.

'Vivid . . . well observed . . . a winner'
***DAILY MAIL***

'Simmering tensions and double crossings will have you racing to the dramatic finale'
***SUNDAY MIRROR***

'This tense and tight thriller builds to an explosive conclusion'
***BEST***

'Slick, gripping and compelling. I couldn't put it down'
**LISA JEWELL**

*Also available by Heidi Perks*

Now You see Her
Come Back For Me

# THREE PERFECT LIARS

## HEIDI PERKS

arrow books

1 3 5 7 9 10 8 6 4 2

Arrow Books
20 Vauxhall Bridge Road
London SW1V 2SA

Arrow Books is part of the Penguin Random House group of companies
whose addresses can be found at global.penguinrandomhouse.com.

Penguin
Random House
UK

First published by Century in 2020
Published in paperback by Arrow Books in 2020

www.penguin.co.uk

A CIP catalogue record for this book is available from the British Library.

ISBN 9781787464117

Typeset in 10.56/15.8 pt Palatino
by Integra Software Services Pvt. Ltd, Pondicherry
Printed and bound in Great Britain by Clays Ltd, Elcograf S.p.A.

The authorised representative in the EEA is Penguin Random House
Ireland, Morrison Chambers, 32 Nassau Street, Dublin D02 YH68.

Penguin Random House is committed to a sustain-
able future for our business, our readers and our
planet. This book is made from Forest Stewardship
Council® certified paper.

*For my mum,*
*for being such a great one.*

# The Night of the Fire

## Monday 13 May

It had taken seven minutes for the first of the fire engines to screech to a halt outside the offices of Morris & Wood, but even by then anyone could have seen it was too late. The fire had coursed through the building at an alarming rate. Red and orange flames were already obscured by a billowing cloud of dark-grey smoke. The sound of breaking glass shattered the air.

She was on the quay across the river from the office, with a perfect view that she no longer wanted, yet couldn't bring herself to turn away from.

To her right a few people had spilled out of The Star pub and the couple of restaurants nearby. It was a warm evening in mid-May, warm enough to be out enjoying the longer evening even though it was a Monday night.

Most of the onlookers had probably protested against the development of the Morris & Wood offices when plans for the building were first proposed to the council. The development had caused outrage five years ago. Ad hoc meetings set up in cafés and school halls had been attended by angry residents from Lymington and beyond, who refused to allow such an eyesore to be built.

*No one*, they had said, *wants to look across the Lymington River from the beautiful quay and see a monstrosity of a glass office staring back at them. Bloody Londoners*, they had murmured among themselves. *They are the problem, coming to the south coast from the city, taking over our town.*

Only a few months later Harry Wood had had them all eating out of his palm. Well, maybe not all of them, but the ones who counted.

And so the plans had been approved, the building work started. Anyone who knew the first thing about architecture should have been able to see the offices would be a thing of beauty – too much so for an advertising agency perhaps?

By then the same residents had begun to forgive Harry Wood for anything. He had recruited locally, was supporting charities close to their hearts. The Lymington Care Home had never had so many minibuses and outings to the New Forest.

Yet once upon a time some of the people now gawping at the fire, as it continued to ravage the building, might have joked to their friends that they'd have liked to have burned it to the ground themselves. Because even after it was built, when its tall glass front reflected the light from the water, dappled against the setting sun, it still left a bitter taste in the mouths of a few. The ones who saw through people like Harry Wood.

Possibly, she considered, over the course of the next few days the police might wonder if there was any link between those early protestors and the fire.

Her heart beat rapidly at this thought, her eyes scanning the small crowd.

Might they think that? Was it possible the police would focus their attention on something so altogether different from the truth?

She pulled back against the wall, hoping to keep out of sight. Her pulse reverberated through her ears, deafening her to the sounds of the commotion unfurling in front of her eyes.

Three fire engines were now parked haphazardly, at least two police cars that she could see, and now an ambulance was pulling to a halt. The scene played out like a silent movie. She could imagine it unfurling in slow motion, even though the reality was frenzied.

There was a taste of salt on her lips and she licked it away, realising tears had escaped without her knowledge. Clenching her arms across her chest, she wrapped them around herself as tightly as she could, almost folding inwards. Her fingers tingled. If she brought them to her nostrils she would smell the fuel on them. She didn't think she would ever forget that stench, its potency making her want to retch.

*Is this what you wanted?* she asked herself.

She pulled a hand away from her chest and held it over her mouth, her mind racing. She tried to imagine what would happen in the morning. How many employees would turn up to find nothing more than a pile of rubble where their precious offices once stood, or if they'd already have been told they no longer had jobs to go to.

Every one of them would no doubt have to speak to the police, tell them what little they knew. She was certain the detectives would be merely scratching the surface when it came to most of the staff, led on a merry dance that took them far away from what had really happened.

There would likely be the odd comment from one or two members of the team who thought they had something of interest to say, but she doubted they'd point the detectives in the right direction.

She focused her gaze on the small gathering of uniforms grouped beside one of the fire engines. A fireman was gesturing, pointing fiercely towards the building, while another one yelled behind him, calling others over. She hadn't imagined the fire would spread so quickly.

Suddenly it was apparent that something was happening. Something urgent, for even from here she could sense the apprehension in the air. It had darkened somehow, become thicker with foreboding.

Automatically she inched forward until she was trapped in the beam of a street light. Her heart pounded even more heavily against the wall of her chest as she strained to get a better view, edging closer still, along the narrow pathway that ran in front of the waterside houses.

Everything told her she should leave. She should be at home with her family. At some point there would be a call about what had happened and, when it came, that was where she needed to be.

And yet at the same time she couldn't tear herself away from the scene.

One of the firemen had now stood aside, allowing her a perfect vision of the stretcher on the pavement. A body was being carried out of the burning building, laid upon the stretcher, and then a circle of people closed around it and she could see no more.

Her body felt like liquid, as if at any moment she would melt away and sink into the ground.

What had she done? It had seemed such a perfect solution. But now she could see that it was by no means an end. It was only the beginning. Now she could see that her actions would strip her of everything that was truly important.

Her family.

She clutched her stomach and bent double, retching on the path beside her. Her hands shook violently.

Revenge and anger had blinded her, and now she might very well lose the two most important people in her life. And it was too late to do anything about it.

***Tuesday 14 May***

**Initial interviews between DC Emily Marlow and the staff of Morris & Wood, following the fire on Monday 13 May**

***Bryony Knight, Account Assistant***

| | |
|---|---|
| Bryony: | Is anyone dead? |
| Marlow: | I'm afraid we can't answer that at this moment. |
| Bryony: | *Can't* answer? (pauses) Okay. Well. In answer to your question, I've worked there for eighteen months. |
| Marlow: | And who do you report into? |
| Bryony: | Well (laughs), it was Laura Denning, before she went off on maternity leave. Then it was Mia, who replaced her, and now – it's both of them! It doesn't really work but ... Do you know what's going to happen? I mean, am I |

|          | going to carry on getting paid? I've got rent to pay and if I can't work … |
|----------|----------------------------------------------------------------------------|
| Marlow: | These are all things you'll have to ask your Human Resources department. As I'm sure you can appreciate, I'm investigating the fire. |
| Bryony: | I know. I just – well, I can't afford to lose the money, that's all. |
| Marlow: | You say you like it there. So you enjoy your job? Have you always been happy at Morris & Wood? |
| Bryony: | Totally. It's an awesome place to work, I mean the offices are – were, I mean – the offices *were* amazing. Shit! I can't believe they're actually gone. Who could have done it? |
| Marlow: | That's what we're trying to ascertain. |
| Bryony: | And you think it was someone who worked there? That's why you're interviewing us all? |
| Marlow: | No, I'm not saying that. I'm just trying to build up a picture of what the staff thought of the company, and how you all felt about working for Harry Wood. |
| Bryony: | Well, Harry's amazing. He's a totally great boss. Everyone loves working for Harry – you won't be able to find one person who doesn't. Harry always stops and talks to you, he's (laughs) … I don't know. He's very good-looking. |

Marlow: So, in your opinion, you think everyone believes Harry Wood is a good CEO?

Bryony: Oh God, yeah. I mean, I don't really know what a CEO does or anything, but if you mean do I think everyone was happy working for him, then as I say, totally. That's why no one ever leaves.

Marlow: I see someone left very recently. Sarah Clifton?

Bryony: Oh, right, Sarah. Yes, of course. I forgot about her.

Marlow: Do you know why she did?

Bryony: Not for sure, but I heard the rumours.

Marlow: The rumours?

Bryony: Yeah. She had issues with her boss, Mike Lewis. But ... well, one day she'd suddenly just gone. She was a very quiet girl. I didn't even realise she'd left until a week later.

Marlow: Did you hear any other rumours, Miss Knight?

Bryony: Like what?

Marlow: Anything at all.

Bryony: (pauses) There are always rumours in an office that big; it depends which one you mean.

### Henrietta James, Senior Account Manager

Henrietta: Harry Wood is a good CEO, I suppose, but I didn't have much to do with him on a day-to-day basis. Of course all the young girls love him. By 'young' I mean the ones in their twenties. Not that I'm old, for God's sake – I'm only forty-two – but you feel it sometimes, you know? When everyone around you wasn't even born when you were leaving school (laughs). Anyway, I think they like him because he's always very nice, and of course he is handsome. Even I can give him that, but I guess they're blinded at that age, aren't they?

Marlow:     How do you mean blinded? Do you think you saw things they didn't?

Henrietta:  I'm sure I did.

Marlow:     Such as?

Henrietta:  (sighs) Such as the way he only really has time for his own, I suppose. The people who work directly under him. He makes a show of speaking to us all, of course, but it always feels a little … *off*. I think he's happiest when he's around the board table with the senior directors.

Marlow:     Mia Anderson is one of your directors, is that correct?

Henrietta:  (nods) That's right. We have five of them now. There had only ever been four in the whole time I've worked there, but Harry kept Mia on. Thank God, if you ask me. It was about time we had someone like Mia.

Marlow:     What do mean, 'someone like Mia'?

Henrietta:  A woman at that level we could talk to. You know, she's only the second woman to sit on the board?

Marlow:  Mainly men are appointed?

Henrietta:  Oh yes.

Marlow:  Do you think this is an issue?

Henrietta:  I don't know. I've never really given it much thought before. I always thought it was just the way it is. Women go off and have babies. That's what they say, don't they? Take me, I went part-time after having kids, so why would anyone consider me for a promotion?

Marlow:  You don't think you'll get promoted because you're part-time?

Henrietta:  I know I won't.

Marlow:  Is that the way it is throughout the company?

Henrietta:  I'm not saying there's anything wrong with the way Harry does things.

Marlow:  I'm not suggesting you are.

Henrietta:  I'm not trying to cause trouble or anything. I'm not saying there's some inequality issue ... I never did buy into all the stuff that—

Marlow:  Yes?

Henrietta:  It doesn't matter. I'm just saying I don't want you to start thinking I had any issues. I don't.

Marlow:  I realise that isn't what you're suggesting.

You say it was nice to have Mia Anderson, because you could talk to her. How about

|            |                                                                                                                                                   |
| ---------- | ------------------------------------------------------------------------------------------------------------------------------------------------- |
|            | Laura Denning? I believe she's the other director you refer to? The other woman who sits on the board?                                             |
| Henrietta: | She is, but I've never really felt comfortable talking to Laura about anything personal. Laura Denning is very – professional, I suppose you would say. |
| Marlow:    | Mia Anderson was brought in to cover Laura Denning's maternity leave?                                                                              |
| Henrietta: | (nods) Laura went off for six months. She came back two months ago.                                                                                |
| Marlow:    | And yet Mia Anderson is still there? Has this caused any issues, in your opinion?                                                                  |
| Henrietta: | (laughs) Oh yes, and that's a whole different story.                                                                                               |
| Marlow:    | In what way?                                                                                                                                        |
| Henrietta: | It didn't go down well at all. The moment Laura Denning walked back in, after she'd had her baby – well, let's just say we all knew there'd be problems. Yes, I suppose after that, things definitely started to change at Morris & Wood. |

# Chapter One

***Two months earlier***

Laura stood in the doorway to the kitchen and watched her husband, Nate, carefully stirring a wooden spoon around a pan that was balanced precariously on the edge of the hob. In his other arm, nestled into his side, was Bobby. Her son's little head lolled against his dad's shoulder and every time Nate moved, Bobby sprang up as if he'd been jolted wide awake.

Laura tensed as she waited for her son's eyes to open. He was fast asleep and while Nate hummed quietly, seemingly oblivious to her standing watching, she felt her eyes moisten.

'I'm off, then.' The words left her lips almost silently, but Nate turned immediately and broke into a smile.

'Hey, gorgeous, you look amazing. And see: it still fits perfectly.'

'Not really.' She ran her hands down the front of her shirt. The buttons tugged over her breasts so much so that she'd worn a vest top underneath, even though the offices were always too hot.

Laura had spent more time in front of the mirror in the last hour than she had in the last six months. Her dark hair had been pulled into a ponytail, then let loose, and was now tied in a straggly bun at the base of her neck. She'd chipped flakes of dry mascara off its wand before applying it to her lashes and had added more grey eyeshadow than she'd ever worn to work previously, all in an attempt to feel more confident. And yet she still didn't know how she'd make it out of the front door.

'You're nervous,' Nate said. 'You're bound to be, going back after all this time.'

She shook her head and attempted a smile, biting her lip as she strode over to where he had switched off the hob. 'I'm going to miss you, little man,' she whispered into her son's warm hair, kissing his head, her lips lingering, too afraid to pull away.

She shouldn't be nervous. She loved her job. Morris & Wood had been her life until Bobby had come along. And yet Laura thought there was every chance she was going to be sick. That it would be a whole lot easier if she called Harry and postponed her return. Just for another week. One more week and then surely she would feel better.

But they had done the maths, and now that her full maternity pay had ended, they were reliant on Laura's salary to pay for the mortgage they'd excitedly stretched themselves to afford five years ago, when she started working for Harry Wood. They both knew that when Bobby came along, it was Laura who'd return to work full-time because, even putting aside the fact that she out-earned her husband by a significant amount, it was Laura who had the career, who had never been able to imagine life without her job.

Nate was smiling. 'You're going to knock 'em all dead. Like you always have.'

'You're biased.'

'I know I am, but I also know how brilliant you are. Particularly with all the work you've been doing to prepare,' he added, nodding at the laptop sticking out the top of her bag. 'It'll be like you haven't been away.'

'Maybe,' she replied, her gaze still on Bobby. It was impossible to believe it would ever feel like that. Not when she'd spent the last six months caring for another human being around the clock.

But Nate was right about one thing. She had put in a lot of hours over the last couple of weeks, preparing herself to dive straight back into her biggest accounts. She felt excited to talk to her lead client, Coopers, about ideas for the TV advert they wanted to start work on this summer. They'd been planning to invest heavily in promotion for their new health-drink brand and she'd been so keen to get her teeth into the campaign. Anyway, surely the moment she stepped out of the office lift onto her floor she would stop feeling so nervous.

'Just go,' Nate told her, turning back to the porridge on the hob, scooping out a spoonful, which he tipped into a small plastic bowl.

'You know that'll be too hot,' she said. 'You need to cool it down first. He can't eat it like—'

'I know,' Nate laughed.

'Call me if anything happens.'

Nate nodded as he pushed the bowl to one side and twisted round to kiss her. 'Hey!' He reached out his hand and ran a thumb across her cheek. 'Why are you crying?'

'I'm not.' She pulled back and laughed, swiping a hand against him. 'I'm just, you know, I haven't left him in six months.'

'Well, this guy and I are going to have a blast. As soon as you're gone, we're going to vacuum the house and put on a load of washing and then – then we're off to the park.'

'Nate, am I doing the right thing?'

'Yes.' He took hold of her arm. 'Of course you are.'

Her stomach felt heavy and twisted. The decision that had always been such a simple one suddenly felt as if it was swamping her. Like she had no other choice. And in that moment Laura wished that Nate's job in IT paid more than it did. Or that her husband had the same degree of ambition she had.

She quickly shook the thought from her head. Deep down, there was nothing she would change about Nate. They were different, and it worked. Laura had often wanted to be more like him and happily throw dinner parties at a moment's notice, or not be remotely bothered when the doorbell rang and a visitor showed up uninvited. But she wasn't that person. She was the one who felt most content when she was controlled and organised; and efficiently running the marketing for a number of clients was something Laura thrived upon. It was why she'd felt she was leaving a part of herself behind, the day she walked out of Morris & Wood to go on maternity leave. And deep down, when she reminded herself of this, she thought how wonderful it would be to find that part again.

Despite this thought, her intermittent tingles of excitement blended with dread as she gazed at her son and told Nate she would be home early. 'Well, early enough to give him tea, do his bath ...'

Nate grinned. 'Just do whatever you have to, on your first day. I won't expect you until I see you.'

'No, but I will,' she said, looking up at him sharply. 'I want to.'

'That's cool,' he continued to smile. 'We'll look forward to seeing you.'

Of course he probably didn't believe her, because she'd so rarely got home before seven in the past, but she would prove him wrong. She wasn't about to let her job take away time with her precious family. She was confident she could make both work, despite what the mums in her NCT group had warned her.

She had brushed off their concerns when, in passing conversation, she'd told them she was returning to work. If anything, she'd wanted to slap the look of horror off Chrissie's face. Not that she was surprised with Chrissie, who passed judgement on everything from colic to weaning, to when was the right time to stop breastfeeding. But none of them were planning to go back full-time. Even Nancy had said she would only do three days if one of them could be working from home. And certainly none of them had even considered the possibility of going back before their full twelve months were up.

Laura knew what they thought of her. That she clearly didn't want to spend time with her son. Of course they never said as much, but she could tell that's what they must think, by the constant hammering of questions, the persistence of *wouldn't she miss him*?

Yes, she was going to miss him. What did they think: that she was a bloody robot? Her heart was tearing in two, and she hadn't even left the house.

Laura had justified herself to the women in her group, time and time again, and all the while they'd made out they weren't judging her, but of course they were. Or it had felt that way.

'As soon as you get to the office you'll be fine,' Nate was saying as he reached behind and passed her a flask. 'Decaf tea.'

She sighed. 'You're amazing, you know that?'

'I do. Now go. You don't want to be late on your first day back. Text me and tell me how you're getting on,' he called as she kissed him and walked away. 'We miss you already.'

Laura held up a hand, but she couldn't look back again.

The offices of Morris & Wood looked out over the Lymington River and to the quay on the other side. It was an idyllic location. Laura hadn't believed her luck when, five years ago, Harry Wood branched out his successful advertising agency to the south coast. She had heard of the London agency long before the first plans were submitted to the council. Laura had been one of the very few who hoped the development would go ahead, because the chance of working for such a prestigious advertising company, which happened to be on her doorstep, was unbelievable. It felt like all the good jobs were in London, and Laura had been wasting away in a small family-run agency that tried its hardest to get some exciting clients, but never quite made it.

She had followed the plans with interest and then, once they were given the green light, had eagerly watched the build and put in her application as soon as she caught wind that Harry was recruiting.

Laura didn't consider what Harry's reasons were for setting up on the south coast – she didn't particularly care. She just hoped she would get a job working for him. She hadn't dared imagine that he would spot how talented she was so soon and, within a year, would give her a promotion, and then another two after that, which would eventually make her a director.

The last five years had been the best of her life, and being on the board meant that she and Nate could finally move out of their rented flat and buy a three-bedroom detached on the outskirts of town. Harry had given her these opportunities and she would never forget that.

The day Laura had found out she was pregnant, her heart had dipped slightly. It was a feeling she'd never once admitted to anyone, especially not to Nate, but as she'd driven to the office that morning, with the pregnancy stick wrapped in toilet paper and buried in her bag, she'd pushed the news to the back of her mind. She knew how awful it was that her first thought had been that she would have to give up her job.

She didn't tell anyone at work for five months that she was expecting. But by that point she had come to the conclusion that her career didn't need to suffer, that a short sabbatical wasn't the end of the world. And by the time she was due to leave, Laura was beyond excited to be having a baby.

This first morning back, Laura took the lift up to the third floor, guilt flooding her body, seeping into every part of her, that she'd once not been delighted at the prospect of having Bobby. Her initial reaction hadn't been utter joy and it was something she'd never be able to change. Since her son had been born she'd reminded herself of this time and time again, and had looked at her son's gorgeous face and felt sick that she'd ever thought that, convincing herself that one day she'd be paid back for those feelings. That maybe she didn't deserve to be a mother and something would happen to put that right.

To say she was a mess, since giving birth, seemed a little of an understatement, Laura thought as she waited for the lift doors to open. When they did, she stepped out onto the floor, her stomach still bubbling. It would be so easy to turn round and go back down, drive home, scoop up her son and tell her husband that he would have to return to work.

Yet she knew she never would.

Laura glanced across the floor nervously. It was before eight and there were only a few people in already, heads buried in concentration. No one looked up, which gave her time to take in the changes. The wall behind the water cooler had been repainted, the configuration of desks to her right had been redesigned into star shapes at awkward angles – no longer rows looking out of the floor-to-ceiling windows that stared over the river.

She strained to see if her own desk was still in the same position, just outside Harry's glass office at the far end of the floor. Had they moved her? She couldn't see from where she was standing, but there was always the possibility someone had decided to put her elsewhere while she wasn't there to defend herself.

Laura could already feel a burn of anxiety at the thought of the conversations she'd have, if that were the case, and suddenly she realised how much harder it was going to be settling back in than she could ever have imagined.

It was no surprise that to her left the display boards had been refreshed with new creatives that she'd not seen before, but it didn't stop her heart sinking. Six months ago more than half of them had been her own work, and now she didn't recognise any of them, bar one in the bottom corner, which had won her and the company a prize.

She told herself she could do this as she started walking across the office, willing at least one person to look up and acknowledge her, so she'd be able to break the silence. It was Henrietta James who appeared first, out of the toilets, stopping short when she saw Laura.

Henrietta's face broke into a wide smile and she glanced briefly in the direction of Laura's desk, before turning to her and declaring loudly, 'You're back!'

'I am,' Laura replied, following the woman's gaze towards where her desk should be, but still she couldn't see it from where they stood.

'Gosh!' Henrietta declared. 'I can't believe how quickly six months have flown.'

'I know,' Laura said as the woman continued to smile at her. She liked Henrietta well enough; she'd always done a good job and worked hard, even though there'd been many times when Laura had squirmed, irritated, as she'd waited for Henrietta to finish a conversation about her weekend with someone, before returning to her desk to complete the work Laura needed urgently. Laura had needed to pull her up on it a couple of times.

'So how are you finding life as a mum?' Henrietta was asking. 'Is he sleeping through?'

'He was,' Laura said, 'but recently not so much.' She smiled to convey it wasn't really an issue, though it had been taking its toll on her and Nate.

'And how was it leaving him this morning?' Henrietta went on, diving straight for the jugular.

'Oh, it was fine,' Laura said, though as Henrietta's eyebrows rose, she wondered if this was the right thing to say. Maybe she was supposed to open up now with the women in the office. She and Henrietta were both mothers, after all. Should she tell her the truth: that leaving Bobby that morning was the hardest thing she had ever done?

But baring her soul didn't sit well, so instead Laura said, 'Well, I should get to my desk.'

Henrietta nodded and stepped aside, and Laura saw the disbelief in her eyes that she had managed to cut her off so quickly. Her thoughts immediately turned to Nate and she decided to call him in a bit. She had a pang of longing, stronger than she would ever have expected. She straightened her back and started to walk towards Harry's office and the place where, hopefully, her desk still sat.

As she neared it, Laura felt instant relief to see it in the same place it had always been – until she realised someone was sitting at it. Someone with a bright-pink pencil pot and a Gucci handbag, a grey cardigan slung over the back of Laura's chair and, for some reason, Christmas paper-chains still hanging over the top of the computer screen, even though it was the third week of March.

Even before the woman at her desk slowly turned round, Laura knew it was Mia Anderson, the person she had hastily recruited to cover her maternity leave. Her thoughts flitted back to the interview and how Mia had nodded, answering Laura's quick-fire questions, so grateful to be given the opportunity to step into her shoes for a few months.

And yet the woman sitting in front of her today had clearly made herself at home, and while Laura should probably have expected Mia still to be here, she hadn't thought for one minute she'd find Mia sitting in her seat like it was her own.

# Chapter Two

Laura stepped forward as Mia turned round, smiling and gesturing to her ear and the earpiece stuck in it as she carried on chatting. 'Of course, that's totally fine,' she said to whoever was on the other end of the phone, her eyes still on Laura as a sheepish grin hung off her lips. 'Yep, it's really no problem, I can get on that straight away.' She raised her eyes dramatically as if the whole conversation was nothing more than amusing, while Laura stood stupidly beside her own desk and waited for Mia to finish. Eventually Mia turned her back to Laura and flipped open a notebook, riffling through until she got to a blank page.

Laura hot-stepped from one foot to the other, her handbag weighing heavily on her left shoulder, her jacket now making her too hot. She didn't dare look about her, as she could already sense that people must be watching and there was no sign of Mia finishing her phone conversation.

She glanced around at a few vacant desks, considering whether to drop her things onto one of them. But no, this was her desk, and Mia was at it. Laura's notepads and pens were presumably still in its drawers, and her files must surely be stacked in the lower cabinet. She couldn't remember ever feeling so painfully embarrassed at work, and she was still dithering behind Mia when Harry's voice boomed across the floor, so loudly that even Mia looked up from her call.

Usually Laura wanted the ground to swallow her when he did so, but in that moment she was grateful for her boss coming to her rescue, giving her something to distract her from Mia's conversation.

'Here she is,' Harry announced as he made his way towards her, reaching out his arms and leaning forward to kiss Laura on the cheek. He grinned and then seemed to register why she was standing awkwardly in the middle of the floor, for he added quickly, 'Come on into my office. Let's catch up.'

Laura followed him through and, once they were inside and Harry had kicked the door shut behind him, he said, 'God, we've missed you around here. The place has nearly fallen apart.'

'Really?' she asked hopefully, despite the fact that she knew this was exactly the kind of thing Harry would say, whether he meant it or not.

'Please tell me you aren't going to be having any more kids,' he joked.

'Harry, you can't say things like that.'

'Oh, come on – you know what I mean.'

'Well, after that birth, I don't think I'm going to be pushing any more out just yet.'

'Okay, too much info,' he said. 'But seriously, it's so good to have you back.' He held her at arm's length, his eyes roaming her face. 'You look wonderful. Motherhood suits you.'

'Thank you.' Laura blushed and pulled away, glancing through the glass window of his office to those sitting at their desks on the other side of it. Everyone could see into Harry's office; she had felt their eyes on her enough times over the years, most likely wondering what was being discussed between them, and probably drawing their own ridiculous conclusions about why she was in there again. Rumours were as rife in Morris & Wood as they were in any other office, and Laura wasn't naïve enough to think she had escaped being the subject of gossip. But this morning no one was watching, not even Mia.

'How's the little one?' Harry asked.

'Bobby's fine. He's six months already. I can't believe where the time's gone.'

'It flies fast, I know. Ella's starting secondary this September. It makes me feel ill. Or maybe that's just the hike in fees.' His mouth skewed into a lopsided smile that made Laura cringe. Harry had a habit of brazenly throwing money into the conversation, and she was never quite sure if he did it on purpose or whether he genuinely had no idea how other people might take it.

'So anyway,' he went on. 'How are you feeling? Ready to get back into it?'

'Totally,' Laura nodded. 'Only' – she indicated out of the window – 'Mia seems to be sitting at my desk.'

'Oh, that's not a problem,' he said. 'She likely forgot you were due back this morning.' His eyes lingered on Mia for a moment, before he turned back to Laura. 'She's done a good job. You were right on the money when you told me to hire her.'

Laura glanced across at Mia too. She had now finished the call and was leaning back in the chair, laughing with Bryony Knight, who was peering over the top of Laura's PC. Bryony was Laura's account assistant and yet there she was, as if she had transferred her allegiances too.

'I want to have my desk back, Harry.' She turned back to her boss. 'I don't want to sit anywhere else.' Laura hoped her words didn't sound as childish as they suddenly felt.

'Of course not.' He waved a hand through the air. 'Don't worry about it. I'll have a word after the exec meeting this morning.'

Laura nodded and released a breath. 'I can't wait to take you through some things I've been thinking about,' she said. 'I have some great ideas.'

'That's what I love about you, Laura,' he replied. 'Your dedication.' Harry gestured to the leather chair and she sat down, waiting for him to head to his own on the other side of his desk as she pulled her notebook out of her bag.

'I want to talk to Coopers about the TV ad first thing, because I want to get that off the ground and hopefully start filming late summer. Honestly, I can't wait to get stuck into this – I've done loads on it.' She flapped her notebook in the air. 'And I was thinking about sponsorship for their premium health-bar range too and …' Laura paused. 'What?' she asked when she noticed the look on Harry's face. His eyebrows were pinched into a point, frown lines dug into his forehead.

Harry ran a hand across the stubble that neatly covered his chin. He'd had his hair cut, she noticed. Maybe a little too short. It was a mixture of light and dark grey, and in places looked white in contrast to his black-rimmed glasses. He was in his early fifties and was easily still the most attractive man in the office.

He leaned back in his chair, the movement making it swivel gently to the side, and crossed a leg, flashing a bright-pink sock beneath his suit trousers. Then uncrossing it again, he shifted forward, steepling his hands on the desk in front of him. 'The thing is, Laura, Coopers already commissioned the TV ads while you were away.'

'Oh?'

'They wanted to crack on with them.'

'But they'd *wanted* to wait,' she protested. 'They said they were going to hold off until I was back. Who's picked them up?' she asked, thinking it was surely not Mia, though she already had the unnerving feeling that Mia was exactly who had been working on them.

'Actually, Mia,' he said, confirming her fears. 'And I have to say she's doing a great job...' Harry trailed off awkwardly when he noticed the shock on her face. 'Like I say, Laura, you were right to recruit her. It was a good call. She reminds me of you, you know – five years ago, when you came here. You both have the same go-getter attitude.' Harry smiled, but it slid away quickly.

'I didn't recruit her,' she said. 'I hired her. Temporarily. She was only a replacement because ...' Laura waved a hand through the air. 'She doesn't have that much experience,' she went on in disbelief, fragments of Mia's interview coming back to her. It was one of the reasons she had taken Mia on: because she wasn't a threat, she was just good enough to keep the job ticking over.

Mia had seemed nothing like Laura in the interview. She didn't have the ambition or the desire for achievement that Laura had always shown. If anything, Laura had worried that Mia was a little too casual about her plans for the future, because she was clearly happy hopping from one temping post to another. She had wondered if Mia might not even hold out the six months needed, because frequently members of the Coopers team changed their minds at the last minute, demanded that Laura work weekends to turn around creatives. Laura thrived on that but she wasn't sure Mia would, and yet she had taken the chance on her because in every other way Mia was exactly what she was looking for. All Laura needed was someone who would keep her job going, with no aspirations to get their hands on it.

Not like Patrick. Laura's colleague, another account director, had made no attempt to hide his desire to take over Coopers, and Laura had worried that if he did, she might never get it back.

'I'm sorry, Laura, I'm sure that isn't the news you wanted to hear.'

'No ... well ...' she stammered. 'I mean, I'm just surprised they didn't wait for me to come back.' She glanced over to where Mia was now standing beside her desk, one arm leaning casually on the top of the computer screen as she spoke with a woman Laura had never set eyes on before. 'She seems to have made herself at home,' she muttered.

Harry pulled back in his seat. 'Laura, Coopers wanted to go ahead, and so of course that's what we did. I'm sorry, but that's the way it is.'

Laura nodded, her eyes stinging with the unexpected pressure of tears. God, surely she wasn't going to start crying? She inhaled a tight breath, bit down on her lip and mentally tried to pull herself together. So this wasn't what she expected, but it wasn't irretrievable. 'Right, well, I'll need to have a chat with Mia.'

'You will.'

'It's fine. I can take everything back from her by the end of the day – I shouldn't need more than that.' Laura had, after all, only had one day's handover with Mia before she'd gone into premature labour in the early hours of the following morning. 'I don't think I'll need her after today,' she said, although as she turned back to Harry she saw that his face had paled.

'Actually, I've agreed with Mia that she's staying on for a bit.'

'What? Why?'

'I've asked her to carry on working here. I thought it would be best to have her see the campaign through. The Coopers team is on board with it—'

'No, no, hold on.' Laura's heart raced as she held up a hand to stop him. 'What do you mean, Mia *seeing the campaign through*? That's not necessary, Harry. She can hand it over to me. There's no need for both of us to be on it.'

Harry dipped his head.

'This is ridiculous. What's going on? She was here to cover me, and now I'm back. Mia doesn't need to be here any longer. What is it?' she snapped. 'I can tell there's something on your mind. Will you just say whatever it is?'

'You won't both be on the account while the campaign's running. Mia's going to be keeping it. For now,' Harry added, after a beat.

'What?' Laura felt the heat creeping up her neck. 'No!'

'She's done a really great job and – I feel crap for what I'm saying – Laura, this doesn't reflect badly on you, I think it's the right thing to do. And it means you can have the time to settle back in.'

'I don't need to settle back in, Harry.' Laura stared at him as her voice rose to a high pitch. 'I've only been gone for six months, and I've kept up to date on all my clients. You know that. We've spoken about it on the phone while I've been on leave. I don't need to be babysat.'

'That's not what's happening.' He shook his head, the frown darkening his already deep-brown eyes. 'It's just that Mia's got her teeth into this and ... Laura, you said yourself, before you went off, that we could do with an extra pair of hands on the accounts.'

'To work *under* me, Harry, not to replace me.' She could feel the rise of her anger soaring through her body as she brushed a hand across her cheek, praying she didn't break down in front of him. Out of the corner of her eye she could see Mia swishing her arms in the air as she spoke animatedly to whoever it was still leaning over the top of the PC.

Mia had told her in the interview that she was moving on, out of the area. Six months was supposed to be perfect because she wasn't hanging around Lymington any longer. Laura hadn't dug into what Mia was moving on from; it hadn't felt relevant. But she'd been so adamant that she was going. 'I cannot believe she has the experience to handle this campaign,' she said now, shaking her head. 'I mean, she came from ...' Laura gestured in the air, trying to recall Mia's previous job. It had been with a marketing company in Southampton, but not one she had heard of. It was a short-term contract that had conveniently just finished, because it meant Mia could start the following week.

'Are you actually telling me she's doing a good job on it?' Laura asked, though she didn't want the answer. 'Better than me?' she went on. 'Is Mia doing a better job than me, is that what it is?'

'No, Laura, it isn't. You know that's not the case.'

She could laugh at the thought that she was once so worried about Patrick Carter covering her job. At least she would have known how to get Coopers back from Patrick. But Mia? She was an unknown entity.

Harry squirmed in his leather chair. The irritating squeak sounded loud in the silence between them.

'She's not replacing you,' he said at last. 'That's not what this is.'

'So tell me what it is then,' she said through gritted teeth. She had to keep it together. With everyone milling about outside the window, she couldn't let herself down, though she feared she might do so. 'It sounds like you've taken my job away from me while I haven't been here. I don't actually think you can do that, Harry.' She could hear the rise in her voice again, the way it was peaking, too high.

'Okay,' he said, leaning back, his face more rigid now, holding his hands up to stop her, like she had gone too far. 'Let's not get carried away. You know I would never do anything like that, Laura.'

'Let's not get carried away?' she repeated. 'Are you kidding me? This is not fair. What you're doing to me isn't fair.' Laura wiped a hand across her eyes again, once more catching Mia in her peripheral vision.

She would not cry. The anger was burning her from the inside, but she would not cry.

'What I mean is that I just thought it was the right thing to do, for now. Mia started the campaign, she's going to complete it. No one is taking your job away from you, Laura. You still have it – nothing's changed. And listen, I wasn't going to say anything today,' he went on more softly, eyeing her carefully as if worried she'd either break down or start screaming any moment, 'but there's a new opportunity on the horizon. It's a start-up; it'll be a big account but it's not concrete yet.'

Laura continued to regard him. She didn't trust herself to speak.

'Someone I used to work with,' he went on, 'and he wants to put a lot of money into building his new company's brand. Laura, you'd be perfect to handle it, but there's no way you could possibly do both.'

She opened her mouth, but for a while no words came to her. She'd been talking to Harry about new opportunities before she had left, begging him for something else that she could invest in, but she hadn't factored in giving up her most important client to do so. Eventually she said, 'But this opportunity isn't even definite.'

'No, not yet. But I'm going to set up some time for you to meet him in the next couple of weeks, and in the meantime you can settle back in. I thought it would help you,' he said, wide eyes imploring her. 'I remember when Janie went back to work after Ella was born. She felt awful every time she had to take some time off when Ella was sick and—'

'Harry!' Laura snapped, 'Nate's at home. You know that. He's given up his job so that I don't have to run home every time something happens.'

Harry splayed his hands wide on the desk in front of him. 'I know that, I know. But please, Laura, this wasn't meant to make you feel worse. I was only trying to help.' He flicked his wrist and she caught a flash of the gold watch peeking out from his cuff.

'You couldn't make me feel any worse if you tried,' she said, her voice on the edge of snapping. 'I want to keep Coopers. I don't want another account.'

'Okay,' he said calmly. 'Okay, let's have another chat about this later. My meeting starts in five, and we can't both be late for it. We'll catch up again later in the day.'

Laura pushed the chair back. 'I want her out of my desk.'

'It's done,' he nodded.

She turned and left the office, tears still pricking the corners of her eyes, though she made it to the toilets before slamming her fists down on the surface beside the basin. Tugging a paper towel out, she dabbed it roughly against her skin, the other hand still curled into a tight ball as she gripped the basin.

She wanted to scream. She wanted to call Nate. She wanted to burst into tears and flee the office, run home before she had to face anyone else. Harry had no idea what she had given up to come back to work. But she had done it because of how much her job meant to her, and because she believed she would be a better mum if she still had her work.

All she wanted now was to see Bobby's face, and the thought that she was missing out on a whole day of his young life for *this* was breaking her. Her already-knotted stomach twisted itself tighter. There were telltale patches of red clinging to her neck, which wouldn't disappear before Harry's exec meeting; and she knew, she just knew, that Mia Anderson would be in that same meeting room and she would have to face her.

Already Laura's bun was looking scruffy, and in the bright light of the toilets the eyeshadow she'd so carefully applied that morning appeared smudged and heavy.

She didn't believe a word of what Harry had told her. There was probably an old friend he was talking to, but in all likelihood he wouldn't have considered Laura for the job until five minutes ago. She certainly didn't think it was the reason he'd allowed Mia to dig her claws into the Coopers campaign.

There could only be one reason why Harry had allowed this to happen. Mia had to be better than her. That was the only thing Laura could think of – her replacement had done a better job in the last six months than she had in five years.

Her fingers clutched the edge of the basin as the door swung open behind her. A petite girl with tortoiseshell glasses paused momentarily as she stared at Laura in the mirror, a thin smile twitching on her lips, before she dropped her head and scurried to one of the cubicles.

What was her name? Susan? No, it was something like Sarah. That was it, Sarah Clifton. She'd joined the company a few months before Laura went off on her maternity leave, and had always seemed petrified whenever Laura asked her to do anything. It was a surprise she was still here, as Laura never had seen her fitting into Mike's graphics team.

She shook her head and looked back at her own reflection. Harry wouldn't have got away with what he'd just said, if she were a man. That was what galled her the most. That and the fact she hadn't pointed out as much, when he said it.

She would make sure she got her client back, if it killed her. By the end of the week Mia would be gone.

# Chapter Three

Mia Anderson had a number of things on her mind on Monday morning that didn't involve work, so for a moment she had forgotten that Laura was coming back. It sounded ridiculous, especially after the conversation she'd had with Harry only the week before, but that was the truth of it. The events of her weekend had taken over, and it had been a relief when she'd left the house early that morning and driven to the office.

As soon as Henrietta had trilled out that Laura was back, Mia felt her stomach lurch with apprehension, because she knew Laura would be shocked to find her still here.

Within minutes Laura had been standing behind Mia's desk while she was trying to have a call with one of the marketing team at Coopers, and it was putting her off-track. She needed to concentrate, but now Laura was shuffling back and forth, and Mia was torn between ignoring her and hanging up the call – something she just couldn't do. Everyone knew how important this TV ad was. She would be presenting the final outline to Coopers in less than two weeks and she had to get it perfect. This was her big chance to prove herself.

Mia had been so relieved when Harry had pulled her into his office a fortnight ago and told her the news that she was to keep Coopers. She'd worked her arse off over the last six months and it had paid off. That night she'd taken some of her new friends from work down to the pub and told them the good news that she was staying on, and they'd been so happy for her. Henrietta James had insisted on buying the first round of drinks, even though she must have known Mia was paid more than she was; and Mia let her, even though she felt guilty about it. In fact she'd been relieved. Her pockets really weren't as deep as everyone most likely thought.

On her desk her mobile began to vibrate. She pulled it towards her and checked the caller. *Mum – Home.* Mia closed her eyes briefly and for a second shut out the incoming call, the voice on the other end of the office line and the fact that Harry Wood had emerged from his office. When she opened them again, the call from her mum had already stopped and Laura was finally retreating.

Mia held her breath as she scribbled some notes, willing the conversation to be over soon, as she waited to see if her mum would call straight back or leave a message. Mia had only been in the office an hour – what was so important that she was calling so early?

By the time she put the phone down she noticed Patrick striding across the floor towards the boardroom and knew she didn't have time to call back. Harry's meeting was due to start and she couldn't be late. She was up first, updating the rest of the directors on how the campaign was going; and today, more than ever, she needed to be on the ball, now that Laura was back. Now there was someone, Mia felt, who was going to be watching her carefully.

That night in the pub, a few rounds down, Henrietta had grabbed Mia's arm and leaned in, slurring into her ear, presumably to be heard over the loud chatter, 'I'm pleased you're staying, but I know someone who won't be.'

Mia had raised her eyes questioningly, even though she knew who Henrietta was alluding to.

'Laura Denning. I have to say, I'm bloody surprised he's done it.'

'Who's done what?' Mia had asked.

'Harry. Given you that account. Everyone knows it's Laura's baby. And Harry and Laura, you know – their past.'

Mia nodded. She'd heard the whispers, and Henrietta's delight in telling her that something had once gone on between Harry and Laura. How did she know this, Mia had asked her? Someone once said, apparently. The usual. No one could really say for sure, and she wouldn't make any judgements until she saw anything for herself, though if they were as close as everyone was saying, it did make

Mia wonder how it was going to pan out, now that Laura was back.

Mia quickly gathered her notes and picked up her mobile, following Patrick to the boardroom. 'Laura's back,' she called out when she had almost caught up with him. Patrick had barely spoken about Laura in her absence; everything Mia had gleaned about her had come from the women she had befriended.

'Yes, I saw,' Patrick said, his face shadowing briefly, making Mia wonder if he too couldn't imagine how this was going to work out.

'It'll be nice to get to know her,' she said breezily. 'I've heard so much about her.'

'I'm sure,' Patrick replied. He wasn't taking the bait.

'About how good she is, I mean,' Mia went on, annoyed that he could put her in the same camp as the others. She might listen to the gossip, but she didn't spread it.

Patrick nodded. 'So how's it going anyway?' he asked as he held the door open for her. 'Everything under control?'

'Yes, I think so,' she beamed. 'I'm updating you all on the ad in a bit anyway, so it'll be good to get your thoughts.' Her heart skipped a beat as she said this, because even though she was confident enough, she didn't relish putting herself out there. And Patrick was such a closed book. She knew he saw himself as Harry's right-hand man, but there had been something so offish about him towards her, right from the start. Mia wondered if at some point the other people around the board table were going to take sides, and if they did, she had a clear picture of where Patrick would go. Straight to Laura's. And if that happened, she feared she might be the one to suffer the loss of a job, because she was the new girl.

Mia straightened as she walked into the room, dropping her notepad and phone onto the table, before pouring herself a coffee from the pot that had likely been standing there for the last hour. The women on the floor, outside the glass walls of the boardroom, might have her back, but if it came to it, were they going to be enough?

Finally Harry arrived, and a couple of minutes later so did Laura. It was odd for Mia knowing she wasn't the only woman round this table any more, as she had been for the past six months. There were seven men in the room – account directors, Chief Finance Officer, Chief Operating Officer, and her. They had danced around her like peacocks when she'd first joined. Each time she spoke, the room descended into silence, a few of the men shifting on their seats. Apart from Patrick, that was, who had a habit of talking over Mia and finishing her sentences.

Laura was now the centre of attention as the men all asked after her and her baby. Mia felt uncomfortable as she stood by the coffee pot at the far side of the room, not knowing whether she should join in the chat or wait until later, when they'd have a chance to speak in private.

In the end she pulled out the chair next to Harry, who was already sitting down, and waited for the meeting to begin. Probably better to remain professional at this point, especially when she had so little first-hand knowledge of what Laura Denning was like.

She had only met Laura twice: once for the interview and then a week later for her handover. The very next day Laura had had her baby, four weeks early. But Mia remembered her well. Her handover was nothing more than a brief run-through of what accounts she would be looking after and the key points of contact, and Mia quickly deduced that Laura didn't answer any questions she didn't want to. She hadn't idled in gossip, had barely looked at Mia as she pulled up information on her computer screen, passed numerous booklets about the companies that she represented, churned out figures, told Mia not to worry about anything that was too far off in the future. Making it clear, Mia presumed, that she wouldn't need to know, because she wouldn't be here once Laura was back.

Mia had tried to take a different tack with her and had asked her about the baby. Did Laura know what she was having?

'A boy. Now this account is unusual in that ...'

Mia couldn't even remember what was unusual about it; she wasn't listening particularly. She had only wanted to press Laura more about the child. 'It must be very exciting,' she persisted, 'getting the nursery sorted, buying the clothes.'

Laura's responses were curt. She made it seem as if she was pretty pissed off that she was having to take six months out of her job, as if the whole pregnancy was just one big inconvenience. She had rubbed her stomach, a frown shadowing her face – not that dissimilar to the one she wore now. But by then Mia had already decided Laura was worrying over something, because she'd had the same feeling in the interview, covering the same questions, like why was Mia only looking for a short-term placement? Was she happy this was only for six months?

Laura, she thought, did not want to let her job go, and so Mia had assured her it was what she was after; that she would be moving on, out of the area. To be fair, she hadn't been totally lying. Because she would have liked to be moving on, even when she knew deep down that it was highly unlikely.

'And you can definitely start at such short notice?' Laura had asked in the interview, telling Mia that she wanted her in five days' time.

'Of course,' Mia had told her, without skipping a beat. She would do whatever was needed.

Now Mia watched Laura hover on the periphery of the boardroom, before Harry finally called everyone to the table. Mia was prepared to give her a friendly smile and wave, but not once did Laura look over at her. She turned back to her notes and scanned her eyes over them, her heart fluttering as it always did when she was about to present. And then it happened again. On the table her mobile began to vibrate, and she already knew who was calling. Sliding it towards herself, Mia looked at the name and knew she couldn't ignore it a second time, because there was no way her mum would be calling her twice if it wasn't urgent.

'I'm sorry,' she whispered to Harry, 'I'm going to have to take this.'

'Oh,' he said cocking his head, unsure what to do.

'I'm sorry,' she repeated, pushing back her chair. 'I'll be as quick as I can.'

As she left the room, Mia wondered if there was ever a time when Laura Denning would be so unprofessional as to leave a meeting just as she was about to present, and decided most definitely not. But then no one around the table had any idea about the parts of Mia's life that would always take priority over work.

*Tuesday 14 May*

**Initial interviews between DC Emily Marlow and the staff of Morris & Wood, following the fire on Monday 13 May**

*Patrick Carter, Senior Account Director*

Patrick:    I can't get my head around what's happened.

Marlow:    I understand this is a stressful time for you, Patrick.

Patrick:    It is. It doesn't feel real. The whole thing's burned to the ground, hasn't it? Was it ... was it an accident or did someone do this?

Marlow:    At this moment in time we don't know exactly what started the fire.

Patrick:    I know you think someone did it. Someone who worked here.

Marlow:    If you wouldn't mind just answering a few questions for me?

Patrick:     I will, but can you tell me the truth. Please? I heard they pulled a body out the building last night. And now neither Harry nor his wife, Janie, are answering their bloody phones.

Marlow:     I'm afraid we can't—

Patrick:     I just want to know that they're all right. I want to know it wasn't Harry, because … you must know if it was or not?

Marlow:     I'm really sorry, Patrick. I'm afraid I can't tell you anything at the moment.

Patrick:     He's a friend, that's all. Harry Wood. He's my boss and everything, but he's a mate too, and if anything's happened to him … This is what doesn't sit right. If someone did start the fire and he *was* in there, well then, I can't tell you one person who would want to do that. It makes no sense.

Marlow:     Patrick …

Patrick:     I just don't know why he's not answering his phone.

Marlow:     Mr Carter, please. Would you answer some questions for me and then I'll see if there is anything I can find out.

Patrick:     Fine. Okay.

Marlow:     Could you confirm your position at Morris & Wood?

Patrick:     I'm a Senior Account Director. I sit on the board. I've been there since the start. Since long before Harry came to Lymington and set up an arm of the agency here. I worked with him in London.

Marlow: Can you tell me what your role entails?

Patrick: I manage some of our most important accounts. I'm responsible for five of them – the ones with the larger marketing budgets.

Marlow: You're pretty high up there then, is that what you're saying?

Patrick: I'm a director. Yes, of course. I'm Harry's deputy.

Marlow: Officially?

Patrick: Not in a contract, if that's what you mean, but Harry involves me in all the decisions. When he's not around, I pick things up.

Marlow: Were you involved in the decision to keep Mia Anderson at the firm?

Patrick: (pause) No.

Marlow: So Harry didn't run that past you?

Patrick: Not that decision. What's your point? Aren't I supposed to be here because of the fact the entire office has burned down? What does it matter whether I was any part of a decision to recruit someone?

Marlow: I'm just trying to get some facts. That's all. You *are* helping, Patrick, and I appreciate you probably have many things you need to be sorting out right now, but your assistance is crucial in

|          | helping us build a picture of what happened last night. |
|----------|---------|
| Patrick: | Fine. Fine. (pause) No, I wasn't involved in Mia Anderson remaining in the job. That was one Harry took on by himself. I suppose he thought she was doing a good job. I don't know, I didn't really get involved in her accounts. |
| Marlow:  | Did the decision upset anyone in the office? |
| Patrick: | Like I said, it was nothing to do with my job – it was Laura Denning she'd taken over from. |
| Marlow:  | And how did it go down with Laura? |
| Patrick: | (laughs) How do you expect? She was pretty pissed. Sorry, excuse my French. She was annoyed. |
| Marlow:  | Thank you, but you don't have to excuse your language for me. How she was annoyed? |
| Patrick: | Well, she thought she'd been replaced, I guess. I suppose she had been. To tell you the truth, I thought Harry was treading muddy water. I'm pretty certain that legally he shouldn't have done what he did. |
| Marlow:  | How do you mean? |
| Patrick: | Well, he took Laura off her job. Gave the biggest client to someone else who'd only been doing it five minutes. |
| Marlow:  | You don't agree with the decision? |

Patrick:    I don't know *why* it was made is what I'm saying. I couldn't actually see the reason for it, but Harry was adamant he didn't have a choice, and that was that. I felt for Laura, to tell you the truth. Anyone else wouldn't have been able to get away with it, I don't suppose, but Harry … (shrugs)

Marlow:    What do you mean?

Patrick:    Well, he still clearly wants to make sure Laura is okay. I don't know whether that's because he's worried she might leave or – you know, if it's because it's her. It's probably both. Harry has a soft spot for Laura, that's all I'm saying. You'll hear it from one of the women in the office soon enough, if you haven't already. The rumour mill is rife, but as far as I'm concerned, there's nothing more to it than that.

Marlow:    So what did Harry do to make sure Laura was okay?

Patrick:    He promised her some new job – some new big client who was supposedly on the scene.

Marlow:    And did that materialise?

Patrick:    (pauses) Nothing's been signed on the dotted line. And in my experience, you don't put in the amount of work Laura has in the last few weeks without having anything signed. She's been putting in more hours than anyone lately and – I don't know – sometimes it can all be just a huge waste of your time. Anyway, as I say, Harry's a mate, but he isn't always ...

Marlow: Always what?

Patrick: He does favours for his own, you know: the men from the directors' clubs he's a part of, from his London days. This new client was one of them.

Harry's bloody good at what he does. That's one of the reasons I followed him down here, but sometimes – oh, I hate talking out of turn about him – I think he believes he needs to do things for certain people. Harry can't always say no. It's his weakness.

Anyway, Laura might have been annoyed about the fact she'd lost one of her main accounts, but she didn't take it out on him. She wouldn't have started the fire.

Marlow: How can you be so certain of that?

Patrick: Laura's not crazy. You set fire to a building and something has to be pretty wrong in the head, doesn't it? No. She and Harry had a good relationship. Always did. She was his golden girl.

Marlow: But she must have felt put out?

Patrick: Yeah. But like I say, it didn't seem to affect her relationship with him.

Marlow: Don't you think that's odd? Surely he was the one who made the decision, after all.

| Patrick: | Only Harry could manage it; he gets away with stuff the rest of us can't. All the women think he's a god, and not just because he's CEO. Like I say, he's a mate and all, but Harry (shakes head), he's on a totally other level. No, he and Laura were as close as ever. |
|---|---|
| Marlow: | How well do you know Harry's wife, Janie Wood? |
| Patrick: | I know her well enough. She comes into the office now and then. Not much, I suppose, any more, but of course she throws the party every year. |
| Marlow: | Party? |
| Patrick: | Yeah, Harry's party happens every May in their back garden; they open up their house to all his employees. Every one of them is invited, even the ones right at the bottom. |
| Marlow: | What do you mean by *the bottom*, Patrick? |
| Patrick: | The lowest pay grade. |
| Marlow: | How kind of him. |
| Patrick: | I don't mean it like that – I'm just saying. He doesn't have to do it, does he? You don't see many bosses opening up their home to everyone. Anyway, Janie's always there. I'm sure she's the one behind it, because I can't imagine Harry getting involved in all that stuff. (laughs) Women like planning parties, don't they? My wife would have a field |

|  | day if I gave her that kind of money to blow on one. |
|---|---|
| Marlow: | When was the last time the Woods held one of these parties? |
| Patrick: | (pauses) You haven't heard anything about it yet? I'm surprised. It was Friday night. Four days ago. |
| Marlow: | Is there something I should have heard? |
| Patrick: | Yes, you could say that. You mix highly charged emotions with alcohol and you're always going to get an explosion. |
| Marlow: | There was a fight? |
| Patrick: | (nods) There was. |
| Marlow: | Who was involved? |
| Patrick: | Mia, Laura, Harry, Janie … The party was a disaster really. |

# Chapter Four

*Two months before the fire*

Janie Wood's washing machine beeped at the same time that the phone rang and the cat leapt through the cat flap with another mouse still twitching in his mouth. 'Urgh!' she yelled. 'You bloody cat! Take that thing out of the house.'

The cat looked up at her with soulful eyes as it dropped the mouse on the floor and patted it towards her with its paw. The mouse didn't move a limb except for its eyes, which found Janie's and pleaded with her either to put it out of its misery or to save it.

Janie stared back at the cat. 'Shoo – go on, get out of here.' She waved her hands until he eventually retreated and then, with one last scowl at her, turned and disappeared.

The mouse continued to look up at her in fear, before it too scarpered. 'Oh God,' she moaned. 'Where the hell have you gone?' She followed it into the hallway, the cat brushing past her legs in haste, only the mouse was nowhere in sight. 'Damn it,' she muttered, crouching down to search under the side table.

She would have to leave it, hope that somehow it would either escape or the cat would have got rid of it by the time she returned. Eventually Janie grabbed the keys, ignoring the phone as she headed for the front door. She checked her watch. She was already running late for coffee with her school-mum friends, and if she didn't get there on time they'd start without her and then she would have to ask them to repeat it all, because she wanted to know what Lucy had said to the head teacher.

And if their coffee meeting ran over, she'd be late for golf, and as much as she thought the instructor was particularly easy on the eye, he had an ugly temper, and she didn't care to be on the receiving end of it.

Janie beeped the car alarm and climbed in. The entire morning had been a game of catch-up. Ever since Harry had snoozed his alarm and woken in a panic. She'd consequently not got into the shower until quarter past, and even an extra five minutes getting out of the house meant the traffic on the school run built up and getting a parking space was nigh on impossible. It meant having to pull up on double-yellows, ignoring Frosty Fiona, who was ready to slap an A4 sheet of paper on the windscreen full of horrifying statistics that she'd googled about road accidents.

If only Lucy didn't have a doctor's appointment straight after drop-off, the four of them could have met right afterwards, but Janie had to concur that the mole had got bigger. And that meant Janie had too much time to kill and had gone home first, which in hindsight was a mistake.

She switched on the engine and Radio 1 blasted out from the car stereo. Janie didn't know why she still listened to the station; at forty-five, she was well past the outer limits of its target audience, yet for some reason she couldn't bring herself to change. She supposed it was because it would be another part of her youth left behind and, more than anything, Janie couldn't bear the thought of that. There were enough things time had stolen from her, and if she had to listen to a DJ who was young enough to be her son, speaking words she only pretended to understand, then that was what she'd continue to do.

As she pulled out of the driveway she wondered who had been calling. Harry, probably. Most likely he'd want to tell her he wouldn't be back for dinner, even though as he walked out the door that morning he had promised her he'd be back by six. Janie glanced at her mobile phone, considering that if it was Harry, he'd surely ring her on that; then she wondered if she cared if he was late anyway, because it only meant she wouldn't bother making anything more than beans on toast and she could eat with the kids.

She'd only just got the salmon out of the freezer. She could put it back in again before it defrosted.

*Jesus, was that really what occupied her mind these days?* she thought as she drove through the much quieter lanes of Beaulieu. For a moment Janie allowed herself to be relieved by the serenity, as her mindfulness teacher had been instructing her to, and for a brief five minutes she felt like it might actually work.

In the early days of moving to the New Forest, five years ago, the solitude had hit Janie hard. It was a stark contrast to the high-powered job and life in London she'd left behind, but then she'd told herself this was exactly what they needed. And yet her head was used to be being busy, a multitude of things running through it at any one time, and what she had found when she first moved to the south was that the peace gave her the space to think about things that were probably more important. And if she was honest with herself, she didn't particularly want to do that.

When the girls started at the private primary school nearby, Janie had flung herself into anything she could find, regardless of whether it was entirely up her street. Over the last five years she had dedicated her time to PTA meetings and bake-sales, which gradually gave way to ridiculously unfounded ideas that she should do courses in creative writing and basket-weaving, and eventually settled on coffee mornings with her friends, yoga and golf and generally living her life through her daughters.

No one could tell Janie she didn't keep herself busy. What she didn't admit was that there was busy and there was *busy*, and while she might have been running around like a headless chicken, she could never say it was satisfying, because she wasn't even using five per cent of her potential.

But that had been the choice she had made. Moving south meant giving up her career and devoting her time to raising two girls, just as her mum had always told her she should.

'You're losing precious time, Janie. They won't be young for long. These years will fly, even if it doesn't feel like it now.' She could still hear her mother's voice as if she were sitting in the passenger seat next to her.

The more her mum had protested, the more Janie dug her heels in, ignoring the guilt that crawled through her veins. She was doing it for her girls, she told herself. Showing them that women don't need to give up their careers.

Though, quite frankly, Janie had already realised that no one should ever have promised women they could have it all, because they couldn't, and the realisation of that only made them feel like they were failing. The idea was laughable really, especially when she considered that some weeks her working hours, combined with Harry's, topped one hundred and fifty. Of course she wasn't having it all; she was losing out on being a mother, replaced by the twenty-three-year-old nanny who was living in her house and bringing up her toddlers.

'It's your choice,' her mum had muttered once. 'That's all it boils down to. Choices.' She had stayed at home to look after Janie until the day she went to university.

Janie later realised that her mum was right. It was all about making choices and accepting them. She had chosen a full-on career, which meant she was supposed to accept that she needed to outsource her childcare. Only she never could.

She glanced at the empty passenger seat beside her and inhaled a breath that seemed to swell in her throat. 'I wish you could see me now, Mum,' she said. 'I finally did what you said I should.' Unfortunately her mother had died six months after Janie moved south and never got to see the so-called choice that Janie had made, to give up her career and be a stay-at-home mum. So-called, because Janie never could reconcile that it was a choice. In the end, by the time they left London and she had given up her role as a defence barrister, Janie didn't believe she'd had a choice at all.

But by then she had been thankful when Harry told her about the site he had found across the water from Lymington Quay. When he was excited about the possibility of branching out his already successful ad agency to the south coast, Janie considered that maybe it was exactly what they needed. And so she listened as Harry told her that he'd been playing with the idea for a while. He already had some big clients based along the M3 corridor, and there were a number of financial companies he'd been speaking to in Southampton and Bournemouth. He could share his time between London and the south. And how about, he suggested, she and the girls move down full-time?

Janie continued to let him list the pros as he sold his argument. Schooling, property prices, they could even have a pool in their back garden. He didn't need to remind her that Lymington had a place in her heart already, as she'd visited often as a child, her dad being a keen sailor.

Harry reminded her that London was not even a two-hour commute, and he could work up there a couple of days a week, maybe rent a flat. He could, by all accounts, carry on living the life he wanted during the week and then have the luxury of leaving it all behind on a Friday.

Janie, however, would have to make a choice, they both silently understood. But by then, in Janie's head, it was already a done deal.

She pulled off the country lane and onto the small gravel car-park alongside Lucy's silver BMW. The coffee shop sat on the outskirts of Brockenhurst, a little way from the school, but she and her three friends all agreed it served the best coffee around, and it was good to talk without the threat of being overheard by another school parent.

She could see all three of her friends gathered around the table in the window, and Janie hurried inside, banging the door wide open as she did. She didn't know when she had got to the stage in her life that she hated being late because of the gossip she was missing, but at some point it had happened.

'Just in time,' Kristen called. 'Lucy was about to tell us about the meeting with Mr Steele.'

'Oh, don't start,' Janie said. 'Let me grab a coffee first.' She threw her bag onto the empty seat, grabbing her purse from it as she rushed to the counter. They were the only customers, as they often were, but there was no sign of anyone to serve them, and in her impatience Janie called out, 'Hello?'

Eventually a young girl appeared and Janie asked for a black coffee.

'I'm sorry I'm late,' she said as she pulled her bag from the chair and sat down without offering an explanation. None of them cared why; they were all as busy as each other, running back and forth between school and the various activities they had during the day. Not one of her small group of mum-friends worked, yet each of them filled their days with so many things they barely had time to breathe. Moments like these were precious – catching up over a coffee and sharing their news, which invariably revolved around the school and their children, and who had fallen out with whom. 'So tell us, what did he say?'

Lucy rolled her eyes and waved a hand in the air. 'Oh, he basically told me this was in *my* daughter's head,' she said. 'That they've been watching Dexter and he hasn't shown any signs of violence in the playground.'

'He didn't actually say that,' Janie gasped as she fiddled the clasp on her purse shut and threw it back into her bag. 'That it was in her head?'

'Not in so many words, but he might as well have.'

'I can't believe they're not doing anything about it. Dexter's clearly insane. I mean you only need to look at his mother,' Kristen chipped in.

'His mother's the problem, isn't she?' Lucy said. 'If they weren't donating so much bloody money to the school, left, right and centre, someone might actually have opened their eyes and seen their son was a lunatic. You know they've invited Mr Steele out on their boat at the weekend?'

'That, and the fact she works full-time of course,' Kristen murmured.

Janie winced.

'Kris, you can't say things like that that,' Lucy said. 'It's got nothing to do with it.'

'Of course it has,' Kristen shrugged. 'She's never there. Dexter's left to the au pair to sort out, who I'm afraid barely speaks one word of English. He gets away with murder, I see it outside the school gate. She's just eighteen and can't control him.'

'Well, you're not going to like my news then,' Anna smiled. 'I'm going back to work.'

'You're what?' Lucy spluttered.

'I know,' she grinned. 'Crazy, eh? But my old boss called and they need someone urgently, and it's something I've been thinking about for a while anyway. Why are you all looking at me like that?'

'I don't know,' Lucy said. 'I mean, of course it's great, if that's what you want to do, but ... Aren't you going to miss all this?' She waved an arm around the empty coffee shop and Janie followed it with her gaze.

Janie's stomach had dipped so deep she could feel it sitting like a lump of rock inside her. She'd never regret being around for the girls the past few years, but sometimes it was hard to ignore the hole stretching and tugging inside. If things had been different ... If she hadn't taken on that case ...

But this was her life now and, as far as the girls went at least, Janie was happy with it. She turned her attention back to Anna, who was grinning and shaking her head.

'I'm still going to see you all, it's just ...' She paused and shrugged. 'I have to do it. You can understand that, can't you?' she asked and her eyes roamed to Janie, who felt immobile as she stared back at Anna. 'What do you think?' Anna asked, reaching out to grab Janie's hand.

The others had stopped murmuring, and Janie realised she hadn't commented on the news. 'I think it's great,' she eventually got out. 'I really do.'

Anna nodded, smiling back at her. 'I knew you'd understand, Janie. I mean, you were always such a career woman yourself. You must know what I mean when I say I need to be doing something just for me?'

'Yes,' Janie smiled. 'Yes, I do.'

'Oh, please don't tell us you're going to get yourself a job too,' Lucy said. 'There'll be none of us left.'

Janie continued to smile and shook her head. 'No,' she said. 'No plans for me.' She nodded at the girl bringing her coffee over to the table and pulled a packet of sugar out of a little porcelain dish, averting her eyes from her friends, whose gaze she could feel on her. 'I need a little,' she said, tearing it open, already feeling a stab of regret. When was the last time she'd taken sugar? Now she didn't even know why she was tipping it into her coffee.

They lapsed into silence, before Lucy piped up, 'In other good news, my mole is actually a wart, so I guess that's something to be grateful for. Everyone up for yoga tonight?'

They all agreed they were, and although Janie knew she wouldn't be able to, if Harry wasn't home in time, she didn't bother saying as much. Her friends knew the possibility well enough.

By the time she left the coffee shop and started her car, Janie realised she was jealous of Anna. And once the thought had entered her head, she feared she might not be able to get rid of it.

She played with the idea that she would miss her girlfriends and their catch-ups, but their oldest girls would be going to secondary school soon. Things were going to change. And really, what did they all talk about that was remotely important? It was so far from the evenings she used to spend with friends in a wine bar in London at the end of a heavy day, when Janie would regale them with tales of her latest cases, drip-feeding them as much information as she was allowed to.

They were always keen to know the ins and outs of her job, because Janie's firm had some big-time clients – but it was Janie's last case there that had particularly piqued their interest.

She knew how to handle difficult questions, how to avoid getting into a debate, but sometimes she would still get drawn in. Janie knew her friends were interested in what she really thought, how she could possibly detach herself. The truth was that she'd learned early on to stop caring about the victims, because if she did care, she wouldn't be doing her job properly. She'd observed how to look at her cases as if they were pieces of fiction.

Only that case, which her friends had questioned her about relentlessly, had caught her in the end. When there was no way of escaping the fact it wasn't fiction – it was reality – that was the point when Janie had to face the question that had begun searing into her every waking moment. How could she carry on doing her job?

Janie drove on, heading towards Lymington, her mind full of the thought that she still dreaded the day she switched on the TV or opened a newspaper and read about the case again. In the last five years thoughts of her career, which had once triggered excitement, had shrivelled away to disgust – and, if she ever allowed the thought in, an element of self-loathing.

It was an unconscious decision to pull into the car park at the quay on her way to golf, and for a few seconds Janie didn't know how she had turned off the main road and headed in this direction. But now she was here and looking across the river to her husband's office.

At the edge of the quay she got a direct view of the shiny offices, though she could only imagine what was happening on the other side of the glass. They could see out, but she couldn't see in – the way the building had so cleverly been designed.

The office looked beautiful. The way the light reflected off the water and hit the glass – all as it was supposed to. That office had been her lifesaver five years ago. Her chance to start again. And yet some days she would look at it and feel hatred bubbling beneath her skin. A hatred that was potentially misplaced, but which also stood for everything she had lost, and for everything Harry still had.

She wondered what was going on inside its four walls right now; how her husband felt, making decisions, giving orders, pulling in another big client or congratulating his staff on a job well done. On the whole, Harry was amazing at what he did – he always had been. His ambition was part of what Janie had fallen in love with. There was something so sexy about success, and Harry had been nothing but successful.

Janie stared at her husband's building as the light bounced off it. Today was one of the days she hated it, but not just because of her reaction to Anna's news. It was also because Laura Denning was back.

# Chapter Five

By the time Laura had extracted herself from the toilets, she was five minutes late to Harry's meeting. The boardroom was already full. From outside the glass wall she could see the jostle for chairs, the banter by the far window. She could hear the laughter erupting through the glass.

There was a time when Laura felt a buzz upon entering the room, but now her stomach was jittering for a very different reason, and she gripped her notepad more tightly as she caught sight of Mia at the far end of the room. Laura's eyes trailed down the length of Mia's grey woollen cardigan. It hung open and unbelted, reaching her mid-calves. Under it she had on an almost-sheer white top, which was pulled out from the waistband of slim navy jeans.

Mia's hair was cut short, tapered into the back of her neck, but hanging lower at the front. It was much darker than Laura remembered. There was something so effortlessly chic about this woman that it made Laura feel dowdy by comparison. She'd been pleased with how she looked that morning, but now she was feeling unsettled. The men who stood around the long oval table were all dressed in either open-necked or polo shirts, as if it were some kind of uniform. They wouldn't even consider checking out what each other was wearing. They probably couldn't tell her what colour their own shirts were, if she asked them to close their eyes. And yet somehow, for some reason, the sight of Mia looking so elegant filled Laura with irritation, because more than anything it sapped away what little confidence she had left.

Mia was smiling at something Harry was saying and eventually he glanced up and caught Laura standing on the other side of the glass. He beckoned her in. A smile was plastered across his face, left over from whatever joke he'd just been sharing, but she could tell that beneath it there was a layer of something else. She wondered how much he was wrangling with his decision, and hoped it was enough that he would come to his senses quickly.

Laura forced a smile as she opened the door and flung it open to a chorus of, 'Hey, you're back. Good to see you.'

She answered their questions about Bobby and agreed how quickly the time had gone by, and silently thanked their financial officer for standing so close to the door that she could direct her attention onto him.

Meanwhile she could sense Mia moving towards the table. As if on cue, she pulled out the seat next to Harry and sat down. Rage bubbled inside Laura. Misplaced maybe, for how could she explain to anyone why she was so disproportionately angry that this woman had taken a seat at their boss's side, for what did it really matter? But Laura realised it mattered a lot – because Mia was there, and she shouldn't be.

As Harry called them all in, Laura dropped her notepad onto the table and took the seat nearest the door. Inside the pad were her copious notes on how she was planning to develop the Coopers campaign, a now-futile exercise that had taken up many hours of her last two weeks of maternity leave, which she could have spent with her son. It both surprised and annoyed her that this was another thought that brought her to the edge of tears; never before had her emotions teetered so precariously close to breaking point. She inhaled deeply, focusing on Harry's words as he ran through last week's top-line figures.

To everyone who worked at Morris & Wood, Harry was some kind of hero. Back in London, before he'd set up another arm of the agency in Lymington, Harry had turned the company into a multimillion-pound, award-winning agency, after taking over from his father and buying out the other partner.

He rarely made decisions that anyone on the board disagreed with, which was why this latest one was so unsettling. Laura scanned the men around the table and wondered what they had thought when Harry told them Mia would be staying on. Did they agree with him? Had they seen her in action and understood that she was too brilliant to lose? Had one of them even suggested it? Laura clutched her hands together under the table – she had never in all her time at Morris & Wood felt so peripheral.

Suddenly Harry's patter was broken by the vibration of Mia's phone, and Mia told Harry she was going to have to take the call. Laura glanced at her boss, who looked bemused, but nodded regardless and picked up again seamlessly as Mia left the room. Out of the corner of Laura's eye, she could see Mia pacing back and forth outside the window and even though it was only a matter of minutes before she re-entered, apologising profusely, Laura wondered what was so important that it took her out of the Monday exec meeting.

And then, just as it seemed the meeting couldn't get any worse, Harry announced that Mia was back in time to present her update.

'Well, we're meeting with the Coopers health-drink marketing team a week on Friday,' Mia began. 'I'm going to be taking them through the concepts for TV, and we hope to start shooting the ad as soon as June.'

Laura squeezed her hands tighter and prayed the others would continue to look at either Mia or the table in front of them and not turn in her direction, as they must have been inclined to do. The air felt sticky and oppressive. The thought that she'd stand out as the only one not called upon for an update was mildly tempered by the idea that if she did open her mouth, no words would come out.

Her body was rigid as she listened to Mia's seemingly eternal presentation, and all Laura could conclude was that somehow, during the last six months, Mia Anderson had transformed herself from a laid-back temp with no ambition into a woman who had clearly earned her place around Harry's board table. The idea of it seemed so implausible that Laura wondered if she had actually read Mia completely wrong when she interviewed her last October.

She willed the next fifty minutes to pass as quickly as possible. As soon as the meeting was over, she was ready to run and, thankfully, being nearest the door, was the first out of it. Yet as she stepped out onto the open-plan floor, she realised she had nowhere to go. Mia bloody Anderson's things were still on her desk and, as tempting as it was to hurl them off, Laura wasn't quite at that stage yet.

'Welcome back, Laura.'

She recognised the voice immediately.

'Sorry I didn't get a chance to say hi earlier. I was on a call and couldn't get off the phone.'

'It's really not a problem,' Laura said as she turned to face Mia.

'How was it, leaving your baby this morning?'

'It was fine,' Laura lied. No way was she going to get into a conversation about her personal life.

'I expect you'll miss him, though, won't you?' Mia went on. 'I mean, it must be a wrench and, you know, worrying over someone who depends on you so much. It's not easy.'

'He's very lucky to be with his dad,' Laura replied curtly.

'Of course.' Mia's gaze didn't leave her, and Laura wondered how much confidence the woman had. 'I'm just saying, I can understand you must be feeling a bit weird this morning.' Mia paused and smiled. 'I think if it were me, I wouldn't be able to stop thinking about him and—'

'Mia, would you mind moving, so I can have my desk back?' Laura interrupted before this woman went any further.

'Right, yes, of course.' Mia hesitated and then, 'I'll do it now,' she said.

As soon as Mia disappeared, Laura headed straight for the lift and rode it down to the ground floor, where she pulled out her mobile and phoned Nate. 'How is he?' she asked, breathlessly, as soon as her husband picked up.

'Hey! Everything okay?'

'Yes, how's Bobby?'

'He's great. He's having his nap.'

'That's good. Did he eat all his porridge?'

'Most of it, greedy little man,' Nate laughed.

'He is,' she smiled, closing her eyes and pressing her fingertips against them.

'Laura, are you okay? You sound upset?'

'No, I'm fine.'

'Bobby's all right, you know. I've been looking after him in the last hour and fifty minutes,' Nate joked.

'I know.'

'Seriously, has something happened?'

'Oh God, Nate. I don't know what to do,' she began, before telling him what had occurred.

'And so what did Harry actually say was the reason?' Nate asked.

'That Mia had started, so she might as well see it through. He said something about easing me back in, and that there was something else in the pipeline.'

'Okay.'

'But it's all crap,' she cried.

'What is? The thing in the pipeline?'

'All of it. What's she done that's so special, Nate? She's clearly done a better job than I have in the last five years.'

'That won't be true.'

'It must be. I can't think of any other reason why she'd be kept on.'

'But maybe there is something else that Harry wants you to work on?'

'Of course there isn't,' Laura protested as she paced to the front door of the empty foyer and then back again to the lift. Her head was spinning and she couldn't clear it. Her stomach was a jumbled mess of knots at the thought of stepping back in that lift and having to face Mia again, because right now she would like nothing more than to run out of the door and not come back.

'Well, maybe he's right,' Nate was saying, 'and it'll be good to ease yourself back in.'

'I don't need to do that, Nate,' she said, her voice rising. 'Harry knows what I'm like – he would never have thought I needed time to get back into it. No. I'm telling you, she's clearly better than I am, and so I'm just going to have to accept that, aren't I?' she said, knowing there'd never be a day when that would happen.

'Laura, you're getting yourself worked up.'

'Of course I am,' she cried, splaying her other hand against her head. 'Mia's a bloody temp, Nate. And she's stolen my job.'

'No, she hasn't, love. By the sound of it, she's doing this one thing and—'

'Oh my God, Nate, will you stop doing that.'

'Doing what?' he said. 'I'm only trying to help you.'

'I know you are, but you aren't. I just want you to be on my side and not keep telling me it's okay, because it actually isn't.'

'I'm sorry.' Nate paused. 'Of course I'm on your side, but I don't know what else to say. It's probably only temporary, and whatever Harry's got in mind might be better. Laura, I don't get what else I can say,' he repeated.

And that was the problem. Nate didn't understand because his job in IT was so different from hers. He had tasks to complete and he got on and did them, and then passed them back to his supervisor. She admired his skills, she really did. She certainly couldn't find her way around a computer like he did, but he didn't understand the complexities of her career. And while she could never expect him to, it meant that sometimes she knew she would never get any useful advice out of him. Right now that only made her feel worse.

'Why don't you speak to one of the team at Coopers?' he suggested. 'Who do you know best?'

Laura shook her head. She couldn't imagine putting herself on the line like that. 'Listen, I need to go back to work,' she said eventually. 'I'll talk to you tonight. And I'm sorry I shouted.'

Laura thought about Mia as she took the lift back up to the third floor, and the way she'd been in the interview, perching on the edge of the chair, her eyes intently focused on Laura. Every so often Mia's gaze had flicked out of the small meeting-room window to the offices beyond, and on a couple of occasions Laura had wondered, frustrated, what she was looking at.

For every one of her questions Mia had given a textbook response, nodding enthusiastically. Laura had put her behaviour down to nerves. No one liked being interviewed for a job, though it had been a surprise when right at the end Mia had given a reassuring little speech as they left the room, about how much she would relish looking after Laura's position while she was on maternity leave.

Ironically it had been those final words that sealed the deal; but now Laura considered that Mia had actually been very determined she was going to get the job. And that those words felt more sinister than comforting.

Laura saw Mia as soon as she stepped out of the lift, hovering by the water cooler, chatting to Henrietta James. Mia's head was bouncing up and down with laughter as she wiped a hand across her face. Had Henrietta actually brought Mia to tears with whatever they were talking about? Laura couldn't remember a time when she had shared a joke with Henrietta, certainly not to that extent, and she realised she was feeling a ripple of jealousy at the sight of the two women being so close.

She glanced around the floor and thought there was not one woman in the office she could call a good friend. There had been once. Saskia. But Laura's fingers had been burned by that friendship, when the lines between work and her social life blurred, and after that she knew it was advisable to keep the women who worked for her at arm's length.

Yet it meant there wasn't anyone else in the office she felt she could confide in about what was happening, while there was every possibility that Mia already could. And that thought made Laura feel suddenly so alone.

She was still standing by the lifts, this realisation dawning on her, when Mia finished her conversation and then turned to have a new one with the quiet woman Laura had seen earlier in the toilets. Sarah Clifton had been hovering nearby, and now that Henrietta had gone, Mia's attention was solely on Sarah instead, but there was a very different dynamic between these two women. The way Mia hung her head, her brow furrowed, one hand lightly touching Sarah's arm, rubbing it gently as she finished talking to her, before her gaze drifted over Sarah's shoulder to Laura.

Laura inhaled a tight breath as Sarah left the water cooler and Mia started walking towards her. Whether she was prepared for it or not, they were about to talk, and Laura knew she was going to have to play this carefully.

**Tuesday 14 May**

**Initial interviews between DC Emily Marlow and the staff of Morris & Wood, following the fire on Monday 13 May**

*Henrietta James, Senior Account Manager*

Marlow: You say things started to change at Morris & Wood when Laura came back from maternity leave. What do you mean by that?

Henrietta: I mean everyone was on edge. There was a tension in the air and we didn't know what to do for the best.

Marlow: Tension between Laura and Mia?

Henrietta: Yes. Mainly.

Marlow: What happened between them?

Henrietta: Well, they both tried to hide it in the office, but then Laura Denning got it into her head that Mia was somehow out to get her. Like she had come for her job on purpose or something.

Marlow: Do you believe that was the case?

Henrietta: Of course not. Laura was trying to blame her because she wanted her account back. Why on earth would Mia do that?

Marlow: I don't know.

Henrietta: Well, she wouldn't. It makes no sense.

Marlow: Yet Laura thought she had. How do you know this – did Laura tell you?

Henrietta: (laughs) No. No, she wouldn't have told me. I overheard her, speaking to Harry. She said she had evidence, but – well, I didn't hear the rest of it. All I know is that Harry seemed to get annoyed with her. He ushered her into his office pretty quick.

Marlow: Harry got annoyed? Did this cause tensions between them, then?

Henrietta: Laura tried to maintain everything was all right between her and Harry, but after that I didn't think it was. I didn't see how it could be. You see, Laura always had Harry's ear and now suddenly he wasn't listening to her. I think we all expected that as soon as Laura returned, she'd somehow manage to talk him round, and Mia would be gone. None of us wanted that, of course. Everyone likes Mia, but all the same I could see where Laura would be coming from, if she had started demanding her job back.

It's not that I don't like her, you know. I hope that's not how it's coming across, it's just Laura is – she's not as easy-going as Mia to get along with. Mia's so much easier to work for. She doesn't mind stopping and chatting, for a start; not like Laura, who's always checking her watch if she wants something from you.

Marlow: You were saying about Laura and Harry?

Henrietta: Sorry? Oh, right, yes. The point is, Laura never did get her way with Harry, did she? Because Mia is still working there.

Marlow: Did you notice any other changes around Laura in the last two months?

Henrietta: Apart from the fact she's always working, even though she has that young baby at home? Mind you, that's no different from the way she always was, but with a child – you know? You'd have thought she would have cut back. I feel sorry for her husband.

Marlow: Nathan Denning?

Henrietta: That's right. I thought we might see him at Harry's party last week, but that was another odd thing. He didn't show.

I did say to someone at the party that I was worried about Laura. I remember doing that. Before everything kicked off, I mean. I said I hope she's okay, because she certainly wasn't looking it by then.

# Chapter Six

*Two months before the fire*

Mia knew this was not going to be an easy conversation, but it was one she had to get out of the way. Yet as Laura's eyes bored through her, she began to wonder whether it would be easier to sidestep the woman and pretend she was heading for the lift. Any earlier confidence was rapidly evaporating.

'Hi again, Laura, I've moved my things.' Mia gestured a hand in the direction of the desk she had just vacated.

'Okay. Great. Thanks,' Laura said awkwardly and then, appearing to pull herself together, she added, 'I hear you're continuing to run with the TV campaign for the time being.'

'Yes. That's right.' Mia smiled at her, as warmly as she could muster when the anger bubbling off Laura was almost palpable.

Of course Laura was angry, she must clearly have wanted to run the campaign herself. It was, after all, bringing in a large sum of money for the company. So Mia understood how Laura must be feeling right now, but at the same time they were going to have to find a way to get on with it.

'I could do with your input actually,' Mia said, watching Laura stiffen as she ploughed on. 'I'd appreciate your thoughts on what I'm presenting – you've known the brand for so long after all ...' She was waffling, but Laura wasn't answering as Mia sucked in a short breath. 'It would be good to see if you can spot anything I've missed.'

'You want me to help you out, so that *you* can present the work to the client?' Laura's eyebrows rose and she gestured to a small meeting room to the side of them. Mia followed her in. When Laura had closed the door behind them, she said, 'Mia, I have to be honest. I'm a little shocked you're still here. You were only supposed to be covering for my maternity leave.'

Mia knew this was coming and yet now they were here, pressed into the smallest of rooms, she didn't know how to respond.

Laura pursed her lips and then said, 'I'm grateful you've been keeping my accounts running, but I've been managing Coopers for the last five years. I know it back to front. Harry knows I'm ready to take it back again, and while I'm sure you've made a great start on the TV campaign, I'll be wanting it handed back to me as soon as possible.'

Mia watched as Laura straightened her back. This was completely patronising – did Laura really have no idea how capable she was?

Maybe it was her own doing, Mia understood that. In the interview she had told Laura what she wanted to hear, because she needed this job and she'd had to get it. What she had quickly deciphered was that Laura didn't want someone who was a threat, she wanted an assistant. Someone who could keep things going for her, and then Laura could walk back in and pick up where she left off. So it wasn't Laura's fault that she didn't know how easily Mia could run a TV campaign, but that didn't mean she wasn't pissed off with the way Laura was talking to her. Especially after she'd already snapped her fingers to get Mia out of her desk.

Mia wondered what she could possibly say right now, when it appeared Harry had told Laura the bare minimum; and if that were the case, then Laura was going to keep pestering her. But at the same time Mia was also wary of Laura and Harry's close relationship and, above anything, she could not lose this job.

'So I'm sorry, Mia, but I won't be helping you run this campaign just so that you can take the credit for it.'

'I realise you've been doing this job for a long time—'

'Only now *you* are.'

Mia held a tight breath. 'Yes,' she said. 'Now I am. And I want to continue doing a good job. Which is why I thought you might help me, but obviously I'm wrong.'

'Do you know, I don't actually remember you having that much account-director experience,' Laura said sharply.

Mia could feel the bite on Laura's tongue and the sneer in her voice. So that was the game she was going to play. Make out Mia didn't deserve to be in this role, as if she hadn't been putting everything into it over the last six months, proving her worth. Clearly Harry hadn't told Laura the reasons he wasn't readily handing the Coopers account back to her, but Mia wished he would, so she could get this woman off her back.

'You wanted a temporary role,' Laura persisted. 'You told me that yourself in the interview. You said you didn't want to stay in Lymington. That was why you were coming to cover me. So what's happened?'

Mia thought for a moment. 'Things have changed,' she said eventually. 'And I'm enjoying working at Morris & Wood. I love the people, it's great experience ...' She trailed off; she didn't need to answer to Laura Denning any more, she wasn't being interviewed. She certainly didn't work for Laura, as much as Laura might like to think she did. They were on the same level. 'Laura, this is the way it is, and I'm sorry you're not happy about it, but I'm running the Coopers campaign. I understand if you don't want to help me, I just thought I'd ask,' she said and she moved past Laura and opened the door.

Outside she caught sight of Sarah Clifton hovering nearby again and while she knew she shouldn't add fuel to the fire, Mia called out, 'Hey, Sarah, do you mind if we catch up on the creatives you're working on for me?'

Mia didn't look back as Sarah nodded, albeit appearing a little confused. Mia took Sarah's arm and led her towards another meeting room, where she'd brush off what she'd just said and turn the conversation instead onto Sarah, who'd been wanting to talk to her privately anyway. Behind her she felt Laura's wrath seeping out of the doorway.

Mia felt drained when she pulled up to the bungalow that night. One day of Laura being back and Mia was not only managing the TV campaign workload, but now had to manage Laura's resentment of her too. On top of that, she'd had to carve out time for Sarah Clifton, who was increasingly reaching the point where she wanted to make a formal complaint against Mike Lewis for harassment, and Mia needed to be there for her. As the only one who knew what was going on, she'd promised she'd be by Sarah's side every step, but right now juggling all three things wasn't easy.

Clutching her Gucci bag to her chest, she checked the road with the broken street lamps before stepping out of the car and up to the front door. It was the smartest door in the street. The only one that had been freshly painted and cared for, and the pale green stood out among the others, just like the small neatly mown patch of lawn beside the driveway did.

Sticking her key in the lock, Mia took a deep breath and held it for a moment before turning the key and pushing the door open. She never knew what was awaiting her on the other side of it and always entered with a sense of apprehension.

But tonight the TV was humming in the background and the smell of roast chicken drifted from the kitchen, and there was nothing that raised an alarm. Her pulse was already starting to slow as she stepped in and called out with feigned joviality, 'Hi, Mum, I'm home.'

In the kitchen her mum turned and smiled at her, wiping a hand across the plastic Bisto apron she'd had since Mia was a child. 'Long day, was it?'

Mia nodded and gave her mum a kiss on the cheek. Today had been long, though there were some days when she lingered in the office later than she needed to. She would never dare tell her mum that, however. Even though she would probably understand that being anywhere but inside these four walls was a breath of fresh air.

Mia wondered whether she'd continue to feel that way, now Laura was back. She'd enjoyed the last six months; Morris & Wood had felt like a comfort blanket in some ways. It was a shame things had to change, but change they must, and at least Mia had the Woods' party in her sights.

'I do so wish it wasn't there you were working, though,' her mum sighed.

'I know you do, Mum.'

Mia's mother had once protested about the development of the offices and still considered Harry Wood to be the enemy. When Mia had got the job, she warily told her mum where she was going to be working, but by then the money was so desperately needed that she thought her mum wouldn't have minded if she went to work for the Conservatives.

'And there really isn't anything else out there you could be going for?'

'No, there isn't. Besides, I like it.' She wrapped an arm around her mum's bony waist and gave it a squeeze. Every time she did so, she felt her mum getting a little thinner. And every time that happened, Mia felt an even greater weight pressing down on her shoulders.

# Chapter Seven

On Friday morning Janie pulled a pair of black capri trousers and a white shirt out of the wardrobe. It didn't escape her that making an effort for a child's assembly was ludicrous but if she didn't, she would stand out. The girls were already waiting by the front door when she descended the stairs, their blazers on, their hats slightly askew. She straightened Lottie's and reached for Ella, who pulled out of her way, making her hat slip even further to one side.

'We're going to be late,' Ella moaned.

'We're not. It's not even ten to.'

'You won't get a good seat. Don't you want to be at the front?'

'Of course I do, but wherever I sit I'll be able to see you. Are you nervous?' Janie asked her eldest.

'No.'

'You shouldn't be. You've practised so hard. You were playing beautifully last night.'

'Ohmigod, I just said I wasn't nervous,' Ella shouted.

'Fine.' Janie held up her hands in surrender and ushered them through the door towards the car.

'Lacey's dad's coming,' Ella muttered when she climbed into the back.

'You know Dad would have liked to come,' Janie said as she slid in too and looked at her daughter in the rear-view mirror. 'It's just that today he has something important to do at work and—'

'I'm not even saying anything about Dad, I simply told you Lacey's is coming. Are you not even listening to me?'

Janie ignored her daughter's tone as she started the engine. Ella wasn't usually remotely bothered if Harry was there or not, but then the evening before she'd overheard her asking him if he was coming, in a way that suggested she was. He'd told Ella he couldn't this time, and then Janie had waited for him to ask her about the piano recital, because the truth of it was she couldn't remember if she'd even told him about it in the first place. She didn't actually think she had.

But Harry didn't ask. Janie assumed this was because he must have thought he'd forgotten all about it, and she decided to let him think that. There was no point admitting it might be her mistake, but she felt guilty that Ella clearly wished her father was there.

She knew she was about to make it worse, but she couldn't help herself when she said, 'Honestly, Daddy really wanted to be there—'

'Mum!' Ella yelled. 'I told you I don't care.'

'Okay. I'm sorry,' she said and they fell into silence. Janie wondered if hormones kicked in again at eleven, or whether they had even stopped after the last surge.

Once they had reached the school playground, Janie kissed Ella hurriedly on the top of her head and waited with Lottie for the bell to go.

'You know you won't get a seat at the front if you don't go in,' Lottie warned her.

'I know, poppet, but I'll be fine.'

'Mummy, why doesn't Daddy ever come to see our shows?'

'Lottie, he does,' Janie said. 'That's not true – he always comes if he can make it.' But even as she said it, she tried to think back to the last time Harry had accompanied her to the school. Even on parents' evening he had rarely been home in time, but always the teachers had brushed it off, because everyone knew how busy and important Harry Wood was, and everyone was more than happy to excuse his absence.

Just like Janie always had been too. Over time, she realised, there had been many occasions when she felt like a single parent. Perhaps that was why she had inadvertently stopped telling her husband about the girls' events. Maybe, she even thought, she found it easier to support them on her own.

There would come a day when Janie would leave Harry. She had known this for some time now, but had always assumed it wouldn't be until the girls were older. When they left home themselves she wouldn't need to worry about what they thought as much as she did now.

She had often wondered what everyone would say when she told them – how surprised they would be. Even her own sister wouldn't foresee it. If Janie were being honest, thoughts of both their families were another reason that made the idea of leaving Harry seem impossible. From the outside, Janie and Harry were still the golden couple they always had been, their marriage the one everyone else supposedly craved. They'd both always attracted people like honeypots.

On the surface, their relationship *was* still the same. They rarely argued, they still had fun with friends, they continued to do things as a family at weekends. It was the layer below where there were cracks. They didn't argue because they didn't have enough meaningful conversations any more, or perhaps because they didn't care enough to get heated about them.

And then there was another layer, way below that. The one that had hardened just over five years ago – the root of all their issues, which was never spoken of. Janie didn't speak to anyone about it: not her sister, not even her best friend Sophie, whom she'd always been so much closer to. Maybe at the time she could have handled things differently and not believed that moving to the New Forest was enough.

A house move and a change of scenery went some way towards plastering over what had happened, but the problem with putting a plaster on was peeling it off. And sometimes it was so much easier just to carry on.

Next to her, Lottie's head nestled into her side and as she reminded herself that she wouldn't leave Harry until the girls were older, Janie also wondered if it would really be that bad. Once the girls had got used to the idea, would they actually miss him?

She kissed Lottie as the school bell rang, before wandering into the hall and finding a seat in the fourth row. Something would happen, if it were meant to.

Janie craned her neck to get a better view around Lacey's large grandfather, who was blocking the scene in front of her. It appeared Lacey hadn't only brought Mum and Dad, as both sets of grandparents were here too – therefore was it any wonder she'd never be able to get a seat at the front, unless she started queuing at eight?

'Mind if I squeeze in?'

Janie looked up and nodded as a mum she didn't recognise gestured to the chair on the other side of her. 'Let me move along,' Janie said and shuffled onto the next seat, from where she had an even worse view of the stage.

'Thanks. I was told to get here early, but I didn't realise it would be this busy.'

'Yep, it's pretty popular. Who are you here to watch?'

'My daughter Amelie. She's playing the cello, of all things.' The woman screwed up her nose and Janie smiled. 'It's bloody awful,' the mum went on. 'She simply can't play it. You'll hear for yourself soon enough.'

Janie laughed. This woman seemed like a breath of fresh air among so many stuck-up parents. 'Janie,' she said, holding out a hand. 'I don't think we've met.'

'Marcia. We're new. We only started this term.'

'Well, welcome,' Janie said and wondered whether she should invite Marcia along to their next coffee. There was, after all, an opening in their small group, once Anna started working again. 'I have Ella playing the piano, and my younger daughter, Lottie, is at the school too.'

'I've also got a son here,' she said. 'Year two: Miles.'

*Miles.* Janie continued to smile, but the hairs on her arms pricked up and for a moment she couldn't find the words to respond.

Marcia continued to talk to her, but Janie's mind had gone to other places. Marcia's son was just a little boy, of course, but that name ... that name had frozen her.

It had entered her head plenty of times over the years, though less so more recently. But the sound of it being spoken aloud – she had no idea her body would react like it had, and it was a relief when the children started filing into the hall. Marcia eventually stopped talking, and Janie turned her concentration to the child who had taken up the seat at the piano and was trying his hardest to thump out a tune.

Marcia nudged her when her daughter stood up, and Janie couldn't help but smile. But her thoughts kept straying and it took all her effort to pull herself back to the present. When Ella took to the stage, Janie shifted in her seat to get the clearest view she could, tears springing to her eyes when her daughter eventually finished playing her piece beautifully. Ella remained at the piano for a moment longer as she looked over to the crowd of parents clapping at the back of the hall, her eyes scanning them until she eventually found Janie. When she did so, her face broke into a smile and it melted Janie's heart that her gorgeous and talented, if slightly headstrong, daughter was so clearly pleased to see her.

For the rest of the morning Janie tried to shake away the thoughts of the man who would now not leave her head. Miles Morgan. She could picture his face as if he stood in front of her, even though it had been five years since she had last seen him in the flesh, or even in a photo. His dark hair, only a few flecks of grey then; the light coating of stubble on his chin; his bright-blue eyes; his height – he was at least six foot two, which made his presence in any room so overpowering. Harry was a man who, everyone admitted, was good-looking, but Miles was one who made you stop and turn.

Janie had always resisted the urge to look him up. To see what he was doing now. But that day, when she got home from the assembly, she couldn't stop herself from opening up her laptop and googling his name to see where he was, whether he was still working at the same company.

It didn't take long to find him, and as soon as Janie saw his picture she took a deep breath, sitting back in her chair, her fingers tapping through images, her breath short and ragged.

She pulled her mobile towards her and scrolled through her contacts. She had a sudden urge to call Sophie, although she could never tell her the reason. She could never admit to her best friend that she had been thinking of Miles, that she'd searched for him online, had seen his face.

'Hey, you,' her friend answered. 'How's things in the deep south?'

Janie laughed, her heart still beating a little too fast. 'Good. All good,' she said.

'How are my god-daughters?'

Janie told her about Ella's assembly and Lottie's ballet classes, and Sophie listened with interest about the children she loved. She would never have her own now. By Sophie's admission, that time had passed, but it didn't stop Janie thinking she would have made a great mum.

'Harry?' she asked.

'Yep, all good.'

There was a beat of silence before Sophie ventured, 'Sure?'

Janie laughed. 'Yes, of course,' she said. 'Life's busy, you know – Harry's working a lot and I'm on the go ...' Her words fizzled out; there was no convincing Sophie, as much as Janie had always tried, that this was the life she was cut out for. That there wasn't something missing from what should be an idyllic existence.

Janie would never find her sister probing like this, making sure she was all right. As far as her sister was concerned, there wasn't anything Janie could possibly have to complain about, when she had a huge house with a pool and, in her own words, a husband who looked like Harry. But then her sister had always been jealous, and Sophie never had been. Not even when their lives couldn't have been more different.

Their paths had set off in opposing directions the day they left school. Sophie had balanced a string of jobs and was now living in a small flat with a struggling artist for a boyfriend who, at forty, was five years her junior. But Sophie had never envied Janie's wealth; if anything, she was more concerned that Janie wasn't someone who wanted to be living off her husband.

'I know you're at work, I won't keep you,' Janie said. 'I just haven't spoken to you in a while.' *I wanted to hear your voice,* she thought. *I wanted to check you're doing all right.*

Their conversations always skirted the subjects that were important to them now, the ones they'd once have dissected at length over a bottle of wine and tapas. They'd never dived into the depths of the choice Janie made five years ago because they didn't have to. They both knew the real reason behind her giving up her career and moving to the south coast, even if neither of them had ever voiced it out loud.

Even when her own husband had buried his head in the sand and lied to himself that his wife was happy to give everything up, it was Sophie who would have understood. But then Sophie was also the only person who was aware of the part Janie had played in it.

***Tuesday 14 May***

**Initial interviews between DC Emily Marlow and the staff of Morris & Wood, following the fire on Monday 13 May**

### *Bryony Knight, Account Assistant*

Marlow:     You said you worked with Laura Denning before she went on maternity leave?

Bryony:     I did. I work with all the account directors – I'm there to assist them.

Marlow:     And you carried on working with her when she came back?

Bryony:     Yes. But it was different.

Marlow:     In what way?

Bryony:     Well, at first she didn't ask me to do much. But then, as the weeks passed, she threw more and more at me.

Marlow:     And you carried on working for Mia Ander-
            son too?

Bryony:     Yes, as much as I could, really.

Marlow:     Did you notice Laura Denning was upset
            when she returned from her maternity leave?

Bryony:     Laura? No. Laura Denning doesn't do 'upset'
            – not like that. I mean, she doesn't cry or any-
            thing. She just gets tougher. Like, bossier. But
            then that's how she gets where she is, I sup-
            pose.

Marlow:     How do you mean?

Bryony:     Well, so successful. On the same level as all
            those men.

Marlow:     Did you think Laura seemed bothered by the
            fact that the main part of her job had been
            given to her replacement?

Bryony:     Of course she did. She was angry. I saw her in
            Harry's office a few times; voices were raised,
            though you couldn't hear what they were
            saying. You know it's very clever, those glass
            offices: you can see everything inside them,
            but you can't hear a thing. They're sound-
            proof. Quite annoying, really.

Marlow:     Do you think she was angry with him?

Bryony:     I don't know whether it was him in particu-
            lar, but you could tell she was annoyed by the
            way she would throw her arms around when
            she spoke. But then, from what I hear, Harry

didn't have much choice. Mia is so amazing at the job. And she's such a lovely person. Everyone likes her, you know? And Coopers love her. That was the point.

Marlow: What was the point?

Bryony: They wanted her to stay on their account. They didn't want Laura back.

Marlow: Laura's main client asked for her to be taken off the account?

Bryony: That's right. They told Harry Wood as much. That's why he had to ask Mia to stay on. I don't know – maybe he would have anyway.

Marlow: Why did they?

Bryony: (shrugs)

Marlow: Did Laura know this?

Bryony: I'm not sure.

Marlow: *How do you know?*

Bryony: I heard it on the grapevine.

Marlow: Is it usual for clients to make demands about who they want working for them?

Bryony: I don't know of anyone else at work who's been taken off an account. But then I guess no one else at Laura's level has ever gone off on maternity leave. The rest of us get our old jobs back, more or less, though a lot of them job-share. Laura would never have done that though. (laughs) She loves her job too much. You know her husband is a stay-at-home

|          |                                                                 |
|----------|-----------------------------------------------------------------|
|          | dad? He's a nice guy. I've met him a few times. I mean, it's an amazing thing to do, isn't it? |
| Marlow:  | What? Stay at home to look after your own children? |
| Bryony:  | Yeah. |
| Marlow:  | You think it's an unusual choice to make? |
| Bryony:  | No, I mean, I don't – well, not all men would do it, would they? I know for a fact my Carl never would. |
| Marlow:  | Well, putting aside the fact that Laura Denning made the brave decision to return to work full-time, is there anything at all you've noticed about her behaviour since she's been back that has seemed a little – different? |
| Bryony:  | Plenty, but … |
| Marlow:  | Yes? |
| Bryony:  | Well, it's like – I mean – is this going on record? Because this is only gossip. I mean, she's not a suspect or anything, is she? |

# Chapter Eight

*Two months before the fire*

Laura had another night of tossing and turning. She hadn't been sleeping well over the past few nights, since she had gone back to work on Monday, and by the end of the week the tiredness was catching up with her.

It didn't help her busy mind that Bobby was waking frequently, and the previous night he had reached an impressive milestone of crying out nearly every hour. Nate had been the one to get up for all bar one occasion. It was part of their agreement. On weekdays he would see to Bobby during the night as much as he could, but then the agreement had been made when Bobby had been blissfully sleeping through.

'He's teething,' Laura had said, blearily, at one in the morning. 'You'll need to get some more gel. I can feel the teeth under his gum.'

Nate hadn't answered. She didn't know if he'd heard, so she wrote it down on a piece of paper and left it on his bedside table, in case she forgot to remind him in the morning.

It had felt like only minutes that she'd been asleep when her alarm blasted. Nate didn't stir and Laura felt it cruel to wake him, so she got up to change Bobby and get his breakfast ready, then eventually had to rouse her husband as she needed to get out of the door.

'I'm sorry, but I really need to go,' she said. 'I didn't want to wake you.'

'No, of course you have to. Sorry, I didn't realise the time.'

'You're shattered. Are you going to be okay?' Laura asked.

''Course I am,' Nate laughed. 'Come here.'

She bent over and gave him a kiss, all the time willing him to get out of bed so that she could leave the house. She was already ten minutes later than she wanted to be.

'He's still downstairs in his highchair,' she said, pulling away. 'I've made breakfast, you just need to give it to him.'

'No worries.'

'Nate!' She lingered. 'I can't leave him there until you're downstairs.' She told herself the traffic would be bad if she didn't go, convinced herself that was the only reason she was agitated to get away.

'Okay,' he mumbled, 'I'm getting up.'

When he still didn't move, she pulled the covers back. 'Will you do it then?' she said. 'I have to go.'

'Okay, okay!' He held up his hands and swung his legs over the bed.

Laura watched him for a moment and then, satisfied he meant it, left him to it. By the time she got in the car it was seven-thirty; she'd be in the office fifteen minutes later, but she already knew she'd be too late. And when Laura stepped out of the lift her fears were confirmed. Mia Anderson was sitting at her desk, laughing and joking with Bryony Knight, who as far as Laura could recall had never been in before eight.

Mia had ended up at a desk near the lift, which meant she was the first person Laura saw every morning as she walked onto the floor. Somehow whatever Laura did to get to work early, Mia was already there. And at the end of each day, when Laura was ready to leave, she was still there. And even though Laura tried to tell herself that Mia surely wasn't doing it for her benefit, she couldn't help but think that maybe she was. That possibly Mia was drawing Laura into a game that she couldn't afford to play, when she had a husband and baby at home. As Mia knew.

'Morning,' Mia called as Laura began walking across the floor. 'How are things? How's Bobby?'

'He's fine,' Laura said, mustering a smile. Concept boards were piled at the side of Mia's desk and Laura couldn't help but glance at them. Coopers' health-drink brand logo was splashed across the top.

'I bet you're pleased it's the weekend tomorrow, so you can see him again.'

Laura felt her stomach churn as she dragged her gaze from the boards and back to Mia. What she really wanted to do was pick them up and look through them. See what ideas Mia was proposing to run with. Part of her wanted to make sure they were good enough, because eventually, she reassured herself, she would be taking back her account. But there was another part that wanted to hate them. So she could tear them apart in front of Harry and say, '*See, she can't do this.*'

'I do see my son every day,' Laura replied, turning her attention back to Mia.

'Oh yes, I know,' Mia waved a hand in the air. 'I didn't mean – I just meant it'll be nice to have two days off.' She paused and then added with a laugh, 'God, I know I can't wait for it.'

Laura stared back at Mia's blank face and thought there was something so insincere about her, and yet she couldn't put her finger on what. Aside from the fact that Mia had lied in her interview about not wanting to stay on, though no one else appeared to think this was an issue.

Harry had spent most of his week in London, but Laura had caught up with him the previous day and voiced her unhappiness again. 'I still don't see any reason why Mia's here,' she had said. 'It makes no sense. She never wanted to be – she said, clear as anything, she only wanted a six-month contract.'

'What she wanted six months ago is irrelevant. She's doing a good job, she enjoys it,' he'd replied.

Laura had watched Harry flicking through his filing cabinet as he spoke to her, his attention elsewhere. Any moment he would change the subject as his mind juggled a number of issues, so she ploughed on. 'But we don't need her. I can manage the work, you know I can. I did it before and I can do it now.'

'Laura.' He turned and threw some papers onto his desk, where they landed with a thud. She cocked her head, goading him to respond. She knew she was the only one who could talk to Harry the way she did. Even Patrick stopped short of contradicting their boss when he knew he was on a losing streak, but Laura had always held her ground.

'You get away with it because you're the golden girl,' Patrick would often joke. If he was annoyed by this, he didn't particularly show it. Patrick was confident enough that he didn't play petty office games with Laura. He might want to get his hands on the Coopers account, but who wouldn't? By virtue of the fact Coopers brought in the most money, they were Morris & Wood's most important client.

But now Laura could see a flare in Harry's eyes, showing he'd had enough, and he went on to say, 'I've made my decision. This is the way it's going to be, and you're going to have to find a way to deal with it.'

He continued to hold her gaze before eventually turning back to his cabinet. Laura's blood pumped furiously through her veins. She could feel the tips of her fingers tingle as if they were no longer attached to the rest of her.

Before, she would have told Harry she didn't care if he'd made a decision – he was going to have to change it. But then *before*, this particular problem wouldn't have happened. And *before*, Laura wouldn't have felt the prick of tears jabbing at the corners of her eyes.

She hated that she wanted to flee Harry's office and keep running. For every time she convinced herself she would get back what was rightly hers, a curveball like emotion would come and knock her off her feet so quickly she didn't even realise what was happening.

Maybe the sleepless nights weren't helping. Nate had suggested that she slept in the spare room, which seemed a rocky path to tread, but she couldn't keep coming into work an emotional wreck.

'Seriously, Laura, it would be great if you could just work with Mia on this,' Harry had said.

That night Laura had called her friend Deborah, who worked in HR for a financial-services company in Reading. 'Can he do this to me?' she'd asked.

'It's a difficult situation,' Deborah told her. 'There are no material changes to your role or your pay. Your status is still the same. To be honest, I don't think you'd have a case, if that's what you're after.'

'That's what I thought.'

'I thought you had a great relationship with your boss?' Deborah went on. 'I can't believe he's doing this to you.'

'Neither can I,' Laura murmured. In the five years she'd been working for Harry he'd never once treated her like this. Even when things with Saskia got bad, Harry had always stood by her, and Laura knew well enough that he needn't have put his neck out for her.

Saskia, her once-friend, had tried to destroy Laura's career, though not everyone saw it that way. Even Laura could now admit that she'd reacted too quickly, too defensively. But still Harry had taken her side.

As far as Laura was concerned, nothing had changed between them apart from one thing. Mia. And now she had no idea how to get Harry to listen to her any more. But by the following morning, when Laura walked into the office and saw Mia's shiny young face smiling back at her, she'd already decided she wasn't going to take this. Somehow – and whatever it took – she was getting her account back.

Laura held her gaze for a moment longer, wondering if Mia was looking forward to the weekend as much as she was making out. 'Bryony,' she said as she started walking towards her desk, 'have you got the direct-mail packs back from the studio yet?'

'No.' Bryony shook her head and started to follow Laura across the floor.

Laura glanced in the direction of the creative studio as they passed, where their art director, Mike Lewis, was hunched over his oversized screen, a large mug of coffee gripped in one hand. He was always in early because he always left by four, but he couldn't make it through the morning without at least five cups of coffee. She watched him push his thick grey glasses up his nose and squint at whatever he was poring over. Mike had a mop of dark hair that sprang out of the top of his head and, combined with his unironed shirts and rolled-up sleeves, he never looked remotely neat.

'They were due back yesterday. Have you chased them?' Laura asked her.

'Yes, I spoke to Mike this morning,' Bryony said. 'He told me he'd look at them next week.'

'Next week?' Laura stopped, the muscles in her shoulders tightening. 'So he hasn't even started them?'

'No.' Bryony paused. 'I didn't think it was that urgent?' she went on, wide-eyed, wondering if she'd missed a deadline.

She hadn't, but that wasn't the point. Laura's name was on it, and Mike would have always got to it by now. 'Did he say why?'

'Well, yeah, it's the TV-campaign pitch,' Bryony answered, as if everyone knew that. Which of course they did. And of course everyone also understood that its work was to take precedence. And if Laura was running it, she would happily have shifted the direct-mail packs for the local estate agency to the following week. After all, they brought in less than ten per cent of her own targets.

But she wasn't running it.

'That's not good enough,' Laura snapped and even though her anger was directed at Mike, she knew it might sound like she was taking it out on Bryony. But in that moment she didn't particularly care. 'Mike, I need a word with you,' she called, as she left Bryony and paced over to him.

Mike was an irritatingly stubborn man; Laura knew if she pushed him, he would retract even further. Her eye caught his screen, and a visual of Coopers' health drinks stared back at her.

'Can I ask you when you're going to get to my brief?' she asked, tearing her eyes away from it.

Mike sighed. 'Which ones?'

'The direct mail for the estate agents,' she snapped back.

'When do you need it by?'

'I was expecting to see something last night.'

Mike shook his head. 'No can do, now. We're all stacked.'

'What do you mean, "No can do"?'

'I mean there's no way I'll be able to get it done today. Not with this,' he said flatly, his head nodding towards his screen.

Laura screwed up her eyes as she assessed her options. She knew she should walk away and not turn this into an issue, but at the same time she didn't know what to do with the ball of rage rapidly building inside her.

Mike had already moved back to his project, rolling his mouse over the desk as he worked his way around the creative. The fact was that Laura had no option. There was nothing she could do but wait until Mike had time to get to her work.

'I'll send it to Sam – he can do it, if you need it today,' Mike said eventually.

'Who the hell is Sam?'

'My work-experience lad.' He nodded in the direction of an empty desk.

'Forget it,' Laura snapped. 'It can wait until Monday.'

Mike didn't bother responding as she charged back to her desk, her blood bubbling beneath her skin. Never had her work been passed to a work-experience 'lad' unless she'd come up with the idea herself.

She pulled out her chair and slid onto it, steepling her hands on the desk in front of her as she leaned forward, resting her chin against them, blowing out short puffs of breath. Beside her, a photo of Bobby smiled back. She reached out and pulled the photo closer, tracing her finger over his happy face.

He was wearing the blue-and-white striped top that she and Nate had bought on a weekend in Cornwall. Five minutes after the photo had been taken a seagull had landed on their table and frightened the life out of her, but Bobby had giggled, reaching his chubby fingers out as he tried to grab the bird.

What was she doing here? The question swept through her so suddenly. She had given up being with her son so soon, and for what? They didn't have to carry on living in their house – they could downsize. Move out of the area. Lymington was so expensive; they could move to Wales, be nearer Nate's parents.

Laura tapped on her mobile and opened up Rightmove. House prices were so much more affordable there; they didn't have to be right on her in-laws' doorstep, and Nate could find work anywhere. She scrolled through the houses for sale, ignoring the feeling that Bridgend was so not what she wanted.

'Moving house?'

Laura jumped and closed down her mobile, tossing it across the desk. 'No,' she said.

'I was going to say: not that bad, is it?' Patrick asked.

Laura smiled thinly and shrugged. She hadn't caught up with Patrick properly all week. He hadn't been in since Monday.

'Yeah,' he went on. 'I can imagine it probably is.'

Laura felt herself turning in the direction of Mia's desk. She had no idea what Patrick thought of Mia, but didn't dare ask when everyone else in the office appeared to love her. There were a couple of women hovering near her desk, listening to Mia, who was gesturing her arms dramatically. Even from the other side of the floor, Laura heard one of them laughing.

'Well, it's short-term,' Laura said. 'As soon as the TV ad's up and running there'll be no need to keep her contract on.'

Patrick frowned uneasily and cocked his head as he looked at Laura.

'What?' she asked.

'Harry didn't say, did he? He made Mia permanent. A week before you came back.' Patrick paused and glanced over his shoulder in Mia's direction. 'I'm afraid she's here to stay.'

# Chapter Nine

Mia sat beside Mike Lewis who was leaning back in his chair, arms folded across his chest, both of them staring at his screen.

'I don't know,' she muttered. 'I don't even know which ones looks better any more.'

*For God's sake, help me, Mike,* she thought. He was the creative director, the one who should be pointing her in the right direction, instead of just sitting there. Waiting for her. She'd been thrown in at the deep end with Coopers; it wasn't that she couldn't do it, but she didn't have history with them – not enough experience with the team to read between the lines of their briefs and work out what it was they really wanted.

'You're going to have to help me out,' she laughed. 'I'll go with whatever you say.'

He shook his head and carried on staring at the screen. 'They're both what you asked for,' he said bluntly. 'It's your call what you give them.'

Mia shifted on her seat. She wished he'd at least look at her, acknowledge that she was asking for his help. 'I could show them both,' she murmured, though she doubted they'd like that. They wanted to be shown one clear direction, and yet here she was, staring at two completely different ways of selling their health drinks, which she'd been pretending were delicious since she'd first tried one six months ago.

The truth was Mia didn't like anything that tasted too healthy, but she wasn't about to tell them that. The Coopers account was critical to Morris & Wood, and if she wanted to keep her job, she needed to do whatever it took to keep them in favour. If it meant gulping down a cold-pressed green juice with a shot of cayenne pepper once a week, then that was the least she could do.

'Fine. Okay,' she said. 'That one. The outdoor campaign. Let's go with that.' She waited for Mike to tell her she'd made the right decision, or even the wrong one, but he did neither. Instead he expelled a puff of air as he leaned forward and started fiddling with the borders as if the whole thing was a waste of his time, even though everyone knew it was the biggest thing he had on right now. Eventually Mia pushed her chair back and stood up, trying to ignore his efforts to make her feel like she really had no idea what she was doing when what she really wanted was to tell him how rude he was.

Mike Lewis was a difficult man to work with, by virtue of the fact that he never looked anyone in the eye. His thick-lensed glasses didn't help, but still, behind them, his eyes would desperately avoid contact with hers. She had come across people like Mike before. In her previous company there were a few like him and they never made the day go more smoothly.

Mike was a prickly character, yet still Mia had been shocked when Sarah Clifton first opened up to her in the toilets about her boss. Mia could see Sarah now, waiting for her. She waved a hand and immediately Sarah sprang to life and hot-stepped towards her.

'Can we talk?'

'Of course.'

When Sarah didn't move or speak, Mia gestured to the nearest vacant meeting room and ushered her inside.

'I've been thinking about what you said.' Sarah spoke quietly.

Mia nodded, her mind stretching back to the conversation they'd had the week before.

'I know you're right, but I don't think I can say anything.'

'Oh.' This took the wind out of Mia. She pulled out a seat at the small round meeting table and sat down. Sarah followed suit. 'I thought we talked it through. I thought you were happy about taking it forward?' She'd been expecting Sarah to tell her she was ready, not that she was backing out. 'You know, if Mike is treating you badly and making you feel unhappy, you can't sit back and not speak up.'

'I know, it's just ...' Sarah's voice drifted away. 'I really appreciate you supporting me and everything, but I spoke to my boyfriend last night and we agree it would be better not to rock the boat.'

'Not to rock the boat?' Mia stifled a short laugh as she leaned forward. 'Sarah, Mike is bullying you,' she urged. 'I want to help, I really do, but I can't do anything unless you're prepared to take this further.'

'I wouldn't have said he was bullying me ...'

Mia shifted uncomfortably on the chair. She didn't like the way this was going. 'But that *is* what you said,' she smiled, her voice softening. 'That's what you told me. Bullying comes in many guises, and what you told me Mike was doing' – she paused and cocked her head – 'is definitely bullying.'

Sarah didn't respond, though her lips parted into a small O.

'You said he makes you feel undervalued when you speak,' she tried. 'You know you should be able to voice your opinions without him shouting them down.'

'I know, I know, but ...' Sarah's words trailed off into an incomplete sentence.

'And he cuts you off when you're talking in meetings?'

Sarah nodded, almost looking ashamed.

'He doesn't ask you to do anything, just leaves you orders on your desk. And you say he hasn't given you any feedback since you started, and then gave you an "underperform" measure in your last appraisal?' Mia reached over and took hold of Sarah's arm. 'This isn't your fault,' she went on, gently but firmly. 'But if we let people like Mike get away with what they're doing, they'll never stop.'

Sarah nodded slowly.

She was right to use the word 'we', to make sure Sarah knew they were in this together. 'He'll carry on bullying other people too, and that's not right, is it?'

'It's just that "bullying" seems such a strong word.'

'Well, we can use another,' Mia said, maybe a little too shortly before adding, 'I'm here for you. I have your back. I totally think you can do this; and what's more, I think you should.' She was trying to strike the right balance. Because there was every chance Sarah was going to bail out.

'Yes. I suppose you're right, but I feel like he hasn't been that bad—'

'Don't,' Mia said. 'You mustn't start making excuses for him. He *is* that bad and he's doing it because of who you are.'

'What do you mean?'

'You know he wouldn't treat any of the male account directors the way he does me. He can barely look at me. Of course he knows he needs to do as I ask—' Mia broke off and waved a hand. 'But I still notice it.'

'Yeah, maybe you're right.'

'I am,' Mia said definitely. 'I am right. And I promise you we're going to be in this together.' She squeezed Sarah's arm. 'If you want, I can talk to Harry on Monday morning.'

'Oh, I don't know.'

*No*, Mia thought, *and your boyfriend will probably talk you out of that over the weekend anyway.* 'Well, it's just a thought,' she said as her mobile beeped with a text. She pulled it out of her pocket and glanced at the screen. Her mum, asking her to pick up some food on her way home. Mia sighed. She'd agreed to go for drinks at the pub after work. It was Friday evening and the thought of heading straight home was unbearable. Especially when they had no plans for the weekend. The idea of having a few gin and tonics more than she should was the one thing Mia was looking forward to.

'I better get back to work,' she sighed and stood up, opening the door. The text made her feel an inordinate amount of annoyance that she had nothing exciting ahead of her, and Sarah's reluctance to address what was happening in the company was another irritation.

Henrietta James was already at the bar when Mia walked in. 'I insist on getting this,' Mia told her. There were too many times when Henrietta already had a card proffered to the bartender by the time Mia reached for her purse, but it was beginning to get awkward. Her salary was higher than that of any of the other staff members who were gathered in a huddle in the corner of the pub, and yet she'd never be able to explain to them that she couldn't afford to get them drinks.

'I'm only staying for this one,' Mia said as Henrietta turned back to her conversation with Bryony, and Mia already wondered how easily she would be swayed. The food on her mum's shopping list was bought and stashed in the boot of her car. She just needed to remember to swing past the car on her way home, if she did end up calling a taxi.

As she waited for the barman, Bryony's voice drifted along the bar.

'... trying to do it all. Have you seen the way she's thrown herself back into work this week?'

'Who are you talking about?' Mia asked.

Henrietta screwed up her nose. 'Laura Denning. Of course you never knew her before. She's always been like this, but I really thought she'd cut back a bit, now she has a child.'

Henrietta was eyeing her, waiting for a reaction.

'Maybe she has a lot of work on,' Mia said. 'Gin and slimline, please,' she added to the barman.

Henrietta leaned in. 'Well, she won't like the fact you're doing so well. Do you think she knows yet? About Coopers not wanting her back?'

Mia glanced at Bryony. 'No, I don't think she does,' she said quietly, though the way gossip spread, she was sure it wouldn't be long.

'She'll be hoping it goes badly, I'm sure of it.'

Mia really didn't have a response for that. Or rather she did, but she wasn't going to say anything. Especially not to Henrietta. 'I certainly hope that's not the case,' she said, as Henrietta raised her eyebrows.

It was ten p.m. by the time Mia eventually got home. The house was in darkness except for a bedroom light at the far end. She was glad she'd remembered to stop by the car, but even more pleased that she'd gone to the pub, because it was nicer walking into the bungalow with the buzz of alcohol fizzing around her body.

Twisting her key in the lock, Mia nudged open the front door and immediately heard raised voices from the far end of the hallway.

She switched on the table lamp and closed the door behind her. No natural light reached the hall, which made it oppressive, and it didn't help that her mum had a patterned carpet and dark-green walls that were cluttered with photos taken over the years. Mia no longer looked at any of them as she walked past and down to the bedroom at the far end.

The door was wide open and she could see her mum in her faded purple dressing gown that was frayed at the hem and cuffs. Her hands were gripped tightly together in front of her. Even from here, Mia could see her knuckles forming white circles under the pressure.

'Mum?'

'Oh, Mia,' she said with relief when she looked up. Mia took a step into the room. Her sister was lying on the single bed, facing the wall. 'She won't talk to me.'

'Then leave her,' Mia urged.

'I can't,' her mum mouthed. The words were uttered so quietly that Mia wasn't sure she'd actually said them aloud. Her eyes were rimmed with tears that threatened to roll down her cheeks, and her thin grey hair was pushed back off her face with an Alice band, which meant she'd either been in bed or about to get into it.

'Jess?' Mia said to her sister. 'Do you want to talk to me?'

When her sister didn't respond or move, Mia took her mum's arm and steered her out of the room. 'Come on,' she said, 'I'll make us all some tea.'

A tear escaped her mum's eye. Mia watched her grab a tissue from her dressing-gown pocket and dab at her skin so gently that it tore Mia's heart in two.

'You shouldn't have to do this,' her mum said, following Mia down the hallway. 'You shouldn't have to keep solving everyone else's problems.'

'You're not everyone else. You're my mum.'

'You know what I mean,' she answered quietly. 'You shouldn't be living like this.'

'Nor should you,' Mia said as she reached the kitchen door and turned round. Her mum's face was blotched red, the skin under her eyes near-transparent, it was so thin. Her arms hung limply by her side, her hands fiddling with the ball of tissue. This was the time her mum should be relaxing and going on cruises, with what little money she had saved over the years, not worrying frantically about her eldest daughter.

And suddenly Mia felt an unbelievable sense of guilt that she hadn't come straight home from work – a guilt that would shortly battle with a tidal wave of anger that their lives had come to this.

**Tuesday 14 May**

**Interview between DC Emily Marlow and Mia Anderson, following the fire on Monday 13 May**

Marlow:     Can you tell me where you were last night between the hours of seven p.m. and nine p.m.?

Mia:         I was at home. My mum's house, I mean.

Marlow:     For the whole time?

Mia:         (pauses) No. Not all of it.

Marlow:     So where else did you go?

Mia:         I went for a drive. On my own.

Marlow:     Anywhere in particular?

Mia:         Not specifically, just around the roads.

Marlow:     Is that something you often do? Go out for a drive on your own?

Mia:         Occasionally. It helps clear my head.

Marlow: So you needed to clear your head last night?

Mia: I was overtired, I think.

Marlow: Was this because of anything to do with work?

Mia: No. Work is fine. It wasn't important, I just ...

Marlow: Yes?

Mia: Sometimes I need to get out of the house. Sometimes it gets too much and I need to be able to breathe.

Marlow: So there was nothing at work troubling you?

Mia: No.

Marlow: It's just that no one saw you in the office all day yesterday. Monday the thirteenth. Were you at work?

Mia: (shakes head)

Marlow: For the tape recorder, please

Mia: I didn't go in yesterday, no. I had an appointment I'd forgotten to tell anyone about.

Marlow: So nothing had upset you?

Mia: Why do you keep asking me that? What would have upset me?

Marlow: Well, for a start, there was the incident at Harry Wood's party four nights ago. I assume yesterday would have been the first time you'd seen Laura Denning again, after what happened?

Mia: (laughs) I wasn't upset about that. At least, not enough to not go into work.

Marlow: And there's the ongoing issue with Laura.

Mia: *I* don't have any issue with Laura.

Marlow:  So it was simply an appointment? That you forgot? Nothing else deterred you from going to the office? Only from what I hear, it's unusual for you. I believe it's the only day you haven't gone in since you started eight months ago.

Mia:  There was nothing else.

Marlow:  It's just that someone did actually see you in the office late that morning. You apparently stepped out of the lift onto your floor and then vanished again pretty quickly.

Is that right?

Mia:  (pauses) Yes, I had forgotten my appointment. Like I told you.

Marlow:  And you didn't think to tell anyone when you were there?

Mia:  Is any of this relevant?

Marlow:  I don't know. That's what I'm trying to find out. I've been wondering whether something did happen in the short time you went into the Morris & Wood offices yesterday that you aren't telling me? The same offices that are now nothing more than a pile of ashes.

Mia:  I told you. Nothing happened.

Marlow:  Okay. So let's go back to last night. You were driving around the roads? Did you stop anywhere?

Mia:  Not that I recall.

Marlow:     Did you drive to the offices?

Mia:        No.

Marlow:     Or anywhere near them? Somewhere you
            might have been able to see the fire?

Mia:        No.

Marlow:     How about the other side of the river? There's
            a very clear view of Morris & Wood from there.
            Did you go to the quay last night?

Mia:        No.

Marlow:     Are you sure about that, Mia?

# Chapter Ten

*Seven weeks before the fire*

'She's here to stay.' Laura repeated Patrick's words to Nate, not for the first time that weekend. 'Now she's permanent, Nate, Harry can't just get rid of her. Why the hell has he done that?'

Nate shook his head. 'I don't know,' he said, following Laura into the kitchen, a bundle of washing stacked in his arms.

'Let me do that.' She reached out to take it from him. 'You know I don't expect you to pick up everything.'

'It's fine. Go and be with Bobby.' He nodded towards their son, who was wobbling precariously on his playmat before toppling onto his back, which made Nate laugh.

Laura didn't move for a moment as she watched Nate load the bedding into the washing machine. Something felt so wrong about him picking up all the jobs around the house, even though it was only what she had done for the last six months.

She turned and crouched down beside Bobby, picking him up and snuggling into him. Laying a kiss on his head, she lingered as she thought about going back to the office the next day, and it was a thought that filled her with dread.

'You've still not spoken to Harry about it then?' Nate asked.

'I don't want to call him at the weekend.'

'So you'll speak to him tomorrow?'

Laura nodded.

'And then you'll know.' He straightened up, rubbing the base of his spine. 'What do you want to do for lunch?' he asked as if that were the end of the conversation, because in Nate's simplistic world as soon as Laura had spoken to her boss she'd be able to move on.

'It's humiliating, Nate,' she said, willing him to understand. 'Getting pushed to the bottom of the pile, like I was with the creative studio. I hired Mia to cover my job and now it's like she's more senior than me.'

Laura had always known that if you wanted to stay at the top of your game you couldn't afford to take time out. She'd proven herself right – unfortunately, at her own expense. While she was bringing a child into the world, another woman had slipped into her place and stolen her job from her.

'Yeah, I can imagine,' he said as he came over and ruffled the top of her head. 'We need to think about lunch. It's already one.'

Laura shrugged. She didn't give a toss about lunch, she wasn't particularly hungry. Her precious weekend at home with her family, and she'd spent the largest part going over and over her job in her head. And as much as she wanted to make the most of their Sunday afternoon, there was a part of her that couldn't, because she knew she wouldn't settle until she was back in the office and face-to-face with Harry.

'Laura?' Nate pressed. 'How about we go out, grab a pub lunch?'

'We won't get in anywhere now.'

'Then please, just help me out and tell me what you want.'

'It's fine,' she snapped as she pulled herself up. 'I'll sort it.' She walked to the fridge and peered inside, her gaze drifting over what little food they had, as her stomach churned, over and over.

The truth was that she was worried about speaking to Harry because she hated the thought of him selling her out. And if he told her that the reason he'd made Mia permanent was because she was doing such a fantastic bloody job, then where did that leave Laura?

She closed the fridge door and pressed her head against it, shutting her eyes. 'I'm sorry, Nate,' she cried. 'I'm so bloody sorry, this wasn't what it was supposed to be like.'

'Hey, it's okay,' he said.

'No, it's not. I don't want to spend my time with you and Bobby thinking about her, but that's all I'm doing. Why the hell does Mia want my job, Nate?' she said, banging a hand against the door and knocking a magnet to the floor. 'I don't trust her,' she said, airing the thought that had been plaguing her all week. 'I don't trust Mia Anderson one bit.'

On Monday morning, as she walked in, Laura bypassed Mia, who was yet again already at her desk, and headed straight to Harry's office.

'Morning, morning,' he beckoned her in cheerily. 'Good weekend?'

'Yes, great, thanks.'

'And how's the little man?'

'Bobby?' she prompted. 'He's doing good, I just ...'

'Is he sleeping through? God, the girls didn't sleep through until they were one, as far as I remember. Neither of them. Of course we had the nanny then – Janie didn't have to worry about getting up in the night.' He shook his head and laughed. 'I wouldn't want to go through that again,' he said, though Laura wondered how much it had actually affected him personally anyway. 'How was the first week back?'

'Well, actually, Harry, that's what I want to talk to you about.'

He nodded, straightening his chair with his desk, and leaned back, crossing his legs. Now that Laura was in front of him, the words she had prepared earlier had dried in her mouth, leaving her with a bitter taste and an inability to find them. For the first time since she'd started working for Harry she felt the need to tread carefully, because she no longer understood what was going on.

She pulled out a chair on the other side of his desk and sat down, inhaling a deep breath. 'I hear that Mia's been made permanent. You didn't tell me.'

'Right.' He shifted slightly, his eyes flickering, enough to tell her that he wasn't comfortable. 'I'm sorry I didn't, I just wanted you to settle back in last week.'

'I'm having a hard time getting my head round it,' Laura said. 'I don't understand why.'

'Well, it's like I said. She's done a great job ...' His words fizzled out as she shook her head. 'I didn't think we should lose her.'

Laura took in his words. The way he skirted round not telling her outright that it was him who didn't want to lose Mia. She wondered how sure he was of the decision or whether it was simply that he didn't want any conflict. There had been a few times when she'd seen Harry back away from an argument, and it was interesting that he might be doing it now.

'But you've basically given her my job,' Laura persisted.

Harry gave a short, nervous laugh as he shuffled again in his chair. 'I haven't at all.'

'You've given her my biggest account,' she said, feeling the heat rising inside her.

'Because I want you to start up something new.' His eyes widened as he pressed further forward over the desk, as if he expected her to be excited about this. 'I told you this. I want you to meet the guy in charge soon, in the next week or so. This comes off, like I hope it's going to, and I promise you, you won't have time for Coopers.'

'But you didn't ask me, Harry.' Laura heard the slight crack in her words, a hint of a whine, but she continued regardless. 'Why can't *Mia* have this new opportunity?'

'Because . . .' Harry gave another shake of his head as he settled back in his chair, and Laura wondered if his pause was because he was trying to find a reason. 'Because I need someone I can trust on this one – and that's you. I know how you work, Laura, I know you'll be able to crack it.'

Laura released a breath, her heart thumping as she considered what he was telling her and whether or not she believed him.

'I need my best person, and that's you,' Harry continued, smiling. He was on a roll now, though Laura knew well enough that Harry had mastered the ability to say what people wanted to hear. And he must have known how desperately she wanted to hear this.

'Has Mia done a better job than me?'

'What?' Harry laughed. 'That's not what this is about. Laura, is that what you think? You think I'm trying to get rid of you or something? The company would collapse if I didn't have you, you know that. You're my best.' His smile had spread into a broad beam now, as if he felt he'd reached safer ground.

Despite this, Laura nodded, her pulse slowing, because whatever lay behind them, the words were still comforting. 'So that's the only reason she's looking after the account for now?'

There was a beat before Harry answered, 'Of course it is.'

Laura knew there was no point pressing him further. They'd only go round and round in circles. She left his office with a slight sense of optimism that she was still needed, but one that was tempered somewhat by the niggling knowledge that she was sure Harry wasn't telling her the whole truth. And Laura knew it was time to finally make the call to Coopers.

She felt nervous as she dialled the number she'd once rung so often and waited for the voice on the other end of the line. 'Tess is on holiday,' the marketing manager told her. 'Can I leave a message and get her to call you back?'

Laura left her name, but the days passed and she didn't hear back, and neither did she hear anything about Harry's new opportunity. And the thought that there was more to it than Harry tried to make out continued to swell.


On Friday, when Mia was due to present her campaign concept to the Coopers team, Laura couldn't get away from the fact with Mia buzzing around the office like it was the only thing everyone wanted to talk about. 'I'm so nervous,' Laura overheard her laughing to Bryony, 'it takes me back to when I was at school.'

Laura didn't think she sounded remotely as nervous as Bryony gushed that Mia was going to be amazing.

Laura's fists were clenched as she hammered away on her keyboard, wishing she could block out the noise and stop her mind from wondering what the creatives looked like. She still hadn't seen them. She had no idea what Mia had up her sleeve, but hadn't the guts to ask. Instead Laura had tried keeping her head down, focusing on the clients she had left, none of which excited her much, while hoping that any day soon either Harry would announce they were meeting the potential new client or Mia would royally screw up.

Her dream career had become nothing more than a job that was paying the bills and keeping her away from her son, and as much as Laura was looking forward to the weekend ahead, she felt a considerable sense of lacking any other purpose than being a mother. And she knew she wasn't doing a particularly good job of that.

Laura still hadn't spoken to anyone from the Coopers team since she had been back, which was why, at two o'clock, wandering past the boardroom, she stopped short, her heart sinking to the depths of her stomach. She hadn't for one minute expected that Mia had invited them to the offices. Always Laura would present to them at theirs, and yet there they were – the entire marketing team sitting together on the other side of the glass.

A flash of heat spread up her neck as she scanned the familiar group of four, jostling in their chairs, swivelling towards Bryony, who had been disproportionately dividing her time between Laura and Mia for the last fortnight.

Her legs felt like jelly as she ducked back, out of their sight, but still she didn't return to her desk. She hadn't seen any of them in more than six months. There had been some contact since she'd left – they'd sent her a gorgeous bundle of baby clothes wrapped up in a blue bouquet. And in return she'd sent them a thank-you card with a picture of Bobby. But other than that? No communication. No return call from Tess Wills, who was now seated at the far end of the table, having clearly returned from holiday.

Laura had worked for Coopers from the outset, had spent so many nights poring over their briefs, working with the creative studio, giving up weekends when they needed revisions made by the following Monday. She hadn't minded. In many ways she felt like she was part of their company, like she worked for them. They had told her that. *What would we do without you, Laura?*

She wouldn't be able to walk past the boardroom now without being seen. Her only option was to slip back the way she'd come, hide, wait for them to disappear and hope to God they didn't walk out and see her, and feel the need to come over and speak to her.

Laura closed her eyes and leaned her head back against the wall. Of course she had another option. She could pull herself together, plaster on a smile and walk into the boardroom as if she wasn't remotely fazed by what had happened. Even as if she were completely on board with it. She could pretend it was under her control, though she had no idea how she could pull off that particular act when her breath was so tightly wedged in her throat. Laura had never been able to hide her emotions easily, but this was ridiculous. This was her domain. She needed to start fighting back.

Inhaling deeply, Laura walked to the doorway and stuck her head into the room. 'Hi, guys, lovely to see you.' The words tumbled out and she wasn't even sure if they'd come in the right order, but all four members of the marketing team were now standing and telling her it was lovely to see her too.

'Laura, oh my God, hi,' they chorused, approaching her one by one. 'How are you?' 'How's the baby?'

'Bobby's great.'

'I didn't even realise you were back,' one said, before the room fell into a momentary awkward silence.

'Yes, I've been back for two weeks,' Laura smiled. 'Thank you all again for your gift,' she added quickly. 'It was gorgeous.'

'Oh, a pleasure.'

'God, of course.' They murmured with relief and continued to regard her, wide smiles on their faces.

'I can't believe Bobby is six months old already,' she said when they lapsed into silence.

'No!'

'I can't believe it, either.'

'Where does the time go?'

Laura couldn't differentiate one voice from the other as they all continued to gape and nod, staring at her and looking vaguely surprised and a little apprehensive.

Her gaze wandered over their shoulders to Bryony, who had stopped pouring tea and was now chewing the side of her thumb.

'Have you got any photos?' one asked.

'Oh yes. Of course.' She reached for her phone and scrolled through a few until she came to one of Bobby lying on his back on a playmat, chubby little fists clenched, mouth open as he giggled at the funny faces Nate was pulling behind her back. Laura stared at it for a moment before handing it over.

'Oh my God, he's so cute.'

'He's adorable.'

'Doesn't he look like you?'

Laura nodded, and once the phone had been passed along the line she took it back.

'You must miss him.'

She looked up, still clutching the phone in one hand. 'Of course.'

'I don't know how you do it, you know – being away from him all the time. I only went back two and a half days a week, and even that was too much,'

'It's not all the time, just while I'm at work,' she joked half-heartedly.

The other woman blushed and laughed too, and suddenly they were thrown into another awkward silence that Laura couldn't ever remember having with any of the team previously. Her eyes panned the room. Usually she'd be sitting at the head of the table, concept boards stacked high, buzzing to talk through her ideas and now ...

'Laura!'

She turned to see Mia, who had now entered the room.

'So sorry I'm a little late, everyone – just getting the final touches done,' Mia gushed as she waltzed in. She was glistening like a bauble in her shiny bright-pink shirt, which she'd tucked into one side of the waistband of slim black trousers. Laura tried to think if she had been wearing that outfit earlier. She couldn't recall it.

Eventually her eyes drifted to the portfolio case tucked under Mia's arms, while the team assured her that her lateness was nothing to worry about.

Mia hung her head to one side and smiled at Laura, and Laura knew this was her cue to leave. Her heart hammered at the thought of retreating, being dismissed again. She suddenly couldn't bear the thought of returning to her desk, all the while imagining what was going on behind the closed doors of the boardroom.

*Wouldn't it be better to know what Mia is doing rather than remain in the dark?* she thought. If she were in the meeting too, at least she'd be able to see it all play out.

'Is it okay if I stay?' Laura asked, without giving the idea further thought.

Mia's mouth hung open before she said quickly, 'Yes. Yes, of course.' A smile fixed firmly on her face.

'If that's okay with everyone?' Laura went on, hoping her heart couldn't be heard as it banged against the wall of her chest.

'You're welcome to stay, Laura,' Tess smiled. 'And I'm sorry I never called you, I was only back in the office today.'

'No problem,' she smiled, pulling out a chair as she caught Mia's head ping up and look across at her.

'So I'm really excited to be sharing these ideas with you,' Mia said as she passed around handouts. 'I'm sorry I don't have enough copies, Laura.'

'That's fine,' Laura replied as breezily as she could muster, as she shuffled closer to Bryony so that she could share hers, then waited for Mia to hold up the first creative. She wondered what the Coopers team was going to think of the ideas. She'd sat in front of so many clients in her time and knew every one of their reactions and what they were really thinking. She knew when they didn't like what they were being shown, or didn't agree with the concept she had decided upon, even when they tried to cover it up. Mostly it took a while for the ideas to sink in, and the good marketeers would eventually see what Laura was suggesting and, even if they didn't wholly agree, they could reach a compromise.

Today heads were nodding and although experience told Laura this was nothing to go on, her stomach still twisted itself into knots.

Mia hadn't once looked in her direction, her focus solely on the clients, as well she supposed it should be, but still Laura was beginning to feel like a spare part. Casually she beckoned to the handout in front of Bryony, gesturing for a closer look. Bryony nodded and pushed it towards her.

She smiled her thanks and flicked through the pack, zoning in on the budgets at the back. As she ran her finger down the numbers, Laura suddenly paused, turned back the sheet and looked through them again.

When she looked up, the room had descended into silence. Laura glanced round the table as everyone gathered their thoughts, waiting for one of them to start the conversation. She knew how awkward this moment was for Mia. She had been through it enough times herself, but she ignored the silence as she turned back to the pack, just to double-check there definitely was a mistake.

Eventually the team began to murmur appreciative thoughts and ask questions, and for a moment Laura couldn't keep up with whether or not they actually liked what they'd seen.

'Well, that's amazing, everyone,' Mia was saying. 'I'm so thrilled you all love it, and I'm really excited to get started on the filming.'

Laura glanced up as everyone appeared to be shuffling papers together, tidying phones away. That was it? No one had even asked for her opinion? Had she actually been passed over, like she wasn't even sitting there?

Laura cleared her throat, because she was going to speak anyway. 'You know, I can see what you're suggesting here, Mia, and I like how brave you're being.'

Mia smiled back at her. 'Thanks, Laura,' she said as she got up.

Laura's pulse raced. She could point out the mistake in private; she didn't have to embarrass Mia, but the fact was that *she* was embarrassed. All the hard work she'd put into growing this client, and no one gave a shit about what she thought of their biggest campaign yet.

'But to be totally honest, I'm unsure how this will actually work on TV.' She raised her voice a little. 'It could be advertising anyone – the viewer might remember the products, but I don't see how they'll recall the brand.'

'It's a fair point,' Tess chimed in. 'But I think it's fine, it can be worked in.'

Mia smiled her thanks at Tess.

'And the actual filming of the ad,' Laura went on, because she was not going to be passed off so easily. 'Of course it will be a lot cheaper filming it outdoors and out of season, as you say.'

Mia nodded. 'That's why I went with this idea.'

'Only I don't see where you've accounted for the weather. I mean if it rains, which of course it could – I assume you've factored in weather insurance somewhere?'

Mia froze as she stared at Laura, her mouth parting as if she were about to speak but didn't know what to say.

Of course she hadn't factored in any insurance, because it would have been in the budgets. Now members of the team had begun murmuring, and while Laura was certain Mia had never run a TV campaign before, she began to wonder why exactly Harry thought Mia was more suitable to look after the campaign than she was? It really wouldn't hurt one bit, she decided, to let Harry know when she next saw him.

Mia's lips moved but no words came out, and Bryony was furiously flicking through her notes, but Laura knew she wouldn't find the answer.

She decided to put Mia out of her misery as Tess asked, 'So how much would this cost?'

'Well,' Laura said, 'you'll need to add another twenty per cent to your budget.'

Ouch! She could hear a collective intake of breath around the table, and she knew then that the whole plan and its budget had been shot to pieces with that one figure. And while she hated the thought that she was taking any pleasure in this rather big omission, Laura couldn't help but feel a little bit satisfied.

# Chapter Eleven

Mia hadn't been looking for another job when she'd come across the advert for the maternity cover at Morris & Wood. But the moment she saw it she stopped abruptly, her fingers caught in mid-air above the keypad of her laptop. It was too good to be true, she'd thought as she'd scanned the advert, her gaze settling on the email address of Laura Denning, the woman whose role she would be covering. She was to contact her personally if she wanted to apply, an irregularity that she didn't stop to consider in her haste to send her CV.

The first time Mia had met the Coopers team she'd hit it off with all of them. Only a couple of months in and Tess Wills had told her, 'It's fab having someone so fun around, Mia. Laura rarely invited us out for drinks or, if she did, she always stayed sober, even before she was pregnant.'

Mia liked Tess. A few glasses of wine were all the Coopers' marketing director needed to confide in her about all sorts of things, like the fact that her husband of ten years had run off with his secretary a year ago. By all accounts, Tess was very quick to proclaim she would never forgive him.

It hadn't been a surprise when Harry asked her to take over the account. By then Mia already knew they wanted to keep her, but it was a relief to hear it. And then, when he confirmed her permanent position, it was another reason to celebrate.

Mia needed this job. More than any of the others sitting around the boardroom table would ever understand.

Twelve months ago she'd had no choice but to move back in with her mum, to the small three-bedroomed bungalow she'd moved to when Mia had finally left home at twenty-three. Over eight years Mia had enjoyed setting up her own future, living her life, but now here she was, back at square one.

Jess had been gone a while when Mia had first left home. Five years older than her, Jess was the one who went to university, who knew what she wanted to do with her life. Not like Mia, who drifted in and out of jobs until she had finally found her niche in marketing.

Those eight years now felt like they weren't part of her life at all, but as if they belonged to someone else. Even the woman who lived in the flat above her – who kept her awake at night, shouting at her boyfriend – even that felt like it had never happened. Those years had held freedom, the promise of excitement, the ability to walk in and out of the shared front door of the flats without having to feel guilt and anger and disappointment.

The job at Morris & Wood gave Mia a flicker of opportunity – the chance to take back some control again. Once she got it, she knew she had to keep it.

She wished she felt more confident about what she was about to present to the Coopers team. The contents of her stomach were doing a merry dance, but she knew once she started talking she would be all right. Or she would have been, if Laura hadn't joined them. Now all Mia could feel was Laura's intent stare, waiting for her to cock up. She knew Laura Denning was here for a fight, and that made Mia feel the pressure even more.

The reason Laura had bypassed Human Resources, when recruiting for her cover, had later become so obvious to Mia. This was a woman who wanted to control, and her return was always going to pose a threat. Mia often wondered what Laura was like out of the office. When you stripped away her hard shell, who was she underneath?

Harry Wood, on the other hand, was as transparent as anyone could be. On the surface he ran his company well, but he wavered over the intricate issues, always deflecting to being one of the boys, careful not to upset the apple cart. He'd been so pliable when Coopers requested that Mia stay on, so ready to relent – an interesting weakness for a CEO.

His wife intrigued Mia. Janie Wood was an enigma. Whenever she came into the office she was always in a rush, avoiding anyone else who might love the chance to talk to her. Mia wondered what a clever, good-looking woman like Janie was doing with a man like Harry. Because strip away his looks and his money, and there really wasn't much else to him.

Mia had read about the Woods in a local magazine after she'd come back to Lymington. Janie, who had once been a successful barrister, now stood by an Aga in her bespoke kitchen, speaking about her husband's success and the wonderful things he did for the local community. Yet there was something about her that had made Mia wonder if Janie was really the type of woman to be sucked in by wealth and her husband's power.

Mia turned to her notes and started to tell the team how excited she was, before ploughing through the presentation that she had spent the last week rehearsing, on the single bed in the box room at her mum's bungalow.

She felt as if she were in a prison, living in that place, but at least she escaped to work five days a week. Not like her sister Jess, who cocooned herself within that bungalow like there was no life outside its four walls.

By the end of the presentation it was clear how fired up the team was feeling. The fact that they loved her ideas flooded her with a warm flush. Finally she could relax, though she didn't dare look in Laura's direction. Just for that moment she didn't want anything to take away her relief.

She wasn't particularly surprised when Laura had something to add at the end of the meeting, but still Mia wanted it to be quick, so that she could get out of the room on a high. She even expected some sort of put-down – she knew she'd be able to handle it – but she could never have prepared for the bombshell about weather insurance.

Mia thanked her lucky stars that she rarely blushed outwardly, because inside she was dying. Budget was a high priority on the brief, and this curveball was going to destroy it. But of course she hadn't thought of insurance, because she hadn't actually run a sodding TV ad before. Why hadn't anyone else in the office thought to mention it to her? What about Bryony, who was now avoiding eye contact, rustling through her papers as if she were looking for the figure in there somewhere.

*You're not going to find it, Bry,* Mia screamed in her head. *Because you never told me we needed any.*

Her heart hammered as she wrestled with an appropriate response. Not including insurance was such a stupid mistake, and it was one that was going to cost them dearly. 'I'm just waiting for some quotes to come in,' Mia lied.

As Tess gawped back at her, it was clear she didn't believe her. Anyway, what use was it waiting for quotes to come in, when she hadn't even factored in a figure in the first place? There was only one person who could dig her out of this hole and that was the person who'd thrown her into it.

Mia didn't have any other choice. She turned to Laura, who seemed faintly amused by Bryony's frantic actions.

Their assistant was diving into pieces of paper like a lunatic, and suddenly Laura's voice boomed across the room. 'Twenty per cent.'

Mia wanted to shut her eyes and close herself off from the open mouths that were hanging wide around her. She didn't want to look at the face of the woman who had thrown her to the wolves so publicly.

Outside the boardroom, Mia's discomfort started to grow into anger.

What was it with some women that made them turn on each other so readily?

Didn't they have enough to deal with, without stabbing each other in the back when they should be on the same side?

Laura might not be happy that Mia was working here, but she should take that up with Harry. And yet, all too often, women like Laura never did. Mia had seen it happen before. It was, after all, what had brought her to Morris & Wood in the first place. And she was not going to let it continue.

**Interview between DC Emily Marlow and Janie Wood, following the fire on Monday 13 May**

Marlow:   I know this is a horrible time for you and I appreciate you helping us.

Janie:   Thank you.

Marlow:   I'm very sorry about your husband's building. It must be upsetting to see what happened. On top of everything else, of course.

Janie:   (pauses) It is.

Marlow:   I hope not to take up much of your time …

Janie:   I do need to get back to my girls.

Marlow:   I understand.

Janie:   They haven't gone into school today, with everything, you know – with what has happened to their dad.

Marlow:     Of course.

Janie:      I don't want to leave them for long.

Marlow:     I'll be as quick as I can. I just have a few ques-
            tions. Janie, have there been any problems
            between you and your husband recently?

Janie:      Problems?

Marlow:     Yes.

Janie:      You mean, in my marriage?

Marlow:     I mean anything at all.

Janie:      What are you suggesting? That I set fire to the
            building? I didn't.

Marlow:     I'm not saying that at all.

Janie:      I would never … I would never do that.

Marlow:     I'm not suggesting you did, Janie. Was it your
            idea to purchase the site for the Morris & Wood
            offices five years ago?

Janie:      It was Harry's.

Marlow:     It caused quite a stir at the time. As I recall, a lot
            of people were opposed to the development.

Janie:      People didn't want something so big being
            built there. They thought it would affect the
            landscape, the view – you know, from the
            quay.

Marlow:     Could you see it from their side?

Janie:      Yes, I could.

Marlow:     Did you ever want to rethink?

Janie:      I take it, from your questioning, you were
            opposed to it?

| | |
|---|---|
| Marlow: | I didn't have an opinion. |
| Janie: | Right. (laughs) Every local had an opinion. I used to think many got involved just because they liked the drama. Because we came from London. |
| Marlow: | But it upset a lot of people? Didn't that ever make you want to pull out? |
| Janie: | No. |
| Marlow: | Yet the plans were withdrawn at one point, weren't they? |
| Janie: | Yes. Briefly. |
| Marlow: | And wasn't that because of you? |
| Janie: | (pauses) No, actually it was because of my husband. He had a change of heart. He thought it wasn't worth the effort fighting it. I was the one who persuaded him it was. |
| Marlow: | Oh? |
| Janie: | That clearly surprises you. |
| Marlow: | It does, actually. Why were you so passionate about it? |
| Janie: | Because … because I was scared that if we didn't carry on, then Harry would give up on the idea of moving south. |
| Marlow: | And you really wanted to? |
| Janie: | Yes. I really did. |
| Marlow: | Janie, can I get you a tissue? |
| Janie: | No. I'm fine. It's just everything that's happened in the last twenty-four hours. It's a lot to take in. |

| | |
|---|---|
| Marlow: | (nods) Can you tell me why were you so keen to move? |
| Janie: | From London? What does that have to do with anything? It's not relevant. |
| Marlow: | If you could answer the question for me. |
| Janie: | I simply wanted to get away, that's all. Make a new start. |
| Marlow: | You had a good job there. You were a defence barrister? You gave that up when you moved, is that right? |
| Janie: | I did, yes, but really I have no idea why this has anything to do with the fire. |
| Marlow: | I'm interested in why you were so keen for the plans to go through. |
| Janie: | It was a good business opportunity. It meant we could relocate. It *meant* we could live the life we're lucky enough to have. That was all it was. |
| Marlow: | Right. |
| Janie: | You said you were going to be as quick as you can. Why are we talking about the build of the office unless you think it was some revenge arson? Is that what you're thinking? Someone who didn't want us building it decided to burn it down? |
| Marlow: | No, that's not really what I'm thinking at all. |
| Janie: | Then what … |
| Marlow: | I believe you recently met up with one of the employees from Morris & Wood outside of the office, is that right? |

| | |
|---|---|
| Janie: | Yes. Once. |
| Marlow: | Is that usual for you? |
| Janie: | No. It isn't. |
| Marlow: | And do you have a friendship? |
| Janie: | With Mia? No. I wouldn't say that. |
| Marlow: | Yet you went out for lunch? |
| Janie: | Like I said, only the once. |
| Marlow: | Who pursued the lunch date? |
| Janie: | She did. |
| Marlow: | Mia invited you? |
| Janie: | Yes. Honestly, where are you going with this? My girls … |
| Marlow: | I'm sorry, we're nearly done. For the record, could you just tell me where you were last night? |
| Janie: | I don't understand: why do you need to know all this? I can't be a suspect, surely? |
| Marlow: | Like I said, it's purely for the record. |
| Janie: | I have yoga every Monday. |
| Marlow: | And where is this? |
| Janie: | In the village hall in Beaulieu. I had to call a friend over to babysit – Anna. She can tell you. I can get you her phone number if you need it. |
| Marlow: | That's no problem for now, thank you. So you went to yoga last night? |
| Janie: | (nods) Yes. |
| Marlow: | What time was this? |
| Janie: | Seven p.m. For two hours. Then I went home, as Anna will tell you. |

Marlow:  Anna tried to get hold of you last night, didn't she? She said she needed to call your husband because you weren't answering your phone.

Janie:  I didn't hear it. Like I said, I was in my class and – please. Are we done?

Marlow:  (pauses) Yes, we're done, Janie. Thank you for your time this afternoon.

Janie:  Okay. Thanks.

Marlow:  Oh, actually, one more thing before you go. You never did say if you and your husband have been having any problems?

# Chapter Twelve

*Seven weeks before the fire*

Janie placed the casserole in the centre of the dining table and sat down in her usual seat, next to Lottie and opposite Ella. She watched her eldest daughter frown as she lifted the lid of the pot. 'Is that chicken?'

'It is. Why are you turning your nose up? You like chicken.'

'I thought you said we could have takeaway on a Friday night.'

'Well, Ella, you've watched me making this for the last hour, so surely by now you've realised we weren't having a takeaway.'

'Don't be like that, honey,' Harry said, playfully elbowing Ella. 'Your mum's gone to a lot of trouble making this for us. It looks lovely.' He smiled at his wife.

She smiled back, then turned to Lottie. 'Tell me about your day, darling? How was netball?'

'Okay. We lost. Twenty to one.'

'Oh dear,' Harry laughed. 'That's quite a difference.'

Lottie shrugged as Janie spooned casserole onto her plate.

'And what about you, Ell bell, how was your day?' he asked.

'Fine.'

'That's it? Just fine?' he said.

Janie watched Ella as she picked up her fork and swirled her meal around the plate.

'You're not hungry?' Janie asked.

'Not really.'

'Is something wrong?'

'The train was packed tonight,' Harry said, seeming completely oblivious to the fact that his daughter wasn't touching her food.

Janie kept her eyes on Ella.

'I had to stand until I got to Basingstoke. Bloody nightmare! I really shouldn't go up on a Friday again.'

Eventually Ella scooped up a forkful of peas and tipped them into her mouth. Janie turned to her own meal and started eating, and with some relief let Lottie ask her dad about his day. She wished Harry wasn't sitting at the table with them, because if that were the case, she would have asked Ella what had happened, because clearly something had. But Ella wouldn't tell her while Harry was wittering on; nor would he let the subject go, if he thought Ella was holding back on them.

She let his conversation drift over her head, intermittently watching her elder daughter, who finally put her fork down, leaving half the food untouched.

'Eat up,' Harry said.

'I don't feel like it.'

'Come on. You've hardly had anything.'

'I'm not hungry.'

'Don't be ridiculous, your mum—'

'Don't force her if she doesn't want it,' Janie interrupted.

Harry looked up at her questioningly. 'She's hardly had a thing.'

'I know, but ...' Janie waved a hand in the air, trying to defuse the conversation.

'Just another few mouthfuls,' Harry said, turning to Ella.

'For God's sake, she doesn't want it,' Janie snapped. 'You can't force her to eat when she's clearly not hungry.' She turned to Ella. 'If you don't feel well, you can go and have a lie-down,' she told her.

'You're pandering to her again,' Harry said, as he chewed on a mouthful of chicken. He had a piece hanging on the edge of his lips, which she couldn't help but stare at.

'I'm not pandering. I can see she's not right.'

'I am here,' Ella cried. 'You're both talking about me like I'm not even in the room.'

Janie took a deep breath as her phone rang. 'You're right. I'm sorry.' If she were a single parent, then at least there'd be no one to contradict her every five minutes.

Janie took a call from Anna, wandering out of the kitchen to speak to her, and by the time she returned, the plates had been stacked in the sink and the back door was wide open. She glanced out of the kitchen window and saw all three members of her family jumping up and down on the trampoline and for a moment Janie couldn't take her eyes off them. They looked so happy. Even Ella was smiling and laughing as her feet landed on either side of Harry, who was curled into a ball, his hands wrapped protectively around his head.

Janie pressed her hands against the granite work surface and felt tears filling her eyes, though she didn't even know what it was that was making her upset. Possibly the thought that she couldn't break them up. Possibly the knowledge that however much she might have wanted to, she wasn't going to be able to do it.

'We're having a movie night,' Harry announced when they came in forty minutes later. 'Your choice.'

Janie shook her head. 'I don't mind what we watch.'

'In that case the girls want *Aladdin* again.'

'Fine by me,' she said, as Harry wavered in the doorway.

'You are joining us?' he asked.

'Of course I am.' She screwed her eyes up at him, matching the way he was looking at her. What else did he think she was going to do? She would never not sit with them, if they were watching a film together. 'I'll make some popcorn.'

Harry nodded. 'Ella's obviously feeling better.'

'Good,' she said as they heard Ella's laughter ringing from the living room. 'I'm glad.'

As Harry left the kitchen, she watched her husband and considered how he could be so present at times and so absent at others, and wondered which way she actually preferred it.

It was late by the time the girls eventually went to bed. Harry had retreated to the kitchen and set up his laptop. Janie picked up a bottle of Chablis and took it through to the living room, where she flicked on an episode of *Luther*.

Now *there* was a man who was never home either, also more dedicated to his job than to his family, yet watching him gave her some pleasure: pleasure she no longer felt when Harry appeared in the doorway five minutes later.

'Sorry about that – I had something I needed to finish. What are we watching?'

'*Luther*.'

'Do you want to watch a film?'

*No*, she thought, *I want to watch* Luther. 'Can do,' she replied.

Harry sat beside her on the sofa and shuffled closer until she could feel his leg alongside her own. In the early days of their relationship her skin had tingled at his slightest touch in a way she'd never felt before. She was thirty when they met, already worried she might not meet someone to settle down with, which fifteen years later was a ridiculous notion. But all her friends were getting married, some of them starting to have kids, and Janie had felt as if she was being left behind.

Harry had walked into the bar where she was sitting with her girlfriends, celebrating her birthday. He looked nothing like the other men in there, making them look like boys in comparison, dressed in an open-necked, pale-pink shirt and black suit trousers. Janie had watched him from the table as he crossed to the bar and leaned across it, a twenty-pound note clutched in his hand. When he looked over his shoulder and caught her gaze, she felt as if time had stopped and everyone else in the bar had disappeared.

They became inseparable. Six months later Harry proposed, and a year after that they were married, and throughout it all Janie never had any doubts, because they were two similar people, driven by ambition, headstrong but so in love. There was a time when Janie out-earned Harry, but he'd never seemed to mind. There was no competition between them, or at least none that she felt until Ella came along.

Having Ella threw Janie's life into instant turmoil. Now they had to make some changes – allowances – yet it was quickly apparent that the thought hadn't crossed Harry's mind that he might have to too. Janie sat him down, said they needed to figure this out, decide between them how they could work around it, when neither of them wanted to give up their careers. Harry had been quick to tell her that of course he would support whatever decision she made. If Janie wanted to return to work full-time, they could afford a live-in nanny. Janie didn't have to worry about a thing.

So it was her decision, she realised. Not theirs. Not a joint one. It was up to her if she wanted to stay at home or go back to work and, regardless of her choice, her husband's life would not change.

Maybe it was her competitive streak that drove her to decide she wasn't going to give up her career, either. Though every day she was the one with the burning hole inside her, telling her she *was* giving up something – being with her girls. Janie had never been able to reconcile herself with that, yet the girls still hadn't been the main reason she'd given up her job in the end.

Unwanted thoughts flittered into her head. Thoughts of Miles Morgan; Sophie.

That time five years ago was as clear as crystal and still made her feel sick to her core when she thought about what had happened. The part she had played in cracking apart her best friend's life. Miles Morgan had been entering her head a lot since the new mum at school, Marcia, had said the name at assembly, and she desperately wished it would stop.

Harry inched closer to her on the sofa. She felt nothing like she once had, with his leg pressing into hers. Now her feelings were consumed by tiredness, and she didn't actually think she'd be able to stay up for another two hours to watch a film, because it was already past nine.

'Is everything all right, love?' he asked.

Janie blinked and turned to him.

'I mean, at home ... everything?'

'Of course it is.'

Harry ran a finger across his bottom lip as he continued to study her and Janie felt herself squirm under his scrutiny. It felt like he had caught her out, yet there was nothing he could bring up that she had done wrong. She hadn't done a thing. That was the bloody problem.

She waited for him to pursue it, but he didn't. Instead he said, 'Getting a bit tricky at work at the moment. Laura's not happy, bless her.'

*Bless her?* Did he really just say that? She shifted her body to face him, but he was oblivious as he rattled on.

'I tried to convince her I don't want to lose her, but ...' he drifted off, shaking his head.

*No, I bet you don't want to lose her,* she thought. Her body was rigid and she tried edging away from him, but Harry was so tightly squeezed against her that it was hard to move.

Janie had always had her suspicions about them. Right from the start, when Harry couldn't stop talking about Laura's prospects, how he wanted to give her a chance. She had watched them both at their annual parties, clocked the way her husband's gaze lingered on Laura as she spoke, how he trailed after her when she walked out of the room.

Laura was both pretty and ten years younger than her. Her long, dark hair was often loosely pulled back and she had a smattering of light freckles on her face that made her look even younger. She always brought her husband, Nate, to their parties – a nice man who, by all accounts, had properly supported his wife in what she wanted to do after having a baby by actually giving up his job. Not just paying for a nanny.

Surely Laura wouldn't give up someone like him for her husband? Janie wondered, as Harry went on. But then would she be that upset if Harry did run off with Laura Denning? At least then she wouldn't have to make the choice.

'I don't know,' he was muttering, and she realised she'd zoned out for a moment and that all she wanted was that she wasn't made a fool of. 'Maybe I shouldn't have kept Mia on, but my hands were tied. I just need to make sure Laura has enough—'

'I'm sure she'll be fine,' Janie interrupted, though she actually thought Harry was completely in the wrong. His hands weren't tied; he'd taken what he'd thought was the easy option. Over the years since she'd met Harry she'd seen glimpses of such weaknesses that others probably didn't recognise. She'd always thought they were rooted in his earlier need to impress his father. Harry had never wanted to take on his dad's advertising agency, he'd wanted to be an artist. A fact he'd once confided to Janie, when drunk. But she saw a flicker of that need in Harry at times

– none more so than when her life came tumbling down around her five years ago. Harry hadn't taken her side then. He'd taken Miles Morgan's. As if somehow he had thought that was the easier thing to do.

Janie sighed as her thoughts returned to Laura. She was certain the woman would have a case, if she ever wanted to take it further. It would be something that would interest Janie to take on, if she didn't suspect the person in question might have had an affair with her husband.

'Were you at the quay today?' Harry asked suddenly.

Janie felt herself blush.

'It doesn't matter if you were – it's just someone saw you, that's all.'

'Laura?' Janie spat out the name before she had the chance to stop herself. She pulled away from him and off the sofa.

'No. Not Laura.' He looked at her, quizzically. 'It was Mia, actually.'

'Oh.'

Mia. Nicely dressed. Stylishly short haircut. Apart from Laura, she stuck out like a sore thumb from the rest of the women, who often looked as if they'd worn the same cardigan for weeks. The new girl. Though Janie supposed she wasn't that new any more. Maybe, she considered, it could be good to meet Mia, finally have a 'friend' on the inside. The woman certainly had something about her, if she'd managed to push Laura to one side.

'Do you want coffee or more wine?' she asked.

'Wine, please,' he said as she left the living room and went up to her bedroom to get a jumper. Grabbing it from the bed, she pulled it on and went to the window to draw the curtains closed, but when she got there something caught her attention. Fingers curling round the edges of the fabric, she peered closer at first, then quickly pulled back. Her hands fluttered against the curtains as she stood aside, her breath short and fast.

There was someone in the bushes. She would have passed it off as an animal, if it hadn't been for the fact that Janie had also felt someone watching her when she left yoga that Monday.

When she stepped forward again there was no longer any movement and she swiftly pulled the curtains together, propelling the room in darkness.

For a moment Janie didn't move. She considered telling Harry, getting him to check outside, but at the same time she knew she wouldn't, because maybe it was simply her mind playing tricks on her. Maybe it was her head being filled with thoughts of Miles Morgan again, bringing back memories of the last time someone was watching her.

# Chapter Thirteen

*Six weeks before the fire*

It still made Laura pause, every morning when she stepped out of the lift, immediately to see Mia chattering away to one of the other women in the office like they were the best of friends. Monday had come round again, and on this particular occasion it was Bryony Knight hanging over Mia's computer screen in what seemed a bizarrely awkward position.

Laura's fingers found the hem of her jacket and played with its seam. She should just turn in the opposite direction and weave around the desks, but she was too fascinated by the interaction between the two women.

Laura couldn't fathom how anyone in Mia's position could be so brazenly open with the people who worked for her. Immaturity and inexperience made her act like this.

She didn't trust Mia, whose hand was now patting Bryony on the arm like she was some kind of dog, and screeching that she was going to '*take her up on that*'.

'This Friday,' Mia laughed loudly as Bryony retreated from the desk with a smile that reached her ears. 'Straight after work.'

Laura wondered what they'd arranged. She also knew that whatever it was, she'd be unlikely to get an invitation and, even though she would never join them anyway, it didn't mean it didn't hurt. Maybe she had brought it on herself, holding them at arm's length. But as she stood and watched the familiarity bubbling between Mia and Bryony, Laura found herself wishing that she could have what seemed to come so easily to Mia.

Eventually Laura released the hem of her jacket, which was now scrunched into a ball, and flattened it down, hovering on the edges of the office floor, watching this woman with ease and charm oozing out of her.

Bryony had turned away, and now Mia's smile had faded and she shook her head, only slightly but enough for Laura to catch, rolling her eyes and letting out a puff of breath as she turned back to her desk.

Laura glanced round her, looking for anyone else who might have caught this small gesture, but the few other staff around were all preoccupied.

It was all so fake. Everything about Mia was an act, including her supposed friendships, and yet no one else appeared to see it except Laura. And as she stood there, still watching this stranger who had come in and stolen her job, she felt an unease washing over her that made her shudder. She had no idea who this person was that she was unwittingly up against.

'Laura, how are you?' Harry stepped out of the lift, which had just reached the third floor. 'I've barely seen you in the last week,' he said, pausing before adding, 'You look good.'

She clenched her fists, glancing across the floor, embarrassed, but when she saw Mia look over, she wondered if it wouldn't hurt to let her know that she was still close to the boss.

'Thanks.' She reached self-consciously for the ponytail that was loosely tying her hair up that morning. She hadn't had time to wash it. She'd barely managed to streak some mascara onto her eyelashes in her haste. She knew she didn't look good, but Harry was watching her with a sheepish grin, and she felt the rush of heat to her cheeks. 'You've barely been here, that's why you haven't seen me,' she said hastily. She was never going to be good at pretending to enjoy his attention.

'I know. Lot going on up in London.' He rolled his eyes.

'Actually I'm glad I've seen you,' Laura said. 'Can we have a chat?'

''Course we can,' he said and stepped back, gesturing for her to lead the way across the floor to his office.

Once inside, when he'd shut the door behind them, Harry retreated to the other side of his desk, glancing at Laura, who was still hovering by the door. 'Everything all right?' he asked, his head cocked, as if he already guessed she wanted to talk about Mia again.

She did, of course, but this time she was armed with facts he couldn't ignore. 'I attended the Coopers pitch last Friday,' Laura started. She watched his eyes dip away briefly as he pulled out his chair and sank onto it. She thought she saw a small exhalation of breath, but she went on anyway. 'I'm not here to criticise Mia's ideas or what work she's put into her presentation,' Laura said. 'But she made a big mistake. She missed out important things from the budget that she should have considered – things that are going to add at least twenty per cent to their spend. I'm surprised Tess hasn't mentioned it—'

Harry held up a hand to stop her.

'Harry, this is critical.'

'I know. And Mia's already told me.'

'Oh?' Laura said, deflated that her big build-up had been flattened so easily.

'She was upset with herself, she wanted me to know what had happened. She called me on Friday night, she was in such a state.'

Laura shuffled on the spot as annoyance built inside her. 'Well, the fact is she *shouldn't* be making mistakes like that,' she said, trying to keep her voice calm. 'It was easy for me to notice it was missing. It's going to cost Coopers—'

'Laura,' he sighed, 'Mia knows all this. She's been working on it over the weekend. I'm not worried about it, and you certainly don't need to be, either.'

She went quiet. Any thoughts she had of how the conversation might go had been shot to pieces. All she could now think was, *What is the point?* What was actually stopping her from telling Harry what he could do with his job? Laura didn't know if she had the energy to fight.

She imagined what Nate would say if she went home and told him she'd quit. Would he be horrified, or would he understand that not only would he need to go straight back to work, but they'd have to put their house on the market, downsize, potentially move out of the area? They wouldn't be able to go to Crete in September any more. They'd have to make adjustments. But maybe it wouldn't be too bad.

Laura watched Harry frowning, as he waited for her to say something, and she felt sick that she could be pushed out so easily. She could imagine Mia's face if she knew Laura had gone, and realised it would be exactly what she wanted.

She shifted on her spot. It would be her family that suffered again if she gave in, and why the hell should they have to? Because of Mia.

The truth was that she had no idea what to do, constantly oscillating between giving up and taking Mia on, and all the time she just wished Harry would listen to her like he always used to.

'I don't believe you can do what you've done,' Laura said suddenly. 'I have rights – to come back to my old job. Legally, you can't do it.'

'Laura, let's not go down that road. Please.'

'But it's true.' She waited, her heart thumping harder now. This was so not how she wanted their conversation to go, especially as her friend, Deborah, had told her she didn't really have a case. She hated begging for what was rightfully hers, but then maybe the threat would be enough to make Harry see sense. Nothing else was working.

'You still have your same job,' he said. 'You're on the same level, making the same salary—'

'You think that's all that matters?' Laura cried. 'Harry, you've taken my most important client away from me. I'm left with *crap*.' She shouted the last word, watching his eyes flicker to his glass walls. But in that moment she didn't care who heard.

'It's not crap,' he said softly, but with a firm tone she'd rarely heard before, as if he was admonishing her, like she were a child. 'And as I told you when you came back, I have a new opportunity. I was going to speak to you about it this morning,' he said. 'The initial meeting's set up for next week. I want you to be there. I'm excited about this.'

He looked excited, she thought, as she watched him shift in his seat, nodding, holding his head on his steepled hands and looking at her expectantly. 'I'll get the details sent to you – you're going to need to clear your diary for it.'

When Laura still didn't respond he said, 'Clearly this is between you and me, but Coopers' – he hesitated, possibly for emphasis, she thought – 'they won't be the biggest client when we win this one, Laura.' When she didn't answer he went on, 'We get this and you can shake off all your other crap.' Harry winked at her and grinned.

Despite what she'd set out to gain, Laura found herself relenting and eventually she muttered that she would come to the meeting.

'Oh, did you get the invite to my party?' Harry asked as she opened the door to leave.

'I did.'

'Friday the tenth of May.' He clicked a button on his mobile. 'God, five weeks this Friday. Better get myself sorted,' he grinned.

Laura doubted there was much he had to sort. His wife, Janie, appeared to do most of it. Laura often wondered how much Janie enjoyed these parties, how she could when she barely knew most of Harry's staff.

'I hope you and Nate will be there?'

'I don't know – I mean, we've not used a babysitter yet.' Right now, Harry and Janie's party was the last place she wanted to be.

'You have to,' he said, his face dropping. 'If you can't get a babysitter you'll have to come on your own.'

Laura shook her head. 'No. I'd want Nate to be there.'

'Of course.' He smiled. 'Well, do whatever you can,' he added, as if his party could in any way be the most important factor in their conversation today.

'When is this meeting?' she asked.

'Oh, yeah. Right.' He scrolled though his mobile. 'Next Monday. Eleven. We're going to meet at the quay. Maybe have some lunch, if we run on that long.'

'Okay.'

'His name's Miles Morgan,' Harry went on. 'I've known him a long time. I hope you'll like him.'

Bobby was already in bed by the time Laura got home that night. She had tried to get back earlier, but even her so-called crap accounts had taken up too much of her time that day. As soon as she walked into the house she crept into her son's room and tiptoed up to the cot. Now she had to make do with staring at his sleeping body, wrapped up in his sleeping bag, flat out, arms splayed at his sides. Laura hovered over him, breathing in his smell, longing to reach down and pull him out of his cot, hold him against her, feel his warmth and his tiny head of soft, downy hair pressing against her face.

It was funny, she realised; she had never thought she would feel like this – so desperate to be with her baby son, so guilty that she wasn't.

Laura gripped the sides of the cot as she watched Bobby, her eyes filling with tears as his eyelids fluttered, and wondered what was going through his mind. What dreams he could be having. She mustn't lean too close in case he woke. Nate had told her Bobby hadn't settled for a while, that he'd had to sit with him in the rocking chair until he did.

She'd known something would give, when she went back to work. She'd had the discussion with her NCT friends months back, when she told them that she felt like a part of her was lost without work. Laura understood that working full-time meant there would be times when she wouldn't see Bobby before he went to bed, or when she'd be out of the house before he woke, and at the time she was okay with that. It was a sacrifice she was prepared to make because she would come home, satisfied and buzzing, able to throw herself into the time she did have with her family.

She had never expected to feel so desperate and vulnerable, and as she peered at her beautiful son, she hated that Chrissie and the other NCT mums were right. She couldn't have everything and she no longer knew what to sacrifice. All she did know was that she definitely wasn't happy.

With a deep sigh Laura eventually retreated and went downstairs, wiping a hand across her face before Nate noticed she was upset. They were seeing the other couples and their babies this weekend and Laura didn't particularly want to face them all, yet it had been in the diary for weeks. There was no good way of escaping it. She had known for a long time she'd never be true friends with this group of women. Their hearts were often in the right place but they didn't understand her one bit, and she certainly couldn't talk to them about how awful her first weeks back at work had been.

Nate handed her a glass of wine as soon as she reached the bottom of the stairs.

'Thank you.'

'You look like you need it,' he said. 'I haven't had a chance to think of tea, with Bobby not getting off to sleep.'

'Oh, don't worry about that. Let's get a takeaway,' she suggested, following him into the living room, where she sank onto the sofa and stretched out her legs. 'I'm so done in.' Laura closed her eyes and leaned her head back.

'How was it today?' he asked. When she looked up, he was flicking through his phone. 'What do you fancy? Pizza?'

'Anything. I spoke to Harry today,' she added.

'Oh?' He passed her his phone. 'Do you want to choose what you want, first?'

Laura sucked in a breath as she took the phone. Nate's mind was clearly on food as he peered over her shoulder, waiting for her to select from the menu. She quickly pointed to the twelve-inch vegetarian pizza she chose every time, then passed the phone back to him and waited for what seemed like an eternity for him to make his choice and place the order.

All the time she sipped at her wine, studying her husband, and when he eventually put his phone down and asked how it went, she couldn't actually be bothered to tell him.

Laura shrugged.

'Did you say anything about Mia's mistake?' he asked.

'Of course.'

'So what did he say?'

'Mia had already told him,' Laura said, blankly. 'Harry didn't seem to think it was a big deal.'

Nate nodded, stretching his legs out next to hers.

'He keeps telling me about this new client, Miles Morgan. Apparently there's a meeting with him next week, but I don't know, Nate,' she went on. 'I don't know if Harry's simply telling me what I want to hear.'

'Maybe you need to see what happens with this Miles guy?'

'I will, but that's not the point, is it? The fact is Mia's still there, lording it around the office, and I'm having to hover about, waiting to see if something comes from a mate of Harry's. She's got away with that bloody mistake – that's what so infuriating. She's working everyone in the office, and they're all falling for it.'

'I don't get why you have it in for Mia,' he said.

Laura's head snapped round to look at him. 'Are you kidding?'

'Surely it's Harry you should be pissed off with. He's the one who's made this decision, not Mia.'

'Haven't you been listening to me, Nate? I told you from the start, there's something about her – she's not the same person who came for the interview.'

Nate gave a short laugh that he turned into a cough.

'Are you shaking your head?' she said. 'You think I'm making it up?'

'No, I don't think that at all. I just have no idea why you're so intent on getting at her, and not Harry.'

Laura's pulse was racing as she looked at her husband. She knew what he thought of her boss; he'd always said he never trusted Harry, and yet he did trust her, implicitly. He knew she would never do so much as flirt with Harry Wood. So why did she feel now like he was accusing her of something?

'I've known Harry years – he's always looked out for me, you know that,' she told him defiantly. 'We wouldn't even be in this house if it wasn't for Harry taking a chance on me. I believe him,' she said, because even though she wasn't entirely convinced by her own words, it was what she desperately wanted.

Nate nodded. 'Okay.'

'What, you don't?'

'I'm not saying that at all. I'm sure Harry's telling the truth. But you don't owe him everything, Laura, simply because he gave you the job.'

'I think this is down to Mia,' Laura said, ignoring Nate and willing him to understand where she was coming from. The fact was that she had to believe Harry, because she *needed* him. All she needed from Mia was for her to leave the company. 'And somehow I'm going to prove it.'

'Oh, Laura,' he groaned. 'Don't go down that road.'

'What?' she cried, pushing him in the arm when he didn't respond. 'What do you mean?'

Nate shook his head. 'You don't need this right now, do you? You've only just gone back after having Bobby. Don't you need to – I don't know – keep things plain sailing for a while.'

'Plain sailing? What are you saying? That I should accept everything that's happened?'

'Well, yeah. For now, anyway. I think you've probably got enough other things going on in your head.' He waved a hand about the room. 'And you're not getting enough sleep. You're probably overtired.'

Laura screwed up her eyes at him. 'You think I'm not up to dealing with it? Because I've had a baby?'

'No.'

'So what do you mean by "not getting enough sleep"?'

'I'm just saying, Laura. Christ, I don't know – you're taking this the wrong way.'

'Because I'm what: too emotional?' she asked.

'Oh, for God's sake.' Nate rolled his eyes and sank back into the sofa.

Laura shook her head as a tear escaped and rolled down her face. She wiped it away quickly before he could prove his point. Eventually she sank back too, and after a moment Nate reached out and squeezed her leg.

'I mean be careful,' he said. 'That's all.'

'I don't think that is all, though, is it?' she said. 'You mean something more than that. Tell me.'

'I mean this has happened before, Laura. And I don't want you starting a witch-hunt, because it won't turn out well.'

'Nate,' Laura gasped. 'I can't believe you even said that. This is nothing like what happened with Saskia.'

**Tuesday 14 May**

**Interview between DC Emily Marlow and Nathan (Nate) Denning, following the fire on Monday 13 May**

Marlow:  You say your wife texted you to say she was going to be late home last night?

Nate:  She did. That's not unusual, though.

Marlow:  What was her reason?

Nate:  She said she was held up at work.

Marlow:  And how often is she held up and late back?

Nate:  Most nights now.

Marlow:  Do you know what time she supposedly left the office?

Nate:  I don't. She texted me at about six p.m., I think.

Marlow:  So three hours before the building burned down she told you she was still in it?

Nate:     Yes. But she wouldn't have been the only one. There would have been other staff still there at six – it's not that late, really. Is it?

Marlow:   And what was her reason for staying on?

Nate:     She said she was meeting the Coopers team members. They're her main account. They *were* her main account, rather.

Marlow:   Only we now know she didn't actually meet any of the team from Coopers.

Nate:     So I hear.

Marlow:   Nathan, I'm sorry to ask you this …

Nate:     Please call me Nate.

Marlow:   Nate. Have you any idea why your wife might have told you she was meeting up with staff from her old account, when it's apparent there was never any such meeting scheduled?

Nate:     I don't. You'll have to ask her that.

Marlow:   For some reason, your wife isn't telling us anything. Either she's covering up for herself or for someone else.

Nate:     (sighs) I wish I could tell you more, I really do.

Marlow:   What time did she get home last night?

Nate:     It was late, it wasn't until about ten o'clock, I think.

Marlow:   And how did she seem?

Nate:     I was already in bed. We didn't speak. We haven't been … we haven't been speaking much lately. After the weekend, I wasn't in

|        | the mood to talk to her last night, so I didn't acknowledge her when she came home. |
|--------|------------------------------------------------|
| Marlow: | Had something in particular happened over the weekend? |
| Nate: | Yes, the party happened. Harry Wood's party. |
| Marlow: | And did you attend it? |
| Nate: | No. I didn't. My wife went on her own. |
| Marlow: | Had everything been okay between you and your wife until the party? |
| Nate: | (pauses) Not really. She's been getting … I've been worried about her. |
| Marlow: | Worried? In what way? |
| Nate: | That she's been … (shakes head) Oh, I don't know, I suppose that she's been getting too 'involved' with someone at work. |
| Marlow: | Involved? You mean she's been having a relationship with someone in the office? |
| Nate: | (laughs) That's not what I mean. Obsessed then, if you want. She's been getting obsessed. The thing is, it's not the first time it's happened, so … |
| Marlow: | Who is this you're referring to? |
| Nate: | Her name's Mia. But this has absolutely nothing to do with the fire, you know that, don't you? I mean, what I'm telling you – there's no way Laura had anything to do with the fire last night. |

Marlow:    Your disagreement over the weekend, was
           it because of your wife's argument with Mia
           Anderson at the party?

Nate:      What? No. No, I don't know anything about
           any argument. No, I was pissed off about what
           happened with Harry Wood.

# Chapter Fourteen

*Six weeks before the fire*

Mia poked her head around Harry's office door. 'Have you got five minutes?'

'I have,' Harry beckoned her in. 'I hope you bring me good news, though.' He gestured to the seat. 'How's everything going?'

'All good, thanks.'

'The TV ad coming on well?'

'Really well.'

Harry nodded and smiled, though his eyes didn't light up the way they usually did. Mia wondered what was on his mind. She had seen Laura in his office earlier, her arms flailing around as she spoke to him. The woman clearly had something to discuss, and Mia had no doubt it was probably her. In contrast to Laura's frantic movements, Harry had been immobile at his desk.

Mia wondered how he put up with it. He was the boss, and yet from where Mia had watched, outside the glass wall, Laura had been the one in control. How she wished she'd been able to hear what was being said.

The rumours about Harry and Laura were partially true, from Mia's point of view. The way he pawed at Laura's shoulder outside the lift, hovering over her just a little too close. It was an unnecessary display from the CEO in such a public space. No wonder the gossip had spread, when it was clearly apparent that he fancied her.

But what did Laura make of it? This intrigued Mia, because as far as she could see there was no reciprocation, yet Laura hadn't told Harry he was too close, or even pulled away.

If it had happened to her, Mia would have turned round and slapped him around the face. Everyone else in the office might think Harry was hot, but Mia didn't get it. She didn't particularly think he had many attractive qualities.

Of course she had never said as much to anyone, especially not the likes of Henrietta or Bryony, because there was no way she would chance it getting back to Harry. Or Laura. The thought of that – Laura would have a field day, if she could report back to Harry that Mia didn't like him.

He was waiting for her now to tell him what she wanted. She'd always been grateful that he didn't dally in small talk; Harry hadn't once asked about her personal life.

'It doesn't look like you're bringing the good news I was hoping for?' he said now, raising his eyebrows.

'Not really, I'm afraid.'

'But you're not here to talk about Coopers?'

'No, that's all going fine. This is a more personal issue that I need to discuss with you.'

'Okay?' he asked cautiously.

Mia straightened herself in the chair. 'I think you need to know there's a lot of concern among the women in the office.'

Harry screwed his eyes up at her and leaned his head to one side. He had no idea what she was talking about, but then of course he wouldn't. He could sit in his glass office with the doors closed and have no idea what went on the other side of it. 'How do you mean?'

'Bullying,' Mia went on. 'I'm afraid someone has confessed to me that she is being bullied, and I feel it right to come to you with this.'

'Bullied? Who?'

'Sarah Clifton, but she's not the only one concerned.'

'Who's she complaining about?' he asked.

'Mike Lewis.'

'Mike?' Harry gave a short laugh. 'You're not serious?'

'I am,' Mia replied, confused by his reaction and a little pissed off that he could think this was anything to laugh about.

'But Mike's ... you know what Mike's like, he's – Christ, what's he actually supposed to have done?'

'He undermines his staff,' Mia said. 'He doesn't listen to what they have to say. He makes them feel like they aren't important.'

'Oh, right.'

*God*, Mia thought, *he isn't taking me seriously.*

'It's the women he does this to, Harry. I'm just pleased they feel they can finally share their concerns with someone.'

*Damn you, Harry Wood*, she thought, as she watched his expression change from shock to confusion, to a mild irritation that she had brought this issue to him.

'Why hasn't Sarah spoken to me herself?' he asked.

Ah, that was the problem. Sarah didn't actually know that Mia was here. As Mia had predicted, Sarah had spoken to her boyfriend again over the weekend and had come in that morning and told Mia she didn't want to take it any further.

'I'm doing it on her behalf,' Mia told him.

Harry raised his eyes. 'Okay, I'll speak to Mike.' He waved a hand in the air as he shook his head. Was he dismissing her?

Mia could feel the anger burning in the pit of her stomach.

'Anything else, because I really need to make a call ...'

'No,' she said, very faintly but through gritted teeth. 'No, there's nothing else.'

**Tuesday 14 May**

**Initial interviews between DC Emily Marlow and the staff of Morris & Wood, following the fire on Monday 13 May**

*Mike Lewis, Head of Creative*

Mike: You still don't know anything more? Staff are talking – asking questions no one can answer. I hear there were people in the building?

Marlow: I'm sorry, I can't confirm anything at the moment.

Mike: It's just that I have a friend who knows someone in the police. He said they pulled two people out, but …

Marlow: As I said, I'm really sorry, but right now we don't have any details.

Mike: (nods) That's okay. I understand.

Marlow:    Mr Lewis, I believe you were accused of bullying someone who worked in your team. A Sarah Clifton?

Mike:      What? Why are you asking – that was nothing more than office gossip.

Marlow:    So you're denying she accused you of harassment?

Mike:      She might have said something, but it was ridiculous. I wasn't bullying anyone. I thought I was here about the fire? Why are you asking me about a girl who doesn't even work for the company any more?

Marlow:    Oh, this is about the fire, but I'm trying to understand exactly what was happening inside Morris & Wood prior to last night. And that means I might be asking some questions that don't always feel relevant.

Mike:      This isn't relevant.

Marlow:    Maybe not. But it might be, and all the same I'd appreciate if you'd allow me to—

Mike:      You're thinking someone who worked at the company did it, then? Set fire to the place, I mean? Who?

Marlow:    It's early days, and right now we're talking to everyone who worked there.

Mike:      Well, it has nothing to do with me. And whatever the girl said about me … it was all fabricated.

|         | I've never heard anything so— (breaks off) It can destroy people, you know, lies like that. |
|---------|---|
| Marlow: | How do you mean? |
| Mike:   | I'm just saying, people start accusing you of things and it sticks. Whether or not it's true, it gets round and then (shakes head), I don't know … |
| Marlow: | Could you speak up, please, for the tape. |
| Mike:   | I said I don't know. I don't know what started it, and I don't know why it was all blown out of proportion. But it was. By Mia Anderson. |
| Marlow: | I was under the impression that an official complaint was made against you and taken to Harry Wood. Is that true? |
| Mike:   | No. There was nothing official. |
| Marlow: | You mentioned Mia Anderson. Wasn't she the one who spoke to Harry about it? |
| Mike:   | Yes. That's the point. It was nothing to do with her. Only she started it, and it snowballed and she wouldn't let it go. |
|         | I was going to give Harry this, you know. (shows letter) |
| Marlow: | What is this? |
| Mike:   | My resignation. I've been carrying it around with me for the last two weeks. To be honest, I don't really want to go. |
| Marlow: | Can you think of any reason why Mia Anderson was so keen to complain, if you believe you did nothing wrong? |

| Mike: | (shrugs) None at all. She was nice as anything to my face. But there was something about her. This fiery spark. I saw it at Harry's party Friday night – the way she blew. |
|---|---|
| | I don't know. I don't really know her at all – not like some of those girls in the office do – but there was something I couldn't quite put my finger on. |

### Bryony Knight, Account Assistant

| Marlow: | In your own words, Mia Anderson was amazing at her job. |
|---|---|
| Bryony: | (nods) She was. |
| Marlow: | But wasn't there an issue with a TV advertising budget? |
| Bryony: | Yes, but that was an understandable mistake. Anyone could have made it. |
| Marlow: | Even someone who had experience in TV advertising? |
| Bryony: | I don't know for sure, but yes, I would have thought so. |
| Marlow: | Did Mia Anderson lead you to believe she had that kind of experience? |
| Bryony: | Of course she had. She had tons of it. Has Mia done something wrong? It sounds like you think she has, by the questions you're asking me. She didn't – she wouldn't have ... I mean, it was no way her. She wouldn't have started the fire. |

Marlow: What makes you so sure of that, Bryony?

Bryony: Well, I just know she wouldn't. She's a lovely person.

Marlow: How well do you know her?

Bryony: I know her really well. I mean, I report to her and everything, but we're friends, too.

Marlow: Tell me about your friendship. What do you do together?

Bryony: Well, you know, we go out for drinks after work, that sort of thing.

Marlow: Anything else?

Bryony: She's more of a friend at work.

Marlow: So, other than a few drinks after work, have you met up with Mia on any other occasion?

Bryony: No, but we've been out a lot of times. Most Friday nights we go down to the pub.

Marlow: What do you know about Mia's home life?

Bryony: Like what?

Marlow: I don't know – you tell me. Anything at all you know about Mia Anderson's personal life. Who does she live with?

Bryony: Well, I know for sure she lives on her own.

Marlow: Oh?

Bryony: In a flat. She has her own place; she laughs about the woman who lives above her, who's always shouting at her boyfriend.

Marlow: Okay, Bryony, I think we're done here for now.

# Chapter Fifteen

*Five weeks before the fire*

On Saturday morning Mia's mother stood at the kitchen sink, her hands plunged into the water as she scrubbed hard on a pan.

'You'll wear your fingers away,' Mia told her.

'Well, these pans won't wash themselves, will they?' her mum answered, feigning brightness in a way she always did when there was something on her mind.

Mia looked at her, hunched over, shoulders taut. She could almost see the cogs inside her mum's brain working overtime. 'Here, let me help,' she said, reaching for the washing-up cloth.

'No, no.' Her mum brushed her away. 'I'm perfectly capable of doing a few dishes. I'm not dead yet.'

'Mum – don't talk like that.'

Her mother stopped, shoulders heaving upwards. She rolled her head from side to side, but didn't speak.

'Your neck's hurting again.' Mia knew what that meant. Her mum had been doing too much, putting too much pressure on herself. It scared Mia to see her like this, because she didn't know how far her mum would stretch before she broke altogether. 'And besides, I want to help,' she muttered, grabbing a tea towel from the side, then picking up a dish from the draining board. 'You can at least let me dry.'

Her mum gave her a thin smile, before turning back to the pan and plunging it into the soapy water again.

They fell into a silence as they stood side-by-side. Mia looked out to the yard at the back, where a few large tubs took pride of place next to a bistro table covered in rust. They really could do with another set, but there wasn't enough money left that month.

'Maybe we could go out this afternoon,' Mia suggested. 'Do you fancy a pub lunch?'

'That would be lovely.' Her mum nodded enthusiastically, but she wasn't smiling. 'Yes. That does sound nice. But I don't think ... I don't know if Jess will come.'

'I'll ask her,' Mia said.

'Yes ...'

Mia clocked the pause, the deep intake of breath. They both knew that her older sister wouldn't want to go anywhere, but it didn't mean they would ever stop trying to persuade her to.

Time had softened their mother. She'd once been so determined, so unprepared for a fuss, yet now she was more than willing to cave in to Jess, not to push her. Mia knew this was possibly the worst thing she could be doing for her sister, but at the same time she couldn't blame her mum. With her ailing health, Jess was too much for her to cope with.

Mia understood that some days it was easier for her mum to let Jess sit in the house all day, because the argument and the fallout were too much to take. There were enough times when Mia wanted to do the same, so she didn't blame her mum for giving in. But she also thought she'd been relenting too much lately, giving in to her eldest daughter's behaviour, and it was a downward spiral. Anyone could see that. Even their mum must.

'It's like Jess is a child again,' she had told Mia once. 'It's hard enough to deal with a three-year-old when she won't do what's best for her, but at least then you can pick her up and strap her into the car when you need to go out. How am I supposed to do that with Jess? She's an adult now. She's thirty-seven.

'Of course Jess wasn't ever that bad as a little one,' she had gone on, and Mia knew what was coming. 'You were the rascal. The one who refused to go to bed, who would lie on the floor of the supermarket, kicking and screaming. Look at us now,' she had said, her words fading to a whisper. 'You don't expect this.'

Mia hated that her mum was living this life. She was sixty-eight. She had been about to give up her part-time job at Sainsbury's a year ago; she'd wanted to take a pottery course. The flyer had been pinned to the fridge for as long as Mia had been back at home. But everything had been put on hold. For Jess.

'I'm going to try my best, Mum,' Mia said as she folded the tea towel and laid it carefully on the draining board. 'It's such a gorgeous day, and we don't have to go anywhere too crowded.'

'No, no, of course, but don't ...' Her mum paused again.

'I won't push it,' Mia said, biting her tongue. As she wandered out of the kitchen and towards Jess's bedroom at the far end of the hall in the bungalow, she knew that if she couldn't get her sister to agree to go to the pub for lunch, then their mum wouldn't go, either. She wouldn't want to leave Jess on her own – not on a day like this. Sunny Saturdays were always so much worse. And yet the thought of them all sitting inside made Mia's fingers curl as she rapped on the closed door and gently pushed it open.

Jess was facing away from her, her finger outstretched, running along the line of her heaving bookcase, until she stopped at one volume and tugged it out. Mia peered closer. *Wuthering Heights*. Such a depressing book, in Mia's mind, yet Jess was drawn to reading it time and time again.

Mia sat on the edge of her sister's bed and waited for her to turn round.

'You look tired,' Jess said eventually when she locked eyes with her sister. 'Are you sleeping?'

Mia shrugged. 'I had a late night. I woke early. But yeah, apart from that, I'm sleeping okay.'

'You're working too hard.'

Mia shook her head. 'I enjoy it.'

Jess stared at her, her gaze intense, her mind whirring with something. 'Do you really?' she asked. It unnerved Mia when her sister studied her the way she did, like she knew there was more going on than Mia could ever tell her. Jess had always had an uncanny ability to sense the things left unsaid, but that ability had intensified in the last year.

'I do,' Mia told her.

'I still don't understand what you see in that place,' Jess muttered, still watching her intently. 'You know how Mum felt about the building when it was being developed. She used to round up signatures, to petition against it being built. You working there is like you're going against her.'

'Mum doesn't mind one bit,' Mia said. There were plenty of things she could have said to Jess. Working at Morris & Wood was surely the least of their mum's worries. Mia's salary had relieved the three of them as much as it could, even if it wasn't stretching far enough.

'You didn't see her at the time. She hated it. She thought it was disgusting that someone like Harry Wood could waltz down here and take over. It's like he was building a bloody shrine to himself.'

Mia shook her head and turned away.

'I'm sorry. I know you're doing this for us.'

*You have no idea*, Mia thought, but she didn't answer.

'Is he still a good boss to work for?'

'Yes,' she said, her voice clipped. She always tried to avoid getting into a conversation with Jess about work or Harry Wood, but sometimes Jess pushed her. 'He's fine, as bosses go. And I don't know why you try to make me feel guilty about working there,' she added, opening her mouth to carry on, but clamping it shut at the last minute.

Mia sighed. It was a constant see-saw of anger that Jess didn't always appreciate what she was doing; and then guilt for feeling that way.

She had often wondered what Jess would say if she told her the truth. How the fact that her mum had battled against the development of the office had briefly tainted her view of taking the job, but an overpowering sense had seized her that this was the one opportunity she could not afford to miss.

When she'd seen the ad, her breath had been momentarily trapped as she read and reread Laura Denning's job description. It was perfect. Too perfect to be true, really. The opportunity had practically fallen into her lap; now all she had to do was ensure she got the job. She had six months of Laura not being there to get her feet under the table.

Neither her mum nor Jess knew the whole truth. She could imagine what they would say to her, if they did. They would tell her to get out.

'How did that pitch go that you were worrying about?' Jess asked.

Mia didn't mention that the pitch was a week ago now; it was nice that Jess had remembered it at all. 'It was fine, to a point,' Mia told her, 'and then I cocked it up. I forgot something major, but I think I've got past it.'

'You always do.' The corners of Jess's mouth twitched. 'My little sister always has a knack of making sure things go her way.'

'Here's hoping,' Mia smiled. She reached a hand out and touched Jess's. 'Come to the pub with us for lunch? We can go locally – we don't have to get in the car – and we can sit outside. You don't have to go in.'

Jess pulled away.

'I know you don't want to, but I'm thinking of Mum. She won't leave you, Jess, you know that.'

'Don't put that onto me.'

'I'm not. I don't mean to. But she looks done in. Honestly, she could do with this. The three of us girls together. Please.'

Jess turned and looked out of the window that faced the road. It wasn't a pleasant view, and Mia often wished Jess had something better to look at, given the amount of time she spent in her room; but then she'd been the one to stop her mum trying to give up her own bedroom at the back. As far as Mia was concerned, that was one thing she shouldn't have to do for her daughter.

'I know how hard this feels for you, but it doesn't have to be,' Mia went on. 'Please just try. If it gets too much, we'll turn round and come straight home. I promise.'

'Okay,' Jess said eventually.

'Really?'

'I'll try, but . . .'

'I know, I know.' Mia stood up and kissed her sister on the top of her head, closing her eyes and lingering for a moment as she breathed in the faint scent of coconut shampoo.

It must seem such a small step for most people, but it was a victory for them, and Mia tried to focus on that, rather than the thoughts that often invaded her head: the events of twelve months ago that had turned their world on its axis. The reason they were all living in this prison.

She eventually pulled away and whispered to her sister, 'I love you, you know.'

## Wednesday 15 May

**Second interviews between DC Emily Marlow and the staff of Morris & Wood, following the fire on Monday 13 May**

### Henrietta James, Senior Account Manager

Henrietta: I suppose they kept it pretty professional in the office – their mutual dislike for each other, that is – though you could tell there were things going on behind the scenes.

Marlow: What kind of things do you mean?

Henrietta: Well, they clearly didn't trust each other's motives. That's why it all blew up at the party. One of them had found out something. I wasn't trying to eavesdrop, of course. But you couldn't help it. They were so loud.

Marlow: Who found out what – do you have any idea?

Henrietta: I can't say for sure, but what started it was when Laura went running over the lawn, yelling at Mia that she was a liar. She was shouting that she knew. That's what she kept saying: *I know about you.*

But, like I say, I couldn't hear all of it.

Marlow: What did Mia do, when Laura was yelling at her?

Henrietta: She looked ... well, she was furious, to be honest. But I mean, you can't blame her, can you? It was embarrassing for everyone – it must have been horrific for her.

Marlow: You think she looked more cross than embarrassed?

Henrietta: Oh, I really can't say. I mean I might be twisting everything all round here ...

Marlow: Your loyalties appear to lie with Mia Anderson.

Henrietta: Of course; well, I don't mean I was taking sides or anything. I really wasn't. But Mia, well, it was all so out of the blue.

Marlow: Did you speak to either of them after their argument?

Henrietta: No. I went to look for Mia, but when I found her she was with Janie Wood and ... well, I didn't want to interrupt that.

But I still don't see what the argument at the party has to do with the offices being set on fire?

Marlow: Maybe it doesn't. Did you happen to notice how much both women had been drinking that night?

Henrietta: (laughs) Well, Laura, yes; I mean you couldn't help but notice how much she'd put away. And with a baby at home and everything. It wasn't right. She was in such a state. To be honest, I was surprised to see her in the office yesterday. I thought she might have been too embarrassed. Though she did come in *very* late.

Marlow: How did the argument end?

Henrietta: Well, eventually Harry had to break it up, but by then everything had gone wrong, hadn't it? You know, I felt so sorry for Janie Wood, after all the trouble she went to. She'd laid out such a wonderful spread – lots of hors d'oeuvres. Have I said that right?

Anyway she'd gone to so much effort, but then she always does. And she looked stunning too. She's a very beautiful woman, Janie Wood. She must have been furious.

You know at first it was strange, because I remember Janie standing behind me, just watching the argument, and she didn't look remotely bothered that they were making such a scene. It looked like she almost found the whole thing amusing.

Though, of course, ten minutes later any smile had been wiped straight off her face. Poor woman. And then there was the whole issue with Harry and … Oh, it was all such a shame and supposed to be a lovely night, but after that – you know, I didn't actually see Janie again? That was a funny thing too.

Marlow:     Henrietta, do you have any idea why Laura accused Mia of lying?

Henrietta:  No. But what I do recall is that at one point Laura said she knew Mia Anderson wasn't who said she said was, and she was demanding to know why the hell Mia had come for her job.

# Chapter Sixteen

*Five weeks before the fire*

Janie was sitting at her laptop trying to focus on preparations for her husband's staff party, but she couldn't clear her head. She sighed as she sat back in her chair and gazed out the window, her hand cradled around a mug of coffee.

Maybe she should take a break from party planning. Do some yoga in the garden. A headstand might help the unwanted thoughts drop out of her head. Searching through Pinterest for pretty platters of food and decorations was certainly not doing it for her, and she was beginning to wish she'd told Harry that she didn't want to host another sodding party ever again. They were nothing more than a chore. In fact Janie had lost any interest in them the moment the first party was over, when she was left with an untidy house, bin bags stacked high in the garden and the feeling that she was the caterer rather than the wife.

Janie wasn't a woman who felt a sense of achievement from throwing a bloody party. She was once someone who made the difference between people walking free or being convicted.

Janie closed her Pinterest board, her fingers hovering over the computer's keyboard. What she really wanted to do was dive into something she had forbidden herself, but parties, and Harry, and a long stretch of the day ahead before she had to pick up the girls, had left her feeling low. And what better place to go to, when you're already feeling like life can't get any worse, she thought sarcastically, than opening up Facebook?

The site pinged into life and Janie typed his name into the search bar, her gaze drifting down the profiles until she came to the third Miles Morgan. She felt the same twinge that she had the last time she'd looked at his face. He hadn't changed one bit.

Clicking on his page, Janie took in the information, looking for what, she wasn't quite sure. A wife? Kids? What he was doing now? That he was still safely tucked away in London?

There was no sign of children in any of his pictures, most of which were of Miles in various luxurious locations, some with a group of men, others with a woman. Janie zoomed in closer on a photo of her. Pretty, long dark hair, deep-brown eyes and a figure to die for, in her tight tops and skinny jeans or shorts. She could be twenty years younger than Miles.

She wondered what version of Miles this woman saw, and whether any of it was the truth. Had he told her what he'd done? Somehow Janie doubted it.

Holding a hand over her knotted stomach, Janie tried to make sense of what she was feeling. But as Miles Morgan stared back from her computer screen, nothing came to her and eventually she deleted her search, so that no one could find it, and closed down the laptop.

Miles wasn't in her life any more. She didn't need to see him ever again. And as she reminded herself of this fact she felt some relief, because it was one thing to look at him on her screen, but the thought of coming face-to-face with him sent a shiver down Janie's spine.

When Harry got home from the gym, Janie could tell he was wrestling with something. She could see it in the way he rubbed at his chin, his attention only half on the girls as they talked about going to the cinema that afternoon, and the film they particularly wanted to see. It still surprised her how keen Ella, in particular, always was to share everything with her father, when Janie got little more than a grunt from her when she tried asking questions.

Now, as she watched their interchange, she wondered if the girls found Harry attentive, because she could tell his response was vague, his eyes blank. As soon as there was a pause in the conversation he picked up his mobile, and eventually the girls left to play outside.

'Anything on your mind?' she asked drily.

'Yeah.' He screwed up his eyes, wrinkling his nose. 'Yeah, there is actually. I've got a bloody complaint to deal with.'

'Oh?'

'One of the women in the office,' he went on. 'Harassment.'

Janie paused, midway through pouring beans into the coffee machine, and turned to look at the back of her husband's head. 'Harassment?' she repeated.

He glanced over his shoulder. 'Not me,' he said. 'It wasn't me. Is that what you thought?'

Janie shook her head. 'No. Of course not.' Though the thought *had* been there, if only for a moment. She let out a small puff of breath and wondered why her husband had chosen a Saturday morning to bring it up with her, when it must have been playing on his mind through the week.

Harry continued to regard her curiously, until she looked away.

'No,' he said firmly, 'it's Mike Lewis.'

'*Mike*'s harassing someone?' Janie asked. 'What's he done?'

'*Supposedly* done,' Harry said, as if she of all people should know there were two sides to every story.

*Yes,* she had wanted to reply, *but there's no smoke without fire.* She of all people knew that, too.

'Anyway.' Harry pulled himself up, as if he realised that he had sounded like an arse. 'It's nothing sexual, as far I'm aware. He's simply treating this particular girl as if she's' – Harry waved an arm in the air as he searched for the right word – 'I don't know, not worthy of being there or something, apparently. Thing is, I have to do something about it now, don't I?'

'*Woman*,' Janie corrected. 'And yes. Of course you do.'

'But it's Mike. We all know what Mike's like – he doesn't mean anything by it. He's just direct, old-school.'

'Old-school? You mean he doesn't know how to talk to women,' she replied. 'He's rude,' Janie went on. 'I talk to him and he responds to you.'

'He's shy, awkward – I don't know,' Harry argued. 'But he's not a bully.'

'So what's she's saying Mike's actually done?'

Harry shrugged. 'I thought it was all going to go away when Mia mentioned it earlier in the week,' he started, making Janie clench that he could think that was the right outcome. 'I've asked her to get the girl to write down some specifics, which it seems she now wants to talk about next week.' He held up his phone as if it were evidence of the fact. 'It all seems so bloody vague to me.' He bowed his head in his hands, then ruffled them through his hair. 'I think I'll go and have a shower. This is the last thing I need right now.'

Janie shook her head, biting her lip as she handed him an espresso, which he downed in one gulp. To Harry, brushing over the fact that Mike could be a little bit odd, and in some ways completely out of order, was easier than having to have a conversation with the guy who'd been working with him for the last five years.

'I don't know what to do about it,' he admitted as he dropped his cup into the sink. 'I have the feeling Mia Anderson isn't going to let up.'

'Why don't you know what to do about it?' Janie asked. 'Surely you need to address whatever the woman is saying.'

'That's the point, really,' he said. 'She doesn't seem to be too—' He broke off. 'I called her into my office to talk and she just clammed up.'

'Probably because she's scared,' Janie said. 'Imagine what it must be like, being pulled into the Chief Exec's office, regardless of what it's about. Add on top of that, it's something personal – you're asking her about someone she probably thinks you're mates with.'

'I'm not mates with Mike.' He looked up at her. 'Mike's a fool; you know what I think of him.'

Yes, she did. Mike Lewis would never be one of Harry's boys. 'I know that, but she's not going to.'

'You think that's what it is – she's scared?'

'I'm sure of it.'

'God.' He rubbed his hands over his eyes. 'This could turn into a right mess. Mia mentioned a "bullying culture",' he went on, forming his fingers into quotation marks. 'I mean, seriously, I've never had anything like this; there's no *bullying culture* in the company.' He spat out the words almost sarcastically.

Janie stiffened. She didn't like where this was going. She had seen it time and time again. It's what had brought people to her to defend them, when ultimately things had gone too far.

During her career Janie had defended men in court who had been accused of harassment or worse. There were often blurred lines – one person's word against another, little evidence. Sometimes it made her job easy. She could get them off on a technicality, when there was no hard evidence. But bullying cultures? When more than one person was on the attack? That could destroy Harry.

'Janie, I need your help, love – you need to tell me what to do.'

*Oh no*, she thought. *No, no, no*. She had done her fair share of standing up for the big boys, helping them get away with whatever they'd been accused of. Ultimately it meant someone who'd been hurt hadn't seen justice.

She could give Harry plenty of advice, but if there were an issue in his company he couldn't ignore it, could he?

*Damn you, Harry*, she thought as she watched him leave the kitchen for his shower, no doubt content that when he came back she'd help him gloss over his problem. He really did have no idea how her last case had broken her, but at the same time she couldn't stand by and watch her husband be ruined.

Janie knew what was likely to happen. The woman who had made the complaint would likely be gone in the next few weeks, but it didn't mean the problem would go away.

She wondered whether Mia Anderson was the type of person who wouldn't let up, as Harry had suggested. And Janie made a decision. She was going to ask Mia out to lunch.

# Chapter Seventeen

It was a sunny Saturday when Laura's NCT group of five couples and their young babies met for a picnic. Nancy had been the one to set up the meet, and had chosen a spot in Brockenhurst by the river, where could they park up nearby and go for a walk. It was organised to perfection, but that was Nancy – she never left anything to chance.

For the next two days Laura had Bobby and Nate to herself and she was going to make the most of this precious family time. 'We could stop at a pub for dinner on the way home,' she suggested as Nate drove through the New Forest. 'We haven't been out to eat for so long.' She couldn't even remember the last time they hadn't sat on the sofa and eaten in front of the TV. The thought of ordering off a menu and having a large glass of chilled white wine at the end of the day already felt exciting.

'Let's see how it goes, shall we?' Nate murmured. 'Bobby's full of cold, and I'm shattered, Laura.'

She flipped her head back against the seat rest and turned to look out of the window. 'We won't be late. I meant we can go at five-ish, on the way home.'

'We're out for lunch already.'

Laura sighed.

'Look, I'm just saying let's see, that's all. We don't have to plan the whole day.'

*I do*, she wanted to say. Because the thought of going home, after the picnic that she wasn't particularly bothered about going to, depressed her for some reason. 'I'm working all week and I want a treat,' she muttered. She didn't want the weekend to pass and for Monday to come round and for them not to have done as much as they could. 'I thought you'd be happy to get out of the house.'

Nate glanced at her out of the corner of his eye.

'What?'

'Nothing,' he muttered. 'It's fine. If you really want to go out, we'll go out.'

'I do, Nate. I'm sorry, I just want to forget about this shitty week. Oh, look, there they are.' She pointed at the group gathered between the car park and the river. 'How come they're set up already – what time did Nancy say to arrive?'

Laura glanced at her watch. They weren't late, but still she wondered how the rest of them managed to have got there and laid out their checked rugs, coolers placed strategically on the corners to stop the babies from crawling too far, or to keep the rugs held down. For a moment she wondered if she'd got the time wrong. All the women were sitting in a huddle, chatting, the men standing. Dave had popped open a can of beer; probably he had another cool box full of them. In the time she'd known them all, Dave had never once assumed anything other than the fact that his wife, Chrissie, would be driving him home.

Nate pulled into a space in the gravel car park beside Nancy's Audi, and Laura took a deep breath. 'This actually feels a bit weird,' she admitted. 'I haven't seen any of them in ages.' She waved back at Nancy, whose arms swung wildly in the air.

'They're your friends,' Nate said. 'This shouldn't be weird.'

They weren't particularly her friends, but she didn't say as much as she stepped out of the car. The women had been good to have around in the late months of pregnancy and in the early weeks after birth, but they were more like acquaintances now, their varied views on parenting having driven an unspoken wedge between them. Ever since she'd told them she was returning to Morris & Wood, she'd felt herself edging further apart from this group of natural mothers, who'd always managed to make her feel like they were doing a better job than she was.

She stood by Nate as he reached into the back for their sleeping son, then asked Nancy as she came over, 'Are we late?'

'Oh, not at all, you're right on time.' Nancy gave them both a kiss on the cheek, stroking Bobby gently on the head. 'We just said at Baby Swim yesterday that if it was a nice morning we'd come down earlier – you know, make the most of the lovely weather.'

And there it was. The first reminder that the other four women still met every week when Laura was at work. Even though she knew Nancy wasn't the type to do it intentionally, Laura felt a pang of estrangement. Of being an outsider.

'Do you want me to get the buggy out?' Laura asked Nate. 'Bobby could probably do with the sleep.'

'Oh, what a shame,' Kay called out from the rug, from which she hadn't moved. 'Joe's looking forward to playing with Bobby. Him being the only other man here,' she laughed.

*Of course he isn't looking forward to doing anything of the sort*, Laura thought. *Because he's only seven months old.* But she smiled and said, 'Yes, boys have to stick together.' She didn't bother getting the buggy out and instead ushered Nate towards the mat, where he put Bobby down and watched him sit unsteadily on his plump nappy before toppling onto his side.

'Oh, bless him!' Chrissie said. 'He's still not sitting yet? Little poppet.'

'Not yet,' Laura said through gritted teeth as she resisted the urge to reach out a hand and punch Chrissie in the face. Out of all them, she was the one Laura no longer liked. Chrissie managed to get a jab in at every opportunity, and it amazed Laura how the others put up with it.

Laura had passed a comment to Nancy once, asking if she'd noticed the way Chrissie was always so competitive, but even Nancy brushed it off and said Chrissie didn't mean anything by it; it was just the way she was.

That was the trouble with this group. She didn't know any of them well enough to be honest with them. Even Nancy. Laura didn't feel like she could take her to one side and open up to her. And it was only going to get worse, now that she had returned to work. The others would continue to meet, their lives would go on without her. She could see that soon she and Nate would only be invited to these gatherings out of politeness.

Laura watched Nate wander over to the group of men and take a beer, laughing and slapping Dave on the back as if they were the oldest of mates. She turned back to the four women, who were discussing feeding and how the pouches of baby food were completely necessary for when you were on the go, though of course nothing could compare to making your own.

Laura didn't agree with this one bit. Bobby had only been weaned a month earlier and he was a fussy eater, and if they could avoid having to fill multiple containers with mushed-up vegetables that invariably ended up in the food waste, then all the better. She knew Nancy didn't agree, either, because on the few occasions Laura had been to her house when they had begun weaning, Nancy had been shoving Ella's Kitchen pouches into baby Lily as quickly as she would take them.

But it seemed even Nancy had taken the side of the home-cooked brigade, as she reached into her cool bag and produced a pot of green slush, which she proceeded to reel off the ingredients for.

Laura's mind drifted. She hadn't had anything to do with the picnic. Nate had been in charge of pulling it together, because he'd been the one to go shopping yesterday. Instead she found herself listening in to the men's chatter, which involved nothing to do with weaning or crawling or growth-percentile charts, and began to wish they hadn't bothered coming in the first place.

It was some time after they'd all eaten, when Dave had drunk at least seven cans of beer (Laura hadn't intended to count them, but his intake had captured her interest), that the men and women eventually started mixing up, and she found herself talking to Nancy and her husband. For a while Laura enjoyed the conversation, which centred around things other than babies, but every so often her ears would prick up at something one of the other mums was saying to Nate.

'You're doing so well,' Chrissie was saying. 'Honestly, Laura mentioned that you'd put the picnic together too.'

She heard Nate laugh as her insides knotted. For God's sake, why was it so hard to contemplate him making a bloody picnic?

'Oh, you really are,' Kay had joined in. 'And Bobby looks so happy. Do you not want to go back to work at all then, Nate?'

'I'm good with what we've arranged,' Laura heard him say. 'But yeah, I guess I'm missing it a bit. My boss emailed this week and asked if I wanted to pick up some part-time work at home, so you know ...' Laura turned and watched him shrug. This was news to her. Nate hadn't mentioned any work, or the fact that he was missing it.

'Well, I think you're an absolute star. I mean, what a godsend for Laura to come home and have her dinner cooked every night, too.'

She heard him chuckle again as her insides clenched tighter. What the hell? Wasn't that all they did for their husbands? It was only what had been expected of all of them since their babies were two weeks old and paternity leave finished.

When she and Nate got into the car to drive home, Laura turned to him. 'You're an absolute star,' she said, cocking her head, rolling her eyes. 'Can you believe Kay actually said that?'

'Well, I am,' he grinned.

'Obviously, but I mean, why does she think it's so bloody impossible for you to do exactly what she does every day?'

'Maybe she thinks men are lesser beings, so she's surprised I'm able to do more than one task in a day.'

'That's not what she meant, and you know it,' Laura muttered. 'She was having a dig. Again.'

'I don't think she was,' he sighed. 'You're imagining things that aren't there.'

'I'm not, Nate – everyone is judging us. Judging *me*, more to the point.'

'You know it isn't just you,' he said, perhaps a little more harshly than he intended, since he looked a bit sheepish as he turned to her. 'I get judged too. You don't think the men question me about when I'm going to go back to work, because surely I'm only doing this for a few weeks, as I can't want to do it for ever. I know what they think, Laura. That being a stay-at-home dad is second to going out and earning the money – because that's what men should be doing. I get judged as well; but I don't let it get to me all the time, like you do.'

'You never said anything.'

'I know. Because I don't let it bother me. Because all that's important is you, me and Bobby, and doing what's right for us as a family.'

'And this is what's right?'

'Of course.' He gave a sideways glance. 'Don't you think so?'

Laura shrugged. 'You didn't tell me your boss had been in touch.'

'It was nothing. He called earlier this week and ran an idea by me. Asked if I'd consider doing some work from home. We didn't agree to anything.'

'And? Do you want to?'

'I don't know. I mean we'd need to make sure it fits in with taking care of Bobby, but I guess it could be good.'

Laura sighed and turned to look out of the passenger window.

'What is it?' Nate asked.

'Nothing's as I expected it would be,' she admitted, willing the tears not to spring to her eyes as they threatened to do. 'I thought going back to Morris & Wood would feel the same as before, but it doesn't. I don't feel like I have a place there.'

'Laura, it's bound to feel odd. You have a baby, you're a mum. Life's changed.'

She shook her head. 'It's not that,' she said in a tight whisper. 'It's not got anything to do with being a mum. I feel like ...' She drifted off without finishing the sentence.

'Like what?

'Like I've been replaced. By someone younger, who's not doing the job any better than I am, except that everyone else thinks she is.'

'Laura, you need to let this go,' Nate said.

She turned to him sharply.

'You've still got a massive job that's taking up most hours of the day as it is,' he went on. 'We barely see you all week. Maybe Harry's done the right thing and given you some space. I can't even imagine when you'll get home, if you get Coopers back. Laura, maybe you need to accept that this is the way it should be for now.'

'Nate, I can't even believe you're saying that. You *know* what this means to me. You know how much I put into that account.'

'I do know that, I do. But you have to step back and look at the wider picture. If you start fighting this, then are things really going to be any better? Sure, you might get your account back, but then what? How many extra hours will you have to put in?'

'I can do it,' she said, though her words came out in a whisper.

'I think something else would have to give and ...'

'Something else?' she asked. 'You think something already is?'

'I'm only saying that I honestly don't know how you'd be able to do it. I don't begrudge you working, Laura, you know that. I've *never* stopped you. But I don't want you missing out on Bobby, either. It would be nice to see a bit more of you in the evenings.'

Laura looked away. It was impossible. She was in a no-win situation. 'I know I could make it work,' she persisted. 'I just want to be given the chance to prove it.'

'I don't know why you're getting so het up about it,' Nate snapped.

'Argh, I know you don't,' she cried. 'I know you don't understand, even though I'm trying to get you to. But don't worry about it. It's fine. I'll work through it on my own.' She flung her hands in the air in surrender.

Nate let out a short laugh and shook his head as he turned towards his window.

'You've no idea how much she's affecting me, Nate,' Laura went on, wiping her hand across her eyes. 'She makes me feel *useless*.' She stared at her husband, waiting for him to respond, until it became clear he wasn't going to.

Laura folded her arms and scrunched herself up as she turned her head away from him and closed her eyes. Something had to give. And if she was going to carry on working, which she couldn't feasibly see a way out of, then she wasn't going to sit back and let Mia keep doing her job.

The more she wound herself into knots about Mia, the more she had the unnerving feeling that there was much more to the woman than she realised. And in that moment she became resolute that in the morning she was going to start finding out who Mia was and where she had come from. And she wasn't going to stop until she did, because Laura didn't trust one word that came out of Mia Anderson's mouth.

'You still want to go out later?' Nate asked eventually.

She shook her head. 'No.'

'Come on, let's not ruin our day.' He reached over and squeezed her hand. 'We can do whatever you fancy.'

'It's fine,' she said. 'Really. You're right, Bobby could do with going home – he doesn't sound well.' She glanced over at her son in the back and reached out for his chubby arm.

'Maybe we should look into babysitters again soon,' he said. 'Go out on our own instead?'

'We'll need one for Harry's party,' Laura muttered. 'He mentioned it during the week. It's five weeks away now.'

'How about asking Louise's daughter, across the road?' Nate asked. 'She's about fifteen. Wouldn't she do it?'

'We don't know her,' Laura said. 'I don't want just anyone looking after Bobby.'

'She isn't anyone,' he laughed. 'She's a neighbour. Anyway, no point worrying about it. If it's going to be a problem, you can always go on your own,' he went on. 'Though it would be nice to come out with you.'

'No. I want you there,' Laura said. 'I'm definitely not going on my own. We've got a few weeks to sort something out. Hopefully by then some amazing Mary Poppins of a babysitter will fly into the area, but if she doesn't, I won't go. I'm not actually that fussed about it anyway.'

'You're a wonderful mummy, you know that? And the most amazing wife. Me and that little man in the back would be lost without you.'

Laura's eyes welled with tears again. 'I know,' she sighed. 'And I'm sorry for getting annoyed. I really don't know what I'd do without either of you.'

# Chapter Eighteen

*Five weeks before the fire*

On Monday morning Laura opened up her PC and found the number for a woman called Katie Burton. She tapped it into her mobile and strolled over to a spare meeting room, where she closed the door behind her, so she wouldn't be heard.

It didn't take long for her to answer. 'Hello? Katie speaking.'

'Hi, Katie,' Laura started. 'I'm hoping you can help me. I'm phoning up about someone who used to work for you.'

'Oh?'

'You gave me a reference for her a few months ago. I was wondering if you might be able to give me a bit more insight.'

'Okay. Well, I'll see what I can do. I mean, this isn't the channel we'd usually adopt.'

'Yes, I realise that and thank you, I'd just like a bit more information.'

'Who are you calling about?'

'Her name's Mia Anderson. I believe she temped for you. She left seven months ago now, so you might not remember ...'

'I remember Mia.'

'Oh, okay, great. Then—'

'But she wasn't a temp,' Katie said. 'I don't know what gave you that impression. I'm sure it wouldn't have been anything in the reference?'

'I assumed she was,' Laura replied. 'Because she was coming for a temporary role here. I thought she'd said as much in her interview too,' she went on, though now she couldn't actually recall whether Mia had or not. Whether she'd been led to think that; and even if she had, did it make any difference?

'No. Mia was permanent. Can I ask why you're calling me? What is it you actually want to know?'

'I just—' Laura broke off. 'I suppose I was wondering if there was anything more you could tell me about her.'

'Has something happened?' Katie asked.

'No. Not specifically.'

'Then I'm sorry, this isn't protocol. I don't know what you're fishing for, but I gave Mia's reference.'

'I know, I know that,' Laura said, desperate for Katie not to cut her off. 'And I also know I shouldn't be calling you, but I wanted to do this off the record. I wouldn't be phoning if I didn't think there was an issue. And I'm sorry I can't tell you more, but please, can you tell me if there's anything at all I should be worried about.'

There was a beat before Katie answered. 'Her leaving,' she said.

'What?' It was the last thing Laura expected to hear.

'Her leaving you high and dry, like she did us. Mia had just received a promotion. A good one, by all accounts, that I'd let six other applicants down on. And then one day she called in sick and never came back.'

As Laura listened, she could tell how much Katie was still annoyed by this.

'She didn't end up working her four weeks' notice because of it, and I wondered at the time if it was because she'd found another job. But then when I didn't get asked for a reference – or at least not until two months later – I didn't think she had.'

Laura shook her head, trying to think back. Katie was right; they hadn't asked for a reference for ages because she'd suddenly gone on maternity leave, and Rebecca from HR had left and everything was so up in the air. It *was* a good two months before anyone had got round to sorting it.

'I was worried about her.' Katie let out a small laugh. 'But then when I knew she'd got another job, I guess I thought no more of it. I just … I don't know what I thought, really. I was too caught up in recruiting our role again, I suppose.'

'It doesn't make sense,' Laura said. 'Why would she give up a good promotion, a permanent role, for a temporary job?'

Katie didn't respond.

'Don't you think it's odd?' Laura persisted. 'It doesn't make sense, does it?' she repeated. Though of course there was one explanation. Mia had her sights set on something else. Something in particular. Laura's job. And for some reason she was willing to risk her career because she wanted Laura's.

'You're right, it doesn't,' Katie said eventually.

Laura hung up the call and wandered out into the office, scanning the floor until she found Mia lingering by the far window, her hand resting on Henrietta James's arm. Her loud bursts of laughter rang out sharply above the murmured conversations, until everything around Laura muffled into one blurred buzzing that rang through her ears.

Mia was befriending these women as if she was making herself indispensable, and it was all Laura could do to stop herself running across the office and demanding to know why she was there, because she didn't like it. She didn't like it one bit.

'There you are.'

Laura turned sharply as Harry walked towards her, his jacket on, one hand tucked into his jeans pocket.

'You ready?'

'Ready?'

He hung his head, brows furrowed questioningly, flicking up his wrist, which in turn made his gold Rolex flash in the light. 'It's quarter to eleven, Laura. We need to get going, if we want to walk to the quay.'

'But I thought . . .' Laura pressed the button on her phone to check the time. 'I thought we were meeting at eleven-thirty.'

Harry shook his head. 'Eleven.' He nodded towards her desk. 'You'd better grab your stuff. Don't want to keep Miles waiting.'

'Shit, okay – give me a minute,' she said, as Harry jostled anxiously from one foot to the other. He was clearly keen to make a good impression on this old friend of his.

'Baby-brain!' Harry joked as she walked away, making a few of the nearby staff chuckle and Laura shudder. She glared at them and then back at him, and wondered how she was going to focus on impressing Miles Morgan when she was so wrapped up in Mia and what the hell she was doing here.

**Tuesday 14 May**

**Interview between DC Emily Marlow and Nathan (Nate) Denning, following the fire on Monday 13 May**

Marlow:    Mr Denning, I know you say you and your wife didn't speak when she finally came home last night, but did she tell you anything about the fire at the Morris & Wood offices?

Nate:    No! Of course not. You're saying that like you think she knew about it. How could she?

Marlow:    She didn't say that she'd seen it?

Nate:    No! She got a call this morning.

Marlow:    Were you there when she received the call?

Nate:    Yes. I was with her in the kitchen.

Marlow:    And you believe that was the first she heard of it?

Nate:    Of course – yes. Of course it was. I don't understand. What is this about?

Marlow:    How was your wife, when she heard the news?

Nate:      Well, I don't know – she was shocked.

           Sorry, I really don't get what you're suggesting. Are you saying Laura was lying? That the phone call was all one big act or something?

Marlow:    We both know it wouldn't be the first time she's lied to you in the last twenty-four hours.

Nate:      She wasn't *lying* about the fire.

Marlow:    Can you tell me what her relationship with Janie Wood is like? Are they friends?

Nate:      Janie? Harry's wife? No, not especially. I don't think Laura has any relationship with her – why?

Marlow:    What's Laura like with her friends, do you know? Is she a very loyal person? The type who would do anything for them?

Nate:      Her friends? I don't understand. I mean she's got a few close ones from school and university that she still sees, but ... Sorry, what's this got to do with anything?

Marlow:    Nate, we have reason to believe your wife knows a lot more about the fire last night than she's letting on. And the best thing she can do for herself is to start talking, because I have a feeling she might be covering up for someone.

Nate:      No way. My wife wouldn't do that. She wouldn't risk that, she ... Christ! Listen, Laura barely has anything to do with anyone in that office. She's not *friends* with them.

Marlow:     Right. But you said earlier she was *obsessed* with someone in the office once – before Mia, that is. Tell me about this person.

Nate:       Saskia? (shakes head) This was two, maybe three years ago. A long time. Laura and she were good friends, but then they had a falling-out. Really, what's that got to do with any of this?

Marlow:     Humour me. What happened to Saskia?

Nate:       (sighs) Saskia's boyfriend worked at Morris & Wood too, but Laura found out he was being made redundant. She didn't tell Saskia it was happening. That was all. Laura was more senior than Saskia. I think Saskia even reported into her. It was confidential information, and Laura decided she couldn't say anything.

Marlow:     By the sounds of it, Laura did the right thing.

Nate:       She did. Only Saskia didn't see it that way and they fell out. And then things took a turn for the worse and Laura became convinced Saskia was out to get her.

Marlow:     Out to get her in what way?

Nate:       She thought she was trying to destroy her career, spreading gossip about … I don't recall all the ins and outs of it, but Laura was certain Saskia was setting her up. But like I keep telling you, whatever's happened with Mia, it has absolutely nothing to do with the fire. My wife's not capable of anything like that.

Marlow: You said Laura isn't friends with anyone in the office any more.

Nate: That's right, as far as I know. After Saskia, Laura found it hard to trust anyone for a while, and certainly at work she didn't. I don't know, she doesn't talk about it, but I don't think she has any real friends there. I don't think she wants to get close to anyone.

Marlow: That's also the impression I get, from talking to her and the other staff. But for me that leaves only one other option. If she's not covering up for anyone for the fire, then …

Nate: Then what, Detective?

Marlow: Then did she do it herself?

# Chapter Nineteen

*Five weeks before the fire*

It was only half an hour after Harry and Laura had left the office when Mia saw Janie Wood appear on the floor. She was immaculately dressed in tailored beige trousers, cropped to skim her ankles, and a long-sleeved white shirt, with an oversized bag weighing down her shoulder. Large sunglasses were pushed to the top of her head and she looked like she'd stepped out of a magazine rather than the office lift.

Mia paused what she was doing, watching Janie out of the corner of her eye. Janie rarely came to the building and, whenever she did, she'd head straight for Harry's office, speak briefly to her husband behind his closed door and then walk straight back out again. She obviously didn't know he wasn't here, and yet today Janie was lingering by the lift as if she was looking for someone else instead.

Janie Wood. The woman had made her life so public with her magazine appearances, and yet even in the articles Mia could see she didn't seem comfortable with it. She didn't have the look of someone who was happy that the cameras were snapping the inside of their house, with its glossy cream kitchen and plump oversized sofas, draped in throws.

Mia had pored over the pictures as she'd sat at the small round table in her mother's kitchen, with its deep-red beetroot stain ingrained into the cheap wood, and thought how their lives were a million miles apart. And there Mia was, working like a dog with nothing to show for it, while Janie swanned around, spending her husband's wealth, no doubt with his Black card cushioned in a designer purse somewhere in that bag of hers. The disparity was almost immeasurable.

Janie was walking towards her and Mia felt herself stiffen. They had spoken on a few occasions, but it was always stilted and clumsy, or at least it was on Mia's part, because she'd never been prepared to see Janie, or to know what to say.

'Mia?' Janie's soft voice had a slight lilt to it. 'Have you got a moment?'

'Of course.' Mia beamed back at her, running her hands down the front of her jeans.

'I just wondered if you had time for a quick lunch? On me, of course,' she added.

'Erm ...' The invitation had taken her by surprise and Mia was immediately flustered, because why on earth would Janie Wood want to take her to lunch, unless there was a specific reason. And if there was ...

'We don't have to be long,' she was saying. 'I'm sure you're very busy.'

'I, er ...' *Come on, Mia, say something,* she berated herself, because on the one hand it felt like all her Christmases had come at once, that she could be lunching with Janie Wood, and on the other: why was she?

'I thought we could have a chat. I feel bad I haven't done it before. You've been here months already,' Janie said.

She sounded genuine, but it didn't feel like a strong enough reason to want to take her out to lunch. And if that was the case, then Mia wondered what Janie's ulterior motive was. When she replied, 'That sounds lovely – and you don't have to feel bad,' she felt uneasy.

They agreed to meet at a sandwich bar on Lymington High Street in half an hour. Somewhere away from the quay, Mia realised. As if there was every likelihood Janie wanted to keep Harry in the dark about what was beginning to feel like a clandestine meeting.

'Harry doesn't know I'm here,' Janie said, confirming Mia's suspicions as they ordered their sandwiches and sat down. She shrugged sheepishly, like it was no big deal, though Mia wondered whether it was.

'Do you think he'd mind?' Mia asked.

'Oh no ...' Janie waved her hand through the air, and Mia shifted in her seat as she waited to find out the purpose of their lunch.

Janie was asking her how she was getting on, what she thought of the job, and so Mia told her she liked it, as she picked the cress out of her egg sandwich. She noticed Janie hadn't touched the wrap that sat intact on her plate.

'How do you find everyone?'

The sudden thought crossed Mia's mind that Janie could be here to ask about her husband and Laura Denning, and it was such a relief that the reason could be something that didn't involve her that she let out a deep breath, before plunging the sandwich into her mouth. She had no idea how she'd answer if Janie did ask outright, although the woman was already moving on.

'So where do you come from?' Janie asked, squinting her eyes as if she was trying to place her.

'Lymington, actually,' she said. 'I was born here. I grew up here.'

'Oh, really?'

Mia nodded.

'It's such a beautiful place, isn't it? Do you have a family?'

Mia assumed she meant children and so shook her head.

'No one nearby?' Janie asked.

Mia put her sandwich back on the plate and swallowed the mouthful. 'Just my mum,' she told her, the omission weighing heavily. It wasn't the first time she'd dismissed her sister as if she didn't even exist.

'You must know all about the development of the offices then?' Janie asked. 'If you've both always lived here?'

'My mum told me bits about it when it was being built.' Mia hadn't shown any interest in the building of the office at the time, and she had wondered why her mum had been so interested in it, when there were clearly more pressing issues their family should be focusing on. Maybe it had been nothing more than a distraction.

Janie wasn't remotely bothered about Mia's opinion of the office build and instead ploughed on with questions about her personal life. Where did she work before she joined Morris & Wood? Has she always been in marketing?

Mia responses were short and flat. She knew how she must be coming across, but what did it matter? They were never going to be friends. Their lunch date felt like an interview, and she was still trying to fathom what she was doing here when Janie insisted she would pick up the bill, as promised, and was already pushing herself out of her seat to leave.

It was as they were walking to the door that Janie suddenly paused and said, 'Harry tells me there's an issue with Mike Lewis.'

Mia could have laughed. So that was it. Janie wanted to find out what was happening, so she could tell her husband how to handle it. So she could find a loophole for him to worm his way out of the issues that he didn't want to face. Mia had guessed Harry would use his wife to help him, but she was determined to create such a watertight case that even someone like Janie Wood wouldn't be able break it.

'There is, but I'm not comfortable discussing it. It's not about me,' Mia told her.

She waited, but Janie merely nodded and said, 'Well, Mia, I hope you do the right thing.'

Then Janie kissed her on the cheek and told her it was lovely to see her and that she hoped Mia was coming to her party.

Mia watched her walk off down the street, her relief that Janie wanted to discuss with her the issue of Mike already dissipating, usurped by something else entirely. And as she closed her eyes and inhaled a deep breath, Mia realised it was fear. Janie had left her on edge. The questioning, from a clever woman with Janie Wood's background. How long would it be until someone found out exactly what she was doing at Morris & Wood?

Janie walked down the street to where she had parked her car and went over the strange conversation in her head. She had wanted to meet Mia because of what Harry had told her. Yet for some reason she'd felt drawn to the younger woman, and sensed that she could do with someone on the inside, who could tell her what it was really like in Harry's castle.

Mia seemed to have her head screwed on the right way. She'd always appeared so much more open and friendly than Laura Denning. Janie had noticed it when she'd been in the office previously. She had watched Mia from inside Harry's glass office and seen her laughing and joking with the other women.

And yet their brief lunch had surprised Janie. Mia was nothing at all what she had expected. Janie had always prided herself on seeing people, on cutting through the thick outer layers that sometimes cloaked the reality beneath. It was what had made her good at her job. She rarely misread anyone – Miles Morgan had been an exception.

Anyone with Janie's knowledge of handbags could see immediately that Mia's Gucci was a fake, the rose-gold bangles that hung around her wrist were the same ones Ella had recently bought from a cheap accessory shop.

In contrast to the bubbly woman she had previously witnessed, today Mia was reserved, to the point of being on edge. And when Janie had asked her about her family life – nothing more than anyone would do, when trying to get to know someone – she had one distinct impression: Mia Anderson was holding something back.

# Chapter Twenty

Laura and Harry were meeting Miles in The Star pub, which had pride of place on Lymington Quay. As soon as they walked in, he stood up and held up a hand in greeting and Laura had to force herself to keep walking. Miles had to be at least six foot two. He was wearing a grey woollen jacket, with a grey V-necked jumper and open-necked shirt underneath. Out of his jacket pocket peeked a blue silk handkerchief. His whole look was mesmerising, and yet he'd managed not to look over-dressed for the pub.

Like Harry, Miles had dark-grey hair, which was styled into a quiff, and a closely cropped beard, and Laura couldn't take her eyes off him. She followed Harry, who was clasping the man's hand with both of his own. From the off, it was apparent the two men went way back, but she guessed they hadn't seen each other in a while, as they told each other how good it was finally to catch up again. Eventually Harry stepped to the side and introduced her.

Laura reached out to shake Miles's hand as he leaned forward and kissed her cheek, and despite herself she was pleased that she'd added another dab of Chanel before leaving the office.

'Laura. It's good to meet you,' Miles said. His steely-blue eyes didn't leave hers. They seem to twinkle as he smiled, and it was only after he finally pulled away that she told herself to get it together.

He offered to get them both a drink, but Harry insisted and she watched her boss walk to the bar. He was a good three inches shorter and, next to Miles, he looked slight – so different from his usual presence, which filled a room. Put them both together and you would automatically look past Harry, and Laura considered that Harry must know this. She wondered how he felt about it.

'Have a seat,' Miles smiled and pulled one out for Laura, his hand lingering on the back of it as she sat down. As soon as Harry came back to the table the two men began chatting easily, names thrown back and forth; some she thought she might have heard of, others she hadn't a clue about, and at no point had she been able to do much more than sit there cradling her lemonade, listening to the conversation like a spare part they'd both forgotten about.

'I'm so sorry, Laura,' Miles eventually said, breaking off. 'You must think we're rude. I always hate it when my girlfriend gets together with her old friends from school and I can't join in the conversation.'

Laura noticed the way he said 'girlfriend', like he was proud of the fact he wasn't married, even though she figured he was easily in his late forties.

'Only Harry and I haven't seen each other in, what – what is it, Harry?' he continued.

'Five and a half years,' Harry said without a beat, raising his eyebrows as he did so, which made Laura wonder if there was a particular reason why Harry knew it was exactly five and a half years since they'd last met.

Miles nodded. 'Doesn't time fly?' His lips were pursed, his expression more sombre than it had been. Laura was desperate to ask what memory had flashed into both their heads, stopping them in their tracks, taking them back to a time she wasn't sure either of them were keen to go.

'So you're looking for someone to launch your new brand,' Harry said, pulling himself together, leaning back in his chair and crossing one leg over the other. He ran his fingers up and down the seam of his suit trousers, a habit of old, Laura knew, from the number of times she'd watched him do it.

'That's right, and so of course I thought of you.'

'Miles here has broken out on his own.' Harry turned to Laura.

'And about time too,' Miles laughed, causing Harry to laugh along with him, only she was more intrigued by their interchange now, and suddenly wondered how easy Harry actually felt in Miles's company.

Harry was pressing forward in his seat again. 'Well, I can't say how pleased I was to hear from you again. You know I'd be thrilled to work with you.'

'I'm glad to hear it, Harry,' Miles beamed. 'And I believe you're the woman for the job.' Miles put his beer down, carefully squaring the coaster beneath it as he leaned towards Laura. 'I'm looking for someone who can put her heart and soul into it, Laura. We're talking budgets in excess of three million for TV alone.'

She held her breath, the air tightening in her throat. That was three times the amount Coopers were spending on their TV campaign. Harry was right. They win this pitch, and Miles's business would be huge. She had little experience in financial services, and none in start-up banking, but she could learn.

'So what do you think, Laura? I take it Harry's told you all about the business.'

'He has. And I can do whatever it takes,' she replied.

Miles nodded. 'We have tight deadlines. For a start, we want our first TV ad to air sometime in September.'

'That soon?' she asked.

Miles nodded. 'Think you can do it?'

'I mean, it's a very tight timeframe,' she said. 'I don't ...' She paused, glancing at Harry, who was looking at her, encouragingly.

'Of course we can,' he finished for her.

'Yes, of course,' she smiled, though a number of things flashed through her head: concepts, plans, actors – there was a lot to put together in a short space of time, and that was even before they started filming and talking to the media buyers. She could already picture herself working round the clock through the long days of summer to get it done. What the hell would Nate say? How did *she* actually feel about it?

An image of Bobby sprang into her head; a flash of guilt. There was no way she could take it on, she thought, flexing her hands, which were beginning to numb. But at the same time she couldn't ignore the fizz of excitement in the pit of her stomach. She hadn't experienced that feeling in a very long time.

'Of course I need you to tender for the business first. Have to do everything by the book.'

There was a pause before Harry readily agreed. 'Completely. Of course.'

She wondered if he hadn't been expecting this, because they both knew what it meant. Spending the next few weeks working her arse off to put together a tender, which might not even get accepted. But if she didn't put in the work, they wouldn't get it. Laura hated tendering for business. It was a thin line between working for free and proving you deserved the job.

'See, I told you I had something up my sleeve,' Harry said as they left Miles at the pub. 'You think you can do it?' he asked, as they walked in the direction of the office. She hadn't seen him this fired up about a new business opportunity in a long time.

Laura knew she had to tell Harry she needed time to think about it. She had to talk to Nate first, make sure he was on board with what it meant, in terms of the extra work. She needed to make sure she was on board with it too. Turning down the opportunity meant she was effectively writing herself out of the game, but at the same time she didn't see enough of her son as it was. 'His timescales are pretty unrealistic,' she eventually said.

'Yeah. That's the problem with Miles ...' Harry drifted off until he finally added, 'He won't budge. And if it isn't us, he'll take his money elsewhere. Quite frankly, it's too much to lose.' He stopped and turned to Laura. 'I don't need to tell you how good it would be for you to take it on. But I mean it when I say if you don't think you can handle this right now, I completely understand. You've got enough on your plate, and I've got other people I can ask who don't have babies they need to think of—'

'No,' she interrupted, knowing exactly who he'd have in mind. There was no way she was going to give this opportunity over to Mia Anderson. 'I'll do it.'

'That's my girl,' he grinned and as they carried on walking back to the office, Laura tried to shut out the voices in her head that were screaming at her she'd done the wrong thing. They were asking her how the hell she thought she'd be able to break this to Nate.

# Chapter Twenty-One

*Four weeks before the fire*

On Thursday night, with no school clubs to attend, Janie made the last-minute decision to take the girls to the quay for hot chocolates on the way home. Now she was watching as they dropped crab-lines, bacon clinging to the ends of them, over the side and into the water. They hadn't meant to stay long, but when they had passed the gift shop Lottie had seen the crab-nets and begged her to buy them.

Janie had been surprised to see Ella almost as excited as her sister. It was the first time in weeks she'd reverted to the little girl that Janie feared she was losing. It wasn't long until Ella would finish primary school, and the thought of what was going to happen beyond that didn't bear thinking about. Phones, WhatsApp groups, retreating into her bedroom every evening ... Janie wanted to hang on to their childhood days for as long as she could, and if it meant crabbing with her girls instead of arguing with them over homework, then that was what she would do.

Ella was bouncing from foot to foot, screeching at Lottie to pull her net up. In turn her younger sister stepped back, laughing as she pointed out a tiny crab, which Ella helped her upturn into the bucket with a plop, making them both laugh harder. Janie smiled and stroked Lottie's dark-brown hair, which hung down her back in a long plait. The sun had warmed it and it felt comforting to the touch. She could feel her youngest pressing into her hand, the way she always did when Janie played with her hair.

Lottie was nothing like Ella. Ella had outgrown the desire to be touched in any way since she was five. Even in reception Janie had barely set foot in the playground when already Ella had run off to chat to her teachers or join a group of older girls. Lottie was the one who had continued to stay by her side, holding on to her top, not wanting her to go.

'Are we going to throw the crabs back in, at the end?' Lottie asked.

'Of course we are,' Ella told her. 'What do you think we're going to do – take them home and eat them?'

'You can eat crab,' Lottie replied. 'Daddy does, doesn't he, Mummy?'

'He does, darling, but Mummy won't be taking any crabs home to cook tonight.' *Or any other night*, she thought, grimacing at the bucket.

'You could call Daddy,' Ella said, helping her sister dip the line over the edge of the quay again. 'You could ask him to come and meet us.'

Janie glanced up at the offices, squinting against the sun, already low in the sky. Her husband was inside, oblivious to the fact that his family were on the other side of the water. If she called him, would he come to the window and look out at them, like he'd said Mia had done a few weeks back?

Ever since their brief meet-up Janie had been wondering about Mia and her closed behaviour, and considered how many more women there were in Harry's office that she needed to be worried about.

'Mum?' Ella had stopped and was facing her, a line dangling from one hand.

'I'll ask him,' she murmured, taking her phone out of her pocket and pressing Harry's number. 'He might be in a meeting,' she added as the call connected, preparing her daughter for whatever excuse he'd come up with, because she knew Harry wouldn't leave work to come crabbing.

When there was no answer she didn't leave a message. He would see that he had a missed call and maybe call her back. 'Sorry, girls, he must be busy.' She put the phone on the wall beside her with a surprising feeling of disappointment, and realised that after seeing him so engaged with the girls, she'd hoped he might carve out more time to be with them. They should be his priority, as they were hers. Spending the evening having fun, which cost less than ten pounds.

Janie shifted position on the uncomfortable concrete. Maybe both their priorities were still wrong? she wondered. Maybe every decision they continued to make was about money and having the best of everything. The biggest house, the most expensive swimming pool, the best education. The most spectacular office for the business.

She continued to look across the Lymington River at Morris & Wood. The glass windows sparkled back at her, an image of her husband behind them filling her head.

Over the years she'd wondered whether Harry realised their marriage had all gone wrong, because after they had moved to the south coast they hadn't discussed what had happened. Possibly he thought he'd fixed it by moving, keeping Janie in a comfortable lifestyle, where she didn't need to think about going back to her job if she didn't want to. Ignoring the part he'd played in it, probably not even realising he'd played one at all.

No, Janie didn't believe that. Harry knew, he'd just pushed it out of his head so that he didn't have to confront it. He knew because she'd told him clearly enough, but all he'd said was, 'What did you expect, Janie? What did you expect?'

She'd expected her husband to understand. To offer his support in some way, but he hadn't. He had been more invested in ensuring there was no blame laid at his door.

She was a defence lawyer after all, so what *did* she expect? That was what Harry had meant. And in a way he was right.

Maybe if Miles Morgan hadn't ever walked through her door all those years ago, she wouldn't be sitting on the quay now, staring at her husband's office, wishing she was no longer married to Harry. But he had, and she had fallen for his charm and readily snapped up his case. And so what use was it deliberating over the what-ifs? There was nothing she could do to change the past. Because that was the only place Miles was now – in her past.

Janie leaned back and sighed. Maybe she should talk to Harry. Possibly he had the right to know that one day they would not be married any longer, she thought as she continued to stare at the twinkling light of the water reflected onto the glass building and wondered what it would be like to tell her husband that she wanted a divorce.

When she looked back at the girls, the cold realisation hit her that she didn't think she could do it. *But I don't love him,* she wanted to say. *I don't love your father.* The guilt of it made her sick. Not because of him, she realised, but because of them. Because if she ever did leave him, it would break their tiny hearts.

'Girls, let's go and get some fish and chips,' she said, feigning brightness as she grabbed their hands to help them return the crabs to the water. It was six-fifteen already and she didn't want to linger any longer.

She pulled herself up, flinging her phone in the bag, and turned towards the car as a shadow flitted out of sight behind it. A shiver ran down the length of her spine and for a moment the sound of the girls behind her, chattering and gathering their buckets together, became a muffled blur.

'Mummy!' Lottie screeched, tugging at her sleeve and banging the bucket into her thigh. 'Can you take it for me?'

Janie snapped back to them and shook her head. She was imagining it. Nothing more. No one was watching her.

**Thursday 16 May**

**Interview between DC Emily Marlow and Anna Halshaw, following the fire on Monday 13 May**

Marlow:   Did Janie tell you she was being followed?

Anna:     (pause) Janie was? No. God, no, not at all.

Marlow:   She tells us she has been, though it appears no one else knew about it. She hadn't told a soul.

Anna:     Who was following her?

Marlow:   We don't know for sure.

Anna:     I'm, I mean I'm …

Marlow:   Shocked?

Anna:     Well, yes, totally. I mean something like that – she must have been terrified. I can't believe she didn't tell me.

Marlow:   That's the thing. Don't you think it's strange that she didn't?

Anna:      I don't know what you mean.

Marlow:    Well, something as important as believing
           you're being watched … it seems odd she's
           only brought this up now.

Anna:      You think she's lying about it?

Marlow:    I'm asking what you think.

Anna:      No. (shakes head) No. Janie wouldn't do that.
           There must be a reason she kept it to herself.
           Janie doesn't lie.

Marlow:    Didn't she lie about where she was on Mon-
           day night, Anna? When you were babysitting
           for her?

Anna:      I'm sure that was a misunderstanding. I
           thought she'd said yoga, but …

Marlow:    And didn't you try to get hold of her at –
           seven-o-five p.m.?

Anna:      I did, yes. As you know.

Marlow:    And in the end you had to call Janie's hus-
           band, Harry?

Anna:      One of the children wasn't well. And it doesn't
           pass me by that I might have been one of the
           last people to speak to him before – before …

Marlow:    Anna, when you phoned him, you said you
           knew someone else was in the office with him?

Anna:      That's what I told your other officer. Because I
           heard Harry say, 'Excuse me a minute,' when
           he picked up. He told whoever it was that he'd

|         | take the call outside his office. I assume it was Miles Morgan. Isn't that the name of the man? |
| Marlow: | It is. And was it just the one person with him, that you know of? |
| Anna:   | (shakes head) I don't know. Why, are you – do you think Janie might have been there too? |
| Marlow: | Anna, had Janie ever mentioned the name Miles Morgan to you before Monday night? |
| Anna:   | No. Never. Why? Did she know him? |
| Marlow: | She did know him, yes. So she's never talked about him? |
| Anna:   | No. Who is he? Is he the person who was following her? Do you think *that* has something to do with the fire? |
| Marlow: | That's what we are trying to ascertain. But like I say, we don't actually know what happened, because it appears no one knew Janie was worried that someone was watching her. |

# Chapter Twenty-Two

*Four weeks before the fire*

'Come out for a drink with me.' Harry was hovering in his doorway. Laura looked around at the empty office, glancing at the clock. Six-fifteen, she realised, her stomach dipping. It was Thursday evening; she'd been late home every night this week so far and had promised Nate she'd definitely be home by six tonight.

But Laura had been engrossed in Google. First she had been looking into Miles's company, setting out thoughts to help her with the tender. At some point that search had blended into another around Mia, and for the last fifteen minutes she had been scouring Mia's sparse Facebook account as far back as 2009, when she had first joined.

It told Laura little. There was no job history, no relationship status and recently a lack of photos altogether.

In fact in the last twelve months Mia hadn't posted or shared a single thing.

Before that there had been a few pictures of her with friends, but nothing that gave Laura much background on her. One woman appeared more than others, a girl called Jessica Louise – a middle name used for reasons Laura couldn't fathom, unless she didn't want anyone to track her down, or possibly because of her work.

There was something about Jessica that looked vaguely familiar, something in her eyes, though Laura doubted they'd ever met, for surely that would be too much of a coincidence.

She had been so engrossed that she hadn't noticed the time or registered the office emptying. For the past four nights, since meeting Miles, Laura had been working flat out and every evening.

She sighed as she shut down the website – the one behind it appearing like a flash. The Venue. The company where Mia used to work. Laura had been looking into what jobs they'd been recruiting for, in the hope she would find the one that Mia was supposed to be promoted into, before she suddenly left. Only one seemed plausible. An account director with a salary £20,000 higher than Laura herself was on. And if this was the job, then it made even less sense that Mia would give it up to cover Laura's maternity, though by now Laura was pretty certain that Mia's purpose for being here was neither the money nor the career opportunity.

Harry hovered nearby as Laura closed down her computer and turned to face him. Maybe she should tell him here and now what she'd discovered from Katie Burton, but then she could imagine his reaction. He would make her feel as if she had a vendetta against Mia for no other reason than she was jealous.

No, what Laura needed was more proof, something concrete. She needed to figure out *why* Mia could be out to get her.

'I really can't,' she told Harry. 'I hadn't realised how late it is. I'm sorry, I need to get home.' She'd told Nate to hold off bathing Bobby because she wanted to do it. Before she had left that morning she'd looked in on her son, listening to his sleepy murmurs, and her heart had ached to hold him close to her. She had fought tears as she eventually stepped out of his room.

Now she was angry with herself for forgetting the time again. She'd texted Nate at six to say she would be a little late, but his response had been a curt *Okay*. No kisses. No *I love you*. She knew he was pissed off that he barely saw her, and she also knew he thought she should be spending more time with Bobby. Which was why she still hadn't told him about the tender and the possible new account.

Laura quite literally felt like two different women – Laura the account director and Laura the mother – and she didn't know how it was possible to merge them together.

There wasn't even any room to consider Laura the wife. She had thought as much that morning when she'd slipped back into the bedroom and watched Nate roll over. She hadn't woken him, there was no need so early, especially when she'd heard him get up in the night again and go to a crying Bobby. She couldn't even say how long he'd been out of bed, as she had fallen asleep again before he came back, exhausted from such long hours in the office.

Less than a month and they were becoming more like housemates than husband and wife, except for the fact they still shared a bed. Though that had been used for nothing more than sleeping in the last few weeks.

'I want to talk to you.' Harry smiled at her, carrying on as if he hadn't heard Laura or wasn't prepared to accept no as an answer. 'Just a quick one down at the quay.'

'I don't know, I really need to get home.'

Harry nodded, perching on the corner of her desk. 'How's Nate coping without you? I've seen you working very long hours. He must miss you.'

'He's coping fine,' she said, maybe a little too abruptly.

'He's a good man,' Harry went on. 'What he's doing at home and ...'

'It's no different from what Janie does,' Laura said sharply. Too late she realised how it must appear that she didn't appreciate everything Nate had given up for her.

She opened her mouth again to tell Harry how much she valued Nate, but already he was speaking.

'One drink, Laura. Please. I need to talk to you about a few things, and I promise I won't keep you late.' His eyes sparkled as if he somehow already knew he would get his way.

Laura pursed her lips, holding her breath. Nate would not be one bit happy; she didn't want to go for a drink, she wanted to go home.

Mia's tinkling laugh rang out from the far end of the office and Harry looked over at her, shuffling off the edge of Laura's desk to stand, and suddenly Laura thought: what if I don't go with him and he asks her instead?

Even then it felt like a ridiculous notion, something two teenagers would worry over when they were after the same boy, yet Laura also knew how much she needed to keep Harry close right now. And she could do with making sure that Mia wasn't.

'Just a quick one,' she said, glancing at the clock again. 'I really can't be long.'

She didn't miss his lopsided smile before he turned to get his jacket, and even though this was all her doing, it irritated her that he'd got his way.

Harry wanted to talk about the new account. He wanted to run some ideas past her and see what Laura thought she could do on the tender. He suggested they have a drink at Le Bateau, a small wine bar off the cobbled path that led down to the quay. Laura asked for a lemonade, but Harry came back to the table with two glasses of Sancerre. She screwed up her nose at him, but took a sip anyway.

'You can't come to a place like this and not have wine,' he said and leaned forward as he started talking business.

'You sound like you want to impress Miles,' Laura told him, fingering the stem of her wine glass. She got the impression Harry would do anything to make sure they didn't lose this opportunity and wondered if there was more to it than simply money.

'This is an important deal for me,' he told her. 'Miles is trusting me with a lot here; he doesn't have to put all his money in one agency. And no, I'm not trying to impress him,' he said. 'Not in the way you think. Not like I *owe him* or anything. We just' – he waved a hand in the air – 'we do things for each other. You make mistakes . . .' he trailed off. 'Well, as I say, you do things like this.'

Laura nodded. She didn't really understand what Harry meant, but she had seen him doing jobs before for so-called old mates.

'There's something else I need to tell you,' he said.

Laura peered over the rim of her glass as she finished her wine.

'Can I get you another?' he asked as she placed it back on the table.

'Definitely not, thanks. Go on, what do you need to tell me?'

'I've had a complaint about Mike Lewis,' he said, pausing briefly. 'That he's been bullying someone.'

'Who?'

'Sarah Clifton.'

'The quiet woman? She works for him, doesn't she?'

Harry nodded. 'You haven't heard anything about it then?'

'No.' Laura shook her head. 'Not a thing. Why? Should I have?'

'Apparently it's the talk of the office,' he said, looking at her steadily as if expecting her to admit she had known about it.

'Harry, I promise you, I haven't heard anything,' she said. It didn't pass her by that she was probably the only one who hadn't heard the rumours. 'If I had, I would have come to you.'

He paused before admitting, 'Yeah, I know.'

'So what's she said Mike's done?' Laura asked.

'Undermining her, making her feel worthless, speaking rudely to her,' he listed. 'I asked for examples, and that's what I got back.'

'So now what?' Laura asked. 'You have to talk to Mike.' She couldn't believe anyone had made a complaint about him, let alone the timid girl Laura recalled hovering in the toilets on her first day back. 'Has anyone else complained about him or was it just Sarah?'

'Well, that's the thing. I'm hearing that a few other women are coming forward and saying they feel undervalued. I'm *hearing*' – he paused – 'that this is how our culture is perceived. I can't believe you haven't heard any of it.'

She shook her head, her mouth agape. 'Nor can I. So who else has spoken to you about him?'

'No one,' he said.

'I don't understand. You said others have come forward.'

'No one's complained to *me* about him. They're speaking to Mia.'

'Mia?' she repeated and let out a laugh, shaking her head.

'That's right, and to tell you the truth, Laura, I don't really know what to do,' Harry said, ignoring her reaction.

'You don't do anything for now,' Laura replied, firmly.

'What?'

'Don't do anything.' She threw her hands up and shrugged. 'We both know what Mike's like, and that it's just the way he is. He isn't a bully, Harry. You know that. This is something that's escalated and got out of hand, and I know she's behind it.'

Harry raised his eyes.

'Mia,' Laura confirmed. 'She's doing this. She's trying to cause trouble. I don't know why she's focusing on Mike, but—'

'Laura, don't,' he said, stopping her. 'You can't make this about your desire to get back at Mia.'

'I'm not trying to get back at anyone,' she said, through gritted teeth. 'But you know that Mike's – Mike's ...' She trailed off, waving her hand. 'Harry, why are you looking at me like that?'

'Nothing.'

Laura glanced down and twisted her fingers around her empty glass.

'It's just that I don't want to see you getting so wrapped up in Mia. I don't want you to make yourself ill again.'

'Harry,' Laura snapped. 'This is so completely different, and if you listened to me you'd realise that I honestly believe Mia is out to get me. For some reason. I have no clue why, but I know she is.'

Harry pursed his lips, releasing his breath slowly. 'Let me get us another drink.'

Laura opened her mouth to speak, but closed it again sharply, sinking back into the seat. What was the point of going over the same ground with Harry when every time he'd shift the conversation? The thought had been crossing Laura's mind lately that if she wanted to get a proper answer as to why she'd been so easily shifted off the Coopers account, then there was only one person she could ask. But the thought of addressing Tess Wills was too humiliating.

'Laura? Another drink?' Harry asked.

She glanced at her mobile, her heart plummeting when she saw the time. It was eight o'clock and she had forgotten to take her phone off silent, after a meeting she'd had earlier that afternoon. She'd missed another text from Nate half an hour ago.

'Shit!' she muttered 'I can't. I really have to go.' She texted back a quick reply. *So sorry. Am on way now xx.*

'Come on then,' Harry said and they left the bar, walking back to the offices where their cars were parked. 'Miles is doing me a big favour putting this opportunity my way,' he went on. It was as if he were letting her know she couldn't cock this up. That if Laura didn't think she could do it, she should say so now, so he could get someone else on the job. Someone like Mia, most likely. He took her arm and pulled her out of the way of a couple walking in the opposite direction on the thin path by the river, as Laura's phone started ringing.

She stared at the screen. Nate.

'You going to answer that?'

Laura nodded uncertainly and eventually picked up. 'Hi.'

'Are you in the car?'

'Nearly,' she said.

'I thought you said you were on your way back.'

'I am – I'm literally at my car,' she lied. It was at least another five minutes before they reached the office.

'Say hi to Nate for me,' Harry said beside her.

Laura felt herself tense as Nate went silent on the other end of the line. 'Nate, I'll be ten minutes,' she said as she hung up, her pulse quickening, picking up her steps as Harry raced to keep up with her.


Eighteen minutes later Laura pulled into the driveway and hurriedly scrambled out of the car. Nate wouldn't be happy and she couldn't blame him. He had never liked Harry, had always said he didn't trust him, insinuating that Harry's intentions crossed a boundary. Tonight would only add fuel to his argument that Harry was seeing more of

Laura than he was. What made it worse was that she didn't even want to go out for a sodding drink with her boss in the first place, and Harry hadn't spoken to her about anything that couldn't be said in the office.

'Then why the hell did you?' Nate snapped when she told him.

'Because he's my boss, Nate,' she cried. 'He asked me to, he told me he needed to talk about work, and I don't know – you know what Harry's like, he's persuasive. I didn't have a choice.'

'You do have a choice,' he snapped. 'And you chose him over me. You know how I feel, Laura; you knew I'd be pissed off, and yet you still went out with him.'

'I didn't *go out* with him – stop saying it like it was anything more than work, when you know it wasn't.'

'Do I?'

'God, Nate, yes,' she cried again. 'Don't even go there.'

He looked away, having the decency, she thought, to look admonished. 'You really don't see it, do you, Laura?' he said.

'See what? What are you getting at?' She grabbed his arm and swung him round. 'What are you saying, Nate?'

'Why do you actually think Harry wants to go out for a drink with you? It isn't to talk about work.'

'Oh my God, are you serious? Did you really just say that?'

'Laura, I trust you – you know I do,' he said. 'But I don't trust him one bit.'

'Nate, he has never so much as tried anything on with me.'

'But you know he would, if you gave him the chance,' he said. 'Don't you?'

Laura shook her head. 'I'm not having this conversation.'

'Then how about the one where you're still prioritising work over me and Bobby,' he said.

Laura slumped on the sofa next to him. 'Nate, don't make me feel bad about this. I don't know what else to do. I have work I need to do. I can't walk away from it, it's too important.'

'And you think this isn't?' he said, waving an arm around him.

'No, that's not what I'm saying. You don't understand,' she replied. 'Ever since I walked back in and found that Mia had taken over my job—'

'Oh, please,' Nate interrupted, hanging his head in his hands. 'Please don't bring Mia into this again.'

Laura pulled back, annoyed. It was true: Nate didn't understand, but he wasn't trying to.

'I know you're busy, I know you want to prove you can do it all – I get that,' he went on. 'But something's got to give, and at the moment all that's giving is me and Bobby. This isn't fair, Laura. Not to me or to Bobby. I am shattered. I am so tired, and I don't mind doing any of it, but sometimes I want to see you in an evening, to remind me that I've got something to look forward to.'

Laura noticed the wetness in his eyes before he swiftly wiped a hand over them.

'Is this actually what you want? To be working all the time?' he asked.

'No.' She shook her head emphatically, tears pricking her own eyes now. 'No, it's not what I want.'

'So why are you? You've been there long enough that you can tell Harry if it's too much.'

'It's not too much,' she said, her throat tightening at the thought that soon there would be even more work. If they won Miles's account, like she was doing everything to ensure, it was going to get worse. 'You make it sound like I'm not coping,' she went on, ignoring this thought.

'I'm not saying that,' Nate sighed. 'But if you haven't got Coopers any more, what's keeping you so bloody busy?'

'It's just—' She broke off. 'My other accounts are demanding,' she lied. 'It's not like Coopers was the only one.'

'That's not what you've said in the past,' he retorted, holding her gaze.

She looked away. She'd put more effort into the accounts she had left than she'd ever done before Bobby, but even they had slipped by the wayside since Monday. Part of her already thought it would be a good thing if they didn't win Miles's account, but at the same time she knew she wouldn't be able to let that happen. She would have to do as much as she could to ensure they secured it, because otherwise she'd feel she'd failed herself.

But the truth was that in the last four weeks Laura could have spent fewer hours at work if she hadn't tied herself in knots about proving her worth, or outstaying Mia.

'I can make it better,' she said. 'I think I know how. You have to trust me.'

'What are you talking about?' he asked, resigned.

'I spoke with someone where Mia used to work this week,' she started. Perhaps when Laura could prove Mia wasn't who she said she was, then she'd get Coopers back. And if that happened, she wouldn't worry about this new account. Someone else could have it. Patrick could do it. 'And she said that—'

'Stop, Laura.' Nate's words were so quiet she wasn't sure she heard them. 'Just stop,' he said again.

She looked at him, her mouth agape.

'You're obsessing over Mia,' he said, turning on the sofa until he was facing her. 'This is Saskia all over again.'

Laura reeled back. 'No.' She shook her head. 'I *know* Mia's taken my job for a reason. I know she has, Nate. She wanted my job and she made sure she got it.'

She wiped the arm of her sleeve across her face, collecting the tears that were sliding down her cheeks. She didn't want to think about what had happened after Saskia's boyfriend had left. How things had got so much worse for her in the following months. How she'd wound up making herself ill. 'This is not the same thing. I want you to trust me on that,' she said.

'All I want is for us all to be happy,' Nate replied softly. 'And I don't think any of us are at the moment. I want you home more, Laura.'

She didn't answer.

'I want you to come home earlier. I need you to. From now on, at least three times a week I want you to commit to leaving at five. That's not unreasonable,' he added.

She continued to stare at him.

'I'm not asking much. I simply need to know that you're still a part of this family. I want you to come back and be here for tea and bathtime sometimes.'

'But I can't ...' she muttered. 'I can't promise I can do that three times a week.' She knew it was impossible. Not now that she had the tender hanging over her. The only way she could do what Nate was asking was by admitting to Harry that she couldn't take on this new project. And if she did that, there was no way he'd risk losing Mia.

Nate let out a laugh, but it was one that suggested he was anything but happy. 'Are you serious?'

'I am – I just ... I can't commit to doing that, Nate. I'm not saying I won't try, because I will, but you can't force this onto me. You know what my work's like; you know I have to work around the clock when the clients demand it – that's the way it's always been.'

'No,' he said, 'that's not the way it's always been. Because everything's different now. We have a baby. *You* have a baby. And besides, you're working *more*, Laura. More than you ever did before.'

'I'm not. I—'

'You are,' he snapped. 'And you know it. Shit, Laura, if you can't even accept that, we've got no bloody hope.' He pulled himself off the sofa and stormed out of the room.

Laura sank back into it, inhaling a deep breath that caught in her throat.

'Okay,' she cried, calling after him. 'Okay, Nate, I'll come home early, three times a week. I'll do it,' she sobbed.

Nate appeared in the doorway again, leaning against the frame as he watched her carefully. 'That's all I want,' he said. 'I just want you to try.'

**Tuesday 14 May**

**Interview between DC Emily Marlow and Laura Denning, following the fire on Monday 13 May**

Marlow:    Okay, let's go over yesterday again. You didn't get to the office until around midday, is that correct?

Laura:    Yes.

Marlow:    And when you came in you were searching for Mia Anderson.

Laura:    I just wanted to speak to her.

Marlow:    Your husband was worried about your relationship with Mia, wasn't he? He thought you were getting obsessed with her?

Laura:    No, he didn't think that. He was a little worried, maybe, but that was only because he could see how upset I was.

Marlow:   But something like this had happened before at work with a woman you were friends with.

Laura:    What happened with Saskia was different. It was …

Marlow:   Go on.

Laura:    It was just different. Saskia had set me up, and my husband knew that, so I have no idea why he's worrying about me now.

Marlow:   How had Saskia set you up?

Laura:    She made it look like I was making mistakes. On one occasion she altered a brief from a major client before it got to me, so I worked on something altogether different and …

Marlow:   I can see this is distressing for you.

Laura:    I really don't know why you're talking to me about her.

Marlow:   But when you returned from maternity leave you thought Mia Anderson was doing the same thing?

Laura:    I've already gone through all this with you.

Marlow:   After the issue with Saskia, you were advised to take some time off from work, weren't you, Laura?

Laura:    I wasn't *advised* to.

Marlow:   It wasn't a suggestion from your boss, Harry Wood, then?

Laura:    He asked if I wanted to, and I agreed I could do with a break.

Marlow: And did you end up being prescribed any medication at this time?

Laura: You told me I was here to help you investigate the fire. I don't see what my past medical history has to do with it. I don't want to answer any more of these questions. I assume I don't have to, do I? I'm not under arrest? I can leave at any time, isn't that what you said?

Marlow: You can, Laura, and that's fine. Let's go back to the night of the fire instead. You texted your husband at six p.m. on Monday evening to say you were still in the office, and that you were meeting with your old account team from Coopers, so you would be late, is that right?

Laura: (pauses)

Marlow: Laura?

Laura: Yes.

Marlow: Was it true?

Laura: (shakes head) No.

Marlow: Why did you lie to your husband about why you were still at the office?

Laura: Because I was working on something he didn't know about and so – I don't know – maybe ... maybe I just felt guilty about being late again. Everyone was making me feel guilty, especially my husband.

Marlow: Guilty about what?

Laura:      About working too much. Do you have children, Detective?

Marlow:    I do.

Laura:      Then you might know what I mean. I can't do anything right. I feel like all the time I'm at work, I should be at home; and whenever I'm there, my workload creeps up to some unmanageable peak. So, yes, maybe I lied to him because I thought he was more likely to accept me meeting the Coopers team.

Marlow:    Laura, other than Harry Wood, you were the last member of staff in the building on Monday night, weren't you?

Laura:      As far as I know.

Marlow:    And a few hours after you left, that same building was burned to the ground.

           (pauses) Do you know who set fire to the Morris & Wood offices, Laura?

Laura:      (pauses) No.

Marlow:    Are you sure about that?

# Chapter Twenty-Three

*Four weeks before the fire*

Janie walked back from the fish-and-chip shop to the car park with the girls, down the cobbled lane, their crabbing buckets still swinging in their hands. Both of them were laughing over a joke that Ella had heard at school, heads dipped towards their packets of chips.

This was what happiness felt like.

She looked up briefly. She didn't know why or what caught her attention, but something made her glance towards the wine bar, tucked almost out of sight on the cobbled street leading down to the quay. Her husband was walking inside.

Janie stopped in her tracks, her heart tapping out a rapid beat. The girls carried on, oblivious, walking a few steps ahead until they too stopped and turned round to see what was keeping her.

'What are you doing, Mummy?' Lottie called.

Janie shook her head, gazing at the door, which had now closed behind her husband, and eventually pulled herself away and caught up with her daughters. 'Nothing,' she smiled. 'Just thought I saw someone I knew.'

'Who?' Lottie asked.

'No one,' she replied at once and pierced her fork into another chip, forcing it into her mouth, past her lack of appetite, resisting the urge to spit it out on the ground in front of them.

He was with a woman. She'd seen her walk in front of Harry, and even though Janie hadn't got a clear view, she would have sworn it was Laura, from the way she walked, the way she wore her hair, scraped back into a low bun.

As the girls started chattering again, Janie's mind whirled, her heartbeat still erratic as she tried to reason with herself that what she had seen was nothing. Harry often went for a drink after work; he had always done business in wine bars or pubs, or the directors' clubs that he belonged to in London. She knew that better than anyone. They were the places he would meet people like Miles Morgan.

She knew that if she asked Harry later if he'd been out for a drink, he'd tell her he had, and would no doubt admit who he was with; it would then be up to her to believe him or not, when he said it was nothing more than work.

As these thoughts fizzed around her head, it didn't pass her by that she no longer loved her husband, so then why did she suddenly feel so empty? So betrayed?

She smiled at the girls again as they turned round to catch her attention. Harry should have been with them. They had wanted their dad to meet them crabbing and he hadn't even returned her call.

Janie tossed the rest of her dinner into a bin.

*Don't make a fool of me, Harry.*

That was one thing she would not tolerate. She might not love him any longer, but she would not allow her husband to humiliate her.

# Chapter Twenty-Four

It was Friday night, and by the time Mia got home and crashed into the house, she expected her mum and Jess both to be in bed. She'd agreed to go to the pub with Bryony and a few other people from work and had drunk more gin and tonics than she had in a long while. Already she cursed the following morning, when she'd have a hangover, but at the time it had seemed like a good idea.

Pausing in the hallway, she listened. The blissful sound of silence, so she went into the kitchen and filled a pint glass with water. There was no alcohol in the house any more. She was the only one in her family who still drank. Her mum used to enjoy a glass of rosé, but not any longer, and maybe this was one of the reasons Mia enjoyed her after-work drinks so much. They were the only time she could forget, even if only temporarily.

She pulled up a chair to the small kitchen table and gulped back the water, sighing as she drained the glass and slammed it down on the kitchen table. She didn't want to be living here, but she had no choice. She hadn't even wanted to move back to the New Forest, and certainly nowhere near Lymington again. All three of them were suffocating in this tiny bungalow.

Suddenly a loud crash from the far end of the hallway made Mia push back her chair with a screech across the lino. She froze, briefly, before running to Jess's room. When she got there she flung open the door, her heart beating fast as she scanned the dark bedroom, feeling for the light switch and flicking it on.

'Jess, what the hell happened?'

Her sister was on the other side of the room in front of a broken mirror. Shards of glass lay around her, and one of her hands was clutching a sharp piece, pressing it into her fingertip.

'Seven years' bad luck,' her sister murmured, so softly she was barely audible, before letting out a chuckle. 'How ironic would that be, to have seven more?'

'Jess?' Mia stepped towards her carefully. 'What happened?' she asked again. When she was at her sister's side she reached out for the piece of glass still pressing into Jess's flesh and gently prised her fingers apart until she could take it.

'It was an accident,' Jess said sharply. 'I didn't – I wasn't doing it on purpose,' she snapped. 'I knocked the damn radio into the mirror. I didn't even want it here. It was you who put the thing on the dressing table.'

Mia ignored her. 'You're bleeding,' she said. 'I'll get you a plaster.'

Jess lowered her head and gazed at the drop of bright-red blood that appeared like a tear on the end of her finger. Slowly she lifted it to her lips and held it in there. 'It's not that bad – I don't need one.'

Mia sank down onto the end of the bed and slowly turned her sister to face her.

'Talk to me,' she said softly, but Jess shook her head.

'No. Tell me something about your life instead,' Jess replied. 'Talk to me about something else. Something from the outside world.' Tears had filled her sister's eyes and Mia fought hard not to reach out and wipe them away.

Mia laughed. 'I have nothing to talk about, other than work.'

'Then tell me about that.'

That was the one thing Mia really didn't want to talk to Jess about, but her sister was searching her eyes, pleading with her to take her out of whatever moment she was currently in, so she had to say something.

'It's fine,' she shrugged eventually. 'Some of the women are a laugh.'

'And you're still glad they made you permanent?'

Mia nodded. Yes, she had definitely been pleased about that.

'So you're happy, then? Because you don't need to stay here, you know. It was never supposed to be for this long.'

Mia didn't know how to answer, because what could she tell her sister? That of course she didn't want to be at Morris & Wood for much longer; this wasn't her dream job, she didn't care about selling health drinks.

In London, she'd once had a job that meant something. What she'd once done had made a difference: working for a charity – helping people. Then she'd had to give it up and move back to Lymington, to her mum's home.

'Of course I'm happy,' Mia smiled.

Jess nodded slowly. She didn't believe her, of course. Her sister could see through her. 'Do you remember when you were little, you wanted to be a pilot?' Jess asked.

'Yes! And then I went on my first flight and threw up.'

'I wouldn't get in a plane you were flying,' Jess laughed.

'I don't blame you. And you wanted—' Mia stopped suddenly, cursing herself that she could be so stupid.

'It's okay, you can say it.'

Jess's eyes were drawn and heavy and didn't mask the sadness that hid behind them. There were too many dark memories and shadows cast over their lives to give either of them much to be happy about when they were together. Even when they were having a laugh, there would always be a reminder.

Sometimes when she saw her sister like this, remembering a time before, Mia's heart fractured into even more pieces. She wanted to hold Jess in her arms and take away everything that had made her into this.

There were other times when she wanted to scream at Jess that she could do something about it. That she didn't need to live in such misery; she could pull herself out of the dark depths to which she'd descended.

Mia knew that wasn't wholly fair, and often asked herself what she would have done? If what had happened to Jess had happened to her? Of course she would never know for sure, when she hadn't had everything taken away from her like Jess had.

'I *want* you to say it,' Jess was urging her now, like it was some kind of challenge.

'You wanted to be a runner,' Mia replied.

Jess was always running. Almost as soon as she was walking, her mum used to joke that she was trying to get everywhere quicker. At fifteen, she was school sports captain and ran cross-country for Hampshire. In her teens she'd be up every morning before Mia had even opened her eyes and would be out of the house, in her trainers, pounding the pavements and the country lanes.

In those days no one used to worry about kids running on their own – down practically deserted pathways, alongside rivers, around the streets – before the sun had even come up. Her mum hadn't blinked an eyelid that Jess wasn't in her bed when she got up in the morning;

she just used to hope she'd be home before the school bus left.

She always was. Because that was Jess – dedicated to her schoolwork too. She was promising in every way imaginable; all her reports foretold that she could achieve anything she put her mind to.

So why *would* their mother have worried about her? Jess wasn't the one who caused her concern; if anyone, it was Mia, the daughter who had to be dragged out of bed, the one who would bunk off school to smoke up in the field with the boys.

'Yes, I wanted to be a runner.' Jess laughed, but it wasn't remotely funny.

Mia's gaze travelled down to her sister's useless legs and the faded blue pyjama bottoms limply hugging the frail bones beneath. She saw her sister naked every morning when she helped her shower and dress, and every day it still sickened her that those once-athletic legs had withered to nothing.

Jess couldn't run any more. She couldn't even walk. And every day it outraged Mia that someone had been responsible for doing this to her sister. And no one had paid.

Mia felt the anger bubbling inside her.

It was anger that always usurped the pity and guilt and sadness. It was anger that drove Mia on, and if she ever stopped, she might agree that it was unhealthy. But she wasn't stopping. Not yet.

Inhaling a large breath, she reached across and took hold of her sister's hands and held them in her own. 'I love you, you know that, don't you?'

'Of course I know that.' Jess's eyes filled up again and she pulled away one of her hands so that she could wipe it across her face. 'And I love you. And I'm so proud of you.'

'For what?' Mia asked, screwing up her eyes.

'For doing what you're doing.'

For a moment Mia held back, studying her sister, wondering what Jess actually knew.

'For giving up everything and living back here, I mean,' Jess said.

'Oh, yeah, right.' Mia let out a breath and smiled.

Sometimes Mia would think God had got it the wrong way round. It shouldn't have happened to Jess. She herself was the lazy one, the one who used to sit around all day in her pyjamas, whiling away the hours doing nothing.

Mia often wondered if the same thoughts had crossed their mum's mind too. The first time she had considered it was one year ago, when they'd both been standing in Southampton hospital, staring at her sister through the glass window, hooked up to machines, her life hanging by a thread, neither of them knowing if she would make it or not.

Mia recalled the words the doctor had uttered to her as she stood next to her mum. 'Your sister is very lucky to be alive,' he told her. Mia had looked through the window, past the tubes and the beeping monitors and the nurses bustling about the seemingly lifeless body beyond, which was supposedly her sister. 'But,' he had gone on, 'if she does pull through, there is every chance she won't walk again. Her legs were crushed by the weight of the car.'

He had carried on talking at them, but his words had started to fizzle and pop in bursts, and Mia could only grab at some of them: *An accident on the road towards Lymington ... Jess's car veered off the road and wrapped itself around a tree ... Believe the accident might have been caused by drink-driving.*

All their worlds had crumbled in that moment. Mia had seen a flash of her sister's future, but still she could never have foreseen how much it was going to affect all of them. How, only a week later, she would be packing up her old life and moving back to her childhood home, because there was no way her mum and Jess would cope without her.

But it wasn't going to end like this. Mia was certain of that. Someone needed to pay for what had been done to her sister.

**Tuesday 14 May**

**Initial interviews between DC Emily Marlow and the staff of Morris & Wood, following the fire on Monday 13 May**

*Patrick Carter, Senior Account Director*

Patrick:    I could tell there was an atmosphere, as soon as I arrived at the party.

Marlow:    What kind of atmosphere?

Patrick:    Janie – she seemed a little … she wasn't her usual self. She's usually so attentive, a great hostess, but last Friday something wasn't right.

Marlow:    Can you tell me how you mean?

Patrick:    I got there late and Janie answered the door, but her mind was elsewhere. I asked her where Harry was and she just stared at me and then eventually smiled and said, 'If you find him,

|          | you'll have to tell me.' She was trying to make it sound jokey, but I didn't get the sense she was happy. |
|----------|------------|
| Marlow:  | And did you find Harry? |
| Patrick: | Oh yeah, he was only out in the garden talking to some of the IT guys. |
| Marlow:  | You said earlier the party was a disaster. |
| Patrick: | Well, it was. Because of the argument. At least that was the start of it. |
| Marlow:  | For clarification, you mean the one between Laura and Mia? |
| Patrick: | (nods) Yes. You could see it was going to come to a head at some point. It was one as much as the other by then – they were both worked up. I suppose it's inevitable, when you mix office politics with alcohol, that something's going to kick off. I'm not sure if Harry's party came at the right time or the wrong one. |
| Marlow:  | Did you hear the argument between Mia Anderson and Laura Denning? |
| Patrick: | Yes. Well, I overheard the start of it, before Mia walked off across the lawn and Laura stormed after her. That part I just watched with horror. They were standing precariously close to the swimming pool, and I knew someone was going to end up in it. |
| Marlow:  | What did you overhear? |

| | |
|---|---|
| Patrick: | Laura yelling at Mia that she knew what she had done. |
| Marlow: | Where were you, at this point? |
| Patrick: | I was heading down to Harry's summer house for a cigarette. The party had spread out a bit, but there weren't many people down the end of the garden. It was a chance to get a bit of peace from my staff either asking me when they were getting a pay rise or telling me they didn't agree with this, that or whatever else I'd said lately. It always happens on a night out, doesn't it? Like they believe it's the right time to tell the boss what they think, simply because they've had one too many glasses of champagne. |
| Marlow: | And where were Mia and Laura? |
| Patrick: | Already down there, though I didn't see them at first, I just heard the shouting. |
| Marlow: | And did Laura say what it was that Mia had done. |
| Patrick: | She said – and I can pretty much quote this bit – 'I've spoken to Tess, Mia. I know how you managed to get your hands on my job.' She meant Tess Wills, the marketing director at Coopers. |
| Marlow: | And then? |
| Patrick: | And then Laura said, 'I know you're lying.' |
| | I wanted to go and check she was okay, but at the same time I didn't know whether to interfere. |

Marlow:     Did Laura say what Mia had lied about?

Patrick:    No.

Marlow:     So what happened after that?

Patrick:    Mia told her to get away from her. She kept
            saying, 'You're drunk, Laura. I think it's time
            you called yourself a taxi.'

            In hindsight, it would have been better if
            she *had* called a taxi, of course. But that was a
            whole other nightmare.

# Chapter Twenty-Five

*Two weeks before the fire*

Laura's days were merging into long weeks, filled with work and not getting home in time to see her son before he was already in bed. She was making every effort to rectify that, or at least she was trying to, promising Nate it was a temporary issue. 'Something has come up at work,' she had said. 'It just needs more attention for the next couple of weeks.'

'Not Coopers?' he had asked, one eye on the TV as she crashed down on the sofa next to him with a large bar of Dairy Milk that she had bought as a peace offering.

'No. Something for a new client Harry has asked me to do. It's good,' she said. 'It's exciting.'

She didn't tell him more, and Nate had nodded and eventually dragged his attention from the TV, breaking off a line of chocolate and putting it into his mouth. 'So you're – you know – you're okay with not working on Coopers?'

'I am,' Laura had lied. It was easier that way. Nate didn't probe any further into the work she was doing for this new client, and neither did she tell him that she was either spending these few weeks working her arse off for nothing or – more likely, given the effort she had put into it – carrying on at this level for the foreseeable future.

Nate didn't ask, because why would he? He had no idea what pitching and tenders involved. She might once have shared with him these excruciating parts of her job, but he wouldn't have taken on board what it meant.

And so Laura didn't reveal that if she won the tender, then the next few weeks would actually turn into months of getting home late, of pouring everything into the tight timescales Miles Morgan insisted on.

Besides, Laura was still telling herself it wouldn't come to that. Because once she could prove that Mia Anderson was lying, she would ensure she got Coopers back, and then she could tell Harry she didn't have the time for Miles's company.

*Then* she could get her life back. And so Nate didn't need to know the details.

Nate turned back to the TV, happy that his wife had seemingly moved on and was no longer interested in the woman who had taken her job, leaving Laura wondering how he could possibly think it was that easy for her. Did he simply want to believe that she was relaxed and confident enough to accept the fact she'd been pushed out of her job on purpose, or did he really not know her at all?

She wondered what Nate would make of the file she had on Mia tucked at the bottom of her wardrobe. In it she had been compiling what little evidence she had. The notes she had made following the call to Katie Burton; pages from Mia's Facebook page printed off; a picture of Jessica Louise, whoever she was. And now there was the complaint about Mike Lewis to add into the mix. Still Laura hadn't plucked up the courage to pick up the phone to Tess Wills, but as time passed she was becoming more and more certain that she might have to ask Tess the mortifying question of why she didn't want Laura working with her any more.

She shuddered at the thought as Nate began yawning, stretching along the sofa as he tucked his feet onto her lap.

'What shall we watch?' Laura asked.

He shrugged, his eyes already flickering shut. She glanced at her watch. Eight-thirty. She'd been back for forty-five minutes and in that time she had crept up to Bobby's room, watched her son sleeping, crept out with a heavier heart and then she and Nate had eaten pasta almost in silence.

'I don't mind. You choose.'

She gave him a playful nudge on the leg, but he reacted by moving his foot out of the way and in less than ten minutes had fallen asleep.

\*

The following morning the alarm went off at six a.m. Laura rolled over to switch it off as, beside her, Nate pulled the duvet more tightly around his body. 'Hey, sleepyhead,' she whispered gently, 'do you want a coffee before I leave?'

Nate grunted and shook his head.

'Okay.' She sat and watched him for a moment, before eventually swinging her legs over the side of the bed and creeping into Bobby's room. They had both been up with their son in the night. Laura continued to tell herself it would stop soon, the nights would get better, but it was taking its toll on both of them and especially on Nate, who had never been one to do well on little sleep. On top of the stresses that work was causing, it wasn't helping the obvious tensions between them.

By seven-thirty Laura was in the office. She sidestepped Mia, whose head was down, busying herself with something at her desk, and headed straight for her own desk, where she opened up the PC and pulled up the presentation she was working on for Miles.

Two hours had passed when she heard the ping of a text alert and, grabbing her phone, she saw Nate had sent her a video.

*Look what our clever son is doing*, it read. Laura clicked on the link and watched Bobby wobbling on his bottom and then eventually throw himself forward and begin to crawl.

'Oh my God!' she cried out loud, holding a hand over her mouth, smiling between her fingers as she watched the full three minutes, then immediately pressed Play again.

Running her thumb down the screen, Laura blinked back her tears. 'You clever boy,' she murmured, so full of pride for her baby.

She wanted to be with him. To be the one sitting on the sofa encouraging him towards her, clapping and cheering like she could hear Nate doing in the background. By the time Laura had watched the video three times, she could barely see through her tears and was picking up the phone to call Nate when Patrick appeared at her desk and asked if she had a minute to help him with something.

Laura dropped the phone and told him she did, though one minute turned into forty-five; and back at her desk, a myriad of emails were clogging her inbox, and by this time she'd been distracted and never did call or even text Nate back, to thank him for sending her the video, or even to acknowledge how much she loved it.

And Laura knew later, when she did make the effort to leave work on time, how bad that looked.

# Chapter Twenty-Six

Mia had barely stepped from the lift when, out of nowhere, Henrietta James appeared, her cheeks flushed red with a cluster of broken veins. Her hair seemed particularly uncared for this morning or maybe she had been running her hands through it. Clearly she had something to tell Mia, and Mia had come to expect it would involve Laura. Which was why it was a surprise when Henrietta said, 'Have you heard Sarah Clifton has gone?'

Henrietta wobbled from one too-high heel to the other, bug-eyed as she waited for Mia's response.

No, she hadn't heard this news. The girl had gone. What the hell?

'I was just wondering ...' Henrietta leaned in. 'Do you think they got rid of her?' she said in a loud whisper.

Mia glanced to the far end of the floor. From here she could make out Harry in his office as he prowled from one side to the other, no doubt on his phone. What she couldn't see was Mike Lewis's desk. 'Surely not,' she murmured.

But what if they had? Was that good news or bad? If they had dismissed Sarah, then she would have a case for unfair dismissal. It would be huge. Mia would need to get in touch with her.

She pretended she hadn't heard the news when she rapped on Harry's door and waited for him to beckon her in. His face was a mixture of calm and apprehension.

'How's it going?' he asked, gesturing to a chair, his mind on something else, by the look of it, as he barely glanced up at Mia.

'Good, thank you.'

He raised his eyebrows, peering up as he fussed with a stack of papers on his desk.

'Actually I wanted to update you on the issue with Mike Lewis,' Mia said boldly. In truth, she had little to update him on. The previous Friday night Mia had sounded out some of the other women in the office, none of whom had had many positive encounters with Mike, but neither did they feel either harassed or undermined by him. At least not enough to join in the formal complaint that she was hoping for.

Mia had even broached the subject that she had found out Patrick Carter had taken some male clients to a strip club in Southampton, which had stirred more interest among the women.

And then one of them told her she begrudged the fact she'd been bypassed for a promotion because she didn't want to work more than three days a week.

These were all things Mia was hoping to use.

'Actually, Sarah Clifton has left the company,' Harry told her.

'Yes, I did hear. She's gone very suddenly.'

Harry shrugged, as if it was no big deal. 'She handed in her notice last week – we agreed she didn't need to work it out.'

'Oh.' Mia's mouth hung open in a wide O. It was Sarah's decision. She must have given up, and now here was Mia looking stupid, unaware, left to pick up the pieces.

Her fingers reached for the desk in front of her and curled around its edge. She felt the anger beginning to rise within her, which to Harry – and most likely anyone else in the office – would appear irrational.

'But this doesn't mean you're just going to drop the complaint,' Mia went on, tightening her grip on the polished oak between her fingers.

'Well, of course I'm still looking into it.' He waved a hand in the air, brushing off her concerns.

Mia could hear her sister's voice as if she were standing next to her. 'Forget it, Sis, this isn't your battle.'

No. Maybe it wasn't her battle. Maybe none of it was, but time had made them into two very different sisters by now, and Mia wasn't going to stand by and refuse to fight.

She was angry with Sarah for giving up, but she was also angry with Harry for turning his back on her as he rifled through the drawers that sat behind his desk, and it took every ounce of determination not to thump her hands down and yell at him not to ignore her.

From the corner of her eye, Mia caught sight of Laura shuffling into the chair at her desk, booting up her computer, and she wondered whether she should be more worried about what Laura was up to than about confronting Harry.

She'd had a text the night before from someone she used to work with. Katie Burton. Telling her that she'd been contacted by someone asking questions about her previous employment with them. Katie wanted to know if everything was all right.

It didn't take a genius to guess it must have been Laura who'd been in touch. If she carried on running around like some sort of amateur Nancy Drew, then everything Mia had worked towards could be taken away in an instant.

Mia exhaled a tight breath and turned her attention back to Harry. She had to be careful. She also wondered if Harry actually knew that she'd met his wife for lunch, because despite Janie alluding to the fact that she had set it up of her own accord, surely Harry had sent her?

*'I hope you do the right thing,'* Janie had said and even though her tone hadn't been menacing, it must have been intended as a threat.

And now Mia didn't know whether she was getting out of her depth, and if she should she walk away before things went too far. But what would that achieve? She had never been someone who gave up easily.

# Chapter Twenty-Seven

*One week before the fire*

Laura hesitated before closing down her PC and throwing her mobile in her bag. The clock had only just ticked past five. A stack of unread emails and an incomplete document left her with butterflies fluttering in her stomach, but when there had been little more than a minimal exchange of words with Nate and some hastily devoured dinners, something had to give. The only thing that was keeping her from leaving now was the fact that she had finally called Tess Wills that day, and now that she had, Laura's need to speak to her was verging on obsessive. Six hours later and she was still waiting for the woman to call her back.

Finally she gave up and left the office. Nate was in the garden when she arrived home. He was carting Bobby along on his hip as he walked alongside the thin border of plants that ran beside the fence. Every so often he would stop and point at a bush or a flower and whisper words in their son's ear that Laura couldn't hear.

She stood by the kitchen window, holding up her hand and pressing her palm against the pane as she watched her precious family. The way Bobby nestled into the crook of Nate's body, like he was attached there. She couldn't make out where one person stopped and the other started, and the sight of them both melted her heart and stabbed it at the same time. How she loved them – more than anything. But how she felt she was losing them too.

The urge to join her boys and announce her arrival at home was superseded by a strange anxiety, which she couldn't put down solely to the work she knew was waiting for her. That hovered on the periphery of her mind like a black cloud that wouldn't go away until she attended to it, but this was something so much more.

It was that Laura didn't know any more where her place was with her boys. She didn't know where she fitted in.

She could count on both hands the waking hours she'd spent with Bobby in a working week. The once-bright smile that had lit up his face when she'd walked in the door at night had been replaced by a new hesitation before he would come to her.

Laura knew this was of her own making, and that she had no one else to blame but herself. And although she longed to drag herself out of the hole she had dug, she didn't see a way to.

Not yet anyway. Not until she got rid of Mia. Then she would make it work. Then she would find the balance she needed to reconnect with her family, she thought resolutely, her hand pressing harder against the pane.

Nate turned round at the bottom of the garden and gave Laura a surprised wave when he caught her standing at the window. She released her hand as he pointed and whispered more words into Bobby's ear, but their son was more intent on pulling the collar of Nate's polo shirt to his mouth.

'I didn't know you were back,' he said, coming into the kitchen. 'How long have you been standing there?'

'Just long enough to watch you giving our son a gardening lesson.' Laura smiled, holding out her hands for Nate to pass her a wriggling Bobby.

'He's hungry. I was about to come in to get his tea.'

'I can do that,' she told him, pressing her mouth against Bobby's cheek and blowing a raspberry against his soft skin until he giggled.

'No, it's all right, I've got it ready.' Nate was already at the fridge, pulling out a container of yesterday's shepherd's pie that he would whizz up in a blender.

She snuggled against her son, the memory of the video Nate had sent her that morning rushing back to her, along with the thought that she hadn't responded to it. 'And I can't believe how clever you are,' she said, pulling back and smiling at Bobby, trying to ignore the flash of guilt that ballooned inside her. 'Crawling like a big boy. Mummy's so proud of you.' She laughed as her son beamed back at her, and then turned to Nate. 'I'm so sorry. It was a gorgeous video. I wanted to call you, but something came up and ...' Her words trailed off. None of them were adequate.

Nate nodded, his back to her as he gave a small strangled sound that sounded like a laugh. She chose to ignore it as she pressed her lips against Bobby's cheek. 'Are you pleased to see me?' she tried.

'Of course,' he said flatly. 'I just didn't expect you yet.'

'I wanted to surprise you.'

Nate nodded.

'You don't *seem* pleased.'

Nate let out a deep breath. 'It's five-thirty, Laura. You left on time – you hardly left early. Don't make out you're doing me a favour.' He rubbed his eyes with the back of his hand and even though his words had jarred, she brushed them off, telling herself that her husband was exhausted and probably annoyed with her about the video.

'I'm not,' she said. 'I – I'm trying to make an effort, Nate. Can you meet me in the middle here?'

He put the container on the worktop and looked up at her. 'Meet you in the middle? Laura, what world are you living in? I've been so far over the middle I'm practically on *your* side. You come home one night before Bobby's had his tea and expect me to jump up and down with joy?'

'I'm not saying that ...'

'Good. Because I really don't feel like doing it, I'm afraid. God, Laura, you have no idea, do you?'

'Okay,' she cried. 'I'm sorry, Nate, I get it – you're pissed off with me.' Laura waited for him to respond, tell her he was sorry, that he was just tired and wasn't really that annoyed with her at all, because he understood that her day was busy.

Instead he glanced at Bobby and then glared at her.

'Bobby doesn't know what the word means,' she hissed. 'Jesus, I really didn't think this was how the evening would pan out.'

'No,' he muttered. 'Neither did I.'


An hour later Laura's mobile rang. She paused before answering, as Tess Wills's name flashed up on her screen. Eventually she picked up. 'Hello, Tess,' she said. 'Thanks for getting back to me.'

'Sorry it's late. I hope this isn't a bad time?'

Laura stepped out of the living room and started up the stairs. 'No,' she said. 'It's fine.'

'What can I do for you?' Tess asked breezily, making Laura's breath catch in her throat.

'This isn't—' she broke off, starting again. 'I need you to be honest with me,' she said. 'Please.'

'Okay.' The word was slightly drawn out, as if Tess might have some idea what was coming.

'I need to know why I didn't stay on your account.' As soon as the words were out of Laura's mouth she felt relieved, and even before she'd heard Tess's answer she wondered why it had taken her almost two months to ask.

When the conversation was finished, Laura hung up. Her jaw was set in a tense line and as she stared at her reflection in the bathroom mirror, she considered calling Mia Anderson right then. Get this done, once and for all.

Only it was clear the woman was a liar. And if they had the conversation in private, then Laura didn't trust what might come of it. Better, surely, that she at least wait until they were face-to-face. And maybe until there were other people around, who would hear that Laura was right. That, for some reason, Mia had really come to steal her job.

## Tuesday 14 May

**Initial interviews between DC Emily Marlow and the staff of Morris & Wood, following the fire on Monday 13 May**

### *Patrick Carter, Senior Account Director*

Marlow:   What happened at the party when the two women walked away from the summer house? You said you watched it with horror. Did you overhear any more of their argument?

Patrick:   No. Not from where I stood. When Mia walked off, Laura turned and saw me briefly. She almost looked through me – I could tell she'd had far too much to drink. I don't think she even saw me. I've never seen Laura like that before. I held out my hand and told her to come back to the house with me, but she stared right through me with these glassy eyes and then stormed off after Mia. I didn't follow, I went to try to find Harry, but I couldn't; and by the time he did appear, all hell had broken loose by the pool. And later, when I eventually caught up with him in the house, there was that whole other situation going on.

Marlow: With Harry and his wife?

Patrick: Yes. They were arguing. Just before he left his own party.

Marlow: Did you speak to Janie Wood after that?

Patrick: No. She was having this conversation with Mia in the hallway, which sounded weird, from the little I could garner, and then – she disappeared. I didn't see her again, and by the time Harry returned I'd already called my own taxi. I didn't want to hang around much longer, even though a lot of the staff were happy to carry on drinking his champagne. You see, this is what I mean when I say the whole night was a disaster. Janie and Harry are friends of mine, but … You know all morning, ever since I heard about the fire, all I keep wondering is whether it had something to do with that night.

# Chapter Twenty-Eight

*One week before the fire*

Janie stood in the doorway to Ella's bedroom, pausing for a moment before she woke her. Ella was eleven, still her baby, and yet she filled the length of her single bed, which remained stuffed with teddies and cushions. When had her daughter grown up to the point where Janie could get so little out of her any more? And yet all she had to do was look at her little girl's room and she felt the tug on her heart strings that they were caught in this trap between child and teenager, and Ella hadn't even started the dreaded secondary-school years. How the hell was she going to get through them?

Janie sighed as she crept over to her daughter's bed and gently shook her awake. Ella snatched the duvet and wound it round herself tighter, and eventually Janie said softly that she was going downstairs to make breakfast, and could Ella please start getting up. Some days all she wanted was to yell at her daughter that *she* didn't want to get out of bed, either. But she also knew that was never a good way to start the day. And then there were moments like today when she wondered how easy her days would be, if the only thing she had to worry about was her girls.

Janie's stomach was unsettled, her mind flittering between past events and those more recent, all of which she'd kept pushing to the back of her mind while knowing it wasn't going to take much for any of them to start unravelling her if she gave them space to breathe.

She knew it might help to talk to someone and part of her wondered if she'd open up to her friends when she met them for coffee later that morning. The bigger part knew she probably wouldn't.

After ordering an Americano, Janie joined them at the window table. She lifted the cup to her lips and blew, peering over the rim as they waited for Lucy to relay her latest story about her youngest.

'So she came home last night with a bite-mark on her arm.' Lucy raised her eyes and placed her own mug carefully on the table between them.

'You are kidding,' Kristen cried. 'An actual bite? Well, the school has to do something, surely?'

'You'd think,' Lucy said. 'Only when I told the teacher this morning, he said he was sorry but he hadn't seen anything happen.'

'That is outrageous, isn't it?' Kristin gasped, her voice rising as she looked round at the other two, who nodded their agreement.

'It is. Something has to be done about that kid,' Anna said. 'Before it's too late. I mean, can you imagine what he'll be like when he's in secondary school?'

'Surely they grow out if it,' Lucy added.

'I don't know,' Anna shrugged. 'Show me the boy at seven and I'll show you the man. That's what they say, isn't it? A seven-year-old's brain is already ninety per cent developed by that time. I think you can tell exactly what type of adult darling Dexter is going to be.'

'Once a bully, always a bully,' Kristen chipped in. 'We'll read about him in the papers one day: he'll have beaten someone up outside a convenience store because they looked at him the wrong way. That happened to someone I went to school with. My mum said she could have told anyone that his future was going to be doomed.'

Janie silently sipped her coffee as she listened to the interchange. It was so nice not to have to think about anything other than everyone else's problems for an hour, but then Anna reached out and took hold of her arm. 'You're quiet this morning. Everything all right?'

Janie nodded. Out of all of them, it was always Anna who noticed when there was something on her mind. She was going to miss Anna when her friend started her job. But right then she wished Anna hadn't asked, because now they were all looking at her expectantly and waiting for

Janie to contribute something to the conversation, and she knew she had to give them something.

In the end the only thing she could think of coming up with was, 'Harry's got a problem with bullying in his office.' The words left her lips before she could stop them.

Her mind drifted back to the conversation she had with her husband, when Harry came home and told her the girl had left.

'Sarah's gone,' he'd said, pouring himself a large glass of Malbec, which he'd picked up on their last trip to France. He studied the glass as he swirled the wine, letting it swish to the top as if he were prepared to let it slosh over the edge and onto the oak table.

'Sarah?' Janie had asked.

'The girl who said she was being bullied.'

'*Woman*,' Janie corrected. 'She's a woman, Harry. You need to stop referring to her as a girl.'

He had continued to swish his wine as he raised his eyebrows, questioningly.

'Any female over the age of eighteen is a woman. You wouldn't refer to the men as boys.'

'What difference does it make?' he had asked, seemingly baffled.

'It makes her sound like a schoolchild. It undermines the issue.'

'I really don't think it does,' he'd said, taking a sip. 'Anyway, the fact is she handed her notice in today. She left this afternoon, after Mike agreed to it.'

'Right.' Janie rolled her eyes.

'It's a good thing.'

'Because it means you can forget about it?' she asked.

'Well, there's no case to follow up now, is there?'

'Other than the fact Mike is still working for you? No, I suppose not.'

'Janie?' Harry hung his head. 'You make it sound like you're not on my side.'

'I just don't think you should paper over it.'

'But Mike – seriously? You know he's an awkward fellow. He can barely look at me half the time when he's talking to me. He talks over *me*, for Christ's sake. I don't believe there's a problem.' He put his glass down and looked away.

Janie had turned back to the oven and wondered whether Mia Anderson saw it that way. Someone should be fighting. She really did wonder if she should try to have another lunch with Mia soon, but then their last meet-up had been an odd occasion and Janie wasn't particularly sure about her after that.

Now, Lucy was asking what the problem was, and Janie wondered why she had suddenly spurted out the news about the bullying at Harry's office and wondered if it was maybe her little way of getting back at him for the fact she'd seen him taking Laura Denning to a wine bar – something neither of them had mentioned.

And then she wondered if it was more than that that had made her spill the gossip. Maybe she was just sick of her husband avoiding responsibility.

'A woman at the office has reported a man for bullying her,' Janie told her friends. 'I don't know much about it.'

'It goes on throughout life,' Anna said. 'I bet that man was a bully at school too.'

'To be honest, I doubt he was,' Janie admitted. She had known Mike a long time. 'If anything, he was probably the kid being picked on.'

'But it doesn't mean they don't have to do something about it.'

'No. No, it doesn't mean that,' Janie said.

'He has to,' Lucy went on. 'This happened to my friend's husband once. By his own admission, he didn't handle it well, and then the woman left the company, so he pretty much thought that was that. Next thing she's gone public. His reputation was ruined.'

'Well, that's not going to happen to Harry,' Kristin laughed. 'Harry has the shiniest reputation in Lymington.'

'Until the day he doesn't,' Lucy said.

Janie frowned.

'I'm just saying,' Lucy told her, 'that you have to be careful. This woman at my friend's husband's company – well, you never know what anyone's capable of, until you push them too far.'

'You must have seen some stuff like that when you were a barrister?' Anna was asking, and Janie snapped her head to look at her friend. 'Cases where things in the office got out of hand?'

'Which reminds me, tell us about your job, Anna?' Lucy said. 'When do you start?'

Janie felt the relief pour through her as the conversation shifted to Anna, who proceeded to tell them she was starting in a fortnight. But it wasn't long before she turned back to Janie again. 'Come on, did you have any interesting cases?' she asked.

Janie's head flooded with images of the case she had spent the last five-odd years pushing to the far corners of her mind. But she shook her head. She'd become good at keeping her mouth shut about that. About all the things that had happened back then. Miles Morgan ... Sophie. The unease rippled inside her, making her feel like she was on a fairground ride.

She knew she was being watched again. She might have been able to pass off the shadow in the car park at the quay a couple of weeks back, but she definitely couldn't ignore the fact someone was lurking near the house when she'd got home the previous night. She'd turned into their quiet lane, almost on autopilot, and done a double take when she'd seen the shadow.

The last time it had happened was when she was involved in the case, which had become a high-profile one, and she understood why someone might want something from her then. But it didn't explain why it was happening again now.

Last night as she'd looked a second time, her stomach had jolted and her fingers twitched against the steering wheel. As quickly as the figure had appeared in her line of sight, it went away again, and by the time Janie reached their gate there was no sign of an intruder.

She'd glanced in the rear-view mirror. The girls were oblivious in the back seat, Ella's head down as she flicked through photos on her phone, Lottie chewing the end of a pencil as she learned her spellings.

Turning off the engine, Janie stretched her gaze further to the bushes that provided a boundary between her long driveway and the road beyond. Someone had been watching her house and now she wondered if they'd recognised her car. Eventually she climbed out and waited for the girls to do the same, all the time glancing around them. Anyone could be lingering in a number of places.

The girls were now hovering by the front door, and eventually Janie clicked the car shut and the alarm in the house off and, with one last glance behind her, let them all inside.

There had never been any danger in the past. No threats. There was absolutely no reason to think someone was watching her again, because why would they be?

Probably, she thought, as she'd flicked on the lights and had a near miss with the girls' school bags that had been dropped in the middle of the hallway, it was all in her head. It was just because she had been thinking too much lately. Her Facebook search for Miles had planted pictures in her mind, and she had even dreamed of him the night before.

Now Janie's phone was ringing in her bag, and yet it took Anna to point it out to her before she realised. 'Oh,' she murmured. She hadn't even heard it. Dipping into her bag, she pulled her mobile out and saw Sophie's name on the screen.

'I better take this,' she said to her friends as she picked up the call. 'Hey, Soph, everything all right?' she asked on instinct, but immediately she could tell it wasn't, as the sound of sobbing filled the line. Janie scrambled out of her seat and went outside the café, pressing her phone to her ear as she said, 'Sophie, what the hell is wrong?'

She was immediately taken back to the last call like this that she had received from her best friend. Five years ago she'd had to leave the house one evening and look for Sophie, whom she'd found soaking wet, sheltering from the rain in a shop doorway, her bright blue wrap tightly wrapped around her. That night she hadn't managed to get her friend to tell her what had happened, but Janie had known. When, twenty-fours later, Sophie eventually opened up, Janie had expected the story, but still she had been shocked by the entirety of it. What it meant.

'Sophie, please, will you tell me what's happened?' Janie begged now.

'Mark's dumped me,' she wailed. 'And he's taken five hundred pounds out of my bloody purse and ...' Her words gave way to more sobs.

'Mark?' The artist boyfriend. Again no shock, only this time Janie felt relief ride through her. Mark was manageable – they could get through this one.

'I love him,' Sophie said, and Janie was surprised, because she herself couldn't see anything remotely attractive in the man, but regardless she listened and told her friend she'd come up and be with her that weekend, if she wanted.

When the call ended, Janie leaned back against the wall of the café and took a deep breath. Holding a hand over her mouth, she shook her head. Maybe it would be good to get away to London for a night. She could take the girls, get some space.

After the night before she might have assured herself there was nothing to worry about – just her mind playing tricks on her – but it wasn't only herself she had to think about any longer. It was the girls too. Her precious daughters could be in danger, and they were everything to her. And she knew she would do whatever was necessary to protect them.

## Thursday 16 May

**Interview between DC Emily Marlow and Anna Halshaw, following the fire on Monday 13 May**

Marlow:    Can you describe your friendship with Janie Wood?

Anna:    We're very close. We've been friends since Janie's oldest daughter started in Year One. I've known her for five years.

Marlow:    And how often do you see each other?

Anna:    Every day, more or less, at the school gate, either at drop-off or pick-up. And then we meet for coffee once a week. There's four of us who get together. We're all good friends.

Marlow:    So you would say you know her pretty well?

Anna:    Of course, which is why what you told me about this person following her is so shocking.

Marlow: And of course the fact that she never mentioned the name Miles Morgan to you before.

Anna: Yes, but there could be many reasons for that. I mean, he probably wasn't significant.

Marlow: He was significant, Anna. But how about her husband? Did Janie confide anything to you lately about him?

Anna: Janie and Harry? You mean, their marriage? No. They were as happy as they've always been. What is this?

Marlow: Or anything to do with his work?

Anna: Oh, well, yes – yes. She told us someone at Harry's office was being bullied. Is that what this is about? Because she didn't tell me much. I didn't get the impression it was a major deal, but God, you never know, do you?

Marlow: One last thing, Anna: did she mention any of the women who worked for her husband?

Anna: (shakes head) Not by name.

Marlow: None that she may have been close to?

Anna: No, I don't think so.

Marlow: Mia Anderson or Laura Denning? You've never heard Janie talking about either of them?

# Chapter Twenty-Nine

*The Woods' party – three days before the fire*

Mia stood in front of the only full-length mirror in the bungalow. It was propped against the wall in her mum's bedroom, positioned so awkwardly that she was always afraid it might fall and break. As she stared at her reflection, her mind was on something completely different from the party that night. It was on Sarah Clifton and what her sudden departure from Morris & Wood meant. It was on Harry Wood and his sparklingly clean reputation. But most of all it was on the fact that she still hadn't achieved what she wanted. That, almost eight months later, the reason she had given up her promising career at The Venue was slipping out of her reach and she was no longer sure what to do about it.

Mia hadn't noticed Jess appearing in her bedroom doorway until she caught a glimpse of her sister in the far edge of the mirror.

'You look nice,' Jess told her.

'Thank you.' Mia screwed her nose up and finally took in her appearance. 'I'm not sure, though.' She was wearing a long, pleated leopard-print skirt that skimmed her ankles and a black chiffon vest-top, which she tugged nervously out from her waistband. Her glittery sandals sparkled on her feet, and a pretty gold chain hung around her ankle. 'I don't know whether it's supposed to be dressy or casual,' she said. 'Harry's invitation didn't say.'

'What are the other women in the office wearing?' Jess asked.

Mia shrugged as she turned from side to side, letting her skirt swish against her legs, wondering if she was going to be warm enough. She had been told that often the Woods' parties spread into the garden, beside the pool with its neat border of shrubbery.

'Well, I think you look lovely,' Jess said and when Mia caught her sister's reflection in the mirror behind her, she saw the glimmer of a smile on her lips, even though her eyes were sunken and rimmed with black shadows.

Mia wondered what was really running through Jess's head right now. Maybe it was nothing more than her little sister looking pretty and dressed up for a party at Harry Wood's house – the man their mum still talked about as if he'd opened a drugs den next door, rather than built an office on Lymington Quay.

Maybe Jess was looking at her and thinking none of this was fair, when she was sitting in faded navy jogging bottoms and an oversized sweatshirt, with nothing lined up for the evening except an ITV crime drama.

'Are you getting a taxi?' Jess asked.

'You sound like Mum,' Mia replied, then frowned and added, 'Of course I am.' They both knew she would never get behind a wheel if she'd been drinking. They both knew all too well the heartbreak and devastation that could cause.

'Is the woman going? The one whose job you have?'

Mia laughed off the comment. 'Yes, I'm sure Laura will be there.'

'Is she still angry with you?'

'Yes,' Mia said. 'Yes, I think she's still out to get me,' she added a little more quietly.

'And who are you out to get, little sister?' Jess asked.

Mia's smile dropped and she cocked her head, her gaze falling on Jess, who was looking at her intently. But by the time she eventually started to ask Jess what she meant by that, her sister had left the room.

It was just gone seven-thirty by the time Mia's taxi pulled up into Harry Wood's sweeping driveway. Other staff from the office were already there. She could hear the murmur of conversation and laughter, a hint of music drifting from the back garden. Glancing at the side-gate, she wondered if she should go straight through, before thinking better of it and walking up to the double wooden door at the front.

It really was a luxurious home. The topiary bushes that lined the driveway were manicured to perfection. Automatic lights flooded the way as the cab pulled up. Even the driver whistled as he drove in.

Janie Wood answered the door and let Mia inside. A smile was plastered onto her face, which was naked apart from black mascara and maybe a bit of bronzer. Janie was naturally attractive, but her smile did nothing to hide the anguish behind it. Mia assumed these parties were not high on her list of things she enjoyed, though she was clearly trying to give the impression she was happy to have her house invaded by her husband's employees. She probably had other things that she could be doing with her evening – friends she would rather be spending time with.

Janie pointed Mia towards the kitchen and asked if she wouldn't mind helping herself to a drink. She had to get something from the dining room, she said.

Of course she didn't mind helping herself, Mia insisted, but she hovered in the hallway as Janie slipped away into the room on their left. The sound of an engine pulling up outside caught Mia's attention. She almost expected to hear the screech of brakes, the way it hurtled up the drive. She peered through the thin slit of window that ran beside the length of the front door and watched as a grey Qashqai pulled up at the side of the drive and Laura stepped from the driver's door, banging it shut behind her and stopping to peer up at the house.

Mia drew back. No husband, she noticed. It seemed Laura had driven herself to the party on her own. Presumably she was intending to stay sober.

Reaching up a hand, Mia fingered the thin veil of curtain that hung loosely by the window and then eventually let it fall. As she backed into the hallway and turned towards the kitchen, she considered her sister's words. *Who are you out to get, little sister?*

If Jess knew what she was doing, then why hadn't she said anything? Why wasn't she trying to stop her?

They'd had a conversation once, maybe a month after Jess's world had come crashing down, sweeping along with it Mia's and their mother's too.

'What are you going to do?' Mia had asked her.

Jess had looked up slowly, her brown eyes ovals as deep as the earth, and in them Mia tried to read what her sister was thinking. But by then she found it too hard to know.

'Forget,' Jess said eventually. 'I'm going to do everything I can to forget.'

Mia had shaken her head. She wanted to tell her sister she couldn't do that, because if she forgot, then someone was getting away with what they had done to her.

And yet she saw the sadness in those brown eyes, and Mia knew it wasn't her place to tell her sister that forgetting was not the solution. In that moment Mia swore that she *would* let Jess forget. But she also knew that she herself never would.

# Chapter Thirty

Janie had been ready since six p.m. Her hair had been washed and styled at the salon and was hanging in soft curls that fell just below her shoulders. She'd chosen a long kaftan in rich purple that fell open at the knees, and had even had her toenails painted to match while her hair was being blow-dried. All this effort for a party she didn't want to throw, but at least it gave her the confidence to open the door to a bunch of semi-strangers that she only saw once a year and welcome them into her home.

The other thing that gave her some Dutch courage was the glass of champagne she held in her hand as she opened the door to one guest after another. But Janie knew better than to drink too much too early. At least one of the guests did that every year and she doubted this one would be any different. There were plenty who liked to make the most of the free alcohol supplied at their boss's expense.

Janie had let Mia into the house and directed her towards the kitchen. She would search her out later, when she got the chance, but for now she had no choice but to leave her stranded in the hallway. Ella had texted from Anna's house, where both girls were having a sleepover, to say Lottie had been crying for the last half-hour because she couldn't find her favourite teddy, Blue Ted.

Janie dipped into the dining room and went over to the sofa in the corner, where the girls had been watching TV before school that morning; and sure enough, there he was, balancing precariously on one arm. She positioned him in front of the cushions, took a photo and sent it to Ella with a message that read: *Blue Ted's perfectly happy watching TV. Love you and miss you both xx.*

She waited to check it was sent, hovering over the phone until a message came back from Ella to say thanks, and that they loved her too. Janie smiled as she read it, looking up sharply as a car came up the driveway far more quickly than she thought appropriate; and as she moved towards the window, she pinched back the curtains with one finger. It was Laura's car, now pulling to a halt by the fence, the door swinging wide open as the engine was switched off. Laura climbed out, wearing dark jeans and a grey blazer. Smart as she looked, she was underdressed for the party, in comparison to the other guests.

Janie let the curtain flutter back into place, but could just about still see Laura as she closed the car door and then stood rooted to the spot in the middle of their driveway, staring at the house. Laura's eyes drifted up to Janie and Harry's bedroom above, before dropping down again and finally landing on the front door.

Janie waited for Nate to join Laura. She peered into the car as best she could from her vantage point, but there was no sign of Laura's husband. She couldn't think of a time when Laura hadn't brought him, though perhaps there was a problem with childcare. Maybe Janie should have gone to the effort of telling Laura she could have brought the baby.

She moved away from the window as Laura disappeared from sight and the doorbell rang, though by the time Janie reached the doorway to the hall, Harry had beaten her to it. The one time her husband had appeared to greet a guest and, although Janie was sure he couldn't have had any idea it was Laura, it felt a little too convenient.

Janie slunk behind the dining-room door as he let her in, and listened to his overenthusiastic welcome as he ushered her inside. 'No Nate tonight?' he asked.

'No.' A pause and then another. 'No. We couldn't get anyone to babysit so ...' She let the end of the sentence hang.

'Oh. Shame,' Harry said, in a manner that didn't sound remotely genuine to Janie as he went on, more enthusiastically, 'but at least you're here. Come on through, let me get you a drink.'

'Thanks. White wine, please,' Laura replied. Janie glanced back at the car parked haphazardly on their driveway and wondered if Laura had already had one.

'How are you getting on with the pitch?' Harry asked her.

'It's going well,' Laura replied with a modesty that grated on Janie, though she detected something else in Laura's voice too, which made her think things might not be going quite that smoothly.

'That's great – really great. See, I knew you could do it.'

'I only hope he likes my ideas,' Laura said. 'If he doesn't ...' Again the sentence was cut short. 'Miles Morgan strikes me as someone who could be a hard man to please,' she went on, her voice fading.

Janie's heart stopped beating. Just for a moment. Her breath caught in her throat before she released it in a sharp puff, poking her head round the doorway in time to see her husband and Laura disappearing into the kitchen.

*Miles Morgan.* Laura had spoken those words so casually. She'd have no idea that the mere sound of that man's name could just have tipped Janie's world on its axis.

She pulled herself out of her hiding place and followed in the wake of her husband's footsteps. So Harry had brought that man into her life again. Did he really have no clue what it would do to her? And not only that – he was doing work for Miles. The man must have been in Lymington. She shuddered at the thought, her mind whirling.

Was Harry planning to bring him to the house?

Janie scanned the kitchen, catching a fleeting glimpse of her husband in the garden, guests milling around him, blurring into one. She clutched the counter beside her, fingers gripping it tightly as she felt the air leave her body. She wanted to cut through the guests to get to Harry and demand that he tell her what was going on. Did he really think so little of her that he could do this to her?

**Thursday 16 May**

**Interview between DC Emily Marlow and Janie Wood, following the fire on Monday 13 May**

Marlow:    What I can't get my head round is that you didn't tell anyone else you thought someone was watching you. Not even your husband?

Janie:    No. I told you. I didn't tell anyone.

Marlow:    Why was that?

Janie:    Because … I don't know. I think I just wanted to pretend it wasn't happening. I didn't want to admit it was.

Marlow:    Not because you didn't think your husband would believe you?

Janie:    No. That's not it.

Marlow:    But you have children in the house. Didn't their safety cross your mind?

Janie:      Of course it did. Of course. My children mean
            everything to me.

Marlow:     Janie, you'll need to calm down.

Janie:      (pauses) My children are my world, but in this
            case – I guess I didn't think there was anything
            to worry about. I didn't feel threatened. Not at
            the time anyway.

Marlow:     And you didn't consider why you might be
            being watched?

Janie:      No. I had no clue.

Marlow:     Tell me about your relationship with Miles
            Morgan.

Janie:      (pauses) There's little to tell.

Marlow:     But he came back into your life very recently.
            In fact, only on Monday. The day of the fire.

Janie:      Yes.

Marlow:     Do you think this is a coincidence?

Janie:      Are you asking me if I think it was him who
            followed me? Maybe, yes. Maybe it was.

Marlow:     You don't sound particularly sure.

Janie:      Like I've told you, I didn't ever get the chance
            to see whoever it was.

Marlow:     Janie, there are too many things that don't add
            up for me.

Janie:      I didn't set fire to that building. I wouldn't
            have done that. You need to believe me.

Marlow:     Yet you were there. You admit you were at the
            quay on Monday night, though you can't give

me any other explanation than that you were looking at the building?

Janie: I know. I just don't know what else to say, because that's all I was doing.

Marlow: And then there are the other people who were also there with you that night, aren't there?

I need you to tell me. What on earth were you doing there with them? Mia Anderson? Laura Denning? Why were the three of you at Lymington Quay on Monday evening while your husband's offices were burning down?

# Chapter Thirty-One

**The Woods' party – three days before the fire**

Laura gripped the wine glass between her fingers as she stumbled on a patch of grass. She had spent the last two hours making small talk, loitering on the edge of conversations and accepting refills whenever someone appeared with a bottle. All the while she'd been keeping an eye on Mia, waiting for the right chance to talk to her.

Mia had been moving seamlessly from one person to another, clinking glasses, throwing her head back in laughter. Right now she was talking earnestly to Mike Lewis, leaning towards him, surely closer than Mike would like. Laura held her glass to her lips as she studied the woman in front of her, wondering what she was playing at.

'Penny for them.'

'Huh?'

'Your thoughts.' Patrick was standing beside her; she hadn't even heard him approach.

'They're nothing much,' Laura said.

'No Nate tonight?'

'No, he couldn't – we couldn't get a babysitter.'

'That's a shame. My daughter can always come over, if you ever need.'

Laura nodded and finished the last of her wine, still holding the empty glass against her lips as she turned back to Mia. It wasn't a shame in the end, as Nate had clearly been in no mood for the party and if he was here he'd only be tracking her, making sure she didn't cause a fuss.

Did she intend to? In truth, Laura had no idea what she wanted the end result to be. What she didn't want was for all the attention to be on her – for everyone to be talking about her long after the party had finished – but then she did want those same people to know exactly the type of person Mia Anderson was. And surely Harry's party, when each and every one of them was here, was the best place for Laura to unmask her.

Patrick was wittering on and Laura wasn't listening, and now all she wanted was for him to leave her alone so that she could go and get Mia. And another drink. She wanted a refill first. Shaking her empty glass, she excused herself and when she emerged from the kitchen, Mia was alone.

Laura drew a breath and took another large gulp of the Sauvignon blanc, which really was going down extremely easily, and gripping the fragile stem of the glass firmly between her fingers, she strode across the decking.

'I know you're lying.' Laura spoke to Mia's back, her words hushed so that no one nearby could hear.

'Sorry?' Mia swung around, her eyes screwed up questioningly. 'What did you say?'

'You heard me,' Laura said plainly. 'I said I know you're lying.'

'I don't want to have this conversation here.' Mia's eyes darted around them at the people standing only feet away. None of them had turned around yet, but they soon would, Laura assumed.

'*I* want to,' Laura said defiantly.

Mia pursed her lips and started walking away, down the lawn towards Harry's dimly lit summer house, presumably knowing that Laura would follow.

Laura blinked; it was hard to focus when it was so much darker down that end of the garden. When she caught up with Mia she reached out with the hand that clutched the glass and pointed it at her. 'I know you're lying,' she repeated. 'I know about you. You're not who you say you are.'

Mia bit on her bottom lip as she continued to watch Laura, but she didn't respond.

'I spoke to Tess. I should have done that a long while ago, shouldn't I?'

Mia gave a small flick of her head.

'You know why I didn't? Because I was so worried about what I would hear.'

Still Mia didn't speak.

'She told me they'd started talking to other agencies. To keep costs down. They only kept the TV campaign at Morris & Wood because they thought we had much better experience at producing ads than anyone else local, and now apparently they're planning to move to some agency near Bournemouth.

'I told her I would have done a good job for her, that I would have kept it competitive. I said if they were worried about budgets, she could have spoken to me; that she could have trusted me. But do you know what she said?' Laura paused. 'Of course you do, because you put the words right in her mouth, Mia. Tess said she didn't know that she could trust me any longer. She didn't think I had her best interests at heart, when I was having an affair with the boss.'

Laura glared at Mia, who reluctantly held her gaze.

'I mean, even if I was, which I'm not,' she screamed, 'what would it matter? How would that ever affect my work? Except you knew it mattered to her, didn't you?' she went on, pointing at Mia. 'Because Tess had confided in you that her husband had left her for his secretary. And so you *knew* that if you wanted to get your hands on my job, then that was a safe little trick to play.'

Mia glanced over Laura's shoulder. Laura didn't need to turn to sense the hush that had descended on the people nearest to them. 'People are looking,' Mia said through gritted teeth.

'Why did you lie about me?' Laura continued.

Mia shook her head and turned away.

'Tell me,' Laura yelled, lunging forward with her hand outstretched again as Mia dodged out of her way. 'Why make that up? What have I done to *you*, Mia?'

'You're making a scene,' Mia hissed. 'You've had too much to drink. This isn't the time or place to—'

'Don't you dare tell me I've had too much to drink!' Laura cried.

A sound rose from someone near to them, a gasp or a laugh, something indecipherable.

'Who the hell do you think you are? You've come into my life and stolen my job from under me, and you stand there, all high and mighty, telling me this isn't the time. It *is* the time, Mia. It's precisely the time. I want to know what I've done to you that— Don't you walk away from me!' Laura yelled as Mia turned her back and began to walk across the garden. She could feel her face tightening, the squeeze of her muscles rippling down her body. There were maybe half a dozen people standing around watching with horror or amusement, Laura couldn't tell which; all she could see was that Mia was desperately trying to get away from them as she strode towards the pool.

Laura's breaths were coming short and fast and she knew that if she followed Mia, everyone else would probably see them too, but in that moment she couldn't give a shit.

# Chapter Thirty-Two

It was almost ten p.m. when Janie caught sight of Mia and Laura standing in the middle of her lawn. A glass of wine hung loosely from Laura's hand as she jabbed a finger at Mia Anderson. Weirdly, Janie's first thought was whether it was one of her Dartington crystal glasses, because she wouldn't have been surprised if Harry had given Laura that. Her second was that Laura clearly looked as if she hadn't stopped at the one glass of wine she'd mentioned having at the start of the night, and she certainly didn't look as if she should be driving home. Did she actually plan to leave her car here? Was she going to be back in the morning to collect it?

Laura's body swayed softly, her feet shuffling as she struggled to regain her balance. At some point in the evening she had shed her shoes and was standing barefoot, her toes curling into Janie's neatly trimmed grass.

By now all the guests had stopped their conversations, distracted by the spectacle unfurling by the swimming pool. At first Janie hadn't realised the two women were arguing, but as soon as she had woven through the people who were gawping on the deck, she had a much clearer view.

Mia was standing ramrod-straight, her eyes flared wide as she stared daggers at Laura. A champagne flute was clutched by her side, and Janie imagined the hand drawing up and swiping the side of Laura's face. She rather hoped it might. Mia certainly looked like she could do so.

Laura's arms, in contrast, were flailing everywhere, and her face was bright red. She was wobbling precariously close to the pool, which Janie noticed was still uncovered, even though Harry had promised he'd cover it before the party. Talking of her husband, she had no idea where he was, and she glanced desperately around the garden in the hope Harry might come and break up the argument before it got out of hand. But there was no sign of him, so Janie wavered between leaving the scene to find him and going over herself.

She was mid-thought when Laura's hand, with the wine glass clutched within it, rose again and then suddenly, through some brute force, the woman managed to snap its stem in two.

Mia's gaze dropped to the ground beneath them as she stepped back. Janie's followed, but when she looked up

Laura appeared not even to have noticed that she might be stepping on broken glass.

Still Harry was nowhere near and, with audible gasps rising from the excited crowd behind her, Janie stormed across the lawn to the two women. She reached out to take the remainder of her precious glass from the hand of Laura, who hadn't even noticed Janie approaching.

'That *is* my Dartington,' Janie muttered as Laura pulled back in surprise. The glasses were a wedding present from her mother – the reason she had set out the cheap ones in bulk – and yet Harry must have bypassed them as he sought out this one for Laura from the cabinet. 'Give me that glass,' Janie said as she made another lunge for it, and still Laura pulled back, opening up the space between herself and Mia.

Janie felt her ankle twist beneath her. The pain shot up the outside of her right calf as she tried to rebalance on the paving stones that edged the pool, but already she feared it was too late. She felt herself tipping forward, unable to stop her fall as she plunged headlong into the swimming pool.

The air was still when she eventually resurfaced. The momentary silence was intense, before shrieks filled her ears, and in the distance a vision of Harry running across the lawn came into view. And as she pulled herself to the side of the pool, all Janie could think was that she was sure the hand that had reached out for her as she was falling hadn't actually helped as it pressed against her back.

\*

Someone had kindly brought Janie a towel from the summer house. She thought it might have been Patrick, but she couldn't be sure as the crowd of guests parted and she made her way through them.

Janie had ignored both women gasping at her, asking if she was all right as she climbed out, but she knew they weren't far behind her, and neither was her husband, who – once he had checked that she hadn't hurt anything but her pride – had jokingly called out that the show was over and told everyone to refill their glasses.

Despite the chill from the water, heat rapidly crawled over Janie's skin. *Ever the host,* she thought through gritted teeth as she approached the back door. *More worried about what everyone else thought.* Though at least by then conversations had started again and she no longer felt everyone's eyes still on her.

Janie was livid. She stripped off the beautiful kaftan and changed quickly into another dress, desperate to get back downstairs so she could find out what the hell had started the argument that had caused her to end up in the pool. When she walked into the kitchen she stopped short as she saw her husband, who had one hand gripped onto Laura's arm as the other was fishing in the bowl for his car keys.

'What are you doing?' She glanced at Harry and then at Laura, who was leaning against the door frame to the hallway, her head back, her eyes semi-closed.

'I'm taking her home,' Harry replied without looking up, as he continued to rifle through the bowl, although he did let go of Laura. Finally he picked out his keys – the *I Love Daddy* key ring swinging playfully from them.

'*Laura?*' Janie asked, stunned.

'Yes.' He jangled the keys in one hand and eventually turned to her. His face was expressionless; it was almost as if he had no idea that walking away from his own party to drive this woman home could in any way be out of order. Or maybe he didn't care.

'Why?' she asked him, her teeth clenched, her wet hair soaking through her top and onto her back.

'Because she can hardly drive, can she?' Harry said quietly, leaning in, nodding in Laura's direction. 'I take it you're okay, love?' he added, as an afterthought.

Janie shook her head in disbelief. 'Then call her a taxi,' she said slowly.

Harry parted his lips, then clamped his mouth shut, his face softening as he gave a small shrug. 'It's fine,' he said, pressing his mouth into a flat smile. 'I don't mind.'

She cocked her head. Did he actually think that was what she was worrying about? The fact he was putting himself out? 'This is your party, Harry,' she said slowly. 'You cannot leave it to drive Laura home. Call her a taxi.' Her words were drawn out as if she was talking to a child who didn't understand her.

'I've only had two bottles of beer,' he said. 'And I won't be long. No one will ever realise I'm missing.'

'I will realise,' she said.

'Seriously, Janie?' He touched her arm. 'It's fine. I promise you I won't be long.' The keys continued to jangle in his hand. She held her own arm down by her side as she fought the urge to reach up and swipe them out of his grip. She could imagine the satisfaction she would get from watching them spin across the room.

Her blood was burning through her veins. *If you go, Harry Wood … if you dare go.* She opened her mouth to tell him how furious she would be if he left this house, but already he had leaned forward, given her a swift peck on the cheek and she realised that if she really had to tell him this, then what was the point anyway?

If they had reached the stage that her own husband's priority was no longer Janie, then why stop him? Clearly it was too late.

She stepped out into the hallway as he grabbed Laura's arm again, hauled her to the front door and disappeared. Eventually the sound of his car engine burred over the beat of music.

'I agree.'

Janie swung round and saw Mia in the kitchen doorway. She let go of the clutches of her dress that she had been balling and smoothed them down her thighs. The heat on her neck was making her itch, and she resisted scratching what she knew must be patches of red crawling over her skin.

'Sorry?' Janie said.

'I agree,' Mia replied. 'He shouldn't have done that. That's what you must be thinking.'

Janie went to speak, though no words came out. She hadn't known anyone else was listening to her and Harry.

'I mean, Laura is clearly drunk, but she could have got a taxi home,' Mia went on, her eyes seemingly penetrating Janie's. 'After all, that's what I'll be doing,' she said, as if emphasising that Harry's favouritism was clear for all to see. 'I'm so sorry about what happened, by the way. I hope you're okay?'

Janie shrugged.

Mia nodded as she looked towards the front drive. 'She has him wrapped around her finger, doesn't she?'

'What?' Janie blurted out, incredulous.

'Laura? I mean, it's hardly Harry's fault.'

Janie shook her head, her gaze trailing over Mia's face, which was full of composure, yet couldn't completely hide something dark lurking behind her eyes. 'What are you saying?' she asked uncertainly.

'I'm saying that we shouldn't always blame the man. If they are led on to believe that a woman is interested in them ...' Mia paused and shrugged, holding her palms up flat.

Janie cocked her head, fury raging through her, but at the same time it was battling with a need to know what Mia was getting at. 'What are you talking about?'

'I'm sorry,' Mia pursed her lips. It looked as if she was trying for a smile, though Janie wasn't sure. Everything about the evening was surreal, and all she wanted now was for Mia to leave her alone so that she could head straight for the champagne, which until now she'd been drinking in moderate proportions.

She needed to bolster herself with alcohol, before any of it started to feel real and she had to face the likelihood that her husband was sleeping with the woman he had just driven home.

'Oh, right,' Janie said suddenly, as the idea dawned on her. 'You're pissed off with Laura. Well, whatever the hell is going on between the two of you, it has nothing to do with me or my husband.'

'There's nothing going on between me and Laura,' Mia said firmly. 'Oh, I'm so sorry. Of course I never wanted to overstep the line when you've invited me into your lovely home,' she went on, 'although I have a feeling I may already have done that. All I was trying to say, rather clumsily, was that I think it's often so easy to blame the man, and a lot of the time it's—'

'Not their fault?' Janie interrupted. 'Is that what you're saying?'

Mia smiled thinly again and this time, in Janie's eyes, she at least had the presence to look embarrassed.

'You think that if my husband is having an affair with someone from his office, then he shouldn't be held responsible?' Janie spat out with a bitter laugh.

'No, actually, I don't think that at all,' Mia replied, her expression now so deadly serious that Janie wondered if she'd caught the right end of the conversation. '*I* think men should be held responsible for every one of their actions.'

She held her gaze, and Janie stared back at her blankly. If she'd been confused moments ago, she was even more so now.

Mia's penetrating glare was beginning to unnerve her.

'And I suppose, as women, we should stand by each other, shouldn't we?' Mia went on. 'Only sometimes that doesn't happen, either. They can be the ones to blame, can't they?'

Janie's mouth hung open. 'Is this all to do with Laura?'

Mia shook her head. 'Oh no. Not at all, Janie. This was nothing to do with Laura. Anyway, thank you for a lovely evening, but I think it's probably time for me to go home, too.'

'Yes, I think it probably is,' Janie said.

Mia nodded. 'Maybe I'm just not as good as you are at putting my point across,' she said as a taxi beeped from the driveway, simultaneously sending a text to her phone. 'Better go,' she added cheerily.

'Wait!' Janie called as Mia walked out of the front door, heading for the waiting car. 'What do you mean, "not as good as I am"?' Her eyes flitted back and forth as Mia climbed into the car and pulled the door shut behind her. Her mind tried to catch up, racing through their odd conversation, attempting to patch together Mia's words, which were clearly intentional. Did she know her?

As the car pulled away, Janie retreated to the kitchen and a text pinging loudly from her phone on the counter startled her. She reached for it and on the screen flashed a photo from Ella of herself and her little sister, clad in pyjamas. The message read: *We're still up!!!*

Janie's eyes filled with tears. She wanted her girls home. She wanted these intruders out of her house.

Mia's words only served to prove that every one of the guests here tonight knew her husband was up to something behind her back. She supressed the scream rising inside her.

Their laughter was grating. The clinking of their glasses sent shivers down her spine. Precariously balanced plates were tipping crumbs onto her floor.

Her daughters weren't upstairs in their own beds because of this crowd of unwanted guests, and all she wanted to do was scream, '*Get out of my house!*'

She wanted her husband still to be here, to deal with them.

At the same time she wanted him never to walk back in their front door ever again.

She wanted, above all, for him not to have brought Miles Morgan back into their lives.

## Friday 17 May

**Interview between DC Emily Marlow and Janie Wood, following the fire on Monday 13 May**

Marlow:   Janie, did you intend to kill your husband on Monday evening?

Janie:     No. Of course I didn't.

Marlow:   Did you set fire to the offices of Morris & Wood?

Janie:     No.

Marlow:   Did you know your husband was in the building when you went there?

Janie:     Please. I didn't do it.

Marlow:   But you and Harry hadn't been getting on well, had you? And you were seen at the quay at the time of the fire ...

Janie:      I didn't … I haven't done anything wrong. I'm begging you – I just want to go and see my girls. They're on their own. They're frightened. This is ridiculous. You must know that. It wasn't me.

Marlow:   Did you know Miles Morgan was also in the office at the time of the fire?

Janie:      No. I didn't know anyone was in there. I didn't even—

Marlow:   So you're telling me you weren't aware that either Miles or your husband were in the office? Where was Harry supposed to be on Monday evening?

Janie:      I have no idea. I don't know. We weren't … we weren't talking.

Marlow:   Because of his alleged affair with Laura Denning?

Janie:      No! I don't know if he was having an affair with her or not. You *know* why we weren't talking. We've been over this already. I was annoyed with him, after the party. You can ask him about that. Things weren't *that* bad between us. Ask him yourself. He may be in hospital, but he's talking now.

Marlow:   We know he's talking now, Janie. And you can rest assured we will be speaking to your husband.

Janie:      Good. Good, because he knew everything was all right between us. Harry knows I would never have done what you're saying I've done. Please. Please – I just want to make sure my girls are okay.

Marlow:     Janie, I need to remind you that this is now a murder investigation ...

Janie:      I know that. God help me, I know that.

Marlow:     ... and that Miles Morgan is dead.

Janie:      I know.

Marlow:     Then you need to start talking to me.

Janie:      (silence)

Marlow:     You see, I can place all three of you at the quay on Monday night, and yet I can't actually figure out what any of you were really doing there. Laura Denning was the last person to leave the office that night unharmed, wasn't she? So, Janie, if you're telling me you had nothing to do with the fire, then you must at least be able to tell me what she was doing there?

Janie:      I already have. I honestly don't know.

Marlow:     Why she didn't go straight home after she left. And why, an hour and a quarter later, she was still at the quay. And *why* she didn't tell her husband that night that she knew there was a fire. You know what I'm wondering, Janie? I'm

|           |                                                                                                           |
|-----------|-----------------------------------------------------------------------------------------------------------|
|           | thinking something might have happened in that office before she left.                                     |
| Janie:    | If it did, then I don't—                                                                                   |
| Marlow:   | You don't know. Yeah, I get it. And then we have Mia Anderson, too. Whom you met for lunch a couple of weeks ago, although it wasn't her who asked you out, was it, Janie? Like you told me before. |
| Janie:    | No. I think maybe it was me.                                                                               |
| Marlow:   | Because you wanted to find out what she was doing at your husband's office?                                |
| Janie:    | No! Honestly, I promise you, that wasn't it at all. My lunch with Mia was completely genuine.              |
| Marlow:   | You didn't recognise the name: Anderson?                                                                   |
| Janie:    | No – I mean, it's not an uncommon name. No, I didn't have a clue then.                                     |
| Marlow:   | But you do now. Why don't you tell me how you knew Mia Anderson before she came to work at Morris & Wood?  |
|           | Janie? Did you not think we would find out?                                                                |

# Chapter Thirty-Three

*The Woods' party – three days before the fire*

Laura didn't think she'd had that many glasses of wine at the party, though she did know it was too many to drive home. She was twisted to her left, staring out of the passenger window so that she didn't have to look at Harry.

Perhaps she'd had a few more than she'd realised. At several points her glass had been refilled before she could stop it. Maybe it was four or five. And she hadn't eaten anything since lunch, so the wine had gone straight to her head, and now the motion of the car was making her feel sleepy and a tiny bit nauseated; and the blurry memories of the night were swishing about in her head, sharp-daggered reminders of how she'd embarrassed herself.

Laura hiccoughed and held a hand over her mouth, feeling the burn of alcohol repeating. She should never have gone to the party. She should have stayed at home with Nate and tried to make some move towards fixing the cracks in her marriage, which had spread all too quickly in the last eight weeks.

She certainly shouldn't have shouted at Mia in the middle of the back garden. Had everyone been watching? She had sensed pairs of eyes on her, but she didn't know if they'd heard. She hadn't been that loud. Or she hadn't intended to be.

Laura had told Mia that she knew she was lying. *Liar*, she had called her. She might have said it more than once. She might have even prodded her in the chest as she did so – she couldn't really remember. All she knew was that suddenly Janie Wood was by their side and the next minute she was in the pool. And Laura hadn't even tried to stop her falling.

She had been mortified when Janie climbed out, her beautiful kaftan drenched as she'd shrugged off her husband, who had tried to help. Harry had in turn pulled Laura into the house instead.

She closed her eyes and let out a soft groan. Did everyone in the company really think she and Harry were having an affair? If they did, she could only imagine what they'd be saying now.

'Are you going to be sick? Open the window, if you are,' Harry ordered.

Why had he urged her into his car? Janie had seen them. Laura knew they'd been talking about her in the kitchen, though their conversation was fuzzy. She should never have agreed, but it was a ride home and Harry was quick to open the passenger door and nudge her into the seat.

'I'm not going to be sick,' she said quietly.

She wanted to scrub out the night, go back to the start of it, do everything differently. She wanted to cry, God damn it. That's what she wanted. She wanted to cry racking great sobs, like a baby. Tears began to fall down her cheeks and she gulped more back.

'It's all right,' Harry murmured from beside her. 'We all screw up from time to time.'

'I've just ruined your party,' she said. 'You don't have to be so kind to me.'

'Stop it, Laura.'

She winced at the touch of his hand on her leg.

'Don't beat yourself up about it,' he said. His hand lingered on her thigh as he gently squeezed it.

'I should send flowers to Janie.' She moved her leg away from him forcefully, though now she was crushed against the passenger door. 'To apologise.'

'That's not necessary.'

'Everyone will be talking about me,' Laura cried.

'Yeah. But only for a day or two. It will all blow over.'

She was relieved to see that he had turned the car into her road and was parking up on the right, outside her house. Harry turned off the engine.

Laura glanced up at the curtained windows and prayed that Nate didn't look out and see her. Opening the door quickly, she swung her legs out. 'Thank you for bringing me home – you didn't have to,' she said hurriedly.

'Laura,' Harry called, too loudly, as he gripped onto her arm, making her stomach twist into knots. She wanted to hiss at him to keep his voice down, but at the same time she couldn't be rude to the one person who was being kind to her.

'You two will work it out,' he said. 'Don't worry about it.'

'What?' she said, turning back to him and screwing up her nose. When had she told him about Nate? *What* had she told him?

'Just talk to Mia on Monday and you can sort out whatever it was.'

'Oh, Mia. Right.'

'Who did you think I meant?' he asked. 'Is everything all right at home?' He nodded towards her house.

'Everything's totally fine. And I'm not sorry about what I said to Mia.' She pulled out of his reach as she sidled off the seat. 'I meant it. She's lying about what she's doing at the company. She's out for my job for a reason.' Even Laura could hear the whine in her drunken voice.

She thought she saw Harry shake his head, but it was such a slight movement she couldn't be sure. 'I know you don't believe me, but I'm right,' she said and slammed the door, stumbling on the pavement as she turned towards the house and up the path, to where Nate stood in the open doorway, arms folded tightly across his chest.

'Oh God.' She swallowed down the trepidation that clung to her throat in a ball, but couldn't budge it. Slowly

Laura tried walking in a straight line up the path and hoped Nate couldn't tell how drunk she was. The outside light caught him in its beam, and she watched as his stare left her and travelled to Harry, still sitting in his goddamn car. Not going anywhere.

Laura looked over her shoulder. 'Just piss off,' she muttered at her boss under her breath.

'He brought you home?' Nate said. 'From his own party?' His eyes flicked over her again. 'What kind of state have you got yourself into, Laura, that your boss needs to drive you home?'

'I'm sorry – I …'

'How much have you had to drink? You drove the bloody car there. Why bother, if you knew you were going to get yourself into this mess?'

'I'm not a mess,' she objected, straightening up. 'I just drank too much to drive home.'

Nate pulled her into the kitchen and filled a glass of water, which he thrust into her hand. She didn't want it – she thought she was definitely going to be sick now – but she held onto it anyway, making every effort to steady herself.

He shook his head as he regarded her, and she felt the bitterness dripping off him. She wanted to roll into bed and fall into a sleep that would, at least temporarily, take away the memories of this awful evening, but she also knew how much bigger they would be when they came searing back in the morning.

'Why did he bring you home?'

'I don't know,' she shrugged. 'I was going to get a taxi, but Harry was there, insisting that he'd drive and ...'

'And he just left his own party?'

'I know. I didn't want him to, Nate; he was offering, and I wanted to get out of there and—'

'Christ!' He shook his head and laughed bitterly, running his hands through his hair. 'This is unbelievable. *You* are unbelievable.'

'Nothing's going on,' Laura cried. 'If that's what you're thinking, you couldn't be more wrong. I wouldn't. I would never ...'

'Go to bed,' he spat. 'I'll be in the spare room. Your son isn't well, by the way; he's been sick,' Nate added as he started to walk out of the kitchen. 'If you care.'

'Oh my God, of course I care,' she said, running after him. 'Nate!' She grabbed his arm, tugging at the sleeve of his T-shirt, slopping water over the carpet as she did so. 'Don't say that,' she sobbed. 'Don't ever say that to me – you know I care about Bobby. What's wrong with him?'

He stood and watched her for a moment before eventually shaking his arm free, but when he spoke his voice was gentler. 'He's just been sick,' he said. 'But he doesn't have a temperature. I'm sure it's nothing to worry about. Get some sleep.'

'You should have called me,' she said, her voice quiet.

'Why?' He paused and looked at her. 'What would you have done?'

Laura opened her mouth to protest, even though she knew there was no point. Nate was right. What could she have done for Bobby that his father wasn't already doing much better? She clutched hold of the bottom of the banister as she steadied herself. 'I'm his mum,' she said weakly as if that were all she had left to offer. But even that no longer felt like it was enough as Nate stared at her coldly and then turned to walk up the stairs.

***Friday 17 May***

**Interview between DC Emily Marlow and Janie Wood, following the fire on Monday 13 May**

Janie:      When can I go?

Marlow:   You've been arrested for murder. The best thing you can do right now is start talking.

Janie:      I don't know what else I can tell you. Please. My girls – I need to be with them.

Marlow:   Your daughters are both being cared for. Like I say, if you're thinking of them, you need to begin telling me the whole story.

Janie:      I *have* told you.

Marlow:   I don't think you have, Janie. (sighs) Right now, all I can think is that if Miles Morgan hadn't appeared back in your life on Monday, none of us would be sitting here. (pauses) Tell me what happened when you saw him in your husband's office. You went out for lunch with him, is that right?

Janie: (shakes head) No. I didn't go. I stupidly found myself walking to the quay with Miles and Harry, but stopped before I actually had lunch. I made my excuses, said I really needed to take Ella's sports bag to school – which was what I'd gone there for in the first place.

Marlow: How did you feel, seeing him again after such a long time?

Janie: I felt so ... wrong-footed again. It was every-thing – his gait, the way he strode across the office like he owned it. I wanted to run at him and punch him in the face. I didn't, though, of course. It's been five years. If I really wanted to hurt him, I would have done it back then. I wouldn't have burned my husband's office to the ground.

Marlow: You were angry with your husband for work-ing with Miles Morgan, though.

Janie: Yes. Of course I was. Because Harry knew. He knew what Miles had done to Sophie. He knew how guilty I had felt afterwards, and yet he was still *mates* with him. He prioritised someone who was good for business over me and my best friend.

Marlow: Tell me what happened with Sophie.

Janie:      (pauses)

Marlow:     Janie?

Janie:      We've been best friends since we were eleven. We sat next to each other on the first day of secondary school and became inseparable. After A levels our lives took very different paths, though. I studied law, Sophie started working for an estate agent. She gave that up when she began waitressing in high-end clubs because the money was better. I mean, our lives were unrecognisable to each other at one point. I was married to a successful advertising exec, two daughters in private education, and Sophie was living in a flat with a part-time boyfriend. But she was still my closest friend.

Marlow:     And one of these high-end clubs was where your husband and Miles Morgan used to drink?

Janie:      (nods) Harry wasn't there the night Sophie called me, though, when she was crying down the phone for me to pick her up. I left him at home with the girls when I went to get her. I had to meet her on a street corner. I won't ever forget the sight of her: mascara streaked down her cheeks, this bright-blue wrap tightly pulled around her as people staggered past. I knew. As soon as I saw her, I knew what had happened.

| | |
|---|---|
| Marlow: | Go on. |
| Janie: | She wouldn't tell me at first; begged me to take her home. It was two days before she finally admitted she had been raped in the club while she was working. Sophie was embarrassed. But then I understood that. I saw enough women in court to recognise the shame, even when everyone told them they had nothing to feel that way about. What I hated was that Sophie was used to men ogling her, and she thought she wasn't worthy of being treated with respect. Just because they were sitting on these plush velvet chairs in their Savile Row suits, buying drinks that cost more than her hourly wages, they thought they could treat her like they had bought her, too. |
| | But that night he had taken it too far and followed her into the toilets, pressing himself against her, telling her he knew it was what she wanted. |
| Marlow: | Miles Morgan? |
| Janie: | Yes. I asked her if anyone else had seen, and Sophie laughed and said of course not. She was so bitter. I wanted to take it all away from her. |
| Marlow: | What did you do? |
| Janie: | I told her we would do something about it. We'd go to the police there and then – it wasn't |

too late. We wouldn't let him get away with it. Do you know what she said to me? She said, 'You haven't been listening to me, Janie. Of course he will get away with it. You, of all people, know that all he needs is to find himself an expensive female defence barrister and he'll walk free.'

Marlow: You think your friend was aiming that at you?

Janie: Of course she was. (laughs) Of course she was, because I had just won my last case. *His* case. The one everyone was talking about, and so I'd done exactly what Sophie was worried about. She told me she wouldn't put herself through a trial to risk everything and not be believed. She wouldn't allow her life to be destroyed, like other women's lives were …

Marlow: Let me get you a tissue.

Janie: (nods)

Marlow: Janie, did you see either your husband or Miles Morgan again on Monday, after you left them at lunchtime?

Janie: No.

Marlow: What about Laura Denning? Did she tell you she had seen him in the office, when you met her at the quay on Monday night?

Janie: No.

Marlow: So what did Laura tell you she was doing there?

Janie:      Honestly? She didn't tell me a thing.

Marlow:   (pauses) Janie, what I still can't get my head round is what you *aren't* telling me? You appear to be covering up something. Or for someone. And I really don't know why – when things are very serious for you – you're still doing that.

# Chapter Thirty-Four

**Monday 13 May – the day of the fire**

On Monday night Janie didn't go to yoga. She'd called Anna to babysit the girls, on the pretence that she was going, but the truth was that she had known the minute she started the car that she couldn't face two hours of relaxation. Not when her head was spinning at a hundred miles an hour. What she needed was just to get away. Out of the house, because she couldn't spend another minute there, pretending everything was okay in front of her girls, when it was anything but. She had been doing that all weekend, and now she was tired. So tired, but at the same time so bloody wired.

The previous Friday night Harry had come home half an hour later, by which time Janie was in bed. The party was still going on downstairs, laughter and music weaving their way up the stairs and the outside walls and in through her window, like creeping ivy. She'd tossed around the idea of staying with the guests, drinking her way through it, but in the end Janie realised she didn't have it in her to pretend any longer. Escaping to her bedroom was suddenly the only option. She couldn't care less what any of them thought. Harry could deal with that, once he'd figured out she was no longer downstairs. She wondered how long that would take him.

At some point he came up to the bedroom and poked his head in. 'You're in here,' he stated.

She feigned sleep as he padded further in, patting the duvet that covered her as if he really had no idea anything was wrong. 'Are you all right?' he asked.

Janie shuffled, pretending to stir, then looked up at him. 'I have a headache,' she lied, dropping her head back onto the pillow. She no longer cared to argue, despite the fact that she was burning inside. She considered there was no point in listening to him telling her he'd done the right thing by taking Laura home, because possibly, in his self-centred brain, he believed he had.

She had no desire to tell her husband he was a thoughtless bastard, because she didn't want to give him the satisfaction of thinking she cared enough to argue.

So she drifted through the weekend as if she were part of a still-perfect family. Her first priority was, of course, the girls, and so it was easier to paper over the deep ridges that for years had been cracking her marriage apart than it was to address them. She was actually pretty adept at it now.

Harry, in his wisdom, had seen fit to disregard the fact that he had fled his own party to drive Laura home. His infatuation with the woman sickened her. Janie had always known that, given a nod of encouragement, Harry would jump into bed with Laura, so in a way did it really matter if he had or not?

They played Scrabble with their daughters. Janie drove the girls to their respective events – ballet and drama classes on Saturday afternoon, two different parties on Sunday.

By Monday morning she was relieved to hear the click of the front door as Harry left for work. By the time she dropped the girls at school, her day ahead was supposed to give her the time to get her thoughts together – a clear space to think. But then, just as she was walking out of the school gate, Ella came running up behind her, yelling that she had forgotten her sports bag.

'It wasn't at home,' Janie said.

'No, it's in the boot of Daddy's car. Mummy, you have to get it,' her daughter pleaded. 'I need it for cricket this afternoon.'

'I've got a hair appointment,' she argued. 'I can't do it.'

'You have to. Please. I don't need it until two o'clock – you can get it by then.'

'Fine,' Janie sighed. 'I'll see what I can do.'

'Thanks, Mummy.' Her daughter beamed and ran off, leaving Janie wishing she'd told Ella it was her responsibility to remember, because now it meant she would have to see Harry.

It was late morning when she walked out of the hairdresser's and called her husband, leaving him a message to call her back. But by the time she reached the Morris & Wood offices she wasn't surprised that she hadn't heard from him.

Harry must have picked up the message only moments before she stepped out of the lift, because he fled across the floor as soon as he saw her. 'I'll go and get the bag,' he said, grabbing her arm and steering her around as he jabbed a finger on a button to call back the lift, which was already descending to the ground floor.

If he wanted to get her away quickly, he was too late because the voice boomed out, calling her name. 'Janie Wood! I was wondering if I'd get to see you.'

The hairs on her arms pricked on end at the sound of the deep, gravelly voice that, when she'd first heard it, had sounded so soothing, so calm and assured. So sexy, she had even thought. So honest.

Beside her, Harry's face was creased into a frown, and his hands fidgeted nervously at his sides.

'Miles,' Janie said. She was surprised by how calm she sounded. 'I didn't know you were in Lymington.'

'You didn't?' he grinned, his head cocked, his brow furrowed as he nudged Harry. 'You didn't tell your wife, when you knew I'd want to see her? Well, no matter – you're here just in time. I'm taking you both out to lunch.'

'I can't,' she said quickly. 'I've got to go, I'm afraid.'

'Nonsense. Janie Wood, I haven't seen you in five years. I insist,' he said. And before she had time to refuse, the lift door was pinging open and Miles was gesturing her into it, with Harry sloping behind.

As Janie would later tell the detective, she had managed to escape lunch with Miles, eventually begging that she really had to get back to the school. She glanced in Harry's direction as she left the two men, and her husband could barely return her gaze. That she had once loved Harry, she thought as she walked away, was a notion that now seemed impossible. Now his pathetic cowardliness made her feel nothing more than sick, with such a burning anger.

She didn't see Harry again that day. Her mind was barely on the children as she picked them up from school, swept them home and fed them beans on toast, because it didn't require headspace.

That night the fire was already ravaging the offices when she saw the other women. It was just past eight p.m. when she noticed Mia first, and then Laura Denning. It had all happened so quickly after that.

# Chapter Thirty-Five

At after seven-thirty p.m. on Monday night Laura stepped onto the pavement outside the offices of Morris & Wood. Rage was coursing through her, racing through her veins, feeding her body until the tips of her fingers were tingling and didn't feel as if they were a part of her any more.

Moments before, she had wanted nothing more than to be back at home with the two people who mattered to her, but now she was out of the office she found she didn't go straight to her car. Instead she stood on the pavement, her jaw so tense that her whole face throbbed with pain as her mind ticked. Back and forth like a metronome went her thoughts. Miles Morgan. Harry Wood. Despite everything that had happened in the offices over the last two months, it was what had happened in the last half an hour that was tipping her over the edge.

\*

Two days previously, on Saturday morning, Laura had woken to Bobby crying. A piercing yell of an alarm call that shot through Laura's sore head like a blade. She'd grabbed a cold flannel on her way to her son's room and pressed it against her throbbing temple, ignoring the urge to stop and be sick, telling herself that really was the last time she would ever drink so much, as wine regurgitated in her mouth.

Pulling her son out of his cot, Laura pressed his warm body against her chest, taking him to the rocking chair in the corner of his room, where she sat down and placed him on her lap, smiling through tears that had sprung from nowhere as he lifted chubby fingers and pressed them against her mouth. 'Hello, my gorgeous boy,' she said. 'I love you so much. Do you know that? I love you more than anything in the entire world.'

It was the truth. The love she felt for Bobby had expanded her heart in ways she could never have imagined possible before giving birth to him. He was her everything. So why was she so intent on wanting more? Why did it feel like she didn't have enough?

These thoughts had continued to plague her over the next two days.

What did it make Laura, when she admitted that the thought of giving up everything she had worked for, her entire adult life, left her empty? That to be all those things for Bobby, she would have to say goodbye to the career she'd always loved?

It made her think that maybe she still wasn't loving him enough.

While she sat motionless in the rocking chair, with the fear that any slight movement would make her feel worse, Nate poked his head round Bobby's bedroom door and asked if she wanted a coffee.

'No. I'm fine, thanks,' she told him. The thought of coffee made her want to retch and she knew that, to get through the day, she would need to pretend. Keep pretending she was coping, when she was anything but.

Laura peered at Nate over the top of Bobby's head. He rubbed one hand through his ruffled hair, as he scratched his leg with the other. His mouth was set rigid, and his eyes didn't mask the anger he must feel towards her.

She'd wanted to cry at him that she knew he was right. Nothing was working as it was supposed to. She had screwed up. She was still continuing to do so, and maybe she needed to accept that she couldn't have it all – or at least she couldn't without falling apart. Without eventually losing something. Or everything.

Laura knew all this, and yet she still hadn't said anything to Nate. *Why is that?* she thought on Monday night as she stood outside the offices, wrapping her arms across her chest. Maybe it was because she hadn't wanted to hear him say that it was time to cut back her hours. To say goodbye to her career as she knew it. Maybe it was because she still wasn't ready to do anything about it, when she still hadn't found out the truth about Mia Anderson.

How far away any thoughts of Mia seemed now there were other thoughts tangling themselves around those, strangling them so that they could no longer breathe. Right now, it was Harry who filled her head; Harry who was filling Laura with such anger.

Earlier that morning, Laura had woken late. Her stomach still felt queasy, even though it was two days after the party, and so Laura had texted Harry and told him she would be working from home.

But by midday she couldn't concentrate, when her unfinished conversation with Mia was spread like sparse pieces of a jigsaw in her brain. Laura had needed to put an end to it, so she had forced herself into work, head down to avoid the inevitable patronising glances as she searched out Mia, who was nowhere to be seen.

As she dumped her bag at her desk, she caught sight of Miles in Harry's office and briefly wondered what he was doing there, when she didn't realise they had a meeting. Harry's face was impassive, but Laura could tell he was tense by the way he stood, one hand leaning rigidly on the desk in front of him. But she hadn't hung around for long. Mia had been her main concern and so she'd continued to search the floor, peering into meeting rooms, stopping to ask Henrietta James if she had seen her.

By all accounts no one had, and neither did it seem Mia had called in. How much all the staff must have hoped that she and Mia would have some kind of showdown in the office, Laura had thought as she checked her watch. It was strange that Mia hadn't turned up. There hadn't been a morning yet when she hadn't been there before Laura. For some weird reason, it was oddly unsettling.

By late afternoon Laura had given up hope of talking to Mia and instead had waited for Harry and Miles to return. They had been out of the office since lunchtime and she didn't want to leave before they'd caught up. She didn't want to admit she had been put out they hadn't invited her to lunch, but she had been.

At six p.m. Laura texted Nate and lied that she was meeting Coopers and would therefore be back a little later than usual. She didn't entirely know why she hadn't told him the truth. Maybe it was because she didn't want to say she was waiting for Harry.

At seven p.m. Harry and Miles eventually appeared. A faint smell of beer wafted towards her as the pair wandered into Harry's office – Harry telling Laura he was sorry they were so late, and did she want to come in and see them now? His face was set even harder than it had been that morning.

Laura nodded. Bobby would be in bed by now, she thought as she gathered her notepad and a pen. Nate would already be annoyed with her.

She followed the men into Harry's office. If Harry had been drinking, he hid it well. He riffled through papers on his desk, his hands moving deftly as he found what he was looking for. He didn't look up when she walked in.

Miles, however, was leaning casually against the door frame, arms folded across his broad chest. His words had an edge to them when he spoke, tumbling out of his mouth in a slur. 'Laura, good to see you again.'

She didn't feel comfortable with the way he was looking at her, his deep-brown eyes holding such a steady gaze as he raised his eyebrows.

Laura gave him a thin smile and turned back to Harry. She wanted him to start talking so she could get out of there and go home.

Suddenly Harry's mobile rang. 'Odd,' he muttered as he pulled it towards him across the desk. 'Sorry, guys, I'm going to have to take this call. Anna's a friend – she's looking after the girls.'

He picked up the phone. 'Excuse me a minute,' he added as Miles gestured a hand as if to give his approval. 'Hi, Anna, everything okay?' Harry asked as he left the office, shutting the door behind him.

'Take a seat, Laura,' Miles said, indicating one of the armchairs as if it were his office and, despite this, Laura found herself feeling for the armchair and backing into it. Miles beamed at her as he perched on the edge of Harry's desk in front of her, crossing his legs at the ankles and folding his hands in his lap. She could feel the edge of his trousers brushing against her bare calf and automatically shifted out of the way.

'I can see why Harry has you working for him,' he said. His eyebrows were pinched into a point again, his mouth skewed. The closer he leaned, the more she could smell the beer on his breath and she wished he wouldn't sit so near.

'Sorry?'

'I mean, I'm sure you'd do a good job and all, but ...' He drifted off, grinning.

Laura fidgeted nervously in the chair. 'I'm not following.' She glanced out to where she could see Harry wandering back and forth as he continued to talk into the phone, slightly too far out of reach for comfort.

'Oh, come on,' Miles said, edging closer again, until she could feel him against her leg once more. 'You and Harry.'

'There's absolutely nothing going on between me and Harry,' Laura replied, contorting herself so that she was out of Miles's reach again. How she could have thought him attractive, she now had no idea, as he raised his eyes in a smug grin that clearly told her he wasn't having any of it.

'Really?' Miles grinned. 'You may want to tell him that.' He cocked his head in Harry's direction.

'Harry knows there's nothing between us,' she hissed firmly, making a move to stand.

'Oho – he also told me you could be a feisty one,' Miles laughed, leaning back on the desk, splaying his hands on either side of him. 'That's fine by me too. I like girls who can handle themselves.'

Laura opened her mouth to speak, but to her confusion found tears pricking her eyes, which in turn made her throat tighten. Unexpectedly she thought of Bobby, and suddenly she felt ashamed. To be sitting here, being spoken to like that by a man she didn't know. She shouldn't be here at all. She should be at home with her husband and her son.

She got up, pushing the chair back. She wanted to tell Miles he was a vile man but if she did that, she would lose the account in a shot. And maybe, for now, it was better for her to slip out of the office quickly.

'What are you still doing here so late then, Laura? The only one left in the office, waiting for Harry. I see it with you girls all the time. You make out you don't want anything but, if you ask me, it's all an act.'

'Oh my God,' she muttered. She couldn't hold her tongue much longer. Her heart thumped. She had to be careful. Her entire reputation could be damaged by a man like Miles Morgan, especially if Harry didn't believe her. 'I was waiting to catch up with you,' she said.

'Well, here I am.' He opened his arms wide.

Laura shook her head, her hands trembling at her sides as she made her way for the door and reached for its handle, hoping she would make it out, that he didn't lunge for her, though Miles was still sitting on Harry's desk and didn't appear to be going anywhere.

'Harry's probably waiting for you somewhere,' he said, peering out of the window, making a meal of looking for Harry, who was now nowhere to be seen. 'Better let your husband know you might be a bit late back.' He grinned as he winked.

'Don't you dare!' Laura suddenly spat. 'Don't you dare insinuate that I would cheat on my husband. Men like you make me sick,' she blurted. To think of everything she had sacrificed for Miles, for Harry, and this was how she was being repaid. Having to listen to crap, to be made to feel like she was nothing.

Miles pursed his lips, straightening himself atop Harry's desk. The smile rapidly slid off his face.

'I won't be doing any more work for you,' she said calmly. Already Laura wondered if she'd later regret her words, but what other option was there? She wouldn't spend another minute in the man's company.

'You're right there,' Miles sang out as she opened the door. 'There is no job, Laura.'

She paused and turned, cocking her head questioningly as Miles's eyes flared in triumph.

'The job's already gone to someone else. As Harry knows,' he added, raising his brows, goading her.

'I don't understand ...' she said, despite her need to get out of the office.

'The work you've been doing for our tender—' Miles broke off, blowing out his cheeks and throwing up his hands to indicate it had just evaporated. 'Harry's not broken the news to you yet, then? No. I know he hasn't. He told me that this afternoon. He said he was worried how you'd react; that you were getting your knickers in a twist over some other girl in the office ...'

'What?' Laura gasped, sickened by his choice of words.

'Maybe I'm paraphrasing, but you get the gist.'

'I don't believe you,' she said defiantly. 'Harry wouldn't let me carry on working on something that wasn't going anywhere. That's ridiculous.'

'I agree,' Miles chuckled. 'He thought he could twist my arm – still try to play for something that wasn't up for grabs. I guess it was too much of an attractive proposition,' he broke off, smiling.

Laura turned her back on him, her heart pounding as she released the door handle and paced to her desk, picking up her bag. She scoured the office for signs of her boss, who was no longer anywhere to be seen. Miles was following her out of the office, the scent of his aftershave preceding him. Grabbing her bag from the floor, she walked as quickly as she could to the lifts, stabbing her finger against the button until one arrived.

Harry had lied to her. He had told her he was looking out for her, but he wasn't. He had made her put her heart and soul, and long hours, into a job he already knew probably wasn't coming to anything. And for what? Because he was too greedy to let it go – only he couldn't be honest with her.

Ever since she'd come back two months ago, Harry hadn't been there for her – or at least not in any way she wanted. He hadn't accepted that he should never have given her job to the replacement. He'd been looking out for himself while he pressured her into doing work for that man.

As Laura stepped out into the cool air she stared up at the building through unblinking eyes, and rage coursed through her. Maybe it was a build-up of everything that had happened over the last two months – the guilt from her own sacrifices, the fear of what came next – but in that moment there was only one person Laura blamed. Harry Wood. And she knew she should have gone straight home to the two people she loved, but right then she couldn't move.

# Chapter Thirty-Six

Mia cupped her hands around the glass as she leaned over the bar. She had watched women do this in films and always wondered how it would feel. To be distraught enough to go to a bar on her own and ask for a neat gin. To knock it back and slide the glass to the barman, and ask for another and then another until her mind was blank. Until every memory that had got her to this point has been wiped out, if only temporarily.

It was seven-thirty p.m. on Monday night and still light outside, but the bar she had chosen was particularly dingy and empty. And instead of her memories being erased, they were floating around her head like they were perfectly content where they were, knowing they'd be able to taunt her for the rest of her life.

She took another swig of gin and felt the burn as it slid down her throat, wondering how many more it would take to obliterate her mind. Erase what had happened that day.

It had been late morning by the time Mia arrived at the office. Jess had needed her, but Mia didn't bother telling anyone she was going to be late; she didn't answer to anyone but Harry, and after his party she hadn't particularly cared about that, either. Harry had driven Laura home, leaving her to call a taxi. She had said too much to Janie. The night couldn't have gone much worse.

Mia was beginning to think she wouldn't be able to hold the job down for much longer. Someone would be onto her soon – find out who she really was. Probably that would be Laura, who was like a dog with a bone. Mia actually admired that in her. Under different circumstances, they might have been friends.

Lately nothing had been going the way she planned, though, and as she rode the lift to the third floor she hadn't imagined it could get much worse. But it did, the moment she stepped out.

As soon as she saw him she had doubled over, gripping a nearby empty desk to steady herself. If only she had been prepared to see him again one day, she might have been able to handle it. But she hadn't. And so Mia had run back out of the office.

Now she tapped the side of her empty glass and allowed the barman to refill it. He was eyeing her carefully, no doubt wondering if he thought she might be a problem. He had every right to be suspicious, but whatever problems she might cause that night, they weren't going to be in his bar.

Mia hadn't gone far when she'd fled the offices that morning. She had only run to the quay. She wasn't sure how long she had been there, pacing up and down the cobbled path, knowing she needed to go back to work, but not willing to return while *he* was in the office.

She had been biding her time when she saw them all together, walking down the street – Harry, Janie and Miles – and shot into a doorway before any of them saw her.

Mia had felt sick as she cowered by the bright-pink door, an entrance to someone's flat. Her fingers trembled as they gripped the edge of the frame to steady herself, praying they didn't walk past and see her.

Would Miles recognise her, if they did? Mia doubted it. It had been a few years and she had changed since then – cut her hair much shorter, lost weight – but she wasn't taking any chances. She waited as they passed, thankfully unaware that she was lurking nearby; and only after they'd gone did she step out into the street.

Her legs felt like liquid as she watched them retreat. At her sides, her hands clenched into fists.

Miles might not recognise her, but he would Jess. Despite the fact that she was now in a wheelchair and a shell of the woman she once was, he'd surely have known her face.

Mia's teeth clenched, her jaw aching where she held it so tightly. There they all were. Together again. Miles Morgan and his awesome defence barrister, who had got him off, even though she knew exactly what that man had done to Mia's sister. The woman who had defamed Jess, crushing every ounce of confidence her sister once had, until Jess told herself she wasn't good enough to work any more. Until she gradually became less and less of a living person; until one day she drank far too much and drove her car too fast on treacherous roads, because she couldn't live with what Miles had done to her, and what he had got away with.

Her sister had lost everything. In turn, so had Mia and their mum. And meanwhile there was Janie Wood walking down the road with that vile man, and she still had everything. Money. Family. Pride in that godawful office, which shone out like a blinding beacon across their beautiful town, like they owned every one of those who lived there.

Janie was the one who really needed to pay.

'You all right?' the barman asked, his gaze drifting to her empty glass.

'No,' she laughed. 'Not at all.'

But he didn't want to know about her worries. And his gin hadn't helped; it had only served to make Mia even more certain that whatever she thought she might be able to do working inside Morris & Wood, it wasn't working. It was revenge she was after, and she needed to up her game.

# Chapter Thirty-Seven

By eight-thirty p.m. the fire was devouring the building. Janie stumbled down the path and towards the edge of the quay. Blue lights flashed their warning as the reflection of the flames licked the surface of the water as if they were dancing on it, while above them plumes of grey smoke billowed in the air.

There was a crowd of people gathered, spilling out of The Star pub and other nearby restaurants, all of them captivated and bewildered by the sight across the river.

Mia was running down the cobbled path, her face a ghostly shade of white, her mouth hanging open as she clutched a hand to the stitch in her side. She stopped abruptly when she saw the crowd.

Laura was hanging on the outskirts of it, immobile, her hands over her mouth, pressed into her face, slightly distorting her view, as if this somehow took away the depth of the horror unfurling in front of her.

It seemed to happen so quickly after that. A hand on Laura's shoulder, making her spin round and nearly lose her balance. Mia clutching onto her, her face blank. Janie inching closer to the two women, step by tentative step.

When each of them noticed the other two, they glanced from one to the other, searching for an explanation as to what *they* were doing here. Each of them mirrored the others' panic in their own faces, and it seemed clear by now that at least one of them must know what had caused the fire.

Mia spoke first. 'Who did this?' She waved a hand in the air towards the offices, as if her question needed explanation. 'Was it you?' Her gaze darted to Janie and her chin jutted defiantly, her finger now pointing in Janie's direction. All of it could, of course, have been an act. No one was sure.

Janie shook her head, her mouth agape as Mia's finger swung now towards Laura.

'No,' Laura shouted, a little too aggressively, for she said it again, this time softer. 'No.'

The truth was they all looked frightened. Something had happened to each one of them that day, and in the days leading up to it, and even if they hadn't lit the match that burned down Harry's office, the thought had been present in all of them that maybe they could have done. Maybe they had wanted to.

'It was you.' A shaking finger prodded at Janie again. 'You.' Mia laughed. 'You did it, didn't you? You bloody well burned down that office. Oh, I can't believe you did it. Because of her?' Now the same finger was thrust in Laura's direction. 'Because you thought they were having an affair? They weren't, you know; she never would have, for what it's worth. Any fool can see that.'

Janie's eyes flicked towards Laura, scanning the woman's face for signs of either denial or confirmation. She no longer knew if she cared what the answer was; it would just be nice to know the truth.

Laura shook her head, glaring at Mia. Everything Mia had told Tess Wills had been part of her act. 'You think I was having an affair with Harry?' she said to Janie.

'Weren't you?' Janie replied, her voice toneless.

'No!' she cried. 'Absolutely not. I love my husband, my family—' Laura broke off. Nate had no idea where she was. He thought she was in a meeting with Coopers, but he must have expected her home by now. She hated that she had been lying to the one person she loved most. 'I would never have an affair with your husband,' she said to Janie.

For some reason Janie thought she believed the woman.

'So what are you still doing here?' Mia turned on Laura now. Somehow she had assumed the role of detective, tossing questions at the two women, deflecting attention from herself – her body soaked with alcohol, her head hazy.

'I was still in the office and then—' Laura broke off and turned to look over the river, to where flames lapped at the sky, the smoke swelling in great puffs of dark grey. Even in that moment she knew not to tell them more than that. Even then she realised she might have been the last person to have seen them, and that if she told the other women her story, she would have a motive.

Janie was shouting. 'Was he in there?' she asked Laura. 'When you were in the office, was he in there with you?'

'Harry?' Laura breathed and turned to Janie. Of course she had to admit he was. They would all know soon enough. 'He was, but that was ... it was over an hour ago.'

Janie looked across sharply at the building. What was Harry doing in there? He wasn't supposed to be. Harry and Miles had been drinking – he had texted her that earlier. That was why he hadn't been home in time, and why she'd called Anna and asked if she could sit with the girls. She'd been angry with Harry that he could have let her down for that man, and yet ...

'Could he still be in there?' Janie asked eventually, as Mia was also asking, 'Was he alone?'

'No – he was with ...' Laura's voice trailed off. How she didn't want to be the one with the answers, for suddenly it felt like the more she knew, the more guilty she must seem.

'Miles Morgan,' Mia finished for her. It wasn't a question.

'Yes,' Laura confirmed as she glanced at her watch. 'But like I said, that was over an hour ago. I left an hour ago,' she repeated, drumming this into them.

For a moment the three women were silent. It was Janie who eventually spoke, as she took a step closer to the edge of the quay. 'They were still in there,' she said, and neither Laura nor Mia knew if this was a question or a statement, so they didn't reply.

# Chapter Thirty-Eight

*Friday 17 May – four days after the fire*

Janie was given a short break. She curled her fingers around her cup of water, pressing them in and then releasing them, listening to the satisfying pop of the polystyrene cup as she did so.

Her daughters were at the forefront of her mind. She wondered what they were doing while their mother had been arrested and their father was in hospital, barely conscious as he drifted in and out of sleep. She wondered what Anna had told her girls, how much they knew about what was happening to her, and whether they thought she was actually capable of burning down their father's office.

The relief of knowing Harry was still alive had been palpable but even that had faded as the days had passed and their futures continued to hang precariously in front of her.

Janie had told DC Marlow her story. At least up to a point. 'We met by coincidence,' she said. 'I saw Mia first, then noticed her grabbing someone's shoulder. When she spun round, I saw it was Laura.'

The detective had wanted to know what the three of them were all doing there, if they hadn't arranged to meet, which Janie continued to insist they most certainly hadn't. This part had been the truth.

She told the detective that Laura had been in the office late – working, Janie assumed. By now it was believed that Laura had been the last person to see Harry and Miles Morgan before the fire. The last person to see Miles alive.

But there was a gap, Marlow kept insisting, between Laura leaving the office and the point when Janie saw her. 'What was she still doing at the quay? Why hadn't she gone home?'

The fact was that Janie had never found out why. She couldn't even remember if the question had been asked. Possibly Mia had asked at some point, as she'd been the one demanding answers, but what Janie was certain of was that Laura hadn't told them. 'I don't know,' she kept replying, though she knew how dubious it sounded.

And Mia? Yes, Janie knew Mia's explanation for being on the quayside for that had come out. It had momentarily distracted her attention from the fact that her husband may still have been in the building.

By now the detective had been able to build up a very clear connection between Mia and Janie. But what Emily Marlow had been demanding to know was why the three women weren't telling her everything. Because she knew they weren't, and yet it made no sense that one of them, at least, wasn't speaking.


What Janie hadn't reckoned on, following that night, was that four days later she'd be sitting in an interview room yet again, only this time under the threat of prison. Marlow was right when she told Janie she couldn't let it go that far; of course her girls were her priority and she would not jeopardise anything for them.

Marlow was offering her a way out – Janie was sure of it. All she needed to do was tell the truth. *'Start talking, for God's sake.'* The detective had said it enough times.

Janie drew in her breath, pressing harder into the cup, crushing it between her fingers.

She would not be charged with the murder of Miles Morgan; she would not give up her life for that man, but at the same time how could she tell the truth?

She looked up at the sound of the door opening. Emily Marlow walked in, her face pinched, her eyebrows knitted tightly together. She didn't take her gaze away from Janie as she strode purposefully to her chair. Even when she slid onto it, she didn't once look away.

Janie shuffled on the plastic seat. She wanted to turn away from Marlow's gaze, but it was quickly apparent that something had happened. Emily Marlow was clearly walking back into the room with knowledge she didn't have earlier, and Janie had a feeling the detective might know exactly what had happened on Monday night.

# Chapter Thirty-Nine

*Monday 13 May – the night of the fire*

Sirens continued to fill the air as the fire blazed behind them. 'How do you know Miles Morgan?' Laura was asking. 'You said his name when you asked if Harry was in there alone, like you expected him to be there.'

Mia's eyes danced as she turned to Janie. She had a gut full of gin, and the headiness of the night was overwhelming. 'Six years ago he raped my sister,' she said, her eyes fixed on the woman she had come for. She waited for a reaction.

Janie blinked, momentarily confused, before closing her eyes and shaking her head with the sinking realisation. 'Oh God, no.'

'You set him free. You stood in the courtroom,' Mia went on, taking a step closer to Janie, 'and told the jury – and everyone sitting in it – that my sister was "asking for it", because she was the type of girl to sleep with someone different every week. Only you knew that wasn't really the case, didn't you?' She pressed forward until her face was only inches from Janie's. 'You *knew* what he had done.'

'I was doing my job.' Janie's words were uttered in a whisper. Tears rolled down her face. When they reached her lips, she dragged them away with her thumb. She searched Mia for signs of recognition, because the woman must have been in the courtroom, watching it all play out. There was a glimmer of something in the high cheekbones, the deep-brown eyes, but her hair was longer then. That was it, Janie thought: she'd had highlighted hair that came down to her waist; and after the case Janie hadn't given her a thought, because she was only a face in the crowd.

'Did you believe him?' Mia was asking. 'Did you actually believe his lies or did you know, deep down, what my sister had gone through?'

'I was defending him,' Janie went on. 'I had to—'

'Do your job; yes, I know, but did you *believe* him?'

Janie had, at first. When Miles had told her about the woman in his office who worked two levels below him, speaking of her with respect; how it had started with flirty comments in the pub one night. And Miles had told Janie that maybe he knew it was wrong at the time, and perhaps his fault; that he should have stopped it.

He'd told her Jess Anderson was needy, often asking for approval of the work she was doing. Miles had buried his head in his hands and said, 'I think maybe I should have known to stay away from her. God, I wish I had, now.'

He'd discovered that Jess had slept with another man in the office only the weekend before, following a night out at work. Just like the one they were having, the night Jess 'suddenly decided Miles had raped her'.

He'd said that maybe Jess liked men with power, and had gone on to say, 'That sounds really awful when I say it out loud. Not that I *am* powerful.' He had laughed and looked sheepish, but Janie had sensed that he most definitely was.

As a barrister, what she could have said to Mia right then was that Jess's guilt or innocence in the proceedings was immaterial. Miles had the right to be defended to the best of her ability, and that was what she had done.

But she couldn't say that. Because she felt sick with herself – as she had when later on Sophie told her why she could never put herself through a trial.

And so instead Janie said now, 'I believed him at first. But no, by the time it got to court ...' She trailed off, shaking her head.

'Yet you stood in court and told everyone how my sister didn't think twice about having a one-night stand, because it had happened the week before. As if that was enough to justify what that man did to her. You said that now Jess's job was being threatened, because Miles was her boss's boss, so she was crying rape to protect herself. You skipped over the fact that the other man was Jess's own age, and someone she'd been having a casual relationship with, because that didn't suit your case, did it?

'Did you forget about my sister after that?' Mia went on. 'As soon as you *won*, did you walk away, pleased with yourself for doing a good job?'

'No,' Janie said firmly, though she didn't expect Mia to believe her.

'You have everything,' Mia was yelling. 'Everything. You want for nothing.'

'I never forgot about your sister,' Janie pleaded. 'I didn't.' But what could she tell Mia? That the guilt of getting Miles acquitted had draped over her like a black cloud, though it wasn't because of what had happened to Jess. It was because of what subsequently happened to Sophie.

The day after Sophie had admitted what had happened Janie had broken down in front of her husband, hysterical that if it hadn't been for her, Sophie wouldn't have gone through what she did.

'You must have known what he was like,' Janie had said to Harry, though she wasn't sure what she expected from him – maybe to be told that he had no idea; or that he was trying to protect her job by not telling her the truth. All she had *wanted* was for Harry to support her, but what he had said was, 'So must you.' In that moment she'd seen a flash in his eyes of something ugly, something that looked like: *Don't put this on me.*

Janie wanted to tell Mia she *didn't* have everything, because from that moment on, something had broken between her and her husband – something they had never been able to get back.

But she also knew it would make no difference to Mia.

'My sister's life is ruined because of you.' Mia was prodding her finger at Janie's chest. 'She lost her job, she lost her confidence. She doesn't leave the house,' she cried, her voice rising. 'She has no friends any more – she does nothing. She's in a bloody *wheelchair* because she couldn't face living any more.'

'What?' Laura murmured, stepping forward. 'What happened?'

'She drove herself into a tree. Only it didn't go according to plan. She survived.'

'I'm so sorry,' Laura said. 'I can't even imagine how hard that is.' She paused. 'But it's Miles you should be blaming. He's the one who did this, not Janie.'

'No. She's right,' Janie said. 'If I hadn't defended him, Miles should have been locked up. He should have got what he deserved so he wasn't able to assault anyone else.'

Laura hesitated. The scene in Harry's office only hours ago hit her again and she wondered if somehow Janie knew. But she couldn't have known, could she? There was no way. And much as Laura had a sudden urge to share with these two women what Miles had just been like with her, she knew that if she did, she would effectively be giving them a reason for her to have lit the fire.

In the end she simply said, 'But if you didn't defend him, someone else would have.'

*Friday 17 May*

**Interview between DC Emily Marlow and Mia Anderson, following the fire on Monday 13 May**

| | |
|---|---|
| Marlow: | This interview is taking place at 1100 hours on Friday 17 May. Mia Anderson, please can you tell me what has brought you into the station this morning? |
| Mia: | I want to tell you what happened. |
| Marlow: | Okay. Go ahead. |
| Mia: | (pauses) |
| Marlow: | Mia, you're doing the right thing. Coming here today, it's taking a lot of guts – I can see that. |
| Mia: | (nods) What's she saying? |
| Marlow: | What's who saying? |
| Mia: | Janie Wood. I know she's in here still. She hasn't told you what happened? |

Marlow:    Janie is currently talking to us.

Mia:       I'm going to tell you the truth, but before I do,
           I need to know something.

Marlow:    Yes?

Mia:       My mum and my sister – will they ... I need to
           know they'll be okay.

Marlow:    How do you mean? Mia, how do you mean:
           you need to know they'll be okay?

Mia:       It's just that I'm everything they've got. I know
           what's going to happen to me and ... I've
           always been there for both of them, after my
           sister's accident, and I don't even know how
           they'll cope. I don't know that they will. I just
           don't know. God, this is a mess. This is such a
           mess.

Marlow:    Mia, listen to me. The more you tell me, the
           more I can help you. Do you understand that?

Mia:       (nods)

Marlow:    So can you tell me what happened Monday
           night?

Mia:       (pauses) I set fire to the offices of Morris &
           Wood.

Marlow:    And did you know anyone was in the build-
           ing when you did it?

Mia:       No.

Marlow:    You didn't realise Harry Wood was in his office?

Mia:       No, I didn't have a clue.

Marlow:    Or that Miles Morgan was with him?

Mia:       No. I didn't know anyone was in there.

Marlow:    Mia, can you tell me why you did it?

Mia:       I wanted to make them all pay.

Marlow:    Including Janie Wood?

Mia:       Yes, including her.

Marlow:    Only now you're confessing because …

Mia:       Now I'm confessing because … You know, I'm not actually a bad person. I never wanted anything that bad to happen to anyone – not like this.

           Now I'm confessing because I just want it to end.

# Chapter Forty

*Monday 13 May – the night of the fire*

Mia wanted Janie to know she was to blame. That if it hadn't been for her defending Miles Morgan, her sister's life would not have been ruined. Jess would still be the same exuberant, clever, confident woman she had been before. She would still be able to run and walk out of the house whenever she damn well pleased.

It surprised her when Janie said Mia was right. That she was agreeing it was her fault.

'But if you didn't defend him, someone else would have,' Laura was saying. But Mia didn't want to think about that, because all these years her anger had been directed at Janie and she couldn't begin to imagine that it was in any way misplaced.

'Listen,' Laura said, 'whatever happened, the offices are on fire and, as far as we know' – she paused and glanced over her shoulder – 'there could have been someone in there.'

Mia felt a shiver running through her body at the thought. Her fear was mirrored in the other women's eyes.

'Did you do this?' one of them was asking her. She thought it was Janie, but her head was spinning and the air was thinning around her.

'It wasn't me,' Laura said. 'I can promise you that.'

'Well, it wasn't me,' Janie cried. 'So was it you?' She was shouting now. 'Mia, did you do this?'

'No,' she breathed out – sharp, rapid breaths. Almost in slow motion, she reached out a hand to stop herself from falling, grabbing onto Laura's arm to steady herself. Beneath her, her legs buckled, unable to hold her.

'Mia, what is it?' one of them asked. And then, 'Who … Mia, who is that? Mia, is that your sister? What the hell—' The words cut off sharply, as realisation dawned on each one of them.

'Oh God, Jess,' Mia muttered under her breath, hoping the women didn't hear her. Thoughts of their conversation earlier that day flashed through her head, the state Jess had been in when she demanded Mia leave her alone. 'What have you done?'

Mia, of course, knew exactly what her sister must have done, but she also knew it was entirely her fault. That afternoon when Mia had seen Miles, Harry and Janie walking down the cobbled path towards the quay, she hadn't gone straight to the bar. Instead she drove home, anger creeping through her veins. She had wanted to get out of town, away from the view of the office – somewhere she wouldn't have a chance of seeing that man again.

Her heart thumped hard as she crashed through the door, tossing her handbag across the kitchen. Mia stood by the table and silently slammed her fists onto it, fighting every urge to scream. Now what the hell did she do?

None of it had gone how she'd hoped. All the plans she'd been carefully laying were being thrown up in the air. First, Sarah Clifton leaving; then Laura and her doggedness; and now – how would she ever be able to walk back into the office again, knowing that Harry was working with Miles Morgan? Wondering each morning if she'd come face-to-face with him again.

'What's happened?'

Jess's voice had startled Mia. She'd turned to find her sister in the doorway.

'And don't tell me nothing, because I can see something has.'

'I saw him,' Mia blurted out. 'I saw him. Today.'

Jess opened her mouth as if to ask who her sister meant, but she didn't say a word.

'That man. That—' Mia stopped briefly. 'Miles Morgan. He was in the office today.'

Jess's mouth widened, every muscle in her face tightening. 'What?' she said in disbelief.

'He was there. With Harry Wood, discussing business – laughing with his bloody wife like they had no cares in the world.'

If Mia was thinking straight, she might have known she shouldn't be sharing this story with Jess, but her stomach was churning so tightly, and her pulse was racing so wildly, that her head wasn't straight in the slightest.

'His wife?'

'Janie Wood,' Mia clarified. 'That's her married name. You know her as Janie Birch.'

She watched her sister's face dropping in horror. 'You knew this?' she said. 'You knew who she was and yet—' Jess broke off, shaking her head. 'You still went to work there?'

'That's *why* I worked for them,' Mia cried. 'That's why I took the job. I wanted to get back at her, Jess. I wanted Janie to lose everything like you did—'

'No!' Jess yelled. 'Stop! Don't you dare. Don't you try to justify it.'

'Jess?' Mia gasped, taking a step towards her. 'I'm doing this for you.'

'For me?' she cried. 'No, you're not. No, you bloody well aren't. If you were doing it for me, you would *never* have gone to work for them. You would have told me who she was. You wouldn't have treated me like a child. How dare you!' she shouted. 'How *dare* you bring them back into our lives – his name into this house.' Her sister's hands were shaking as she clutched hard to her chair.

'Jess, I'm sorry, but you're not listening to me. I was going to get back at her. I was going to—'

'Stop!' Jess screamed, bringing her hands to her head, digging into her scalp with her fingers. '*You're* not listening to *me*. I never wanted to know what the man was doing, where he was. I never wanted to know any of it, because if I did, then I had no clue what I would do about it. I wanted to *forget*, Mia.'

'None of us are forgetting ...'

'And now we can't, can we? You've made sure of that. Get out,' she cried. 'Please, just go, Mia. Get out. Leave me alone.'

'I'm not leaving you in this state.'

'Yes, you are,' she hissed. 'For once, do what I'm asking of you.'

As the fire raged behind her, Mia walked slowly across the quay towards her sister. Jess's hands were balled in her lap, her body shivering. Mia crouched down beside her and took one of Jess's hands in her own. 'Don't say a word,' she whispered to her sister as the other two women approached. 'Don't say anything.'

Jess glanced over Mia's shoulder, her face expressionless even when she saw Janie. 'What have I done?' she said eventually. 'Mia, what the hell have I done?'

'Shush,' Mia told her, squeezing her hand tighter. 'Stop now,' she urged, but she already knew it was too late.

'I have to go to the police.' A single tear rolled down Jess's cheek. Mia lifted the hand that still gripped her sister's and wiped the tear away, her heart thumping.

'No, you don't.' A voice behind them made both sisters turn. 'None of us do.' It was Janie. 'You can't,' she hesitated. 'You tell them what you've done and you'll be locked up for certain, and you don't deserve that. Not one bit, and yet there'll be nothing you can do about it.'

For a moment everyone stared silently at Janie.

'I, for one, haven't seen you here tonight,' she went on.

Mia blinked, and Janie turned to Laura, who took a breath before eventually adding, 'Nor me.'

Mia held a hand over her mouth as she looked from one to the other and then back at her sister. Her thoughts whirled, but there was something she was becoming sure about. She was not going to let anything happen to her sister. And if these two women were prepared to help, then maybe they stood a small chance of getting away with it.

But if they didn't, if something happened to make one of them break – which she knew was the more likely scenario – then Mia herself would take the blame. Because if it wasn't for her, this would never have happened.

'There was someone in there,' Jess said. 'I saw them being pulled out.'

Janie suddenly turned to the building, fishing in her back pocket for her mobile. 'Shit!' she murmured, tapping her phone, pressing it to her ear. 'Was it Harry? Was it my husband?'

Mia couldn't deny that her own concerns weren't what might have happened to Harry, but that she might not be able to rely on Janie to keep quiet, if Harry Wood was dead.

'It might not be him,' Laura was calling after Janie, as she began running off. And all Mia could do was pray it wasn't; pray that Harry wasn't dead, because Janie and Laura were the only chance she and Jess had.

# Chapter Forty-One

*Three months after the fire*

Laura hung up her mobile and placed it on her bedside table. Beside her, Bobby lay flat on his back, arms splayed on either side of his head. The curtains were drawn and the window open, but still the summer sun flooded the bedroom with warmth and light. It had taken him a while to drift off for his afternoon nap, but Laura hadn't minded. She had waited until he fell asleep before she called Patrick back, knowing that even if she didn't get hold of him until later, it wouldn't matter.

In the last couple of months her bedroom had become a makeshift office. Two plastic crates were stacked by the wardrobe, filled with folders and client information. It wasn't ideal: she would have to decide what to do long-term, if she was going to carry on working. She had wondered about building an office at the end of the garden or changing the spare room, but that would mean selling the double bed and squeezing in a sofa bed, and right now Laura wasn't happy to commit even to that. Just in case one day soon she decided she didn't want to work at all.

Beside her, Bobby flung an arm out to one side, his tiny balled fist knocking her thigh. Laura slid down the bed, propping herself on her elbow so that she could curl gently around her son. She watched his eyelids flutter, wondering what he could be dreaming about, what was filling his head. Gradually her mind drifted to the conversation she'd just had with Patrick. They needed to make a decision about recruiting, and sooner rather than later.

It was funny how the two of them had managed to pull together in the aftermath of the fire. She hadn't imagined it possible when Patrick first called her, a week after the fire, and said he needed Laura to help him keep the business running, 'Just until Harry is up to coming back,' he had said, as if he somehow knew she might not want to be there much longer.

She wasn't even sure that Harry did want to come back to work at all. Laura had eventually visited him in the hospital a week after the fire, when Mia had confessed and the questioning had subsided. By then he was more alert and accepting of visitors and though they all knew how lucky he'd been to get out alive, Laura could tell how much Harry was suffering, not only from the pain but from the sight of his burns.

She hadn't stayed long and over the weeks their contact had mainly been over the phone. Both she and Patrick felt that Harry was keeping them at arm's length and in many ways Laura was grateful for that. It was hard to face him when she was still hiding the truth about the night.

Laura's first reaction was to tell Patrick she wasn't interested in working for Morris & Wood any longer. She'd wanted to walk away and forget everything about it that had led her to this point.

Nate had found her a few days later, sitting in a darkened living room. 'Talk to me,' he said as he sat down beside her. He had been tentatively stepping around her since the fire, as if he didn't know whether he trusted her or not. It wasn't until four days later, when Mia walked into the police station and gave her confession, that Laura saw a glimmer of relief on his face.

Laura had longed for Nate to believe her when she told him there was no way she had anything to do it. She'd told him she'd walked out the building at seven-thirty p.m. and had not looked back. That much was true. She could never be capable of burning down an office; she was angry, but never that mad.

But she also understood that she couldn't expect her husband to believe her, when she hadn't told the whole truth from the start; when she'd later had to admit that she had been there – on the quay – and had known about the fire before the call the following morning, but had been too scared to admit it, when there was a chance she could get away with pretending she hadn't known.

Nate had been furious with her for lying, but eventually accepted her fear.

She *was* afraid. She'd been afraid for her part, her silence, and even now the events of the night still ate away at her. How she'd found out that Mia had been at Morris & Wood for Janie all along; and that taking her job had never been anything to do with Laura. Laura had simply been in the wrong place at the wrong time – her job had come up, and Mia was right there waiting for it.

Laura had been in the wrong place on Monday night too. How she wished she'd never been at the quay; that she hadn't learned the truth about the fire, and hadn't been willing to keep quiet.

The day Nate asked her to talk to him, he was no longer worried that she'd done it, but he was still worried about her.

'What do you want me to say?' she had replied.

'I want you to say whatever it is that's going on in your head. I want you to stop shutting me out,' he had told her.

'I'm not doing that.' Laura had shaken her head, folding her knees up and wrapping her arms around them. Gently Nate had prised her hands apart and taken hold of them in his own. 'I have been talking to you,' she said. 'You know how I feel.'

'I know you think the answer is to close yourself off from the job you once loved.'

Laura had laughed, softly. 'I can't believe you're saying that, after everything. Now you're suggesting I carry on? I'd have thought you'd be pleased I don't want to.'

'I'm not pleased about anything, if you're not happy,' he said. 'You know I never wanted you to give up your career.'

'No,' she said quietly. 'I do know that.'

'I think you need to listen to what Patrick is suggesting and, between us, we'll see if we can make it work. You can work from home – do your hours around caring for Bobby – and then I can start working part-time again.'

Laura had squeezed her husband's hands in response, tears pricking the corners of her eyes. She didn't deserve Nate. Not one bit; and yet here he was, springing back into the loyal husband he had always been.

In the days afterwards, they had talked about many things. Laura listened to how he really felt about the hours she'd been working, and in return she told Nate how she'd been feeling about Mia, and what it had done to her confidence.

But Mia was out of the picture now, as Nate pointed out to her. Mia was currently in the remand wing of prison, awaiting trial. And Harry wasn't fit to run his company at the moment. At the time of Patrick's first call to Laura, Harry was still in hospital; and maybe, Nate had said to her, maybe she *could* make a freelance career work.

Laura had mulled over the idea for a few days, before finally picking up the phone to Patrick and listening properly to what he was proposing. There were going to be some tough months ahead, in the wake of the fire – Mia's upcoming trial, decisions to be made as to what was going to happen to Morris & Wood.

Patrick had admitted he needed Laura, in a moment of surprising honesty, and her heart had beat a little faster at the thought, as she let him tell her how he couldn't make it work without her. 'I've talked it through with Harry, and he's happy,' he had said. 'In fact he wants you there. I think you should do it for him.' Although those were the words that could have swung Laura the other way.

*Harry.* She hadn't been able to sift through her feelings for the man she had trusted as her boss. Laura had always looked up to him, had never imagined he wasn't anything but on her side, and yet he had let her down. But then the guilt of what had happened to Harry would creep in, until some days it overwhelmed her.

She told herself she wasn't taking up Patrick's offer for Harry; she was doing it for herself. Laura didn't really know which was true. Instead she focused on how she could make it work. And now, three months down the line, she realised she had.

She and Patrick had kept on a majority of their clients as they worked remotely, keeping in touch with each other as regularly as necessary. In the last few weeks Patrick had even rented office space, though he hadn't pushed her when Laura told him she wasn't ready to join him, and that she wanted to keep working from home so she could be with her son.

Laura knew things might change soon, and when they did she would have to tackle how best to adapt to them, but for now the situation was working. And if she was honest, the last three months had in some ways been a blessing. They had given her the chance to see that she could be a mum and have a career, and she could be good at both.

Nate tapped lightly on the bedroom door as he pushed it open. 'I didn't know if you were still on a call,' he said, sliding onto the bed beside her and Bobby, resting a hand on her leg. 'All going okay?'

'Yes,' she said. 'Yeah, I think it is.' She smiled at her husband and reached for his hand, squeezing it in her own. 'Thank you,' she murmured.

'What for?'

'For everything. For still being here.'

Nate laughed as he lay down alongside her and wrapped an arm across her chest. 'Where the hell else would I be?'

She closed her eyes, enjoying the comfort of her husband and son next to her, though every time she was lulled into this security, her heart would jolt at the thought of the trial looming closer. Of Mia. Of the fact that they had all lied.

As far as Nate was concerned, there were still patches of her story missing; and every day since that night, Laura told herself she should come clean, but each night she promised to do it the next, and then the next, until she was caught in a vicious trap that she no longer knew how to escape from.

Once the trial was over, she told herself now, she would tell her husband the truth about Mia and her sister and what really happened. And she would pray that when the time came, he continued to understand.

# Chapter Forty-Two

Janie placed a cup of tea on the dining table in front of her husband and pulled out a chair to join him. She curled her fingers around her own cup as her gaze wandered out to the garden to some far-distant spot, beyond where the girls were playing on the trampoline. She had promised them both they would go out for the day, and although the August rain had subsided, as yet they hadn't made it out of the house. There were still another three weeks of the summer holidays, yet somehow the days had passed them by. She regretted that they hadn't made enough of them.

Of course it couldn't be helped, when Harry was still recuperating, but she couldn't stop herself thinking selfishly that it would be nice to get a week away, as they had planned, before Ella started secondary school.

She turned towards her daughter, whose long limbs flew into the air as she landed on her back and bounced straight back up onto her feet.

'What are you reading?' she murmured to Harry, lips pressed against her cup as she took a small sip of the too-hot tea.

'Just an email. From Patrick.' He closed his phone, snapping the case shut and pushing it across the table.

'Everything all right?'

Harry nodded. 'They seem to be doing a good job.'

'Which is what you want,' she prompted.

'Yeah. Yeah, it is.'

She knew Harry struggled with what was happening to his business. They'd needed to discuss it often enough over the last couple of months. Harry's lawyers were all over it, but there was a mountain of paperwork, decisions and conversations that sometimes got too much for him to handle on his own, when he was only two months out of hospital.

On top of that, Janie had listened patiently as Harry dissected his feelings about working, oscillating between one extreme and the other. On the one hand, he would tell her, he had no desire to go back – not when the place had nearly killed him. 'Maybe this is a chance for me to do something completely different,' he would say. 'We can use the money to do whatever we want. We could go travelling.' In these moments Harry would be in a brighter mood as he focused on the positives of the situation that had befallen them.

'We can't go travelling,' she had told him more than once. 'Ella's at senior school now.'

'Yeah, we can – of course we can,' Harry would insist. 'We've got nothing stopping us. Nothing keeping us in Lymington, if I sell the business.'

They last had this conversation a week ago. Harry didn't want to go back to work at this point, although Janie knew his opinion would change again soon, and they would start the circle again. And when they did, Harry would be unsettled, feeling worthless, as if there was no point to his life.

'You wouldn't understand, Janie,' he had said to her. 'I was running that company for most of my working life, and now look at me.' He had gestured at his face – scarred, still raw from the burns.

Janie had wanted to tell him that of course she understood, but she had bitten her tongue. What did he think she had been through over the last five years? She had been completing this same circle since the moment they decided to leave London.

But Harry clearly didn't realise this, and maybe that was partly her fault, because she had never told him. Now they had drifted so far out of reach of one another that she considered there was no longer any point mentioning it.

Instead Janie had continued to do what she always did and carried on, paddling furiously beneath the surface, but above it pretending everything was all right. She was mainly doing this for the girls, because it had been hard for them, with their dad hitting rock-bottom in the early weeks after the fire, refusing to leave the house. Janie had plastered on a cheery smile and continued to tell them this was a perfectly understandable and temporary reaction, and all the while she pushed her own feelings to one side. They could be addressed later down the line.

But she had come to a point, after that last conversation, when she needed to speak to someone. And eventually she had picked up the phone and called Sophie. 'I was going to leave him,' she admitted in a burst. 'Only now I can't.'

Sophie had listened as Janie talked, and when she finished Janie said, 'I'll never forgive myself, you know.'

'For what?' Sophie had asked.

'If it wasn't for me, you would have taken Miles to court. He would never have got away with what he did to you.'

There was a beat before Sophie said, 'No. I'm not sure that I would have.'

'What do you mean?'

'I don't know that I would have put myself through that, it had nothing to do with you. Not really. If I'm honest I told myself at the time that the best way for me to deal with what he did was to try to forget it ever happened.'

Janie was silent for a moment. Then, stunned, she asked, 'And did you?'

'No,' Sophie said. 'But it's finished now. He's dead,' she said bluntly. 'And going back to you and Harry, you don't ever have to feel guilty about what decision you make. You just have to make the right one for you.'

Only it wasn't that simple. Because what was right for Janie might not be right for the girls. And anyway, despite all that, how could she? 'What would everyone say?' she had cried down the phone to her friend.

Of course Sophie told her what Janie would tell any of her own friends – that it didn't matter what anyone said; her true friends would be there for her, no matter what. But the platitudes didn't help.

And so Janie carried on watching Harry scurry around in circles, listening to him debate what he was going to do.

The funny thing was, she realised, as they sat in the kitchen that morning and the girls continued to play on the trampoline in the sun, he hadn't once asked her what it was she wanted.

In fact, since Ella was born, she couldn't actually remember a time when it had been about her. It had always been about Harry.

Finally she turned to her husband and said, 'We need to talk.'

His gaze flicked up from the phone, which he'd dragged back to him.

'I don't think I've been totally honest with you,' she said. Her hands shook against the cup that was still poised at her mouth, and eventually she put it down on the table and held it there.

'Okay,' he said cautiously.

Janie opened her mouth, still not entirely sure what she was going to say. Because until that moment she hadn't known that she was going to bring up again the details of Sophie's rape at the hands of Miles Morgan.

To his credit, her husband listened. And as the girls continued to play outside for another hour, Janie managed to tell her husband exactly what had been going on in her life for the past five years, from the moment she'd told him about Sophie to the point when she knew she was being followed.

When she finally finished, she picked up her cup and drank the cold tea while waiting for him to speak. She didn't miss the tears that had appeared in the corners of his eyes, or the hand that she no longer recognised as his wipe them away with the tip of his thumb. He no longer wore his wedding band. He had been tearful then too, when he'd told her he couldn't, a week after the fire, though at the time Janie had stared coldly at him, thinking that was surely the least of their problems.

'Why are you only telling me all this now?' Harry said.

She wondered what was going through his mind as he asked her. If she'd told him when it first happened, they might not be sitting here now, in their current situation. If she had told him, he might never have brought Miles back into their lives. The fire might never have been started.

Is that what Harry thought? That this was her fault? He wasn't accusing her, but she couldn't get the thought out of her head, because Miles's actions had been the catalyst for the fire. Of that she was certain.

'I don't know why,' she replied eventually. 'I was angry with you. I think I blamed your attitude, because I didn't want to carry on blaming myself for what happened to Sophie.'

'I thought you wanted to leave your job. I thought you weren't happy,' he went on. 'I *thought*,' he said, 'that I was doing the right thing for you by moving down to Lymington, because you didn't want to work any more after ...'

Janie didn't answer.

'Why weren't you honest with me?' Harry asked.

'I don't know,' she said, in a much quieter voice this time. 'I just didn't talk to you, and then it kind of snowballed.'

Harry sank his head into his hands. 'You never told me you were being followed,' he said. 'I mean, why wouldn't you even tell me that? It affects the girls too.' When he looked up at her, his eyes shone with fear. Everything could have been so much worse.

'We know who it was now,' she said. 'And I believe Mia when she says she never intended to hurt me or the girls.'

Harry gave a short laugh as he shook his head, dropping his hands to the table with a thud. 'That's ridiculous; you clearly can't believe a word that woman says,' he replied, his scarred face contorting with anger.

'No, you're right,' Janie said quickly, to defuse the situation before it blew up. 'You're right – I don't.'

Although the truth was that she did actually believe Mia. Even though Mia wanted to avenge her sister, Janie knew she would never have hurt her or the girls because she had seen it in Mia's eyes when they spoke, on one of Janie's visits to prison.

But of course she could never tell Harry about them, either. And at some point Janie also knew she would have to stop visiting Mia, but not yet. Not just yet. For now, it was something she still needed to do.

'So what do you want to do?' Harry asked. His expression had changed again, no longer angry, but now more worried.

'I want to go back to work,' she said. 'I've been thinking for some time that I want to help women – encourage them to speak out about harassment in the workplace.' It felt such a great contrast to her previous job, but in many ways so similar. 'I want to show Ella and Lottie it's important to stand up for themselves,' Janie went on. She wanted to show them that this was far more important than defending the men who took away their rights.

Harry nodded slowly. 'Okay,' he replied. 'I get that.'

'I don't want to work full-time, because of the girls ...'

'I understand.'

Janie nodded too.

'But what do you want—' He broke off, his eyes on her. 'What about us? Are you ever going to get back what you think you've lost?'

Janie turned away and watched Lottie clambering down the steps of the trampoline. Behind her Ella stood, clutching a netball, shouting something at her sister that Janie couldn't hear. All of a sudden the ball left her hands and landed with a thump on the top of Lottie's head.

Janie winced as she waited for tears from her youngest, which – to her surprise – didn't come.

'Janie.' Harry reached over and took hold of her hand, and by instinct she pulled it away. For a moment they were both silent as they looked at the table, their hands only inches apart, though it felt like an interminable gap between them.

It was easier when they weren't talking so honestly, Janie thought. When there were no questions from Harry that she had to answer, when she could drift through the days, pretending.

'I don't know,' she said.

Harry held a hand over his mouth, rubbing his lips with his fingertips. His eyes searched hers. 'Do you want to try?' he asked eventually.

'I don't know,' she said again, more quietly, with a small flick of her head.

Beside her, Harry stilled. The air between them was deathly silent. Janie closed her eyes. She knew it was going to be a long stretch ahead. If she left him now, how would he cope? Would he lay that on her? Would he beg her to stay, because he wouldn't be able to do this without her? In many ways she could imagine her husband doing just that, and yet Harry eventually said, 'I love you, Janie. I want you to be happy, and if that's not with me ...' His words broke and she felt the sorrow balling tightly in her throat as her mind flooded with too many thoughts to bear. 'I think we need to be honest with each other.'

Janie nodded. She would be honest with him. Not about everything, maybe. Not about the fact that she was seeing Mia, and that she'd been giving her family money, to help with Jess. But she would finally be honest about what she wanted.

# Chapter Forty-Three

Mia glanced up as the visitors rolled in. She had begun to recognise most of them now and always had to watch every one of them enter the room, before her mum finally appeared at the end of the line.

She looked older than ever today. Her frail body was even more stooped than usual and her face was pale, deep eye sockets shadowed with dark circles, but then Mia supposed she looked no better herself. Her hair was growing out, shapeless strands touching her shoulders now, the roots showing, and her nails were bitten low and ragged.

'How are you, love?' her mum said as she sat down.

'I'm good,' Mia told her, though they both knew this was a lie. 'How are you?'

Her mother looked at her and Mia saw a flash of something in her eyes, though she couldn't identify it at first. 'Keeping going. The traffic wasn't as bad today – took less than two hours,' she said, as if this was in some ways a bonus.

'I don't like you doing so much driving.'

'Nonsense,' her mum tutted. 'I'm getting used to it, anyway.'

'How's Jess?' Mia asked, hopefully.

'She still wants to come and see you.'

Mia turned away, studying the other visitors intently.

'She doesn't understand why you won't let her,' her mum persisted, the words spoken a little more sharply, enough to make Mia glance back. 'I don't understand it, either. You two, you were always so close. So close and now—' She broke off, leaving the unfinished sentence hanging. 'Do you blame Jess for your being in here?' her mum asked, not for the first time. 'You can tell me the truth, love. I would understand.'

All her mother had tried to be was understanding, and it was breaking Mia's heart.

'Because you would never have been seeking revenge in the first place, would you?' she went on. 'It would never have got as far as it did.'

'Do *you* blame Jess?' Mia's words came out more abruptly than she'd intended. She hadn't even meant them to, but she'd wanted to shut the conversation down.

'Mia!' Her mum pulled back, holding a hand over her mouth.

Mia wanted to reach across and hug her, tell her she didn't mean it, yet she stayed stubbornly rooted to the seat, her gaze drifting away and across the room. 'That's not the reason I don't want to see her,' she said eventually.

'Then please, love, tell me what I can say to her.'

Mia gave a small flick of her head and her mum sat back, breathing out deeply.

'You think Jess can't handle it?' she asked. 'Is that it? You think she won't be able to deal with seeing you like this. Well, she will. After all, I can,' her mum said, her voice cracking as she laid a hand over her heart.

'She's only just started going out again,' Mia said quietly.

'That's what this is? You're scared it will put her off?' Her mum leaned forward again, grappling for something to grab onto that would make her understand Mia's obstinate refusal to see her sister. 'It's not going to do that. She's doing so well, this wouldn't ...' Her sentence fizzled out, as if she wasn't sure she believed it.

Mia straightened herself and splayed her hands on the table between them. 'Tell me what you've been up to this week.'

Her mum pursed her lips and took a moment, as if she was trying to recall what they'd been doing. In reality Mia knew she was wondering how much to say.

'Go on. Please,' Mia urged, because she *did* want to know.

'Well, last week we took a picnic to the beach. We went all the way to Sandbanks – over on that ferry you both used to love when you were kids.' For a moment she was caught in the memory and her eyes sparkled as she spoke of it.

Mia nodded encouragement.

'Jess loved it there, but then it started raining, so we came back and went to the cinema. Oh, and then Thursday she got us tickets to the theatre. Can you believe that? They had one of those London shows come to the Mayflower. Jess spotted it online; she said it was one she'd wanted to see for ages.'

Mia smiled. 'That's brilliant.'

But the light drained from her mum's eyes as she said, 'It doesn't feel right.'

'Yes, it does. You should be thrilled Jess wants to do all this.'

'How can I be thrilled? How can I be happy about any of it, when you're here? I don't seem to be able to live my life without one of my daughters in a prison, do I?' As soon as the words were out of her mouth, her mum's face dropped. 'Oh dear God, I shouldn't have said that. I'm sorry, love, I'm so sorry. '

'It's fine,' Mia brushed a hand through the air.

'No. It isn't fine at all. Why on earth do you want to hear all these things we've been up to, when you can't – you can't even ...'

'I *do* want to hear them. I love knowing what you and Jess are doing. I want to know she's beginning to live her life again.'

*Don't you think that's why I'm in here?* she thought, though she didn't say it.

'So you need to make sure she carries on,' Mia urged her. 'Show her how much there is to live for. This is no more than Jess deserves, you know that. She deserves a bloody life at last.' Mia's eyes welled with tears as her mum closed her own.

'What's the point of it all?' she said, so quietly.

'What do you mean, Mum?'

'I've gained one daughter and lost another, so what's the bloody point?'

'Mum, you can't talk like that.'

'This is what I don't get.' She shook her head, opening her eyes and searching Mia's. 'I don't get it at all. How you can talk about your sister with all this love, but then refuse to see her?'

Mia flattened her mouth and dipped her head. She didn't want to go into this again.

'Are you still letting those other women visit?'

Mia shook her head. 'I only saw Laura twice.'

Laura had visited near the beginning, and Mia had been grateful for the chance to talk about what had happened that night. To tell her again how indebted she was for Laura's silence during those first few days of questioning.

She'd also thought Laura had come because she'd wanted to hear Mia explain again how she'd never been out to get her. There was something so fragile about the woman, whom Mia had always been led to believe was so strong.

After two visits it was clear they had little left to talk about.

'And what about Janie Wood?' her mum asked.

'I've seen her a few times,' she admitted. 'The barrister she put me in touch with is amazing. Are you still okay – you know, you're still getting the payments?' Mia asked.

Her mum nodded. 'It isn't right though, her paying us.'

'She wants to. And while she does, take the money, Mum. You know you need it, and they don't.'

'That doesn't matter,' her mother laughed. 'It doesn't make a difference if they need it or not. She shouldn't be paying us, especially not after what happened to her husband.'

'Mum,' Mia urged, 'Janie wants to do this; and it's for Jess, for her to get help. It's only for a few months, so please, promise me you'll use it.'

Mia had been grateful for Janie's money and contacts, though she couldn't deny she'd been playing on the woman's guilt. Janie's reaction to realising who Mia was had been superseded by everything else that unfurled the night of the fire, but it had become clear during later visits how heavily her part in Jess's demise weighed on her. The impact of her job was suddenly all too clear to her.

It wasn't until the third visit that Janie admitted to Mia that Miles had done the same thing to her best friend, and Mia wondered if they would have been in the same position if that hadn't happened. If Janie had learned that Mia had been trying to exact revenge on her one night while her husband's offices were burning to the ground, would she have been so supportive if she didn't have Sophie preying on her conscience? Mia honestly didn't know.

Janie had wanted to know why Mia had been watching her. 'What were you trying to do to me?' she had asked. 'When you were outside my house – the girls . . .' She hadn't been able to get the sentence out.

'No, no, I'd never have hurt them,' Mia promised her. 'I never wanted to hurt any of your family, not like that.'

Janie had nodded slowly, her head hanging questioningly. 'Then why?'

'I wanted to know something about you – anything at all that could help me make you pay. You were never at the office; you had nothing to do with the business; no one knew the first thing about you, really. But there was nothing about your life that wasn't driven by money, and so all I could do was work out a way to destroy that, if I could . . .' Mia shrugged. It all sounded so childish and amateur now, so unlikely to work; and all those months earlier, when she had seen the advert for Laura's job, she had convinced herself it was the opportunity she needed.

'You and Harry were so' – she waved an arm – 'you had everything. Your lives were so glossy, and ours—' Mia broke off and laughed. 'They couldn't be more different. I wanted to bring down Harry's company, including his reputation. I had no idea how at first, but then when Sarah told me she was being bullied . . . It was only a glimmer of opportunity, but it was enough.'

'You could have ruined Mike Lewis's life too.' Janie said it plainly, like she wasn't trying to admonish her, just state a fact.

'I know. There were always going to be some casualties along the way,' Mia said, and she knew she sounded heartless as she looked away. 'The fact was I didn't think of any of that – I just wanted to get you back. Women *are* treated differently there, you know,' she added, as if this was some way of justifying her actions. 'They're not promoted. Harry and his boys, it's all mates doing favours for each other.'

Janie nodded.

'I wanted to tarnish his reputation and lose him important clients. I figured that if Coopers believed me—' Mia shook her head. 'I thought that if you lost your income, you'd be losing the most important thing. But despite all that, I am sorry for what happened – to Harry. I never wanted ...' she drifted off again. 'Things spiralled.'

It had been two months since Janie told Mia she wanted to help financially and now Mia turned to her mum and said again, 'Please, just take the money.'

'Okay.' Her mum held her hands up. 'Fine.'

Mia sat back in her seat and studied her mother. She couldn't bear to think how much of a toll the last three months had taken on her, and it was only going to get worse when the trial began.

Eventually her mum spread her hands across the table and Mia reached out for them, feeling the pressure of her mum's fingers as they wrapped around hers. 'I wish there was something I could do. I don't want you here, Mia.' Tears bubbled in the corners of her eyes until they slid down her cheeks. Mia watched them roll off the end of her chin, dripping onto the table. 'I wish I was here instead of you.'

'You can't do that, Mum.'

'No. There's nothing I *can* do,' she said. 'That's what breaks my heart. I would swap places with you in a heartbeat, if I could.'

'I know you would.'

'I realise you never intended to kill that man,' she said, as she'd said in every one of her visits. 'I know you would never have done that. It was pure impulse.' She smiled ruefully. 'You always did have a quick temper.'

'I know, Mum,' Mia replied.

'Please, darling, please let Jess come and see you. As soon as you see her, you'll know she can cope. Please. Do it for me. Then I can close it off.'

Mia shut her eyes, shaking her head a fraction. 'Okay,' she said eventually. 'Okay, let Jess come.'

But as soon as the words were out of her mouth, she already wondered if she'd done the right thing.

# Chapter Forty-Four

Mia had been refusing to see Jess, but not because she blamed her sister for being in prison. She had made that decision herself. Rather, Mia worried that any day now Jess would decide to tell the truth. And if her sister saw her here, there was a greater chance of that happening.

Mia had often wondered if, deep down, her mum knew the truth, or at least suspected it. She had seen a flash of something in her eyes that she hadn't understood at first, but later realised it was the same look her mum used to give them as children. When she knew one of her daughters was lying.

It broke Mia's heart that her mum thought she could do something like start the fire, but at the same time it would break her heart to think Jess had. It was a no-win situation.

Mia glanced around the room, at every other woman waiting for her visitor to arrive.

She had no idea what to expect when she saw her sister. She didn't want to talk about the night of the fire, though; she wanted Jess to tell her more about her life now: what she was doing, how much she was enjoying living again. Mia wanted to see the life back in her sister's eyes.

Still she knew it was a lot to ask, as she watched the first three visitors making their way in, catching her breath when she caught sight of Jess, a security guard holding open the double doors for her.

Mia lifted her hand in a wave, but when Jess turned, it wasn't just life that Mia saw in her eyes.

Jess paused when she saw her, her face open, a small smile on the edge of her lips. She blinked once and inhaled a deep breath before she began moving again. All the time she didn't look away from Mia.

As Mia followed her movement, her head was filled with all the things her mum had been telling her about: Jess's desire to throw herself back into the world again; picnics on the beach, a trip on the Sandbanks ferry, the cinema, the theatre – suddenly it all dawned on her.

Mia clung to the edges of the table in front of her. She wanted to leap up, run over, push her sister back out of the room before Jess could tell her what she had so clearly arrived to say. But instead Mia froze, her breath shallow as she watched her sister making her way towards her.

Jess hadn't been doing any of those things because of what Mia had given up for her. She had been doing them to make the most of the freedom she had left – a last hurrah.

Mia knew why her sister had wanted to visit so desperately. She knew exactly what Jess was going to tell her today, and she also knew there was nothing she could do about it because she had seen that look in her sister's eyes before. Many years ago now, when Jess could run and would let nothing get in her way.

Mia shuddered. Her sister was here to tell her that she would admit what had really happened that night. It was clear that Jess had never had any intention of letting her sister go to trial, or take the blame for something she hadn't done.

While Mia had been sitting in prison for the last three months Jess had been doing what Mia and their mum had been begging her to do for the last five years – living her life again. Just one last time.

And what broke Mia's heart the most was that she knew Jess hadn't been to the theatre or the beach or any of those things for herself. She'd done it all for her mum and sister – the two people in the world who meant everything to her.

# Acknowledgements

To all the many, many wonderful mums I know and those in particular who I greatly admire but who don't always realise what an amazing job they're doing – this book is for all of you.

My thanks go to my two wonderful friends Deb Dorman and Donna Cross who have helped me shape the stories of Laura, Mia and Janie. And to all my other friends who continue to be such a huge support. I am so lucky to have you all.

To my lovely readers, reviewers and book bloggers, and everyone who has been generous with their time and comments: thank you. Without you I wouldn't be able to do what I love. And I really do love doing it.

And to the amazing and talented people I work with both at home and over the seas: my ever fantastic super-agent Nelle Andrew who I would genuinely be lost without and my two editors who continually amaze me with their ability to turn the book around for the better at each edit. Emily Griffin and Jackie Cantor, you have both made my experience of writing this book an absolute pleasure.

The teams at both Century in the UK and Gallery in the US – thank you all for your support in marketing, PR, proof reading, designing brilliant covers and getting the book into stores. I have to pinch myself that I have such great people working behind my books, and I know that any success is a massive team effort.

And finally to my family, this time with the added support of Pickle the cat who helps me by sitting on my laptop and biting the end of my pen. To my mum, for picking up the phone and crying when she'd finished reading because she is so proud of me. And to my husband, for continuing to be my other biggest supporter, who never doubts me and loves to think that the characters are written around him. (Harry isn't you, John!)

And, as always, my two precious children. Bethany and Joseph, you are my world. Words will never be enough to tell you how much I love you and how proud I am of you, but I am, every single day. Thank you for allowing me the time to work on my book when I needed to and for basically being the two kind, loving and generous little people you are.